REIGN IN HELL

WILLIAM DIEHL

REIGN IN HELL

ARROW

Published by Arrow Books in 1998

1 3 5 7 9 10 8 6 4 2

Copyright © William Diehl 1997

The right of William Diehl to be identified as the author of this work has been
asserted by him in accordance with the Copyright, Designs and Patents Act,
1988

This novel is a work of fiction. Names and characters are the product of the
author's imagination and any resemblance to actual persons, living or dead, is
entirely coincidental

First published in the United Kingdom in 1998 by William Heinemann

Arrow Books Limited
Random House UK Ltd
20 Vauxhall Bridge Road, London, SW1V 2SA

Random House Australia (Pty) Limited
20 Alfred Street, Milsons Point, Sydney, New South Wales 2061, Australia

Random House New Zealand Limited
18 Poland Road, Glenfield
Auckland 10, New Zealand

Random House South Africa (Pty) Limited
Endulini, 5a Jubilee Road, Parktown 2193, South Africa

Random House UK Limited Reg. No. 954009

A CIP catalogue record for this book is available from the British Library

Papers used by Random House UK Limited are natural, recyclable products
made from wood grown in sustainable forests. The manufacturing processes
conform to the environmental regulations of the country of origin

Typeset by SX Composing DTP, Rayleigh, Essex
Printed and bound in the United Kingdom by
Mackays of Chatham PLC, Chatham, Kent

ISBN 0 7493 2284 5

To my beloved friend
Mister Magoo
Who asked nothing more than love
Always in my mind
Forever in my heart
1983–1996

And for Virginia
Who shared his love

Here we may reign secure, and in my choice
To reign is worth ambition, though in hell:
Better to reign in hell, than serve in heav'n.
        —John Milton, *Paradise Lost*, 1667

Acknowledgments

My deep appreciation to Glenn Brazil, ATF, retired, Buddy Harris, Federal Law Enforcement Training Center, retired, Todd Scott, of SOS in Brunswick, GA, and to Cheryl Williams, for their guidance and help in researching this book.

My thanks to the staff of Travel Montana, Montana Department of Commerce, for introducing me to one of America's truly wonderous states and for their help.

To Morris Dees and the Southern Poverty Law Center for their continued vigilance. To Dennis Covington, whose book, *Salvation on Sand Mountain*, cleared my perception. To Kenneth Stern and his book, *A Force Upon the Plain*, must reading for anyone who is interested in the politics of hate. And to Alan Bock for his enlightening book, *Ambush at Ruby Ridge*.

To Linda Grey, Clare Ferraro, Amy Scheibe, and Kim Hovey at Ballantine for their enthusiasm, support, and friendship.

To Peter Gethers, my editor, for his fine tuning, encouragement, and friendship over the past eighteen years.

To Owen Laster, who defines the word gentleman, for steering my career through all these years, and to Helen Breitwieser for her always cheerful help and enthusiasm, and to all the others at William Morris who provide constant security.

To Harrison Latimore, Larry Krantz, Pat Robert, Lucy McIntyre, and Shana Parver for wonderful characters.

To Lorenzo for doing it right and for doing it from the heart.

And to Stan Pottinger for his political insight.

To the team that keeps the wheels rolling: Brett, Rod, Cathy, Glen, and Larry.

To Temple and Shawn, with wishes for a lovely and loving future.

And for Virginia, who has made it all worthwhile for the last twenty years.

St. Simons Island, GA
July 31, 1997

REIGN IN HELL

BOOK ONE
SNAKES

Better to reign in hell than serve in heav'n
But better still to reign in both.
—D. J. Enright, *A Faust Book*, 1979

One

The dusty RV wailed along the flat interstate, its tires whining on the hot pavement. Behind the wheel was a gaunt, reed-thin driver, his thinning black hair whipping in the furnace of hot air that streamed through the open window. He sucked on a bottle of water to keep from dozing, arcs of sweat staining his white shirt. It had been unmercifully hot since they left Omaha, heading south and then due west on Interstate 80, with towns and small cities – Kearney, Cozad, Gothenburg – blurring past them as they paralleled the river. He drove straight into the sun, into the hot June afternoon, whizzing past the Nebraska farms and fields, uncluttered, lonely, and dull in their sameness.

As was his wont, he bitched to himself as he drove.

What's the use havin' air-conditionin' if he don't let me turn it on?

A few miles later. Shaking his head.

Never knew nobody loved the heat like this one. Must be a hunerd-ten out there, he wants the damn window open.

Another couple of miles.

Nobody t'talk to. Won't let me play the radio when he's sleepin'. One of these days I'm gonna just doze off . . .

Nodding to himself.

. . . bug off the road, we'll both end up wrapped in this RV in the middle of godforsakennowhere . . .

Tapping the flat of his hand on the steering wheel.

. . . damn buzzards eatin' our eyes out.

Brother T was stretched out on a futon spread across two seats. He was uncomfortable sleeping in the main suite, as he called it, while the RV was on the highway, preferring instead the double seat behind the driver. He was napping, getting his strength together for the confront. That's what he called the meetings, *confronts*.

'What we're doin', Mordie, we're confrontin' the devil,' he would say. 'Gonna whip that fire-scald, son-bitch to his knees again t'night,' he would say. 'Praise God, praise JEE-sus.'

Like they were going to war or somedamnthing.

But the driver wasn't complaining. It was the best job he ever had, even though he hated driving the flat plains where you could close your eyes for ten minutes then open them and appear to be in the same place you were when you shut them.

Suddenly he perked up.

'Shhhew,' he said under his breath.

There was a sign far ahead, dancing among dervish heat monkeys. He squinted through his sunglasses: 'Brady two miles.'

'Thank you *Jay-sus*,' he said aloud, mimicking his boss in his own rolled-out south Georgia accent.

Behind him, Brother T stirred. He leaned up on one elbow and craned and twisted his neck, popping the muscles, a husky man with long blond hair that hung down to his shoulders and a heavy beard.

'Where we at?' he asked in a voice that was low as a whisper and harsh as a file.

'Smack dab in the middle of the Lord's oven.'

Brother T cupped the palms of both hands under his jaws, raised his eyebrows, and very lightly rubbed the sleep from the corners of his eyes with the forefinger of each hand.

'Sometimes I think Gawd jes' took ten square acres of Kansas, Xeroxed 'em, and laid 'em out end on end all over the whole damn middle of the country.'

4

'Sounds like you're flirtin' with blasphemy there, Mordie.'

'Flirtin' with the truth, what I'm doin',' Mordachai answered, coming to a stop and turning right onto a narrow two-lane blacktop.

'What's the name of this place again?'

'Brady. 'Bout twenty miles this side a North Platte.'

'That doesn't tell me a thing.'

'We've driv a little over two hunerd miles. Over halfway 'cross Nebraska since we left Omaha. It's flat, hot, and I ain't seen another car for at least an hour.'

Brother T opened his eyes and stared through orbs the color of milk. Stared at absolutely nothing. 'You ought to feel right at home. Sounds like south Georgia.'

'No trees. Nothin' but hay growin' everywhere.'

'Wheat, Mordie, wheat. Hay is what it becomes after it's shorn from the bosom of the land.'

'I'll trade a hunerd miles of whateveryacallit for one tall pine tree.'

'Unhappy, Mordie?' Brother T admonished gently.

'Jes' bitchin'.'

Brother T chuckled. 'Good for the soul.'

'And I'm soppin'. Since you never sweat, I drip fer the both of us.'

'Jesus is the great leveler.'

'Easy fer you t'say, you ain't the dripper.'

'True. Cold's more your fashion.' Brother T shivered involuntarily at the thought, rubbed his arms, then felt around the floor for the ice cooler. He snapped it open, took out a can of Coke, bent the tab under, and took a long swig.

'Ahhh,' he said. 'My mouth was as dry as stale toast.'

Near the cooler on the floor were four flat, varnished boxes. A sound came from one of them. Briefly. Like a babe in its sleep rolling against a rattle.

'Easy, children,' Brother T said softly, leaning over and brushing his fingertips across the smooth top of one of

5

the boxes. 'Curl up and go back to sleep.' Then to Mordachai: 'What are my arrangements?'

'You're staying with one'a the preachers, name's Harmon Jasper. Got a room fixed up in his barn for a farmhand but the feller quit and moved to Lincoln.'

'Any family?'

'Wife.'

'Children?'

Mordachai paused for an instant.

'Mordachai . . .'

'Daughter in high school.'

'How old?'

The driver stared uncomfortably at Brother T in the rearview mirror before he said, 'I dunno. Fifteen, sixteen.'

The preacher took a swig of Coke. Then he stroked his long blond locks with one hand and smiled.

'All the publicity you been gettin' on the radio,' Mordachai said, 'and the state papers, we could maybe see a hunerd er two hunerd folks tonight. But out here in the middle a nowhere, hell, we won't scratch doodley. Times're so bad, nobody's got two nickels to rub t'gether.' He paused for a moment, then added, 'If we'd a stayed outside Omaha a couple nights, bet we woulda had a thousand people every night, maybe took in four, five, maybe even ten thousand a night.'

'You know I don't like the big towns. Press is too nosy.'

'People don't give two hoots 'bout that. You got apostles, T, *apostles*. They know lies when they read 'em.'

'I appreciate your ardor.' The preacher leaned back and took another deep swig from the can. 'Besides, we've had some good one, two thousand dollar nights lately.' He leaned back in his seat, his glazed eyes flicking sideways occasionally. 'Tell me what you see.'

'A drought. Fields all wilted, ground cracked and

6

dusty, heat squigglin' off everything . . . farmhouse off the left, coupla oak trees givin' it shade and behind it's the barn, got a advertisement for chewin' tobacca painted on the side . . . can't tell what kind, it's all faded and cracked.'

'How picturesque.'

'Everybody out here's hard-timin'. Ya might throw in a word for some rain, t'night.'

'Excellent idea.'

Brother T leaned his head back, like a wolf baying, and his voice rose suddenly, still harsh and tormented, but quivering with emotion. 'I beseech you, sweet *Jee*-sus, in the name of my *suffering* brothers and sisters . . . bathe this thirsty dust with your tears . . . and give life to its parched earth and wilted fruit.'

'*Amen, Lord, a-men!* Which Book's that from?'

'My very own treasury of injunctions,' Brother T answered, and chuckled.

The Jasper place was a pleasant if somewhat spartan white frame farmhouse, boxed by the porch that surrounded it. A dusty red Chevy pickup was parked beside it, and a sturdy barn that looked recently painted stood behind it. Fifteen or twenty skinny pigs rooted and wallowed in a sty at one side of the barn. Behind all that, a field of scorched grain spread across the flat land toward the town of Brady, a few miles away, a large cluster of low buildings surrounded on four corners by silos, which from a distance, in the clear but heat-heavy air, looked like sentinels guarding a prairie fortress.

The big tent was stretched out, fifty yards or so from the house at the edge of a parched field, its canvas side flaps rolled up and tied. A vague and inadequate breeze stirred the grass around it. Nearby, several vehicles of all makes and models were parked haphazardly along the road and on the grounds.

There was a sense of revelry here, of people escaping

7

from the moment in anticipation of comradery and redemption: a dozen women and children scurried about, chatting and laughing and setting out plastic plates and eatingware on four long tables; a young teenage girl in a blue dress spun around and danced to a song in her head; a small boy sat on the ground staring mutely at a squirrel in one of the oaks, while other children played tag around one of the larger trees; two men in shirtsleeves attended pieces of chicken sizzling over charcoal on twenty-gallon drums that were halved and perched on sections of old train rails; four women fussed over a table abounding with bowls of biscuits, coleslaw, baked beans, corn on the cob, chocolate layer cakes, and pitchers of freshly made lemonade.

At the edge of the dirt road leading to the farmhouse, a mobile sign announced:

Revival Meeting 7:30 P.M. tonight
BROTHER TRANSGRESSOR
Pastor, Church of Christ Wandering
'Preparing for Parousia'
All you can eat country dinner, 3$
6:00–7:30

Mordachai walked across the hard earth, flapping his damp shirt against his chest. He asked someone where he could find Jasper and was pointed to a short, rather beefy man with sparse brown hair and skin as tanned as leather. Jasper's handshake was as vigorous as it was earnest.

'I expect a good turnout,' he said enthusiastically, in a flat, nasal twang. 'Folks comin' down from North Platte and churches hither and yon. Could get maybe three hundred.'

'Well, that'd sure make Brother T happy.'

'Is that what he prefers to be called, Brother T?'

'That'll be jes' fine.'

'And you are . . . ?'

8

'Brother Mordachai.'

Strange-looking fellow, Jasper thought. Mordachai towered above him, tall and lean as a cornstalk, with a long, narrow face, a sharp nose, and flashing eyes that mirrored the fading sun. Sweat had formed a dark stain on the front of his wrinkled white shirt and under his arms, and he kept sweeping his disheveled black hair away from his eyes.

'Come along, like you t'meet the missus and our daughter,' Jasper said, and led Mordachai toward the small group of women arranging the food. 'We need this revival, brother. This drought's the worst I can remember. People's faith gets shaky when things go bad and don't get better. I prayed the good Brother would bring his message to us.'

'And the Lord answered yer prayer, that's why we're here, Brother Jasper. Brother T heard yer prayers and took heed of yer call.'

'Me and m'family are doubly graced that the good Brother is going t'spend the night in our home. We don't have air-conditioning, I'm sorry to say. Just fans.'

'The hotter it gets, the better Brother T likes it.'

'Praise the Lord.'

'Oh yeah, praise *Jay*-sus.'

Mordie had parked the RV behind the tent, as close to it as he could get to make Brother's entrance as easy as possible. The preacher was sitting in the revolving easy chair near the large window on one side of the RV when Mordachai returned. He had showered and his tresses were lustrous, the color of corn silk. He was wearing a shin-length, earth-colored caftan with a cross embroidered across the chest and full sleeves that hung halfway to his elbows. The preacher's braille Bible lay in his lap, and a bunch of Concord grapes lay in the palm of one hand. He picked them off one at a time, squeezing and sucking the meat from each while staring toward the sounds of people talking and children laughing and a dog playfully barking.

'And how're things with Brother Jasper?' he asked as Mordachai, wiping sweat from his forehead with the palm of his hand, slumped in a chair.

'He's tickled white-eyed. *Shew*, sun's already on the line and it's still hell out there. I hope yer gonna do a rain dance fer 'em tonight.'

'I might just do that. Me and my friends.'

'Tell yuh what, if it did come down rainin', you could probably get elected governor a Nebraska.'

Brother T smiled. 'Interesting notion. What time's the confront?' He leaned on the first syllable, pronouncing the word *con*front.

'Preacher Jasper'll take the floor at seven-thirty, do a little warm-up with the locals, bring you on about 7:45.'

'Good. Should be through by nine. Maybe earlier, if it starts raining.'

'Yeah, right.' Mordachai laughed.

'Tell me about the Jasper girl. Did you meet her?'

'Uh-huh. She's helpin' serve the food.'

'Describe her,' Brother T said, still staring toward the sounds.

'Not your kind, T.'

'*Describe* her.'

'Kinda short, five-three er -four, light brown hair. She's got light eyes, blue'r green, couldn't really tell. Maybe 110 pounds.'

'You know what I mean,' the preacher rasped.

Mordachai hesitated and looked down at the floor. 'She's got . . . nice, full buds. Tight little body.'

'What's she wearing?'

'Cotton dress. Blue.'

Brother leaned close to Mordachai's ear and his voice lowered to a whisper. 'And is she sanctified, Mordie? Could you tell if she's sanctified?'

'Hell, I don't know whether she's . . . out here I reckon

10

so. Small town, y'know, and she couldn't be more'n sixteen. Prob'ly.'

'What's the young lamb's name?'

'Penny.'

'Penny. Lovely. And bright as one, I'll bet.'

'Seems pretty smart. A Bible thumper, I can tell ya. Quoted somethin' from Psalms, but I don't remember what it was.'

'Splendid. How about the mother?'

'Aw, Jesus, T . . .'

'I'm just curious about my congregation, Mordachai.'

'Well, she definitely ain'tcher type and she *definitely* ain't sanctified.'

Brother T laughed. 'Why don't you suggest the young lady fix me a plate and bring it on over here.'

'Aw look, T . . . things're going real well fer us. We don't need no trouble. Why doncha jes—'

'Shut up, Mordachai. Shut up right now and do what I tell you.'

Rebuked, Mordachai winced and stood up. 'Gotta change m'shirt,' he said sullenly.

'Hurry along with it, then, I'm hungry.'

He watched the scene as through a milky glass, without tint or hue. Gray images floating past his field of view. To his right, Mordachai was checking the tent and instructing the small advance staff. He closed the shutters of the venetian blinds and peered cautiously around the edge, watching her through the narrow slit between sill and shutter, squinting his eyes to focus better. Finally he reached up and, using his forefingers, pushed the gray-tinted contact lens down under the lower lids of his eyes. His vision cleared, color painted the scene before him, and he focused on the young girl piling food on the plate; watching her study each ear of corn before selecting just the right one, sucking chocolate from a piece of cake off a finger, caressing her cheek with the frosty side

11

of a glass of lemonade; listening to her almost childish laugh; entranced by the impudent way she tossed her head to one side, thrashing her face with her brown-blond hair. The artery in his throat began to pulse, his breath became labored. He watched every move she made until she headed for the RV, then he leaned back in the chair and forced the contacts back up over his eyes, closed them and waited.

A minute passed. Then he heard her footsteps outside the door of the RV. She tapped lightly.

'It's open,' he said, softening his tone as much as possible. He kept his eyes closed, heard the door open and the voice.

'Brother T?'

'Yes?'

'I brought you some dinner, sir.'

'Well, thank you, my dear.'

He sat up in the chair and motioned her in. She entered cautiously, almost reverently, staring around the dimly lit living room of the RV. It was pleasantly furnished and religious paintings filled almost every available space on the walls. Obvious paintings – the Last Supper, Christ with his arms outstretched and his heart aglow, a crucifix – then she saw him and she gasped in awe. She stood like a post, the plate trembling in her hand.

'You must be Penny,' he said.

'Y-Y-Yes sir,' she stammered, her voice as soft as a wind chime.

He was seated by one of the large windows in an easy chair, his fingers tracing the raised braille icons as he read the Book with his fingertips. She stared, fascinated by the flowing hair framing the aesthetic face, the look of strength and serenity, the sackcloth caftan. Her eyes moved to the picture of Christ, and the comparison was immediate. He smiled, then he opened his eyes and she was so astonished she almost spilled the lemonade. He was staring directly at her with milky, ambiguous, unfocused eyes that seemed to

12

peer into her heart and soul and read her mind.

He reached around to the side of the chair and swung a small table on rollers in front of him.

'Put it right here,' he said.

She obeyed, setting the plate and glass on the table and putting the plastic knife and fork beside the plate.

'Sit here beside me,' he said, and when she had pulled over a canvas-backed chair, he added, 'I want to look at you.'

'Look at me?'

He reached out toward her voice, found her cheeks with his fingertips and slowly began to trace her soft skin. She closed her eyes as his fingers flitted over the lids, caressed her nose, stroked her lips. Her breath came faster and she could feel the blood flowing up into her face.

'Perfection,' he whispered. *'Thou art the rose of Sharon and the Lily of the valleys. Behold thou are fair, thou hast doves' eyes, thy lips are like a thread of scarlet, thou art all fair for there is no spot on thee.'*

'Song of Solomon,' she murmured.

'Have you been saved? Are you in grace?'

'Yes.' Trembling, her voice as vague as mist.

'Then I will speak at you from the pulpit, and later I will anoint you with the oil of redemption.'

He slid his hands down her throat and slowly withdrew them.

'Now be with me whilst I eat.'

They started coming about six-thirty. Mordachai saw it first, a cloud of dust boiling toward them along the dirt road and trailing more clouds behind it, like smoke from a tail of fire. 'What the hell's that?' he said.

Brother was resting on the cot in the rear of the RV. 'What's what?'

'Looks like a dust storm blowin' down the road.'

'It's the parade,' Brother said.

'Whaddya mean, parade?'

13

'Comin' to the freak show, Mordie. They're not comin' for salvation, not comin' to be saved. They're comin' for the show.'

'Aw, c'mon, don't start that ag–'

Brother jumped up and swung his legs to the floor. 'Makes no difference. We stroke 'em good before we're through. Don't make any difference what gets 'em in, it's what happens when they get in that counts.'

'Jeez, wish you could see this, Brother. That cloud a dust must be a quarter mile long.'

Brother walked to the window, stood behind Mordachai, and squinted through the window. A whirl-wind of dust was moving toward them.

'Been listenin' to the radio?' he asked.

'Ain't had time,' Mordachai said. 'I never have time 'fore a confront, you know that. Too much t'do.'

'There's a front moving in.'

'Hell, there's a front movin' up the road towards us, looks like.'

'You're not listening, Mordie.'

'Yeah, yeah, a front . . .'

'Looking for it to hit here about eight, eight-thirty.'

'We seen fronts before, T, fronts don't mean rain.'

'It's raining in Kansas. Town called Cedar Bluffs. Where's that?'

Mordachai shrugged to himself. He opened a drawer and pulled out the Hammond road atlas. Leafing through it, he found Kansas and ran his finger along the roads and byways.

'Whaddya know, here it is. Due south a here, maybe . . . sixty, seventy miles.'

'And what's that cloud of dust tell you, Mordie?'

The thin man peered out the window, stared at the cloud as it rose, then began to dissipate, then swirled back toward them.

'Wind blowin' this way?'

'Blowing this way, right up from Cedar Bluffs.'

14

'Son-bitch.'

'Let me tell you, tonight we're gonna pray for rain like we never prayed before. We're gonna pray and sing and dance and offer up for rain tonight. I want you back near me, just outside the tent. You're an old farmhand, Mordie, you can taste rain in the air. If it's comin' this way, gimme a sign, bang that tambourine of yours. That's when we'll offer up, and if that rain comes, my God, they'll shell up everything they got. Hell, they'll shell up their *wedding* rings.'

Mordie leaned forward and cupped his hands beside his eyes. 'Jeez, T, there must be twenty, thirty cars comin' up the road.'

'Why of course. It's the parade, Mordie!' Brother T raised his hands over his head and his voice trembled in a mock sermon. 'Brothers and sisters . . . get your prayers answered . . . get all you can eat . . . see the *freak* show . . . all for three lousy bucks.' He lowered his arms and chuckled. 'What a bargain. Deal of the year.'

The cars streamed almost bumper-to-bumper into the field across the road from the tent Harmon Jasper had blocked off for parking. A school bus rented for the occasion arrived with thirty-five anticipants from a Church of God congregation forty miles away. There were four- and five-car caravans from other churches in the area. One, a black, late model touring car, pulled up near the tent and a young man in military fatigues got out and approached Jasper. They spoke for a minute or two, then the farmer pointed toward the RV. The soldier opened the rear door of the sedan and two men got out, one in fatigue uniform, the other in a dark business suit. They walked toward the RV.

'Looks like we got us some VIPs, Brother.'

Staring over his shoulder, the preacher saw the two men opaquely.

'See what they want.'

'Right.'

15

Mordachai met the two visitors as they neared the van. There was some jabber and then Mordachai led them to the RV. He tapped and stuck his head in the doorway.

'They's two gentlemen from the state a Montana would like a word with ya, Brother T.'

The preacher picked up his Bible and sat in his easy chair.

'Show them in, Mordie.'

Mordachai led them into the living space. The man in uniform was the shorter of the two, five-ten or so, ram-rod straight and obviously in excellent trim, his skin browned by the sun. He snapped his overseas cap off, revealing black hair trimmed close to the scalp. His expression was as rigid as his bearing and he wore the eagles of a colonel on his collar. The other man was a bit over six feet. His brown hair was neatly trimmed; his face had the florid look of a man with persistently high blood pressure. His linen suit showed signs of a long drive. Despite the heat, both men were dry as a desert carcass.

'Brother Transgressor, my name's Lewis Granger,' the taller one said. 'My associate here is Colonel Shrack.'

'An Army man, Colonel?'

'Montana Patriots.'

'Is that a football team?'

Granger laughed, but the colonel saw no humor in the remark.

'State militia,' he snapped.

'Sorry. I don't know a lot about sports *or* the militia.'

'No offense.'

Brother T held his hand out between them and Granger shook it. The colonel walked quietly behind Granger, staring into the veiled eyes of the preacher, studied the room, checked it all out. He did not take the preacher's hand.

'Welcome to our humble church,' T said. 'Are you seeking sanctification?' Then he smiled. 'Or perhaps . . . a donation?'

16

'We like your message. Like what you have to say, Brother. You speak our language.'

'I speak the language of the Lord, Mr. Granger.'

'With a little politics mixed in,' Granger said with a smile.

'My mission is to make sure my flock is informed. Life is choices, gentlemen. I like to think my followers have all the options.'

'I'm surprised you haven't had trouble with the IRS,' Granger said. 'They get nervous when politics and religion get mixed together.'

'I am a church. I live by donations alone. All we own is this vehicle. Mordie keeps excellent books, always available to them.'

Granger looked back at Mordachai, nodded, then turned back to the preacher.

'I'll get to the point,' he said. 'We've attended your service several times. Missouri, Kansas, last week in Omaha. You always leave a town while your audience is still building.'

'I go where the Lord leads. And where we're welcome.'

'You seem to have an aversion to publicity.'

'Publicity corrupts the best of men.'

'I like that. I like that a lot, sir.'

Brother sat and stared vacantly at a space between Colonel Shrack and Lewis Granger, his peripheral vision tracking the man in the camouflage fatigues as he perused the interior of the RV.

Granger filled the silence. 'All that's well and good, sir. I wouldn't suggest otherwise except . . . well, your message really needs to be heard by more than a few hundred people a night, wouldn't you say?'

'Whatever God wishes.'

'I've had a few talks with God, too, Brother. That's why I'm here. God told me your message needs a wider audience.'

The colonel suddenly spoke up. 'You should be speaking to everybody who's oppressed. People forgotten by their government, or those being betrayed by it.'

Brother's expression did not change. His milky eyes stared straight ahead. Granger leaned closer to him, his eyes bright with anticipation. 'How'd you like to reach a couple million people a week with that message and never have to drive a mile?'

Brother smiled. 'Well, that would indeed be a miracle, wouldn't it, Mordie?'

'Praise God. A miracle indeed.'

'Think that would make God happy?' Granger asked.

'I don't know, God doesn't discuss His frame of mind with me.'

Granger laughed. 'I like your sense of humor, Brother.'

'*A jest's prosperity lies in the ear of him that hears it, never in the tongue of him that makes it.*'

'Is that from the Bible?'

'Shakespeare.'

'Well read, too,' Granger said, then stopped, embarrassed by the faux pas. 'Sorry . . .'

'You needn't be. A figure of speech. Actually Mordie does the reading. I just listen.' He let another awkward pause linger, then said, 'What did you have in mind, Brother Granger?'

'A radio show, Brother. I own six stations myself but I'm part of a network that has thirty stations in the northwest. Montana, Idaho, Utah, Wyoming, Colorado. Very conservative viewpoint, jells right along with yours. We've been looking for a religious program, one that would combine the Christian viewpoint with our political agenda.'

'And what is that?'

'Awareness,' Colonel Shrack said in a flat, authoritative voice. 'Wake the sleeping tiger.'

Granger looked sharply at Shrack and made a motion with his hand to tone it down.

'We are talking about AM and FM,' Granger said. 'Reach about two, two and a half million people.

Excellent programming, a Christian, conservative view-point. Our biggest night is Wednesday. What we'd like you to do, Brother T, is consider an offer. A radio show. One hour every Wednesday night at seven P.M. We'll provide you with a fine chorus, testimonials, a born-again preacher to introduce you properly every week. If it's as successful as we think it will be, we could expand it, hopefully syndicate it. Think about it. Down the road, maybe thirty minutes every night heard by millions of people who are hungry to hear the truth as God sees it.'

Brother said nothing. He sat near the end of his chair, back rigid, hands folded in his lap.

'Of course, we'll pay you and your staff generously.'

Brother waited.

'And you would share in the profits from advertising and donations.'

Brother waited.

'No personal photographs, publicity, just the way you like it. It will add a touch of mystery. We'll tape your sermon and dub in the chorus and introduction later. You never have to show your face.'

Granger stared at him. The preacher still said nothing.

'Do you understand what I'm saying, Brother?'

'Of course, Mr. Granger.'

'It's Lew. Call me Lew.'

'And you're going to be my employer, Lew?'

'Not at all. It will be your show, sir. Your words, your thoughts. We'd like to think that, uh, we could occasionally suggest a Bible verse or two which might give you inspiration. Perhaps suggest a topic for a sermon now and then, but only if you agree. No censorship. We are all firm believers in the Constitution.'

The preacher stood up and felt his way into the kitchenette.

'Anyone care for a lemonade?' he asked, opening the refrigerator door and taking out a gallon jug of pale, pink juice.

19

'We wouldn't want to impose,' Granger said.

Brother started to screw off the top of the jug but Mordie rushed to his side.

'Let me do that,' he said.

Brother laughed. 'I didn't want our guests to think I'm helpless, Mordie,' he said. But he waited while his aide filled a tumbler and placed it in his hand.

'Thanks,' he said, and made his way back to his chair, checking the patch on Colonel Shrack's shoulder as he went by. Crossed bayonets on a blue field, their hilts shaped like crosses. He couldn't make out the words that bordered the shield, but the banner that unfurled around the two blades spelled SANCTUARY in red.

'I'm to understand that you are offering me my own one hour radio show and also will pay me and my staff and give me a percentage of the profits and that you will in no way censor my sermons. Is that correct?'

Granger nodded, then quickly added, 'Correct. We'll be glad to let your attorney work out a suitable contract and–'

'I don't have a lawyer, sir. Never had need for one. I'll pray on this. In the meantime, you can work up what you think is a suitable contract and Mordie and I can look it over.'

'Then you're interested?'

'I'll discuss it with the Lord. Leave your card with Mordie so we know how to get in touch with you.'

'We're spending the night at a motel outside of town. Perhaps . . . breakfast tomorrow so we can continue to pursue this?'

'Perhaps. Mordachai will let you know.'

'Excellent. We appreciate your time, sir. And your consideration.'

'How soon would you like to start this radio show?' Mordie asked.

'Sooner the better.'

He handed Mordachai an envelope.

'A little donation for taking up your time . . . and perhaps to convince you we're serious. A pleasure, Brother T.'

He reached out and took the preacher's hand. The colonel said nothing as they left.

'Jeez, T, you like to froze those guys out,' Mordachai said, watching the two men stride back toward their car.

'Oh, I don't think so,' the preacher answered, and smiled.

Mordie opened the envelope and took out its contents, spreading one hundred dollar bills on the table like a hand of cards. He whistled.

'Ten big'uns, T. A thousand bucks.'

'Showin' off,' the preacher said with a chuckle.

'Way to a man's heart.'

'Way to a man's back pocket, ya mean. Dangling a little bait in front of us.'

'Wonder what's with that military fella.'

'You remember reading to me about the Sanctuary of the Lord?'

'Kinda. I read everything in the damn paper to you but the want ads. Them, too, sometimes. Can't remember everything.'

'Paramilitaries, Mordie. Very outspoken.'

'Why would that colonel come along with the radio fella?'

'Because they're such staunch Christians. They are children of the Book.'

Mordie laughed. 'Don't josh me.'

'They got a holy war stuck in their craw.'

'A holy war?'

'God, Mordie, you read me about 'em at least once a week. They're trying their best to provoke a confrontation with the government.'

'They's just crazy damn gun freaks playin' soldier boy on weekends.'

'Oh, I think not, Mordie. I think their mission goes far beyond that. What's the time?'

'Quarter a seven.'

'I think I'll revise my sermon a little. Give these boys a taste of what they want.'

'You think they're gonna be out there in the crowd?'

'Of course. Probably tape-recording the whole thing.'

'Hell, that ain't legal.'

The preacher laughed. 'I'm sure that concerns them.'

'What d'ya know, they're gettin' dinner. You're right, they're stickin' around.' He paused a moment. 'Helluva'n offer, T.'

'It can be refined. And we'll see what their paper looks like.'

'You think they already wrote up that contract?'

The preacher smiled. 'Tell you what they didn't do, they didn't come all the way over here from Montana to shoot the shit, Mordie.'

Three hundred people packed the worship tent, fanning away the heat with newspapers and their hands. Harmon Jasper nodded to Penny, and she walked nervously to the front of the makeshift stage. She smiled sheepishly as, behind her, two teenagers, a girl on guitar and a boy on harmonica, struck up a slow, almost mournful beat. Penny's voice trembled but it was clear and sweet.

In the RV the preacher stood next to an open window and listened, stirred and aroused by her innocence.

'Oh yes,' he said to himself.

When she finished, Harmon Jasper stepped up to the microphone. The two young people struck up 'I'll Fly Away.' The layman began a jig. The congregation started to clap their hands. A few voices joined the musicians.

> *'Some glad morning,*
> *When this life is over,*
> *I'll fly away . . .'*

By the second verse the congregation was in the mood.

22

Foot-stomping and clapping, they all joined in the song.

Brother T closed the window and chuckled to himself.

'Time to dance,' he whispered. He gathered up his cane and Bible; his other props were already in place on the stage. He took Mordachai's arm and they walked to the tent. As the singing ended, Brother T pulled back the flap and entered the tent, tapping his cane ahead of him. The congregation fell silent. Brother T walked alone onto the platform. He stopped when he felt the edge of the makeshift stage. He dropped the cane to the floor and his milky eyes stared out at the audience.

He held the Bible high over his head.

'Praise GOD!'

'Praise GOD!'

'Praise JESUS!'

'Praise JESUS!'

'The word . . .' his voice rasped, 'is GOD!'

There were a few 'Amens' from the audience.

'These are HARD times, friends. Hard, hard times.'

'Amen!'

'These are times that strain your faith. . . .'

'Amen!'

'This is the time of Job.'

'Amen!' *'Amen!'*

'But . . . and hear me well . . . if you would deny God, then you best leave this place *now*, because God IS the word, and if you don't believe *that* you can walk right out the door. Go out and get in your car and go home and stand in the darkness . . . because that's all you got without God's love.'

'Hallelujah! . . . Amen!'

He paused for a few moments.

'I am here to tell you if you believe, the Lord God will come through for you. He will stand by your side. He will guide you through this abyss. David tells you in Chapter Two: *Is any among you afflicted? Let him pray! Is any sick among you? Let him call for the elders of the church;*

23

*and let them pray over him, anointing him with oil in the
name of the Lord . . . the prayer of faith shall save the
sick, and the Lord shall raise him up. . . .'*

'Amen . . . . AMEN!!'

'Well, brothers and sisters, *we* are afflicted. Our hearts
are sick. Why? Because this land is dying around us . . .
only one thing can save us, one thing, brothers and sisters
– *FAITH*. Faith in the Lord because, dear hearts, only
faith will keep you strong. Only prayer will bring relief.'

'Amen!'

He threw the Bible down on the floor. It landed flat,
spewing dust as it struck the platform.

'I don't *need* the Bible to talk to you tonight. Don't
need scripture. Don't need David, Mark, Luke, or John
to tell you what's comin'. You read about it every day.
See it on your television. You see it when you look out the
window. They're burning a hole in the sky and the sun is
burning up our fields and dryin' up our streams and
who's lettin' em do it? Who's coverin' it up? Your
government, that's who. And who is the government?
The people you put in office. They're afraid of offending
the big business boys because they get all that PAC
money and lobby money from 'em. And when your fields
're fallow and your streams're dust, who's gonna come
take your farm away from you? The IRS, that's who. The
Infernal Revenue Service.'

The audience had fallen silent.

'They're givin' away our wilderness to the sawmillers.
Look at your children . . . go ahead, look at 'em right
now. Know why? Because they're gonna suffocate to
death if we don't stop 'em. The trees put the oxygen in
the air, and without it we're all gonna die. The government's mollycoddling the polluters with their *mon*-
oxides and their *di*-oxides, telling 'em, 'C'mon in, stink
up the land, poison the water and air.' Want to talk about
Armageddon? Brothers and sisters, it's right out there . . .
in your burned-out land. Parousia is all about us. The

24

Devil himself has brought his hell fires up and spread 'em across God's bountiful land. Tain't fair . . .'

'*AMEN!*'

'T'aint right . . .'

'*AMEN!*'

'Pay one man for ploughin' under his crop and take another man's farm away from him when times're hard. God is angry. God is sick of having His creation destroyed by greed.'

More 'Amens.'

'*I CAN'T HEAR YOU! I say, GOD IS THE WORD.*'

'Amen!' 'Amen!' 'Amen!'

'Do you trust God? Do you trust the Lord?'

'Yeeees!'

'Good God A'mighty, He is with us tonight!'

'*Amen!*'

'God is here in this tent with us, neighbors. God loves us all, every man, woman, and child here together. We offer up this tune, it's kind of the history of the world in three minutes. You know, brothers and sisters, every time I hear the news, this song makes more sense.'

The harmonica and guitar laid down the beat, a fast, foot-stomping beat. The guitar player closed her eyes and started singing:

> '*So often when men are blessed*
> *with prosperity,*
> *The goodness and mercy of God*
> *They no longer see.*
> *They sing the prayer with Him,*
> *And offer up their pleas,*
> *Then they turn away from God*
> *And do just as they please.*
> *Just as an eagle,*
> *Serves her nest,*
> *So that her young ones*
> *Will have her best . . .*'

The singing gathered energy. The louder they sang, the faster he danced. Hop, hop, skip, hop, hop, skip. Somewhere off to one side a woman raised both hands over her head and began speaking in tongues, then another joined, and another. The frenzy was building. The preacher danced toward the varnished boxes on the table near the pulpit.

Eyes widened, the tempo picked up. Nervous energy swept through the crowd.

As he approached the boxes, he saw Mordachai come into the tent. He was smacking his tambourine against his leg, looking back outside, up at the sky. He smacked the tambourine faster.

Brother T looked into one of the boxes. Two sand-colored rattlesnakes lay on the bottom of the box. He flung open the lid of the box. The furous rattling from within was drowned out by the singing, by the 'Amens,' by the voices babbling in a strange unknown language.

The preacher raised his voice above the chaos:

'Mark, Chapter Fifteen. *And these signs shall follow them that believe; in my name shall they cast out devils; they shall speak with new tongues; and they shall take up serpents . . .*'

He plunged his hand into the box, grabbed one of the two rattlers by its middle, and lifted it out. He danced away from the box, petting the snake, feeling its muscles rippling against the palm of his hand, sticking out his tongue and letting the snake's flitting tongue touch his.

The congregation went wild. Electricity seemed to flow from the rattling serpent into the crowd. He saw Penny, in the second row, eyes closed, head back, wildly clapping her hands. The preacher raised the snake over his head and continued to do his spastic jig.

He reached into the box, took up the other snake. He draped the first rattler around his neck, held the second out with both hands.

'Lord, your beleaguered servants beseech you, bring us the rain. We remember your words in James Five, dear

God. *Fear not, be glad and rejoice: for the LORD will do great things. For, lo, he that formeth the mountains, and createth the wind, and declareth unto man what is His thought, The LORD, The God of hosts, is His name.'*

He heard the first pop on the tent above him, then another. He took one hand away, keeping the snake at arm's length with one hand while he reached for the other, which seemed entranced as it dangled around his neck.

'Be not afraid, ye beasts of the field: for the pastures of the wilderness do spring, for the tree beareth her fruit, the fig tree and the vine do yield their strength. Rejoice in the LORD your God and He will cause to come down for you . . . the rain. And the floors shall be full of wheat, and the vats shall overflow with wine and oil . . .'

Then more drops. Like machine-gun fire, they began to pelt the tent. Outside, geysers of dust burst around the raindrops as they splattered the hard earth.

The preacher reached for the first snake, started to take it from his shoulders, and as he did the snake was roused from its stupor. Its head suddenly snapped up.

The neck curled back.

The hinged jaws sprang open.

The preacher saw it in slow motion. Mouth open almost 180 degrees. Fangs glistening with venom. Then it struck, a tawny streak, and bang! The fangs buried deep into his forearm.

It felt like someone had hit him in the arm with a baseball bat. He could feel the fangs puncturing deep into the muscle. Fire raced up his arm. The other snake turned its head toward the arm that held it, began to curl back.

The preacher grabbed the first snake just behind its jaws, squeezed, and ripped it out of his arm.

The crowd gasped. Several people screamed. Those close to the platform backed away.

'Don't stop!' the preacher yelled. 'Sing louder. Bring it down!'

Outside, Shrack, Granger, and the young sergeant watched from their car as the snake struck.

'Jesus!' Shrack said. Granger just stared in mute horror.

Pain streaked up the preacher's arm and gnarled his shoulder. The venom burned deep in his flesh. His arm began to go numb. He thrust the first snake into the box. It slithered into a corner and coiled up, getting ready to strike again. He dropped the second snake on top of it, distracting it for a moment, and closed the lid of the box.

Mordie and Harmon Jasper rushed to his side.

'Keep it going, keep it going,' he gasped to Jasper, and to Mordachai, 'Get me outside.'

Jasper grabbed the mike and began singing louder as Mordie led Brother T through the rear flap of the tent.

Lightning cut a jagged, orange path across the sky. The rain poured down.

'I'll get ya to the RV.'

'No,' the preacher said, his voice pinched and weak. 'Over on the table. Want to feel the rain. I'm on fire.'

'How bad is it?'

'Forgot how bad it hurts.' He was gasping for breath. 'Squeezin' my chest.'

Mordie swept paper plates, bottles of ketchup, and napkins off the tabletop and helped the stricken preacher lie down. He lay on his back, ripped open his caftan almost to his waist. His arms fell out at his sides as though he was embracing the fury of the storm.

'Feels good, Mordie. Rain feels good.'

'How about you. How do you feel?'

'Numb. I feel . . . far away.'

'Hang in there, old buddy.'

'Keep 'em singin', Mordie. Get the baskets goin' around. Tell 'em I'm out here for them – doing battle with the Devil.'

In the touring car the three men watched the drama playing out next to the prayer tent.

Shrack took out a cigar, tore off the wrapper, and bit off the end, spitting the nip of tobacco out the window. 'He should have a doctor on hand when he pulls that shit,' he said.

'He won't accept medical help,' Granger said. 'It's a test of faith.'

The colonel lit the cigar with a Zippo lighter, slowly twirling it in the flame until it was evenly lit. 'You ask me, he needs a new wiring job. If he isn't dead already.'

'If that's what he believes, that's what he believes. I don't ever argue with a man's beliefs. That's between him and God.'

'Sticking a crazy rattler in your own face? Helluva way to play up to God. Then refuse a doctor?' He shook his head.

'You don't take up snakes unless you believe you're sanctified. In his heart he believes if he dies, he goes straight to the arms of the Lord. He lives, it means the Lord loves him that much more.'

'You believe all that Bible-thumping bullshit, don't yuh, Lewis?'

'Well, I still admire the words, but I fell from grace a long time ago.'

'Actually, I only remember one verse from the Book, but it stands me well,' Shrack said.

'Which one's that?'

' *"There is nothing better for a man than that he should eat and drink, and that his soul should enjoy good in his labor."* '

'Ecclesiastes,' the young sergeant said. 'Chapter Two.'

The colonel smiled bitterly. 'Very good, son. My old man did enough Bible-barking for the whole damn state of Montana. Pumped it into me morning, noon, and night until the day I left home for the Army. If I made a mistake in spelling or misquoted the Book, he'd take me out to the barn, cross my hands, tie 'em at the wrist, hang 'em over a hook, and whale my ass with a two by four, all the while quoting the damn Bible at me. He did on me until I was sixteen and too big to mess with. When I came back from 'Nam, I never went home again.'

'You came back to Montana and never went to see your family?' the sergeant said.

'My mother died while I was away,' the colonel said, staring through binoculars at the preacher lying still as a tree trunk on the picnic table. 'The old man married some seventeen-year-old a couple months later. I didn't need some pimply-faced Jesus freak giving me shit.' He puffed on his cigar, then added, 'Know what surprises me? What surprises me is the snakes are the McCoy. I figured he bled the venom before the service . . . but, the good brother over there, he's one sick puppy.'

'Excuse me, Colonel. Thing is, he believes,' the sergeant said, without turning around. 'Put himself in the hands of the Lord, sir. *Then shall the dust return to the earth as it was, and the spirit shall return unto God who gave it.*'

The colonel stared at the back of the sergeant's head for a few moments and said, 'If you say so, Sergeant.'

'It was Solomon said it, sir, not me.'

'*In my name shall they cast out devils; speak new tongues; take up serpents; and if they drink any deadly thing, it shall not hurt them,*' Granger said. 'Also Ecclesiastes.'

The colonel looked at Granger with surprise.

'Actually, I did a little reading about snake handlers,' Granger said.

'You memorized that?'

'I thought it might come up.'

'You're a shrewd son of a bitch, Lewis,' the colonel said, still watching the picnic table through his binoculars.

'That's how come I own all those radio stations and banks, Harry.'

The preacher's legs began to tremble and his whole body started to spasm.

'Christ, he's taking a fit.'

'Fightin' the Devil,' the sergeant whispered with awe. 'Hallelujah.'

'Hallefuckinlujah, my ass. He's gonna just lay there and die right in front of our eyes.'

A thin stalk of a man in a white suit came out of the tent and walked toward the picnic table. Mordie stopped him before he got to the preacher's side.

'Best leave him alone, brother. Just keep prayin' on him.'

'I'm a doctor.'

'He don't want no doctor. Don't *need* no doctor.'

The doctor stared down at the preacher. In the oblique light from the nearby tent, he saw a man whose skin was gray, whose breathing was erratic and labored, whose arm was swollen the size of an orange, who was shivering almost as if in seizure, and whose eyes seemed almost to be hemorrhaging. Foam bubbled from the corners of his mouth. Behind the doctor the young woman, Penny, left the tent and walked to the picnic table. She stood in the rain and looked down at Brother T with a combination of fear and awe. The doctor took his wrist, looking for a pulse, but the preacher jerked it away.

He spoke in short gasps.

'God's here. I feel his presence. He will guide me through the tunnel or take me to paradise.'

'I'm afraid I don't take the Bible literally,' the doctor said.

'Then what have you got?' Brother T asked, and smiled. *'He that believeth and is baptized shall be saved; but he that believeth not shall be damned. Mark Fifteen.'*

The preacher opened his mouth, letting the raindrops pelt his tongue and throat.

'Ahhh.'

31

He began speaking very fast, speaking in the cadence of words and sentences, except what came out was gibberish.

'We need to call an ambulance. He's going into shock.'

'No!' Mordie said. 'I know you wanna help, but this is the way of it. He's in the Lord's hands now.'

'He's going to die.'

'If that's the plan . . .'

'I just can't stand by and–'

'What's the matter, Doctor, you forget how to pray? Go back inside and pray for him. He'll come through. Ain't the first time.'

'He's been bitten before?'

'Twice since we been together, once before that.'

'My God!'

'God is right. It's God's show. Go back inside and talk to Him.'

The doctor turned slowly and walked back through the rain to the tent. Penny stepped closer to the preacher.

'Best go inside, missy.'

'I can pray just as easy out here in the rain.'

She took the preacher's hand. His eyelids fluttered and closed. Mordachai could feel the heat rising from his fevered body. The raindrops pelting him almost sizzled when they fell on his flesh. His lips barely moved and words sputtered out, run-together words, garbled words, like the possessed ones speaking in tongues inside the tent.

'Cachungcachungcachungcachung . . .'

'What's that? What're you tryin' to say, T?'

'Cachungcachungcachungcachung . . .'

He was trapped inside his own nightmares. An observer, watching his own past. He sees a highway flashing in and out through a snowstorm. A sign: Crikside, five miles, and a few moments later another leading up a Kentucky mountainside. And then a chopper coming from

32

nowhere, hovering over him in the raging snowstorm.

The preacher squeezed Penny's hand, still jabbering, the words tumbling over each other. She couldn't make sense of the babble.

'. . . camefromnowhere . . . almosthomealmostthere-thenthere'sthis . . . this*chopper*right . . . overthecar . . . Vail . . . hadtobeVailthat . . . goddamnjunkyarddog-neverletsgo . . . chopperinthisblizzard . . .'

The car skids off the muddy mountain road, and he runs through the woods to the mine shaft. Number Five. And suddenly there's Vail, pointing a gun at him and he's walking away because he knows, he knows, no way Vail will shoot him in the back. And then the platform beneath him starts to give way. Old rotting timbers hide under the snow. Below them the shaft goes straight down, 1,500 feet. He's terrified. He remembers his eighth birthday and the total fear he felt when he stared down from the elevator, down into that black hole. His father taking him down in that creaking elevator, descending into that bottomless pit, 1,500 feet straight down. Why? Because all the men in Crikside go into the mines when they're eight years old. Now boarded up for years, the timbers are rotting underfoot and he's walking faster, and it's rotting out and falling away under each step until the cover collapses. He drops six feet and lands on the rotted elevator under it. And it, too, begins to creak under his weight and fall apart. He drags himself across the floor as it tilts, the rotten wood shredding as his fingers dig in. Splinters rip under his nails, piercing the quick. As the floor falls away under him, he rolls franti-cally onto the platform that serves it. He leans against the platform wall, eyes closed, gasping for breath, waiting, waiting for the debris to hit bottom. He stares up through the hole in the snow, still shaking with fright.

And he hears it.

Cachungcachungcachungcachung.

And then he sees it. Sees the chopper as it passes over the hole.

'Made it,' the preacher said, quite clearly.

'Do you understand him?' Penny asked.

'Just talking crazy,' Mordachai answered.

'He said something about a veil.'

'Didn't make any sense t'me.'

He walks five miles over the mountain to Crikside.

The town is deserted. Beleaguered by snow, it is at a standstill. Darkness falls early in the deep valley, particularly here, where the trees blot out the last of the sunlight. He sits among trees on a ridge overlooking the town and little details begin to rush back. Even after eight years he remembers details about everything. The white sign at the edge of town. POPULATION: 212. The narrow valley with a single street half a mile long. On one side, Morgan's Creek and the railroad tracks leading up one side of the mountain to the mines. On the other, the steep walls of the valley trap the town. Company stores and company housing – seventy narrow, two-story frame houses, alike except for paint and trim – line both sides of the street for a half a mile or so, then it curves and rises out of the valley. Everything here belongs to the company, except Rebecca's house. The people own nothing. Their vision is defined by bad weather, poverty, geography, and fear of the outside. Simple people, ferociously patriotic, God-fearing, loyal, their faith fanatically rooted in the fundamentalist church, their fervor rooted in the flag, their loyalty rooted in a company that would exploit them to their graves.

Stupid people.

So much for Crikside.

Rebecca's cabin is just below him, on the opposite side of the roaring stream from town. It sits back in a bay of pine trees, a small A-frame structure with a large window overlooking the creek. A narrow wooden bridge leads to it.

He considers his luck. To the world, he is dead. It will be weeks before they even look for his body, if indeed they bother. He has to get some clothes and food and do it without leaving a trace. He needs a new identity. As soon as this storm is over and the weather clears, the police will come to the house. Snooping, looking for bits and pieces, filling in the blanks of the Aaron and Rebecca story. He has two, maybe three days to get out of there.

As darkness falls he goes down to the cabin. The key is where she always leaves it, in a magnetic box stuck under the aluminum drip pan near the back door. Had to be careful. He talks in whispers to himself. 'Can't leave a trace, can't tip 'em off I was ever here.'

The windows are boarded up. It is completely dark except for two or three narrow beams of light streaking through cracks in the boards. He stands inside the door, picturing the layout of the small house. A sleeping loft over the kitchen in the rear of the peaked great room. A bath and closet upstairs, a lavatory downstairs. Bookcases on the right, stereo across the room.

He must be careful not to disturb anything, not even the cobwebs.

He removes his wet shoes and socks and walks barefoot on the cold wooden floor to the kitchen, where he puts them in the sink. He feels his way up to the sleeping loft and checks the closet, finds a down quilt to sleep under. He retrieves an old radio, its batteries long dead, and a flashlight, also dead. And some candles. He lights one. Books are jammed into shelves that line one wall. There are several stacks of records, some antique 78 rpm's. The room is remarkably free of dust. Things seem to be left exactly where she had used them last – three years earlier.

He goes to the bookcase, recognizes a title and picks up

the book, opens it, finds a phrase that he had underlined in pencil many years before, a Chinese proverb: 'There are only two perfect men – one dead, the other unborn.' He carefully moves some books from a shelf and pulls out a loose board.

He reaches in the dark space and feels the metal money box. Their getaway money, now just his. He takes out the cash and replaces the board and books. He goes upstairs to the bed and counts it in candlelight.

Eight thousand, two hundred dollars.

Thank you, darlin'. Thank you, darlin' Rebecca.

He makes a list of basic necessities.

He sits in front of one of the boarded-up windows, staring through a narrow slit, watching the small hamlet.

He waits until after midnight before he leaves. He takes Rebecca's rucksack with him. He lurks in the darkness between two houses. He is next to Charlie Koswalski's clinic. Doctor, undertaker, optometrist. He stares in the window at the waiting room. Then he sees something. He tries the window. It doesn't move. He checks the lock – nobody ever locks their windows in Crikside. Open. He taps the window jamb, knocks frozen snow loose, and slides the window open. He enters the waiting room and squats down in front of a display on the counter.

Sunglasses. Oh yeah.

They'll never look for a blind man.

The hardware store is across the street, a long, squat building with a tin roof and a dim interior with an array of pickaxes, oil lamps, harnesses, work clothes, boots, flannel shirts, the like. Then there's Walenski's drugstore and the city hall, and then Clyde Boise's rambling old grocery store. Farther up the street is Miranda's Emporium, which sells mostly women's and children's Sunday clothes, and across the street from that is Early Simpson's café, bar, and a liquor store. The frame house next door is boarded up although the sign is still out front: *Avery Daggett Legal Advice and Office Supplies.*

The street is empty. He darts from the shadows to the opposite side of the road. The back door of the hardware store is unlocked. He takes batteries for the flashlight and radio. He carefully packs the rucksack, taking the clothing from the back of the shelf: two sets of long johns, a pair of heavy walking boots, gloves, two flannel shirts, two pair of work pants, a heavy jacket, a box of paper clips. Then he moves down to the grocery store. Once again he takes items from the back of the shelves where they won't be missed: canned goods he can eat cold, tuna, deviled ham, fruit, soda crackers, peanut butter, strawberry jam, a bottle of apple juice, aspirin. The rucksack is full. He is back in the cabin in less than an hour.

He goes in the bathroom, lights several candles, closes the door. He spreads paper towels on the floor, makes himself a snack, and tunes in the radio. An announcer is recounting the story of Rebecca and Aaron:

'This is not a legend, not a glamorized myth like the story of Bonnie and Clyde. This is a modern day horror story about two mass murderers that started ten years ago in the little town of Crikside, Kentucky. Now Rebecca, a psychotic schoolteacher, lies in the Cook County morgue, and her pupil and lover, Aaron Stampler, is dead in the bottom of the very coal mine he feared as a young boy. . . .'

Stampler smiles. It has a nice biblical ring to it.

He lies back on the bed, remembering Rebecca. He remembers the two-room schoolhouse where she taught eight grades in one room. And he remembers her wearing a denim jacket over a flowered shirt, an ankle-length skirt, and black boots. He remembers her thick, flaming red hair streaked with gray and pulled back in a tight ponytail. No jewelry or makeup, she was beautiful without it. He sat in the corner of the room, longing for her,

37

getting hard thinking about her. He was thirteen at the time.

She teaches him everything, encourages him to read, and when he is fourteen, she opens the world to him.

She is sitting cross-legged on the floor and he is reading to her. She knows it is coming, has been coming for a long time.

'Kin I touch you?' he says in a trembling voice.

'Don't say 'kin,' say 'can.' '

'Can. Can, can, can . . .' he says.

She unbuttons her blouse slowly.

He lies on the bed, adrenalized, his heart throbbing, his mouth dry, remembering how he reached out to her, his fingertips barely touching her skin, spreading the shirt open, gazing in awe at her breasts, his hands an inch away from her nipples.

'It's all right,' she says in a whisper, and she takes his hands in hers and places them on her, and he feels her nipples harden under his palms.

The only way out is the milk truck, if the milk truck from Somerset still comes every morning. The first night passes and no milk truck. But it is still snowing. Maybe tomorrow. He catnaps during the day, fearful of every sound. The second night he wraps his shoes and socks in paper towels and packs them in the rucksack, dresses warmly, cleans up all traces of his presence. He takes only her walking stick. He will be ready if the truck does show up. He goes out into the dark night and hides in the shadows near the grocery store. And waits.

An hour before dawn he hears it, chains grinding up the ice and snow on the road. It parks in front of the grocery store and the driver starts unloading the milk crates, taking them around to the back of the store. He makes a run for it, hides among the stacks of crates in the refrigerated truck. He hears the footsteps of the driver crunch-

ing through the snow, hunches down deep inside the truck, hears the door slam shut.

The driver stops at a truck stop for coffee near the toll entrance to the Cumberland Parkway. He slips out of the truck, taps his way into the restaurant. It is crowded and he waits by the door. A couple is seated nearby. The man leans across the table, nods toward Stampler, and then approaches him.

'Excuse me, brother, the place is crowded but my wife and me has room at our booth. Be pleased if you'd join with us.'

So far so good.

His name is Isiah Shackleford and he is a fundamentalist preacher. He and his wife Lee Ann are on their way to a small church outside a little Tennessee town called Bybee, where they will spend the winter preaching. They can give him a ride into Manchester, where he can catch a bus to Chattanooga and on down to Atlanta. He tells them his name is Travis.

Along the way, Stampler and Isiah get into a Bible-quoting match.

'Say, brother, you do know your scripture.'

'All my ma would read to me until I was in my teens,' he lies.

He wonders about the wooden box covered with a blanket beside him on the floor of the backseat. Then he hears the chattering.

'Whatcha got back here making that racket?'

Isiah pauses for a few moments before he answers.

'Snakes, Brother Travis. Hope you're not skittish. They're locked up safe and sound.'

'They your pets?'

'We take up snakes, Brother Travis. Church of Jesus Christ Wandering. Take a little strychnine occasionally, too.'

'Mark Fifteen,' he answers. 'And these signs shall follow them that believe; in my name shall they cast out

39

devils; they shall speak . . .'

The Shacklefords join him.

'. . . with new tongues; and they shall take up serpents.'

'Why don't you come into Bybee for the night? I'm sure one of the congregation'll put you up,' Isiah suggests.

'Good home-cooking,' Lee Ann promises.

Why indeed. Perfect.

He stays for two months. Isiah preaches every night to thirty-six parishoners. Within a week he is giving witness. By the second week he is delivering sermons. He sleeps in the spare room of a family named Fortside.

Over dinner one night he hears the name Enigma for the first time. Their preacher has just died of a snake bite.

The first night he sees Isiah dancing this crazy dance with three rattlers and a moccasin around his neck and one in each hand. The man is in ecstasy, in another world.

Stampler is drawn to the snakes, as a sinner is drawn to the Devil.

Everything is going along fine until the wife comes to his bed one night. She is ravenous in her lovemaking. It is his first sex in almost four years.

The next night their fifteen-year-old daughter drops in for a visit.

Time to move on.

He is on his way to freedom. He remembers the name.

'Enigma,' he says aloud.

He was breathing harder, his mouth gulping for the raindrops. Suddenly he opened his milky eyes and said, quite clearly, 'Enigma.'

'What's enigma?' Penny asked.

'Little town down South. Where he got his start. His first church. I was there the night he first came, just went up there and took up those two rattlers, held 'em up and

40

started preaching like I never heard before. Didn't even have a place t'stay. I took him home with me, fixed his dinner. Been taking care of him ever since.'

He remembers Enigma. Every detail. Getting off the bus. Cup of coffee in the bus stop. Practicing the blind thing. Feeling the edge of the cup and guiding the cream to the cup. Asking the waitress, 'Could you tell me where the Church of the Lord is?'

'Wouldn't go down there, mister. They're crazy. Let rattlesnakes and copperheads run around in there while they're praying.'

'Snakes don't bite blind people.'

Waitress, unsure, 'Aw c'mon. That ain't true. Is that true?'

'Well, I never been bit by one.'

Laughter.

Crumbled up macadam on the side of the road. An old hardware store. Handmade pews. Paintings of Christ in faux wood plastic frames. Men in white shirts buttoned to the top without ties. Galluses attached to belted pants. Work shoes. Women in cotton dresses, some buttoned to the chin. Flat shoes. No makeup. Unadorned hair. Hardship chiseled in the lines of all their faces. A man and woman on the platform playing guitars. The almost-words of the tongue-speakers, eyes closed, hands raised to the Almighty.'Abbada ba soshashashe . . .' And the singing. 'O Lord, show me the liiight . . . O Lord show me the liiight . . .' Tap-tap-tapping through the small crowd to the platform, and the preacher jigging, then stopping. Staring down at this blind man in the cheap black suit, stumbling as he steps up on the platform. The children, rattling in their handcrafted, varnished boxes with brass hinges, rattling with the music, leading him to them. He drops the cane, feels for the lid of one of the boxes, and opens it. Two six-footers the color of sand, quivering tails, black eyes, red tongues feeling the air.

He reaches in, grabs one of the diamondbacks a foot from its head, lifts it out. Strokes it. He does the jig. Lift one foot. Hop two beats on the other. Switch feet. Hop, hop. Switch. Hop, hop. Switch. Open the box again. The other child begins to coil. His heart batters his ribs. His mouth is dry and his throat is tightening. Hop, hop. Switch. Hop, hop. Switch. Going to the light. Going to the light. They wrap around his forearms, tails rattling in front of his face. Muscles swelling and contracting in his hands. What a rush!

I am God. I am God and the Devil and all the saints and all the sinners. The power of nature is in the palms of my hands.

Euphoria.

Brother T moved his arm, reached out as if he were try-ing to touch something.

'M-M-Mordie?' he stammered.

'It's Penny,' she said.

'Are you an angel?' he asked. 'Come to lead me to heaven?'

'No s-s-sir, just Penny.'

'You led me through the tunnel of darkness,' he said. 'I saw you in my madness.'

He raised himself on his elbows, and as he struggled to sit up she put an arm around his back and took his hand.

'Are you safe now?' she asked, her voice accented with fear.

'It'll pass.'

'I thought you were going to die.'

'God had other plans. God blessed me tonight. I am sanctified.'

'Praise the Lord.'

He struggled to a sitting position and shakily swung his legs over the side of the table onto the seat. Bile scorched the back of his throat and he leaned forward, almost falling off the table. She steadied him and he felt the warmth of her body against his.

'May be sick,' he said, and put his head down. She held him until the nausea passed.

He became aware of his surroundings, of the voices still singing in the worship tent, the rain falling through the trees, his own heart pounding in his ears.

'How long did that last?' he asked.

'An hour, maybe.'

'Sometimes it takes all night.'

With her help, he struggled off the table and stood in the wet grass. His legs were unsteady, and his knees began to shake.

'Maybe you best lay back down.'

'No. Help me inside.'

Penny led him back into the tent and helped him to the platform. He was shivering and his legs were unsteady, but he moved up to the edge of the platform and took the microphone from Harmon Jasper.

'God led me here tonight,' he said in a quivering voice. 'God put me to the test and brought the rain and led me through the tunnel. Praise be the Lord in His wisdom, praise be the Lord for His bounty. Praise God!'

The congregation moved toward him, shouting 'Amen' and 'Praise God' and 'Hallelujah.' They reached out to touch him, their eyes glistening with tears of gratitude and adoration. They touched his soaked caftan and his outstretched hands.

In the back of the tent Shrack, Granger, and the young sergeant watched the pilgrimage of farmers and business-men and wives and children moving to the front of the worship tent.

'Well, Harry?' Granger said.

'Let's hope he makes breakfast,' the colonel said.

Behind Harmon Jasper's house the preacher lay naked under a cotton sheet on the soft mattress Mrs. Jasper had

43

provided in a stall near the rear of the barn. They had fashioned it into a small room for him, with a lamp and a table beside the bed. The crowd was gone, leaving behind a generous contribution. The tent squatted empty at the edge of the field. The only sound was the rain still spattering intermittently on the roof, the only odor the pleasant smell of wet hay. Brother T stared at the ceiling and took in deep, long breaths. His arm throbbed painfully and the aches in the joints in his legs and arms were profound.

Should I thank God or the Devil? he wondered. *Whoever. That snake hitting me was the miracle. It made believers of the whole damn bunch. Hallelujah and amen.*

He heard the barn door squeak open and waited. A moment later she appeared in the stall doorway. An angel in a white frock shimmering in the lamplight.

'It's me, Brother T,' she said softly. 'It's Penny.'

'My rose of Sharon,' he said. 'My angel of mercy.'

She smiled, embarrassed and flattered by his words. 'I brought you some milk, and Papa sent you one of his nightshirts.'

'Everyone is so kind. So generous.'

'It was you who was generous, giving yourself up for us. I never saw such bravery.'

'I was in the hands of God,' he said, sitting up. He let the sheet drift down to his waist.

She stared at his powerful arms and chest and felt a familiar trembling below her stomach. He began to shiver, and she came to him and helped him put on the nightshirt, pulling it down over his head, her hands running across his hard body.

'The Lord blessed me tonight,' he said, taking her hands in his. 'I was sanctified, as you are.'

Her hands were trembling, not out of fear, but with anticipation.

He slid his hands up her arms to her shoulders and then her neck to her cheeks until his fingertips were brushing

44

her lips. He could feel her heart pounding. He drew her very tenderly to him, felt her breasts swelling against his chest, felt her breath against his throat. His arms surrounded her.

'I will bless you as I was blessed,' he whispered. 'I will anoint you with my seed and share God's love with you.'

He lowered her to his bed.

Two

Sheffield, Illinois, was sixty miles south of Chicago, an affluent town of seven-thousand-plus mostly middle and upper middle class citizens who either commuted into the city every day or worked in a burgeoning electronics industry that provided higher than average income in white-collar jobs. The town itself had preserved the look of the fifties, its main street lined with locally owned businesses that were supported by the locals. A shopping mall and fast-food center was located a few miles from town, but there was a sense of loyalty by the people of Sheffield to businesses owned by their neighbors and friends. There was very little crime in Sheffield. It was an anachronism in the late 1990s, a town that tried to hold on to its history and values while progress swirled about it.

It was a perfect place for the trial, although the locals were largely annoyed by the press that swarmed in, filling its old four-story hotel, the motels on its outskirts, and the three above-average downtown restaurants. News vans with satellite dishes mounted on their roofs crowded the parking places around the courthouse, a stately old building that had recently enjoyed its one hundredth birthday.

The Sheffield Café, up the street from the center of attraction, had become the gathering spot of the media. They absorbed space, drinking coffee and devouring the daily specials. The locals at first complained bitterly that these out-of-towners had taken over, but now, on the eve of the trial, they ventured forth, mixing with the press, listening to theories and rumors and generally getting caught up in the excitement of the biggest event in the town's history. The sixteen jurors and alternates who were to be sequestered when the trial began had achieved the status of local celebrities.

Jack Connerman sat at a small corner table in the café with a view of the courthouse down the street. The magazine writer had been in Sheffield for two days, talking to the locals and soaking up local color. The small table was covered with notebooks, local newspapers, and a legal pad on which he was scratching out notes, referring constantly to his research. He was so deeply focused on his task he didn't see the tall woman enter the restaurant, look around, and walk to his table.

'Jack Connerman?'

Startled, he looked up sharply and whipped off a pair of old-fashioned horn-rimmed glasses. He recognized the dark-haired woman immediately. Decked out in a black suit and white silk blouse, she was stunning; prettier in person, less officious, perhaps, and softer than she appeared on television. She was carrying a forest-green leather briefcase.

'Ms. Azimour,' he said, standing and offering his hand. There was nothing soft about her handshake.

'Sorry to interrupt, are you on deadline?'

'Nope.'

'Good. May I join you for a minute?' she asked pleasantly.

'Please.'

She sat down across from him and smiled when she looked at the mess on the table. He slid the notebooks and papers into a pile and laid the legal pad on top, face-down.

'You needn't do that on my account,' she said.

'I don't own the table,' he said with a boyish grin. Connerman was a lean man with graying hair and a youthful face that belied his forty-eight years. He was dressed haphazardly in a wrinkled tan poplin suit and a pale blue shirt open at the collar.

'How's the food?' she asked, checking the menu. 'I'm starving. Airline food tastes more and more like cardboard every day.' There was a trace of British in her accent.

'Like Mom used to cook,' he said. 'They make a mean Reuben.'

She flagged a waitress and ordered a Reuben and a glass of Budweiser.

'I just got in an hour ago,' she said. 'Couldn't get a room at the hotel. They've got me in the Sunflower Motel, which is in Kansas someplace.'

He laughed. 'You're spoiled,' he said. 'You're about fifteen minutes from town. Couldn't pull any rank at the hotel, huh?'

'I don't think they ever heard of World Wide News over there.' She shook her head. 'I like to be where the action is.'

'Well, this is where the action is during the day. At night everybody gathers in Harnicker's Steak House right over . . .' He turned and pointed across the street. '. . . there. It becomes a bar when they close the grill at nine.'

'Been here long?'

'Two days.' He paused for a minute, then asked, 'Can I do something for you?'

'I understand you're Martin Vail's official biographer.'

He laughed heartily. 'Unauthorized only,' he said.

'Everybody says you're the Vail expert.'

'I've been covering him off and on for about fifteen years.'

'I hear you've done twenty or thirty magazine stories on him.'

'Four is more like it. Plus some columns.'

'Freelancer?'

'Contract writer for *City Magazine*, and I do a column for the *Trib* on Sundays. Op ed.'

'Are you friends?'

'Well, let's put it this way, he's never taken a poke at me.'

'He takes pokes at people?'

'Figure of speech.' Connerman took out his wallet, leafed through some business cards in one of its pockets, took one out, and handed it to her. Vail's name was printed in the right-hand corner. In the center of the card were two words: NO COMMENT.

'That tough, huh?' she asked, raising an eyebrow.

'Well, he's not real verbal.'

'Think he'll stand still for a one-on-one interview?'

Connerman threw back his head and laughed so hard half the eyes in the restaurant looked over at him.

'If that's what you're after, you made a long trip for nothing.'

'I've been told that before.'

'That what Castro told you?'

'His hatchet men did. Fidel was easy once I got past the bodyguards and hangers-on.'

'Quite a coup.'

'Did you see it?'

'Oh yeah. And I'm not even interested in Cuba.'

'Everybody so far says Vail's a real pain in the ass.'

'He's a cool guy, just doesn't do a lot of talking outside the courtroom. He has a real hard-on for lawyers who try their cases on the courthouse steps.'

'I'm interested in why.'

'Why?'

'Why he decided to take on Western Pulp and Paper, and Atlas Chemical.'

'There's a lot more to it than that.'

'Not as far as the national press is concerned. Do you know both their stocks took a nose dive over this?'

He nodded.

'Is this guy Vail running for governor or something?'

'Vail doesn't do anything for show. And he's never run

for public office in his life. Doubt he ever will.'

'He was D.A. in Chicago before he became Attorney General. How did that happen?'

'He was appointed chief prosecutor in Chicago and became D.A. when his boss died of a stroke. The governor appointed him Attorney General when his predecessor was caught, uh, in delicto, as the saying goes.'

'That made headlines all over the world. I mean the ex-Attorney General's indiscretions, not Vail's appointment.'

The waitress brought her Reuben and she attacked it like a field hand on a fifteen-minute lunch break.

'What do you want from me, Ms. Azimour?'

'Call me Valerie, will you?'

'Okay.'

'You're not a fountain of information yourself, Jack. Okay if I call you Jack?'

'Everybody does.'

'I just want to get a handle on this guy. Why would he take on two of the most powerful corporations in the world?'

'Like I said, there's more to it than that.'

'Such as . . .'

'A whole county gone rotten. This is a RICO case, Ms. . . . Valerie. He's looking to take down four commissioners, a couple of state environmental boys, a bank. And he's probably going to give the daily newspaper up there a 200,000-volt jolt before he's through.'

'I repeat: Why?'

'Well, for starters, three major corporations colluding to bribe public officials and state investigators, diverting money from all kinds of government programs and using it for their own purposes, laundering money through banks they controlled, covering up one of the worst pollution problems in the country, and corrupting a local newspaper and its reporters to lie to its readers so the people wouldn't know what was going on.' He paused for a moment and added, 'On the other hand, maybe he just got pissed off about something.'

Now it was Azimour who laughed, holding a napkin over her mouth as she did. 'Hot-tempered Irishman, that it?'

Connerman leaned back in his chair and stared at her. 'What do you know about Vail?'

She shrugged, then opened her briefcase, took out several magazines and a folder of clippings, and dropped them on the table in front of him. 'Confession time. I've read all your stuff on him.'

He moved the items around with a finger and nodded. 'Well, I'm flattered. Now you know everything I know.'

'C'mon.'

'What else can I tell you?'

'I'd like to get inside the guy. What makes him tick, what kind of personal life does he have, why did he take this on? I mean, he's going up against a couple of real sharks, the toughest corporate lawyers in the country.'

'Maybe that's why he's doing it,' Connerman said with a slight grin.

'Doesn't worry him, then?'

'Are you kidding?' He shook his head. 'I'll give you this. When Martin Vail goes into court tomorrow, he's going in to win, to win big, and there's no question in his mind about that.'

'You do know this guy pretty well, then?'

'Well, we've kind of grown up together, professionally I mean.'

'In what way?'

'I've sat through a lot of his trials. He's matured from an arrogant, hard-nosed defense attorney to a tough prosecutor to a guy who really believes in constitutional law.'

'Mr. Self-Confidence, huh.'

'Put it this way, I doubt he's lost five minutes of sleep over those corporate sharks you mentioned. Vail's one of

51

the best lawyers alive. And I'll bet you every penny I make on this story you don't get more than three words out of him. The first one will be "Hello."'

'You're really sold on this guy, aren't you?'

'I admire perfection.'

Vail guided the black sedan into the underground hotel garage and parked near the service elevator. Police lines kept the press out of the garage. He called the desk on his cellular phone.

'Hi, it's Martin Vail. I'm at the service elevator. Thanks.'

He snapped the phone off, stuck it in his pocket, and sat in the car until the doors opened. He got out and scampered into the cubicle.

'Any problems, Jerry?' he asked the plainclothes detective who operated it.

'Nah. Coupla hotshots sneaked into the hotel earlier today, but we nailed them before they got through the lobby.'

'You do good work, Detective Fennerman.'

'I do okay for a small-town cop.'

'Ever want to move up in the world, let me know. I still have a little pull with the Chicago department.'

'No thanks. The last homicide we had here was four years ago. And the last drive-by shooting we had was a teenager shooting the bird at one of his buddies.'

Vail chuckled. 'I'd stay here, too, Jerry.'

He got off on the sixth floor. The team had taken over half the upper story of the hotel, and carpenters had blocked off the hallway. The only way to get to the A.G.'s headquarters was by guarded elevator.

Naomi Chance, who literally ran the operation, smiled when he walked into the main suite. Behind her, clerks were busy arranging evidence, tagging files, getting everything ready for the next day. Vail's office was in an adjoining suite.

'Hi, boss, have a nice trip?'

'If you call spending the day at Joliet Prison a nice day, yeah.'

'Okay, was it successful?'

'The missing link.'

'No kidding? That good, huh.'

'I made Jimmy 'the Doc' Fox an offer a month ago. Today he decided he liked it.'

Naomi looked concerned. 'You're not making a deal with that scumbag, are you?'

'Jimmy Fox is doing ten to twenty for second-degree murder. He's done five, so he's up for parole in another two. We put him in a country club like Statesville and guarantee he'll walk in two years.'

'A stone killer?'

'All I'm doing is moving him out of Joliet. He's clean there, he'll do the deuce and go out anyway.'

'And what did he give up?'

'I'll fill you in after I take a shower. Gotta get the prison stink out of my nose. Anything new here?'

'Shaughnessey called,' Naomi said casually.

'You're kidding.'

'He's on the third floor – the Presidential Suite, naturally. Asked if you'd drop by for a drink.'

'The night before the trial and he wants me to stop by for a drink?'

'He actually was pleasant to me. Usually he treats me like I have something catching.'

'Shaughnessey is something catching.'

She laughed. 'Want to tell him you don't have time?'

'We hear from Abel yet?'

'That's the second message. Dinner with the mysterious gentleman at seven-thirty at the Coq d'Or. There's a private dining room in the back. Dermott and Abel are bringing him over to make sure he isn't followed. They were worried about bringing him here.'

'Smart.' He looked at his watch. It was four-thirty.

53

'Call Shaughnessey. Tell him I have fifteen minutes at five.'

She laughed. 'Jesus, Marty, you're going to piss him off before you even go down there.'

'I just want to make sure he knows the Attorney General of the state outranks a two-bit state senator.'

'What do you think he wants?'

'He's a PAC whore. He's going to try to make a deal for his pals.'

'You think Dillmore is worried? Next to Jane, he's the toughest corporate lawyer in the state.'

'This is a criminal case.'

'That's why he's got Neil Jarmon at the table with him.'

'Naomi, Shaughnessey has a deal up his sleeve. Bet a dollar.'

'I can't afford the bet on what the state pays me.'

'Yearn for the old days down on Gaylord Street?'

Naomi had been with Vail since he started building a reputation as the most feared defense advocate in the state, seventeen years ago. They had worked out of Vail's house in a restored section of town until he became D.A.

'Are you kidding? The money was good, but the clientele . . .' She let the sentence dangle.

'Hell, Naom, the clientele's the same as ever, just on the other side now.'

Vail went into the bathroom and palmed cold water on his face. Naomi was there with a towel when he finished.

'How old is old Roy now? Shouldn't he be retiring soon?' she asked.

'I'm not sure. Sixty, sixty-five, somewhere in between. And he'll never retire. He'll be like Strom Thurmond, a toothless, senile old fart drooling in the legislature.'

'He's sure ballooned up in the last couple of years. Looks like Jabba the Hut.'

'I'll tell him you said so.'

'Don't you dare.'

There had been a time when Roy Shaughnessey's reputation as the most feared politician in the state was in doubt. The former Chicago ward heeler had risen from a state representative to Attorney General, then Secretary of State. He was the state's political high priest, the bludgeon that kept young upstarts and newcomers in the state house in line, but he had made a bid for governor and had been so soundly defeated that his power had begun to wane. Ambitious young political gunslingers, thinking he was washed up, challenged him. Big mistake. Shaughnessey had backed Cleveland Briggs, an unknown, in Briggs's bid for the governorship against a former ally turned enemy, the incumbent, Harold Gross. Shaughnessey had managed Briggs's campaign, called in years of political favors, threatened, cajoled, and charmed votes, and handed Briggs a stunning upset. He had weathered forty years, five administrations, and the sniping of the tyros, and proven he was still the master politician. He couldn't live long enough to call in his political IOUs around the state. Young Democratic hopefuls seeking national office traveled from all over the country to take him to lunch or dinner, hoping to get his advice for the price of the meal.

And Governor Briggs owed him big-time. He was the whip that toughed through the governor's favorite legislation and who got the votes to kill anything Briggs opposed. More than one old war-horse trembled when Shaughnessey called on the phone or stopped by for a chat.

Martin Vail was the one thorn that remained firmly implanted in his side. Ironically, Vail had risen from the state's most visceral defense attorney to D.A. and then to Attorney General because of Shaughnessey. The irony was that Shaughnessey had talked him into switching from the most dangerous defender in the state to Chicago's chief prosecutor. It was politically expedient to get him on the state's side, and a wise move, except that

Vail's first action had been to indict a corporation and two city councilmen for under-the-table dealings, and he narrowly missed indicting Shaughnessey, who had successfully shielded himself from the corporation. To get Vail out of his hair, Shaughnessey had talked the governor into naming him Attorney General – the unfortunate incumbent, Oscar Levinson, having been caught by an enterprising paparazzo in a pinafore and high heels, cavorting with a thousand-dollar-a-night hooker who was wearing a strap-on dildo. He had resigned before the morning edition hit the street.

Now they were at odds again. Vail had indicted the CEOs of two of the largest industrial giants in the country, the head of the Environmental Safety Division, two of his field agents, four county commissioners, and the head of the most profitable land development company in the state – all either heavy PAC contributors or ardent supporters of the governor and most of his allies in the legislature. The charge was racketeering and included the corruption of elected officials, money laundering, misuse of state funds, violation of state environmental laws, and various other felonies. The final irony was that Vail himself had rewritten the racketeering statute, using as a model the federal RICO statutes with most of its loopholes plugged. Then he had successfully lobbied his bill through the legislature. He did it with little fanfare. Most of the legislators barely read the amendments.

The case had attracted national attention since it involved two of the country's major industries, which were charged with, among other things, knowingly violating antipollution laws and bribing investigators from the ESD to cover up the dangerous levels of pollutants they were releasing into the air, water, and earth. That was just the tip of the corruption iceberg. They had formed an unholy alliance with the developer, and for years the three corporations had ruled the county at their whims, owning politicians, controlling an embarrassingly unethical daily newspaper with advertising, even avoiding millions of dollars in taxes by owning the tax assessors. The tentacles of this amoral alliance had reached out deep into the county, corrupting zoning boards, health boards, department heads, even controlling both local political parties. They indulged themselves in all the worst aspects of power and destroyed any person or thing that challenged their empire.

Vail had spent eighteen months and the energies of all of his young staff, known as Vail's Wild Bunch, to build a sweeping RICO case against the presidents and general managers of all three corporations, four of the seated commissioners, two deposed commissioners, three state employees, the county manager, and six members of the health board. The case had quickly attracted the national press and was going to be nationally televised.

Vail was now regarded as a dangerous and uncontrollable loose cannon by the political structure.

He couldn't have cared less. Which is why he was the only man capable of unnerving Roy Shaughnessey.

Normally a bulky man anyway, booze, good food, and soft living had turned Shaughnessey into an immense Buddha. His hands were pudgy, dimpled melons. His face was a balloon with hooded eyes that glittered with avarice. Massive fingers were locked and folded over his chest, the thumbs rubbing together constantly. His cholesterol lips were curled contemptuously in what the unsuspecting might have mistaken for a smile, and he was bald as a bullet.

He dominated a love seat in the center of the living room of the Presidential Suite. A matching sofa faced it on the other side of a coffee table the size of a billiard table. The wet bar in the corner was as well and expensively stocked as the pub at the Ritz. When Vail entered the room, Shaughnessey waved him in and pointed to the opposing settee.

'Fix this gentleman an old-fashioned and then take a hike for a while, George,' Shaughnessey said to the bartender without looking at him. George threw together an old-fashioned, brought it to Vail, and left without a word.

Shaughnessey sighed and shook his head.

'What the hell am I gonna do with you, Marty? Every time I give you a break, you turn around and kick me in the nuts.' Shaughnessey's voice was a half-whispered growl.

'Funny, I thought the governor appointed me to fill Oscar's term.'

Shaughnessey lowered his chin and raised his eyebrows. 'Don't let's play games, okay? Whatta you want, the governor to come up here from Springfield and kiss your ass because you're busting the balls of some of the biggest political contributors in the state? You think that kinda showboating sits well downstate?'

'Roy, I don't give a big rat's ass what sits well downstate. I'm doing my job.'

'Your job. Your fucking *job*! Destroying a county, throwing hundreds of people outta work. That's not your goddamn job. I was A.G. myself once, as you'll recall. I know what the job of the A.G. is, and that ain't it.'

'The job is what I decide it should be.'

'Bullshit. This case is gonna cost the taxpayers two million dollars before it's over.'

'Well, hopefully the fines will alleviate their pain.'

'Jesus, ya never change.' Shaughnessey leaned forward and changed his tactics. He willed himself to smile at Vail.

'Look kiddo, supposing I was to tell you I'm authorized to make a hard offer in settlement. Save the taxpayers more expense and free you up to do other business.'

'We're talking about felony upon felony upon felony here. People are going to jail, Roy. You'd be advised to distance yourself from them. Shit rubs off.'

'Tom Lacey is on the President's Economic Board, for Chrissakes. And Harold Grossman is honorary chairman of the National Cancer Association.'

'I'll make you a bet, Shaughnessey. Before the trial's even over, the President will accept Lacey's resignation, which is already written and signed – all they have to do is date it. And the cancer people will probably put a contract out on Grossman.'

'You always were an optimist. You actually thought Stampler had a split personality. Bought right into that scam, didn't you?'

Vail smiled and shook his head. 'I keep forgetting you're the master of the cheap shot.'

'Well, what the hell. He conned the judge, the prosecutor, everybody. Which reminds me, how is Ms. Venable? You two ever planning to get married?'

'It's never come up, Senator.'

'What's it like to be shacked up with a woman makes a couple of mil a year while you're still sucking the public tit?'

Vail didn't take the bait. He shook his head and smiled ruefully. 'I forgot you have no class, either.'

Shaughnessey's sneer vanished. His eyes glittered with anger. Finally he said, 'I'm just here to try and resolve a nasty situation. Nobody wants these mills closed and nobody wants nobody to go to jail. I told you I got an offer. You wanna hear it?'

'Must've made you pucker up when you found out Patricia Robert is going to be the judge. Not one of those dirty old men you've had on the payroll since they learned to write. An honest, tough lady you can't touch.'

'I asked you, you wanna hear the offer?'

'You're making an offer because you can't fix the judge, you can't buy the prosecutor, and you can't get to the witnesses. We have an even playing field for a change, Roy. How does it feel?'

'You wanna hear the fucking offer or not?'

'You just don't get it. This isn't about the money. I want everybody to know just how corrupt one county can get and how it happens. We're sending a message. If some of the county's *leaders* do some time and there are nice fines so the people of the state get something back, that's all gravy.'

'I'll go back and tell 'em we got a snot nose for a prosecutor and he's in it for headlines. That'll go over big in appeal – if we have to go to an appeal, which is remote.'

'We? I thought you were interceding in the public interest. Tell you what to tell your pals. Go back and tell them no deal – unless they'd all like to sign full confessions and throw themselves on the mercy of the court.'

Shaughnessey's sneer returned. 'Now what would be the percentage in that?'

'No public exposure except the confessions themselves, and no prolonged trial where they're the top of the news every day for a month or two.'

'They're gonna beat you, Marty. They're gonna hang you out to dry just like that time . . . what, twenty years ago? That's what this is really all about, isn't it? Getting even. Don't get mad, get even . . . the Irish lullaby. You got press from all over the country watching this. Your balls are gonna shrink to the size of field peas when they clean your tank.'

Vail shrugged. 'Maybe they are already,' he said, and laughed. He walked to the door, stopped, and turned back to the politico. 'Get smart, Shaughnessey. Put a lot of distance between yourself and these jokers. Just like the President and the cancer people are doing. No fee for the advice.'

'I'll give you some of the same. You're through in this state. You'll never hold public office again and every judge in the state'll stomp your dick in the dirt every time you go into court. Better tell your old lady to keep her day job.'

'She'll be relieved to know that, Roy. See you in court.'

The Coq d'Or was the best restaurant in town, good French food and an excellent chef. Vail got there first, sneaking into the private dining room through the kitchen. Three of his investigators were in the kitchen, two dressed in chefs' apparel and one wearing a waiter's uniform, who nodded toward the door to the private room.

It was a small, comfortable room with a large table that seated eight, although there were only two place settings at one end. There was a dish of peanuts and pretzels and a bottle of red wine on the table. Vail sat down and nibbled on the peanuts. Five minutes crept by before the door opened. Abel Stenner and Dermott Flaherty entered first, ushering Herman Kramer, who paused in the doorway.

Kramer, the former administrator of Grand County, wore a tight-fitting seersucker suit, white shirt, and a blue and red rep tie. A man in his late forties with very little hair, he was heavyset, with a double chin, and had the look of a man who had recently put on weight. His wary eyes darted around the room, then finally settled on Vail, who sat at the table and stared at him through his own cold, gray eyes.

Kramer came in, and Flaherty and Stenner stepped outside and closed the door.

It was just the two of them.

'Mr. Kramer, I'm Martin Vail.' He stood up and extended his hand. Kramer shook it cautiously. His hand was shaking.

'I'm not sure I should even be here, Mr. Vail. Mr. Stenner and . . .'

'Flaherty.'

'Flaherty, yeah. They said it was to my good to come over and have dinner with you.'

'Have a seat, Mr. Kramer.'

'I maybe should have called Mr. Jarmon.'

'Not a good idea.'

'I just don't know. I mean, why are you interested in buying me dinner?'

Vail smiled. 'Friendship. Cordiality. You won't believe this, Mr. Kramer, but I'm interested in your well-being.'

'Yeah right, that's why you got me indicted for everything but stealing the Statue of Liberty.'

'This isn't a deposition, Mr. Kramer. It's perfectly legitimate for the two of us to have dinner together. But if you're uncomfortable . . .'

'I thought I pretty much told your lady everything at the deposition.'

'Ms. Parver and I are a little hazy on some things, Herman. Okay if I call you Herman?'

Kramer nodded with trepidation.

'Good. Call me Marty. Anyway, I thought we could iron them out before you get on the witness stand. I want to be fair to you.'

'Why you worried about me?' Kramer asked suspiciously.

'You seem like a nice man. Nice family, nice kids. I never like to see the little guys get hurt.'

'Nobody's going to hurt me. I got the best lawyers in the country.'

'You really think Roger Dillmore and Neil Jarmon are on your side?'

Kramer leaned across the table and said sarcastically, 'They are my lawyers, *Marty*.'

'No, they're lawyers for Tom Lacey and Harold Grossman. That's who's paying them and that's who they're there to protect. You really think they give a hoot in hell about Herman Kramer?'

'They know I–' He stopped in mid-sentence.

'They know you what?'

'Can we get a drink before dinner?' Kramer said, changing the subject.

'Sure.' Vail pushed a button under the table and the

staff member dressed as a waiter entered with menus.

'What're you drinking, Herman?'

'Vodka martini with an olive, straight up.'

'And you, sir?' the waiter asked.

'Perrier on the rocks. We'll order when you get back.'

'Very good, sir.'

The waiter left.

'You don't drink?'

'I just had a drink with a friend of mine. Roy
Shaughnessey, maybe you've met him.'

Kramer did a double take. 'Mr. Shaughnessey's a
friend of yours?'

Vail took a handful of peanuts and popped them into
his mouth. 'Actually, Roy was responsible for me becoming Attorney General.'

'You're kidding.' Kramer looked worried.

'You know him?'

'We met once.'

'Gave you the pep talk, did he?'

'Huh?'

'You know, nothing to worry about. It's in the bag. That
kind of thing.'

Kramer didn't answer.

'Roy's a very persuasive fellow, Herman. He could sell
a refrigerator to an Eskimo. I guess he sold you that there
was nothing to worry about. They treat murder like it's a
parking ticket.'

'Murder?'

The waiter came in with their drinks, a basket of bread
and butter.

'Go ahead, Herman, anything on the menu. I'm having
a Caesar salad, steak, medium rare, and a baked potato.'
He broke off a piece of French bread and took a bite
without butter. Kramer ordered mushroom soup, lamb
chops, and french fries. Vail ordered a bottle of '90 red
Sancerre to go with Herman's meal.

'The bread's great, Herman.'

'What was that about murder?'

'I think it's murder, what Western and Atlas and the Lakeside Company did to Grand County. How's the family?'

'Taking it kind of hard. Kids in high school can be cruel, y'know. They keep telling the kids I stole money from the county. I never stole a dime. . . .'

'Nobody said you did. We said you misappropriated funds.'

'I didn't get anything out of that.'

Vail leaned over toward Kramer, smiled, and said softly, 'Don't shit a shitter, Herman.'

'What . . . ?'

'You think we – the A.G.'s office – made all this up? That we were guessing? C'mon, you know how close to the bone we are. Anyway, that's not why we're having dinner.'

'Why *are* we having dinner, Mr. Vail?'

'Marty.'

'I think I'll stick with Mr. Vail.'

'I want to talk to you about your future.'

'My future's fine. Got a good job, got it for life . . .'

'That's what Lakeside's telling you? That's where you went to work when you left the county, right?'

'That's right, in the real estate department.'

'And you're in for life.'

'That's right.'

'They must think very highly of your management skills.'

'Guess they do.'

'How long did you work for the county again?'

'Eighteen years.'

'And what were you making when you left?'

'Ninety-two five. Why?'

'Making a hundred and twenty-five at Lakeside, right?'

'So?'

Vail waved his hands. 'Just asking. You must be *very*

good at what you do.'

Dinner came and the waiter had trouble opening the bottle of wine. The cork broke off and he finally shoved part of it into the bottle. A geyser spewed out all over the waiter's shirt. Vail looked down and rolled his eyes.

Herman bowed his head and said grace.

Nice touch, Vail said to himself.

'One twenty-five,' Vail said, continuing the conversation. 'That's a lot of money for a guy who misappropriated funds, lost records—'

'That's what you say,' Kramer said angrily.

'I'm sorry. Allegedly did all those things.'

'Maybe I ought to call Mr. Jarmon . . .'

'Mr. Jarmon's job is to put you at ease, Herman,' Vail said, and started to eat. 'Mr. Jarmon's job is to make sure you stick to the story they've manufactured. Mr. Jarmon's job is to protect their clients. I'm sure he wouldn't tell you you're looking at perjury and possibly accessory to murder after this trial is over.'

Herman almost threw up. '*Murder?* What— What—' he stammered.

'We'll get to that. I have some questions about some of your answers in the deposition with Ms. Parver.'

'No, no. What's that about murder, what do you mean?'

'Remember a fellow named Doc the Fox?'

He turned pale. 'Fox?'

'Yeah. Doc the Fox. His real name is Jimmy. Maybe you knew him as Jimmy Fox.'

'I don't—'

'He's doing life in Joliet for killing a man named Morgan.'

'Bob Morgan.'

'Right. Remember him now?'

'I knew Bob Morgan for a couple of years.'

'I mean Jimmy Fox. You remember Jimmy Fox, don't you?'

Beads of sweat bubbled out of the pores along Kramer's brow. His fork with a piece of lamb was poised in midair.

'Short guy, kind of skinny. At least he is now. I guess five years in Joliet will take it off you.'

'I don't remember . . .'

'Let me reconstruct it for you. You drove up to a little town called Tallman. A motel called the Bavarian Inn. It was a Thursday night. Ten o'clock. Room, uh . . . 111, on the first floor. The room had a connecting door to 112. You tapped on the connecting door, Jimmy Fox opened it, ID'd himself with his driver's license, and you gave him a package. Is it coming back to you?'

'I think maybe he's talking about somebody else.'

'According to the hotel's computer records, you registered in your name. Herman A. Kramer. Paid with your personal credit card.'

Kramer's mouth was dry. He gulped down half a glass of water and followed it with a sip of wine. 'It isn't . . . coming, uh, back to me.'

'Like signing the contract with the county and not reading the small print? You remember that, don't you, from your deposition?'

Kramer licked his lips and took another drink of water. 'Yeah. Kinda. That was a while back. What, four, five months ago? Anyway that was, you know, just an oversight. Let me tell you, Mr. Vail–'

'Marty.'

'Marty, right. Okay, sorry.' He chuckled nervously. 'Y'know, I rarely ever missed a day. Had the flu once, that's about it.'

'That's admirable, Herman. You had a contract with Grand County for what?'

'First was for three years, renewed it for seven, then six.'

'And your contract with the county stipulated that you were fully aware of all the state laws involved in performing your job, right?'

'Look, I straightened all that out. About not reading the contract before I signed it and all that. I straightened that out.'

'And you understand the law now?'

'Oh yes, I do understand it now.'

'Suppose you explain it to me.'

'Well, it means . . . say, you can't take monies from one government pot and put them in another. What I mean, you can't move these monies around at whim.'

'So, you have a government grant for educational purposes, you can't put those funds in, say, the general fund, correct? Or anyplace else *but* the purpose for which they are assigned, correct?'

'Yes. I straightened all that out.'

'Not really, Herman. See, that's where we have one of our problems. You stated earlier that you didn't understand that rule.'

'I understand it now.'

'But you didn't at the time of the deposition, even though it's the law, and when you took the county administration's job you took an oath which included a statement that you *knew* the law and were familiar with your responsibilities.'

'Uh . . .'

'See, where we have this new problem is that your job as administrator required . . . *required* that you understood and would abide by the laws and procedures in dealing with state and government funds. As administrator you frequently dealt with designated state and federal monies. And in order to carry out your duties lawfully and legally, you *had* to know what the rules were.'

'I told you I straightened that out.'

'Uh-huh. One more time, Herman, you accepted the job as administrator without being aware of the legal responsibilities of that job. When you told Ms. Parver in your deposition that you were not aware of the consequences of mixing funds, you were committing a felony. Didn't Jarmon straighten you out on that?'

'Felony?'

'It's a violation of the state RICO act to accept a position which involves handling regulated monies if in accepting that position you attest to the fact that you do understand all regulations that go along with the job. So if you lied about that and then misappropriated such funds, you are guilty of two felonies – misappropriation and perjury.'

'Perjury!'

'Either you lied when you said you didn't understand the law when you accepted the job, or you committed a felony if you did understand the law, and went ahead and misappropriated those funds.'

'I don't know what's going on here.'

'I'll tell you what's going on,' Vail said. 'You think you have all the big shots behind you? Wake up, Herman. They're going to dump you faster than you can cook a set of books, because they are going down and they're going down hard, and unless you get smart, you're not only going down with them, when this trial is over we'll have to take you down for accessory to murder. And perjury. You're looking thirty, forty years hard time in the eye. No parole.'

Herman put his fork down on his plate. 'Maybe I better call Mr. Jarmon,' he said in a half whisper.

'Mr. Jarmon doesn't give two hoots in hell about you. Mr. Jarmon would dance in the street if you took a gun right now and blew your brains out.'

'You don't know what you're talking about.'

'Jarmon's only interest in you is to keep you in line. Make sure you keep lying on the witness stand. You think he'll take care of you when the trial's over? Who's gonna pay his thousand-dollar-a-day fee? Western Pulp and Paper? Atlas Chemical? Get smart, Herman, the tooth fairy's dead. But . . .'

Vail took out his cellular phone and laid it in front of Kramer.

'If it'll make you feel any better, give Jarmon a call. Then I'll pay for dinner and be on my way, and the next time we'll talk is when you're sitting in the box.'

'Box?'

'The witness box.'

'He says I may not even have to testify. He says he may not even call me.'

'If he doesn't, I will. Think about it while you finish your lamb chops.'

'I'm, uh . . . I'm getting full.'

'Losing your appetite?'

Kramer did not answer. He stared down at his plate and absently stirred the remaining food with his fork.

'What am I doing here?' he whispered finally.

'I want you to wake up. Realize your only responsibility here and now, in this room, is to Herman Kramer and nobody else. Right now you're looking at several counts of malfeasance, misappropriation, perjury . . . it goes on and on. But I'm more interested in the good old boys that are behind this. The boys Dillmore and Jarmon really represent. The boys that told you what to do and when to do it. You just did what you were told to do, isn't that right, Herman?'

No response.

'And I want you to think about Jimmy Fox and the package you delivered to him at the Bavarian Inn in Tallman. You know what was in that package, Herman?'

Herman slowly shook his head.

'Ten big ones. Ten thousand dollars. That's what it cost to ice Bob Morgan.'

'I never looked in the package, Mr. Vail, I swear to God. I didn't know what it was for.'

'Who gave you the package?'

Kramer's Adam's apple bobbed like a cork on a fishing line.

'Who gave you the package and told you what to do that night, Herman?'

'They'll kill me, too,' he said hoarsely.

'Nobody's going to kill anybody else. You do the right thing, nobody will touch you. That I will promise you.'

'What do you want me to do?'

'Simple. Tell the truth. Don't take the Fifth. Just tell the truth. It's easy. You don't have to remember any lies, don't have to be afraid of making a mistake. You just tell it the way it happened.'

'How about all those charges? How about the murder thing?'

'I can't make any promises. But if you tell it the way it happened, I will promise you this. I will work with the judge to see that you don't do any time.'

'Including the murder case?'

'Who gave you the package?'

'Jeffrey Summers.'

'The vice-president of the Lakeside Company?'

He nodded. 'Jeffrey Summers.'

'Anybody see him give it to you?'

'There was one other guy there.'

'Commissioner Stewart.'

'You knew that, too, huh?'

'He made the original contact with Fox.'

'We were in Sid's car in a parking lot behind the theaters in the shopping mall. It was about eight-thirty at night.'

'What did they tell you?'

'Just to drive up to Tallman and check into the Bavarian Inn. Sid said he made the reservations. He said Jimmy Fox would identify himself with a driver's license. Then give him this package and come back.'

'Real friends, Herman. These are the people who are going to get you off, huh? They set you up as a murder accessory.'

'I never wanted to get mixed up in all this. Mixing the

funds and everything. But they had the power, Mr. Vail. They ran everything. It was like . . . they could fix anything. Everybody was under their thumb.'

'Bob Morgan wasn't.'

Kramer looked at Vail and tears welled up in his eyes. 'You say I helped get him killed.'

'You didn't know what you were doing. Forget that. Just spit it out when you get in the box. Say it like it happened. Let me tell you what's going to happen next, Herman. We finish our dinner, I pay the bill, and Mr. Stenner and Mr. Flaherty take you home. After you leave tonight, I'm not going to have another word with you until I cross-examine you. You think about all this. Talk it over with your wife. You don't mention our meeting with anyone. And remember, it's never too late to start over.'

'Can I get in that witness protection thing?'

'You do the right thing. Then we'll talk about your future. It's your decision. Finish your dinner.'

'Ladies and gentlemen of the jury, my name is Martin Vail. I am the Attorney General of the state of Illinois. First of all, let me thank you for sacrificing your time and the time of your families to serve on this jury. I will not delude you, this will be an arduous and time-consuming experience. But in the end, I hope it will also be a gratifying, illuminating, and satisfying endeavor for all of you.

'The case I bring before you was indictable under the statutes of the state Racketeering Influenced and Corrupt Organizations act, otherwise known as RICO. It will be a complicated case and so I will endeavor to explain and to illustrate why the crimes I will present to you violate this act. I know most of you probably think of racketeering as involving gangsters – the Mafia, drugs, gambling, and prostitution – but under the RICO act, racketeering activity is defined as *any* act or *threat* involving murder, kidnapping, arson, robbery, bribery, extortion, embezzlement of state funds, bank fraud; tampering with a witness, victim, or an informant; laundering of monetary instruments, violation of the state environmental laws, or any other felony connected to the above activities.

'Sounds like a mouthful, doesn't it? Well, it is. This state has the toughest and most comprehensive RICO law in this country.

'And this case involves a great many of the crimes included in that act.

'The victims of these crimes were the taxpayers, home owners, and voters of Grand County. People like you, who trusted their elected officials and their business leaders and were betrayed, victimized, and in some cases put in deadly jeopardy because of that trust. The acts we will prove are despicable and often beyond comprehension.

'The state will prove by a preponderance of hard facts, supported by circumstantial evidence, that the defendants in this case, over a period of the last ten years, conspired to violate most of these laws with ardent contempt for those who trusted them.

'Some of these defendants are people of prominence, important people; some of them even famous. Some of the defendants are elected officials. Some of these defendants are state and county employees – your employees. Some are felons with long prison records.

'In order to prove this case, we must prove that at least two of these racketeering acts involved *all* the defendants. In other words, the people named in this indictment worked together to knowingly weave a web of deceit, lies, and criminal activity over a period of years that cost the taxpayers and voters of Grand County millions of tax dollars, damaged their health and well-being, and controlled their wages and property values. The defendants cheated on their taxes and deprived the people of the county of their rightful voice in their own government.

'We will show that three corporations colluded to carry out these acts. That they systematically and knowingly poisoned the air, water, and land of the county, subverted hospital records that revealed tragic birth defects and deaths caused by these violations. That they endangered the lives of their friends, their neighbors, and their own employees. That they bribed county and state officials, covered up dangerous violations of the laws that protect citizens from pollution, which endangered the health of all the people in the community. That they violated the local zoning ordinances for their own benefit and the benefit of their coconspirators. That they corrupted department heads, newspaper reporters, lawyers, doctors, and other citizens like yourself in order to continue this illegal and criminal enterprise. And finally, that they misappropriated state and federal funds to their own benefit.

'I will take you back ten years to prove to you that this racketeering activity is insidious and perpetual.

'We will prove to you that three men, chief executive officers of three of the most powerful and respected corporations in America – Tom Lacey of Western Pulp and Paper, Harold Grossman of Atlas Chemical, and Warren Smith of the Lakeside Company – knowingly and maliciously collaborated and directed these activities . . . a pattern of greed and violation of public trust that is shocking, sickening, and a tragic comment on the immoral abuse of power. A pattern so insidious that we demanded and got a change of venue here from Grand because we could not trust the judges and law officials of Grand County.

'Do not be deceived by the positions or titles of these people, by their fame or their charm. They are criminals whose crimes destroyed the home place of innocents like yourself, people who trusted them and were deceived, deluded, and betrayed by that trust. We will show that when challenged by innocent people hoping to make a change, these men, with their venal and fragile egos, often responded by maliciously destroying the lives and careers

73

of those who dared to question their methods. No one was immune to their avarice and arrogance.

'I ask you to study the evidence carefully. I implore you not to be deluded by names and titles. I ask you to put yourself in the position of the citizens of Grand County.

'We will guide you through this maze of deception, fraud, and duplicity with charts and exhibits showing how these crimes were connected. So, while the law itself may be hard to understand, the facts will not be.

'Finally, I ask you to bring down a plague on these felons and send a message to the rest of the country that the decent people of the land will no longer abide criminals who disguise themselves as leaders of the community.

'Thank you for your attention and for your time.'

For five weeks Vail and his cocounsels, Shana Parver and Dermott Flaherty, presented witness after witness, court documents, bank records, evidence heaped on evidence that gradually built a net around Grossman and Lacey and the Lakeside Co. Employees testified about midnight acid dumps in the rivers, accidental spills that were downgraded, toxic levels in the plants that were covered up. Darryl Hamilton, an inspector for the state's Environmental Safety Division, admitted he had been wooed by Lacey himself at a party and then bribed to falsify environmental reports. Newspaper reporters testified that their stories were altered or killed. Commissioners were bribed with everything from a new set of false teeth to a farm in Ohio. In the vortex of this eddy of corruption were the four county commissioners. If the big shots were the orchestrators of the deceit, the commissioners were the players.

By the time he finished presenting his case, Vail had still to produce hard evidence directly connecting Warren Smith, the president of Lakeside, to the plot. There was plenty of circumstantial evidence, but Vail knew that his case depended on tying all three of these companies together.

Herman Kramer would do that. He had accepted bribes from executives of the company, diverted grants from the educational fund into the general fund and from there into public works, where they were used to clear land, build roads, widen streets, even fill lakeside wetlands, all so that Lakeside could develop, develop, develop. Herman Kramer was the little guy who knew it all. He was the link.

The first witness Neil Jarmon called was Herman Kramer.

What the hell, Vail said to himself.

Kramer did not look at Vail when he took the stand. Jarmon, a slick young New Yorker in an Armani suit, wasted no time. After the preliminary questions, who, what, why, he started his questioning with a stinger.

'Mr. Kramer, in your job as county administrator, did you ever knowingly misappropriate or divert funds in violation of Section 2365 of the state code?'

'Sir, I refuse to answer on the grounds that it may tend to incriminate me.'

Vail was jarred back in his chair. The little bastard was copping out. He glared at Kramer throughout the interrogation, but the wit-ness looked straight ahead as he recited his answer to the next twelve questions.

'Sir, I refuse to answer on the grounds that it may tend to incriminate me.'

Before Kramer's last refusal, Vail knew what he had to do.

'I have no further questions, Your Honor,' Jarmon said.

'Mr. Vail?' the judge said, nodding toward him.

Vail looked at his watch. It was 4:55. He stood up. 'Your Honor, I have no questions at this time.'

There was a rumble of discontent in the courtroom, mostly from a citizens' group that had traveled 120 miles from Grand County to attend the trial.

'However, I request that Mr. Kramer remain in sequester.'

'Objection,' Jarmon said. 'Mr. Kramer is here, ready to testify now. If Mr. Vail has no questions at this time, Mr. Kramer should be excused.'

'Your Honor, it's five o'clock. I'm just asking for an overnighter. I'd like Mr. Kramer to show up and be sequestered in the witness room first thing in the morning, when we can get a fresh start.'

Judge Patricia Robert, a handsome woman with a sardonic sense of humor and an inate sense of fairness, thought for a moment and said, 'Not an unreasonable request. I remind the jury not to discuss this case. Mr. Kramer, I expect to see you here bright and early. Court is in recess until nine A.M.'

She rapped her gavel and left the bench.

'Do you think he told Jarmon everything?' Shana asked.

'No. I think Jarmon thought he was being very clever. Kramer just did what he was told.'

'Why would Jarmon do that?'

'First shot of his cannon. He was thumbing his nose at us, telling us we aren't getting anything out of any of his witnesses.'

'So now what do we do?' Flaherty asked. 'We need Kramer to tie in Lakeside and Warren Smith.'

'Outfox them,' Vail answered.

By now Jarmon was retrying his case on the front steps of the courthouse, and the media was glued to his every word. Vail, Parver, and Flaherty left the courtroom through the prisoner's entrance and sneaked out the side door. Abel Stenner was waiting in the car.

'Abel,' Vail said. 'I've got a little job for you.'

Kramer was in the witness room a little before nine. He was nervous to the point of hyperventilating. Vail would be all over him and he knew it. Hell, all he did was what Jarmon told him to do – take the Fifth to Jarmon's questions.

'But everyone will assume I'm guilty,' Kramer had whined when Jarmon ordered him to plead self-incrimination.

'So what?' Jarmon had answered. 'They can't do a damn thing about it. You just do what I tell you to do and don't worry.'

But Kramer was worried. Had he shut the door Vail had opened to him?

At exactly nine o'clock the door to the witness room opened and Abel Stenner entered the room. He looked around and then ushered in Jimmy 'the Doc' Fox.

Kramer was jolted in his chair. His lips trembled as Stenner led Fox, shackled hand and foot, to a chair, told him to sit down. Fox sat and stared blankly at the wall across the room.

Kramer twitched nervously in his seat. He heard the judge enter the courtroom, heard her bang her gavel. Then suddenly the wiry, hawkish prisoner turned and looked straight at Kramer through pale, ice-cold blue eyes. His expression did not change.

'Long time no see, Herman,' he said in a flat, harsh voice. Then he resumed his stare at the wall.

The clerk opened the courtroom door. 'Mr. Kramer, you're up.'

Kramer stood. He was trembling and he rubbed sweat from his palms. As he went out he heard Fox say, 'Right behind you, Herman.'

'Good morning, Mr. Kramer, I trust you had a restful night,' Vail began.

'It was okay,'

'Good, then we can get a nice, fresh start.'

'Yes sir.'

'As I recall, you took the Fifth on thirteen questions yesterday afternoon. Isn't that correct?'

'I guess. Yes.'

'Now that you've had a chance to think about it, maybe we can start over.'

He stood directly in front of Kramer, hands in his pockets, cool and relaxed.

'Where'd you go to college, Herman? May I call you Herman?'

'Yes. Sure. I went to the University of Illinois.'

'Did you finish?'

'I got my master's in Business Administration.'

'You were fifth in your class, weren't you?'

'Yes, that's right.'

'Graduated magna cum laude.'

'Yes.'

'When was that?'

Kramer thought for a moment and nodded. '1973.'

'And you married just after you graduated?'

'That's right.'

'Get a good job?'

'Yes sir, I worked for Hildebrand and Cairo in St. Louis.'

'Tax consultants.'

'Yes sir.'

'Then what?'

'I was hired as assistant administrator in Torrence County. And then two years later, the administrator quit and I moved on up.'

'And how did you find your way to Grand County?'

'I'd been there three years and they – the people from Grand – approached me to see if I was interested in a change.'

'Who came to you?'

'Commissioners Sid Stewart and David Cutler.'

'What were you making at the time?'

'Thirty-two.'

'And what did they offer you?'

'Sixty-six five.'

'Quite a raise.'

'Yes, it was.'

'Anything else?'

'A car.'

'Uh-huh. That was what, fifteen years ago?'

'Sixteen.'

'So, you were about thirty-one, thirty-two then?'

'Thirty-one.'

'Two sons?'

'Yes. Chip and Barry.'

'So when you went to Grand County you were sitting on top of the world, weren't you?'

'Yes, I was.'

'Proud of yourself. Sixty-six thousand five hundred in those days was good money.'

Kramer nodded. 'Still is.'

'And how were you treated?'

'Great. We were invited to picnics, fishing trips. Things went very well.'

'Get a house?'

'Yes sir.'

'How much?'

Jarmon jumped to his feet. 'Objection, Your Honor. Relevance.'

'Attorney Vail?'

'Foundation, Your Honor.'

'Okay, counselor, I'll cut you a little slack. Don't build a house. Overruled, Mr. Jarmon. Answer the question, Mr. Kramer.'

'Sixty thousand.'

'Boat?'

Kramer nodded. 'Thirty-two thousand.'

'Another car?'

'Yes sir, for my wife. A Honda Accord.'

'Another what, twenty thousand?'

'Twenty-two.'

'Your boys were in private school?'

'Yes.'

'You got in pretty deep, pretty fast, didn't you, Herman? How did that happen?'

'Sid introduced me to a car dealer and I got all interested and he told me, 'Don't worry, it can be arranged.' The bank gave me good loans. They were very helpful.'

'That was Fidelity Trust?'

'Yes.'

'How did you get tied up with them?'

'Mr. Summers introduced me to Charles Thornton, president of the bank.'

'That would be Jeffrey Summers, vice-president of the Lakeside Company?'

'Yes.'

'How did you meet him?'

'He, Sid Stewart, and some of the other commissioners went fishing a lot.'

'Any women, gambling, drinking?'

'None of that. Some beer on the boat.'

'So now you had a new sixty-thousand-dollar house, your wife had a car, you had a new boat. Both boys going to private school. That's a heavy load to carry.'

'Pretty heavy.'

'And did there come a time when Sid Stewart asked you to do a job for him?'

Kramer paused for a moment before saying, 'Yes.'

'Was there anything out of the ordinary about this job?'

'Yes. He asked me to write a check and transfer half a million dollars from the educational fund into general.'

'The general fund, that is.'

'Yes.'

'And that's a felony, isn't it, Herman?'

Kramer nodded.

'And both of you knew it was a felony, is that correct?'

Jarmon, red-faced and angry, jumped to his feet again. 'Objection! Mr. Kramer cannot testify to what Mr. Stewart did or did not know.'

'I'll rephrase,' Vail said. 'How was this request for transfer put to you, Herman?'

'We were on the boat.'

'Your boat?'

'No, Sid Stewart's boat. I was sitting in the back. Sid came back and sat beside me and he made some chitchat and then he said, "How's the money holding out?" and I said things were tight, and he said, "Maybe your car note can be taken care of." I said, "What do you mean?" and he said, "I need a favor. Nothing big. But we need to cover a shortfall." Then he told me if I could move $600,000 from the education fund into the general fund and then channel that into public works, the car note would be satisfied.'

'He said that, it would be "satisfied"?'

'Just like that. Yes.'

'Wasn't that risky? Wouldn't people know that had been done?'

'I also had to fix the books to cover the transfer.'

'So you committed two felonies – you illegally transferred funds and cooked the books to cover the transfer – and Commissioner Stewart, Mr. Summers, and Mr. Thornton took care of your car note.'

'Yes.'

Jarmon slammed his hand on his desk. 'Objection, Your Honor. That's pure supposition. Guesswork.'

'I'll rephrase,' Vail said. 'Did Mr. Summers ever mention the transaction to you?'

'Yes. A week or two later he told me the Lakeside Company was deeply indebted and if he could ever do anything for me, just call. He also told me to drop by and see Charlie Thornton. That's what he said, "drop by." So I did, and Charlie told me Lakeside had purchased the car and they were leasing it to me for a dollar a year. And I signed over the pink slip.'

Kramer was on the stand for two days. After his testimony, two other defendants caved in. The defense was chewed up and spit out.

Doc Fox never testified.

At seven-thirty the twin-engine plane dropped out of the rain clouds, swept low over the highway, and landed on the single macadam strip that served Sheffield. Vail stood under an umbrella at the edge of the hard stand as the plane taxied over and parked.

Jane Venable had left Germany the night before, flown all night, and taken a private plane to Sheffield. She climbed out of the plane looking like she had just walked out of the beauty parlor. Her green silk suit didn't have a wrinkle. She brushed her hair away from her face and smiled. The black patch over her eye, the eye she'd lost in an attack by Aaron Stampler years before, was tantalizing, as always. Amazing, he thought. She stepped down and threw her arms around him, and he dropped the umbrella. In the early morning rain, their kiss was immediate and passionate.

'God, I've missed you,' he said.

'Still love me?' she asked, taking his face in her hands.

'More than ever. Know what I was thinking?'

She laughed. 'I hope I do.'

'I was thinking we could go back to the hotel and have breakfast in bed.'

'Don't you have to be in court at nine?'

'Nope. We're waiting for the verdict. Finished up yesterday afternoon.'

'Oh no! Congratulations. I'm sorry I missed your summation. I flew all the way from Germany and missed it. Were you brilliant as usual?'

'As usual.'

'Gonna win, Vail?'

'I never predict.'

She wrapped her arms around him and kissed him. It was a hungry kiss. They held hands as they walked to the car. She laid her head on his shoulder.

'Six weeks. Never, *never* again will I leave you for six weeks. Not even three weeks. It was agony.'

'No handsome German duke chased you around?'

'Several. I told them I had to go back to the hotel and watch my husband on WWN. They were all over this trial.'

'Yeah. Some old bag wanted to interview me.'

'Ohhh . . .'

'Naomi blew her off. I never even talked to her.'

'What was her name?'

'Nazimova, something like that.'

'Valerie Azimour?'

'Yeah, that sounds right.'

'An old *bag*. The hottest thing on television. Men drool over her. Old bag my ass.'

'Janie, like I said, I never met her.'

'Good thing.'

'Hungry?'

'Starved.'

'Then I guess we'll have to eat first.'

He ordered a pitcher of fresh orange juice, eggs Benedict, coffee and lots of cream and sugar, while she got out of the clothes she had been wearing for ten hours. When she came out of the bathroom, she was wearing a black silk robe that set off her fiery red hair.

'Wow,' he said.

She smiled and twirled around, her hair caressing her face. 'Picked it up in Paris. Sneaked off for a weekend.' She tossed him a pair of black silk bikini shorts. He held them up and looked over them at her.

'Suppose I got in a car wreck wearing these?'

'Nurses would be lined up outside your hospital door. And I'd be inside with an AK-47.'

She pushed him back on the bed and lay on top of him, supporting herself on her elbows.

'Want me to call down and hold all calls?' he asked.

'You're waiting for a verdict to come in, Marty.'

'Shana or Dermott will have the details.'

'You're nuts.'

'I'm horny as hell.'

'Not as horny as I am.'

'Wanna bet?'

'Bet you a thousand dollars I come first.'

'You always do.'

'Don't be supercilious.'

'What's that mean?'

'Smug.'

She spread her legs so she was straddling him and moved slowly on him, and then finally opened the robe and leaned forward. He ran his tongue around her nipple, then sucked it into his mouth. She groaned, raised up slightly, barely touching him, and began moving in slow circles on him, feeling him growing hard under her.

'Oh God, how I do love you, Martin Vail,' she whispered huskily.

She was cradled in his arms, his face was buried in her hair when the doorbell rang.

'Room service,' the muffled voice said.

Jane sat up on the edge of the bed and pulled her robe on. 'Don't bother getting up,' she said.

'I can't get up,' he said, pulling the covers over him. 'I'm naked.'

'Where are the bikinis?'

'I don't know. Somewhere under here.' He looked under the covers.

She went to the door and a cherub-faced teenager wheeled a hot tray into the room.

'Morning, Mr. Vail,' he said, and nodding to Jane, added, 'Mrs. Vail.'

She put her hand over her mouth and faked a giggle as the waiter passed.

'I'll forge your signature,' she said, accepting the bill.

'I could arrest you for that, you know.'

'Waste of time,' she said, scrawling his signature under the tip and ushering the waiter out. 'I've got the meanest lawyer in the world.'

'Mean, huh.'

'But lovable.'

'I suppose we have to eat now.'

'Eggs Benedict are deadly when they're cold.'

He got up, and pulled on the silk bikini shorts. 'What do you think,' he said, striking a pose.

'I think the paparazzi would give a fortune for a shot of this.'

He pulled chairs over to the table and they sat down to eat.

'I was starving,' she admitted.

'I'm still horny.'

'Martin, you're always horny.'

'Look who's talking.'

She giggled and sipped her orange juice.

'What am I going to do with myself in a month?' Vail said. 'I'll be out of a job come November.'

'You'll think of something.'

'I haven't so far. Nothing serious, I mean. I've thought about writing a book. Maybe teaching at Chicago Law. Nothing sounds interesting, though. Going to be hard to top this case.'

'How about private practice? You could set up a firm. You've got Naomi, Shana, and Derm and Meyer. Abel doesn't want to retire, he's an action junkie just like you. They all are.'

'We've talked about it but nobody wants to go back to the defense side.'

'Why don't we take a month or two off? I've got some time coming after I finish this German job, another two, three weeks. We can go out to the cabin for a month, just the two of us. It's a perfect time of year.'

The phone rang.

'Oh *fuck*!' she snapped.

He answered it, listened for a minute, and said, 'On the way,' and hung up.

'We've got a verdict,' she said flatly.

'Thirty minutes.'

She sighed. 'I flew all the way from Germany and I can't even finish breakfast.'

'I gotta take a shower.'

'Not without me you don't.'

'I only have thirty minutes.'

'Well,' she said, brushing against him, 'like you said, Shana and Dermott will have the details.'

Jane sat in the first row directly behind him. She reached over the rail that separated spectators from participants and laid her hand gently on his elbow. Not a tremble.

The jury filed into the ancient courtroom.

Judge Robert looked over at them and smiled. 'Good morning, ladies and gentlemen, have you got a verdict for us?'

The foreman, a woman in her early fifties with silver hair and a pleasant smile, said, 'We have, Your Honor.'

'And how do you find?'

It was a clean sweep. Guilty. Guilty. Guilty. Guilty. Guilty. And so on. The real victory came when the judge read the sentences and fines.

Western Pulp and Paper, Atlas Chemical, and Lakeside: fined thirty million dollars each.

Western and Atlas were ordered to shut down until they could prove they were operating within EPA standards.

Lacey, Smith, and Grossman were each sentenced to two-to-five years. They stood stone-faced and in shock as the judge read the bad news.

The four commissioners got five to ten.

Herman Kramer got a suspended sentence and community service.

Shana and Dermott held the press conference.

Jane and Martin went to the hotel and got back in bed.

Valerie Azimour never got her interview.

Three

Johnny Baylor slumped down in the seat of his darkened car, a cigarette cupped in his hand, watching the night depository of the Seattle Bank and Trust. He was across the street in the parking lot of an all-night diner. Nobody had paid any attention to him. Nobody he knew had come by the diner. He waited until the street was empty and drove across the road, pulled up beside the bank, reached out, opened the steel slot, and dropped the envelope into the depository with a gloved hand. Then he got out of there.

Driving away, he checked the rearview mirror. No cars behind him. So far, so good.

Half an hour later the dispatcher at Pacific Armored Transport saw the familiar red Camaro clear the main gate. The dispatcher was surprised as he peered into the surveillance monitor and saw the car pull into the operations parking lot. Johnny Baylor got out of the car, reached into the trunk, took out a fly rod and creel, and carried them to the heavy steel entrance door. The warning bell jarred the sprawling security building. Baylor leaned closer to the camera and smiled. 'Hey, Patch, wake up,' he yelled into the mike.

'I hear ya,' the dispatcher said, checking his watch. It was a little after three A.M. 'What the hell're you doin' here this early?'

'I got the runs. Been up all night. Figured I may's well come on in now as sit home.'

'What's with the fly rod? They're not bitin' in here tonight.'

88

The dispatcher pressed a button and the door buzzed open. Through a series of video monitors, he watched Baylor enter a steel corridor.

'I'm going fishing for the weekend,' Baylor said as the first door closed behind him and he approached the second door in the narrow, bugged, monitored, bullet-proof corridor. 'Don't wanna leave my stuff in the car.'

The dispatcher buzzed again and the doors to an elevator slid open.

The dispatcher laughed and said, 'You think somebody's gonna stiff your car in this friggin' fortress?'

He waited until Baylor entered the elevator and activated it. As it descended to the underground nerve center, Baylor looked up at the video camera and stuck out his tongue. When the elevator opened, Baylor faced another door. He swept his ID card through a slot and waited until the dispatcher popped that lock. Baylor entered the communications center, walked past the locker room, the lavatory and showers, and the lounge, to the semicircle of bulletproof glass that gave the dispatcher a full view of the garage and the two entrances leading into it. Monitors lined one side of the room, and the electronic board in front of him gave him access to all radio equipment and all surveillance cameras on the property.

The beefy, older man swung around in his revolving chair and appraised the younger man.

'Looks like a cat dragged ya through an alley,' he said, and chuckled. 'You young bucks're all alike.'

'Too much Tex-Mex and Corona,' Baylor moaned.

'No senoritas?'

Baylor smiled sheepishly. 'That, too.'

'Montezuma's revenge . . .'

'I hope I can hold it in until we make the first drop.'

'First run's forty-five minutes out,' the dispatcher said. 'Sheesh!'

'Wait until five to check in. You know how freaky they are about overtime,' the dispatcher said. 'Good flick on the early show. *The Spoilers*. Grab a cup a coffee. I just made it.'

'You kidding? One sip of coffee and I'd blow up. I'm gonna change clothes.'

Baylor went to his locker, opened the combination lock, took out his uniform, hooked the hanger over the latch of the locker next to his, and put the fishing rod and creel in the back of his cubbyhole. He changed into his uniform: black pants, white shirt, loosely knotted black tie, black leather jacket with the company seal over the left breast. He hung his jacket and pants back in the locker. Then he knelt down, opened the fishing creel, and lifted out a tray of lures. Beneath it was a small Psion 3c computer, a black box six and a half inches long, three and a half inches wide, and less than an inch thick; a minimodem, which was an oval tube only six inches long with a phone cord attached; and a cellular phone. He put the computer in one jacket pocket, the modem in the other, and slipped the small cell phone into his back pocket. He replaced the tray and closed the creel, secured his locker, and went back down the hall to the lounge. Without turning on the light, he stretched out on the couch, positioning himself so he could see the dispatcher, who was leaning back in his chair staring at John Wayne and Randolph Scott beating hell out of each other on the small TV screen in the corner.

But Baylor wasn't watching the dispatcher. His eyes were hooked on the top right-hand drawer of the dispatcher's desk, at the keys dangling from the lock.

He's done the maps. He knows the first drop's forty-five minutes out, so he's done the maps. Just wait him out. He'll leave the keys in the drawer, he always does.

Still so far, so good.

Fifteen minutes later the movie was over. The dispatcher stood up and stretched. He ground his fists into the small of his back and worked out the kinks, then walked across

90

the hallway and stuck his head in the door of the lounge. Baylor appeared to be sound asleep. The dispatcher liked Baylor, an ex-Marine who had been wounded in Desert Storm. He was an honest-to-God war hero, a first-class hell raiser, always on time and always in a good mood. The dispatcher strolled down the hall toward the refreshment room.

Baylor rolled silently off the couch and moved to the doorway just as the dispatcher entered the alcove. Moving quickly into the operations room, Baylor opened the drawer. The maps were there.

He could hear the dispatcher rustling the coffee mugs.

He took a transparent grid out of his pocket.

The dispatcher was washing out the mug.

Baylor spread the grid over the map and traced the route with his finger while jotting down several coordinates on a slip of paper with his other hand.

He heard the door of the microwave slam. Now the dispatcher was heating up his cinnamon bun.

Baylor dropped the map back in the drawer, sneaked back to the lounge, and flopped down on the sofa. A moment later the dispatcher came back down the hall with his coffee and roll.

Baylor waited a half hour and then joined the dispatcher.

'How ya feelin'?'

'Gotta hit the john. If I'm not back in half an hour, call the medics.'

'You take anything for that?' the dispatcher asked as the kid walked toward the rest rooms.

'Ate a bunch of Saltines,' Baylor called back over his shoulder.

'White bread's better. Soaks all that stuff up.'

Baylor entered the spotless tiled rest room, went to a stall, locked the door behind him, and sat down on the toilet. He took out the computer and snapped it open, revealing a small keyboard and a screen built into the flip lid. He took out the modem and snapped the tiny plug into a socket on the side of the computer. Finally he plugged the cellular phone into the modem. He turned on the computer, typed a number into his cell phone, and, when it squawked, entered the fax mode on his computer and typed:

'MOSES.'

'BULL RUSHES,' came the answer.

'INPROG . . . D101.6; H301.2 . . . F300.6; H301.2 . . . F300.6;D226.3 . . . I406.1; D226.3 . . . I406.1; F304.0 . . .'

When he finished feeding the coordinates into the machine, he waited. A minute passed, then the message came back: 'F300-I406.'

Baylor's finger traced to the coordinates.

Hamley and Irving, perfect.

He looked at his watch and started to type in the ETA when he heard the door to the lavatory open. He subconsciously held his breath.

'You okay, kid?' the dispatcher called out.

Baylor's shoulders sagged with relief. 'Yeah, fine.'

He typed in '720 . . . END,' and quietly closed the cover.

'I was thinkin', I can call in a standby if you'd like.'

Baylor unplugged the modem and cell phone and put the rig back in his pockets.

'I think eatin' those crackers worked, Patch. I'll be fine.'

'Three million smackeroos in nice, crisp twenties, fifties, and hundreds, Mr. Rosario,' the dispatcher said with a leer. 'Sign right here.'

'Why is it always me?' Rosario sighed, taking the clipboard and scrawling his signature.

'Privilege of power, Captain Rosario. You are the man in charge, the custodian of three-point-three mil. The man responsible for seeing that this marvelous cargo . . .' He picked up a packet of hundreds and drew it under his nose, sniffing it adoringly. '. . . is delivered to West Coast Tool and Die and to three branch banks over on the peninsula.' He dropped the packet back in the bag. 'Have a good day, old buddy.'

'Screw you, Patch.'

The dispatcher laughed and went back into his office. The two guards, Solomon and Weldon, climbed into the steel compartment of the armored car.

'Sure is hot in here, Rosie,' Solomon said.

'I'll switch on the air conditioner,' the driver said. 'Keep your eyes open, boys.'

'Always do,' Weldon said as Rosario slammed the heavy steel doors shut.

The two guards locked and secured the doors. They settled down on the hard bench that ran down one side of the chamber. Solomon sucked on a squeeze bottle of ice water. Weldon, as usual, turned to the crossword puzzle of the *Post Intelligencer*, folded it carefully, and perched it on his knee.

Rosario climbed into the cab and pulled the heavy door shut. Baylor was already strapped in the shotgun seat. The heavy engine rumbled beneath the cab. Rosario switched on the air.

'Lock and load,' Rosario said, and Baylor pushed the button that activated the cab's interior locking system.

'How's the stomach?'

'I'm fine,' Baylor said, taking out the envelope containing the route map and tearing it open.

'Why bother with all this security?' Rosario said. 'Dick Tracy back there just spouted off the whole damn customer list. I'm surprised he didn't call one of the morning talk shows and announce it publicly.' He snatched up the radio mike and pressed the button with his thumb.

'You awake in there, whatsisname?'

'Been sittin' here starin' at the phone, waiting for your call, Captain, my captain.'

'We're locked in and clear. Open the pearly gates.'

'What's the code word?' the dispatcher asked.

Rosario sighed. More games. 'Password, my ass.'

The dispatcher laughed. 'Drive carefully.'

Heavy steel doors ground back on their tracks and a shaft of early morning sunlight streaked through them into the garage, growing wider as the doors opened. Rosario checked his watch.

'I got 6:31.'

'Check.'

'Call you from checkpoint one.'

'Not if I call you first.'

He was a good dispatcher. He would spot-check them every five or six minutes, even though the book only called for ten-minute spot checks in addition to the routine call-ins they would make from the designated checkpoints on the route map.

Rosario drove out of the underground garage while Baylor checked the red line sketching their route. 'Get over to 520 and take it to the 405, then head south,' he said.

'South on the 405,' Rosario repeated.

They were on their way.

Baylor was getting nervous. They were reaching the turn point and the dispatcher hadn't spot-checked them for seven minutes. They were two minutes from Hamley and Irving.

'Go down another block and take a right on Hamley,' Baylor said.

'What's the matter with Patch? He's running us all over town.'

'He's paranoid.'

'We're better off on a crowded interstate than these deserted back streets.'

'There's nobody here in the warehouse district at this hour, Rosie. We're about ten minutes from our first drop, he's bringing us in the back way.'

'Twenty-two years I been doggin' these iron horses

around, nobody ever even *looked* like they were thinking of knocking us over.'

'Always the first time.'

The gnarled voice of the dispatcher interrupted their conversation.

'Miss me?' he asked.

'Oh yeah,' Rosario said. 'I just wiped away a tear.'

'You should hit West Coast Tool and Die at about 7:25, right on schedule.'

'That's because we're perfect, Patch,' Rosario said.

They were approaching Irving.

'We turn up here,' Baylor half mumbled.

'Talk to you when we get there.'

'Not if I call you first.'

'Har-de-har-har. Ten-four.'

'Same to you.'

Baylor pointed through the windshield. 'Left at the next corner.'

'Okay.'

Rosario turned onto Irving. On both sides, three- and four-story warehouses lined the street, deserted in the early hours after dawn.

'We got a baby-blue van behind us,' Weldon said suddenly on the intercom.

'Is he following us?' Rosario asked, checking his side mirror.

'Parked. Aimed in the other direction.'

'I see him. Looks harmless enough. Keep an eye on him.'

'Gotcha.'

Rosario picked up a little speed as he headed down the deserted street, still watching the van in the mirror.

In the rear, Weldon watched the van through the tiny slit in the rear door.

'They ain't goin' anywhere, Rosie, must be a–'

The explosion cut off the sentence. Jarred, Rosario saw the manhole cover five feet in front of the truck blow straight up, followed by a flash of fire. He swerved but it was too late. The truck's right front wheel slammed into the open manhole. Its heavy tire, moving at thirty miles an hour, smacked the opposite side of the gaping hole; the sharp edges sliced into the tire, and it blew. Rosario was slammed forward. His head smacked the steering wheel and a deep gash split his forehead.

At the same moment, the steel cover dropped from above them and smashed into the bulletproof windshield. The back wheels, barely touching the pavement, squealed and burned rubber as Rosario's foot jammed against the gas pedal.

Baylor, his arms stiffened against the dash panel, took the brunt of the crash in his shoulders. He grabbed the radio so Rosario couldn't get to it, and hit the button unlocking the cab doors.

Outside, smoke bombs attached to light poles were remotely activated. Smoke burst from the bombs and boiled up around the truck.

In the back, Weldon and Solomon, caught completely unaware, were thrown back against the forward bulkhead of the steel box. Solomon was knocked unconscious, and Weldon, dazed, struggled to his feet and grabbed a shotgun off the rack on the side wall. He staggered toward the rear of the truck.

In the front, Rosario stared over at Baylor, saw the mike in his hand.

'Call Patch, tell him we been hit,' he stammered. The door beside him suddenly swung open. A gloved hand reached out of smoke and jerked Rosario out of the seat and into the street.

Rosario, his eyes streaming from the smoke, stared through the mist at a figure in fatigues wearing a gas mask.

'You son of–' he started to say. The figure shoved a shotgun against his chest, pushed him back a foot, and blew a hole through his chest.

In the back, Weldon staggered to the rear doors. Smoke obliterated his view. Then he saw figures moving through the dense clouds. A moment later the two back doors were literally blown off their hinges. The explosion slammed Weldon back against the bulkhead of the truck. Half conscious, he saw two men framed against the ruined frame of the doorway, saw the shotgun swing up, heard and saw the flash that killed him an instant later. He did not hear the shot that killed Solomon.

Three men jumped into the back of the truck as the van, its side door standing open, pulled up hard against the doorway. They started throwing bags of money into the van.

Baylor, still dazed by the crash, pulled himself with both hands to the doorway of the cab.

'Got a mask for me?' he gasped.

The shotgun swung up a foot from Baylor's face. He saw the flash, felt the gale of heat sear the flesh from his face, but he never heard the blast.

'Sorry, soldier,' a voice muffled within the gas mask said. 'Fortunes of war.'

He rolled Baylor's body over and took the computer, modem, and cellular phone out of Baylor's pockets.

High above them, a tramp flopping in a deserted third-floor loft was shaken awake by the explosions. He peered fearfully over the sill of the window and looked down into the middle of the block. He saw smoke bombs attached to light poles, spewing swirling eddies of smoke in the middle of the block. Suddenly, a van burst out of the man-made fog and screeched around the corner. The tramp cowered below the windowsill, afraid that he'd been seen. Cautiously, he rose up and looked back down at the street.

The smoke slowly dissipated and he saw below him the crippled armored truck, its back doors lying in the street, and two men sprawled beside it. One had no face.

Four

Near a peak of the rugged Bitterroot mountain range, a solitary man perched on a snowmobile, studying the slope below him through binoculars. He knew and loved the sounds the cruel wind would make as it swept past him down the steep mountain slope toward the pass, moaning over the rocky tor, whistling past sharp stalks of high winter grass, crackling through the bright green shrub brush and pine limbs in a half-mile-wide bay of pines, then bursting free of the trees, gaining momentum and howling across a steep, snow-deep meadow, churning up wisps of flakes in its wake.

He panned the glasses down into the pass, following the road south as it curved slightly for a couple of hundred feet, then made a sharp turn due east for several hundred yards before cutting south again. The road had been cleared but the wind brushed it with fresh snow from the slopes. It was a desolate and forlorn V-shaped chasm between two mountain ranges, beautiful in its seclusion.

A moment later the unnatural roar of a second snowmobile drowned out the wind. It swept over the crest of the mountain and pulled up beside the first. The two men, both dressed in white camouflage suits, their faces snug behind ski masks, huddled against the cruel gale.

The first man pushed his tinted snow goggles onto his forehead and studied the sky. The sun was dropping below the mountain peaks, and behind the mountains gray clouds were boiling up.

'Getting dark,' he said. His breath steamed through the

round mouth hole in the mask. Bits of ice ringed the hole where his breath had condensed and frozen.

'What's the matter, Dad, too cold for you?'

'That'll be the day.'

The boy smiled and followed the older man's glance. 'Gonna get us some more snow,' he said.

'Yep. Let's take a pass through those pines.'

'Okay. I'll take the high side along the ridge. Maybe we can spook us a buck.'

'Meet you at Widow's Peak.' The father laughed. 'Keep an eye out for rangers – and try not to shoot me.'

'I was gonna say the same.'

'Getting pretty frisky for a sixteen-year-old.'

'Yeah.' The young man laughed and spun off, whipping the machine sideways and sending a geyser of snow over his father. He headed up the sharp incline to the top edge of the pine stand.

The father headed down the side of the mountain. The slope was so steep he leaned hard into the hill to keep it from sliding out from under him. He guided the machine along the lower edge of the forest and twisted the throttle, expertly skirting the trees before stopping at the edge of a precipice. A hundred yards below him was the first curve in the road. He moved quickly, first tying a length of heavy rope around one of the larger pines and dropping it over the edge. He took a small square packet from one of his saddlebags, stuffed it in his jacket, then dropped quickly over the side of the cliff. He slid down about fifty feet, carefully studying the face of the cliff, and abruptly stopped next to a flat niche in the rocks. The package was wrapped in oilskin and sealed in a plastic Baggie. He lodged the package carefully in the niche and then took a small tube about four inches long from his pocket and twisted it into the package. Then he pulled himself back up the cliff.

His son was waiting at Widow's Peak – the south end of the woods where the forest funneled to a point and ended at hard rock.

'See anything?' the young man asked.

His father shook his head. 'I don't think there's a living thing up here. It's too damn cold.'

'I didn't even see a rabbit track.'

'Let's head home.'

The father turned his snowmobile and headed off through the trees with his son close behind. They had gone almost to the end of the pine stand when the older man suddenly raised his hand. He slowed, and then stopped and rolled off his snowmobile into the snow. His son followed.

'What–' the boy started to say, but his father held a finger to his mouth. He reached into a leather rifle holster and slid his rifle out. The gun was fitted with a silencer. He crawled about twenty feet through the snow, stopped behind a fallen tree, carefully laid the barrel of the rifle on the stump, and sighted through the scope. He focused it. Four hundred yards away he followed another snowmobile as it roared out of another stand of trees below them and to the north.

The boy took out his binoculars and sighted on the figure. He crawled beside his father and said, 'Whatcha doin', Pop? That's Floyd.'

'Quiet up,' the father snapped under his breath.

The boy leaned closer to his father and said in his ear, 'Floyd's not gonna bother us.'

The father recognized the Forest Service logo on the side of the snowmobile and the number 6 above it. Chip was right, it was Floyd Tracy. He moved the cross hairs up until they were steady over the ranger's heart. His hand tightened a bit, taking the slack out of the trigger.

'What're you doing?' his son whispered frantically. 'He's our friend, he knows we're not poachers.'

The boy's mouth went dry. He lay in the snow watching the barrel of his father's gun panning slowly as the ranger waded through the snow and scanned the mountainside through binoculars.

The father's mind was racing. *If he sees us, do I take him out? What will I do with him? What will I tell Chip?*

The boy nudged his father and whispered in his ear.

'Over to the left at the edge of those trees. That's what he's looking for.'

The father swept his gun sight north. Trudging knee-deep through the snow was an enormous eight-point buck. It was taking its time, sniffing the air with its ears twitching, nibbling on the low foliage in an adjacent pine stand.

'Beautiful,' the father whispered. He swung the gun back and watched Floyd through the scope. *Okay, pal, go home,* he said to himself.

The ranger swept his glasses across the face of the mountain one more time, then remounted his snowmobile and roared off to the north.

The buck, startled by the sound, bounded through the snow, heading up the slope. The young man turned on his side in the snow and rested on one elbow.

'What was that all about?' he asked.

His father did not answer. He rose to his knees, took one more look below him, and said, 'Okay, he's gone.'

'Why were you pulling down on Floyd?'

His father slid the rifle back in its holster.

'You told me never point a gun at anything unless you plan to shoot it,' the boy continued.

'Hell, I was just having some fun, Chip. Practice makes perfect.'

'Remember when you caught me aiming at one of Mr. Henderson's chickens with my .22? Was the day after I got it – my first gun – and you locked it in the rack for two weeks. That's what you told me. "Don't ever bear down on anything unless you plan to shoot it," you said.'

'That was four years ago. You got some memory, Chip.'

'Some things stick with you.'

'Gonna take my gun away from me?' the father said, and chuckled.

The boy thought for a moment and said, 'Nah, I ain't big enough yet. Maybe next year.'

They both laughed as they stood up and brushed the snow off their clothes.

'Tell you what, we pick up that buck's tracks and you get first shot.'

'That's all there'll be, one shot. One shot and he's gone.'

'Better make it good, then.'

'Better find him first,' the boy said.

'I'll go down behind him, drive him up the ridge toward you. Be sure to use a silencer, don't want to start an avalanche up here.'

The father threaded his way through the trees, led on by the pointed tracks. Finally he saw the tan animal zigzagging his way through the trees, bounding through the snow. He stayed twenty or thirty yards behind it, glancing occasionally up the hill.

Above him, Chip, too, saw the buck and sped up, weaving past trees until he got ahead of it. He stopped, jumped off the buggy, and pulled his rifle out. The deer was running up the hill about thirty yards from him. He laid the barrel of the rifle against a tree, tracked the running stag, picked him up, and set the cross hairs on its chest. Then he yelled, 'Whoop!'

The deer, startled by the sound, stopped for a fatal instant, its ears twisting toward the sound. The boy squeezed off his shot, watched the deer jerk, its eyes looking terrified. It backed up a step or two, then its hind legs gave out. It thumped down on its haunches. The front legs collapsed and it crashed forward in the snow.

His father came up through the trees and stopped beside the fallen animal. Chip joined him.

'Straight to the heart.' His father leaned over and felt the body of the deer. 'This guy's been eating well. Must be four hundred pounds.' He looked over at Chip, his eyes crinkling as he smiled under his mask. 'We'll be eating venison steaks for the rest of the winter.'

From the storage space under the seat of the snow buggy, Chip took out a folded canvas tarpaulin and together they spread it out on the downhill side of the deer. They slid one edge under the carcass, then hoisted and shoved until it was well wedged under the dead animal. Then they rolled the deer over onto the tarp. They folded the tent over it and tied it in several places with thick rope, then attached tow lines to the back of both snowmobiles.

'We gonna dress it out tonight?'

'No,' the father answered. 'We'll put it in the meat shed. I have a meeting at the church.'

As they mounted their snowmobiles, the father reached out and touched his son's arm. The boy looked over at him.

'Beautiful shot.'

'Thanks,' his son said proudly. He paused and added, sarcastically, 'When I aim at something, I shoot it.'

'Big shot,' his father said as they cranked up their machines.

They headed up the slope toward the back side of the mountain, towing their prize behind them.

Five

The driver of the olive-drab eighteen-wheeler leaned forward until his nose was almost touching the windshield. Large snowflakes battered the truck, and the windshield wipers merely turned them to slush. He could barely see the Humvee fifty feet in front of him. His relief driver was studying a map that was stretched across his legs. He had a narrow halogen flashlight between his teeth.

'We're comin' up on that pass they told us about, Sarge.'

'Call Riley and advise him. Tell him we can just barely see his tail lights.'

'Roger.'

'Jesus, why the hell did they send us down this road?'

'They said it was gonna be clear,' the young PFC answered.

'So much for GI fuckin' weather forecasters.'

The Army convoy was delivering a cache of arms and ammunition from an armory outside Spokane, Washington, to the air base at Mountain Home, Utah. The route would take them into Missoula, Montana, then south on U.S. 93 into Utah to Interstate 84. The trip from Missoula south took them through the Bitterroot Valley. The road was defined to the west by the towering Bitterroot Mountains, a ragged border between Montana and Idaho, whose ten-thousand-foot peaks were often faced with sheer granite walls. To the east the Bitterroot River bordered the road, and beyond it were the glistening peaks of the Sapphire Mountains. Rugged country.

The road coursed due south until sixty miles south of Missoula, where it took a sharp ninety-degree jog to the east for about the length of a football field, then turned back south again. The dogleg was known as Lost Trail Pass, an historic, narrow, V-shaped chasm between the Bitterroot and Anaconda ranges, discovered in 1804 by Lewis and Clark in their search for the Northwest Passage. On a clear day the valley would have been a picturesque leg of the drive. But a front had unexpectedly shifted, and now, in the middle of nowhere, a winter storm was upon them. In the dead of night the storm had reduced their progress to thirty miles an hour. The trip, which should have taken eight hours, was going to take twelve or thirteen – if they did not have to stop.

'Jag One to Jag Two, do you copy?'

'Whatcha want?' a harsh voice snapped back.

'We got a dead left turn coming up in about ten minutes. Just thought I'd advise. Also we can hardly see your headlights.'

'We read you. I'll copy you when we get to the turn,' the radio voice replied. 'Holding steady on thirty.'

'Rodge and out.'

'Any coffee left in that thermos, Martinez?' the sergeant asked.

'Yeah, sure.' The PFC tipped a gallon thermos, leaned it against his foot, and poured coffee into a mug. 'Here ya go.'

'Thanks. Shit, this night is *never* gonna fuckin' end.'

He was wrong.

Three miles ahead of the convoy, ghost figures dashed through the trees and positioned themselves in the rocks that bordered 93 where it made its jagged path through the pass; specters in white camouflage, white ski masks, and white helmets, moving quickly and with precision. The wind, confused by the snaking mountains, whined past overhead. In the narrow valley it was eerily quiet.

The leader was on the north side of the pass. His radio crackled to life.

'Apache to Monty.'

'Read.'

'Ten minutes.'

'Read.'

'No other traffic north or south.'

'Roger, out.'

He snapped his walkie-talkie to life.

'Squads ready?'

'Ready, One.'

'Ready, Two.'

'Ready, Three.'

'Ten minutes,' the leader said.

He snapped the walkie-talkie off and handed it to the man beside him, then took a .50 caliber Eagle pistol from its holster and charged a round into the chamber. He could hear automatic weapons clicking in the darkness. He waited stoically, as cold as the weather.

A few minutes later he heard the convoy downshifting and growling as it approached the sharp curve. He rose up and peered through the trees, saw the lights of the three vehicles a few yards away.

'On one, launchers,' he whispered into his walkie-talkie.

He waited until the rear Humvee turned into the pass, then snapped his thumb on the walkie-talkie button.

'Three, two, one . . .'

In unison, two rocket launchers fired their missiles into the front and rear Humvees.

In the truck, the sergeant and the PFC were jolted by the sight of streaking flame as it whistled from the darkness and ripped into the side of the front Humvee. The Humvee exploded, sending its driver tumbling head over heels into the road. The other three GIs were ripped by shards of metal from the ruined vehicle. In his rearview mirror, the sergeant saw the rear Humvee also take a direct hit and burst into flames.

'Jesus Christ!' the sergeant in the semi screamed, slamming on his brakes.

Two specters in white appeared from the darkness and leaped on the running board of the truck. The sergeant stared in horror at the white ski masks with their obscene mouth holes, saw the pistols an instant before the two attackers each fired through the side window. The PFC was knocked against the door of the passenger side. The second shot tore through his skull, splashing blood on the window. The first shot at the sergeant hit him in the throat. He gasped and a mist of red blood plumed from his mouth. The second shot hit him in the right eye.

'Clear,' one of the shooters yelled. The passenger door opened and both bodies were dragged out of the cab as the first shooter jumped behind the wheel of the big rig.

'Ready to roll,' he yelled into his walkie-talkie.

The leader walked out onto the road and marched past the rear Humvee as his men swarmed over it and fired shots into the four wounded and dead soldiers in the demolished vehicle. He checked his watch as he walked. Two minutes.

Excellent.

Four of the ghost troopers stood over the front Humvee and fired shots into the already riddled men, while another sprayed foam from a fire extinguisher on the wreckage. They quickly dragged the victims out and laid them on the shoulder of the road.

At the rear of the ruined convoy the bodies of the GIs were also dragged to the side of the road.

The leader reached the driver's side of the semi.

'Roll,' he said.

The driver put the big rig into gear and drove into the back of the burning Humvee, shoved it off the side of the road, and kept on going.

*

In the darkness, the leader heard the solemn sounds along the side of the road.

Ziiipppp. Ziiippp . . .

He walked down the row of dead soldiers, each one stuffed into a forest-green body bag and zipped closed.

Except one. One of the ghost troopers looked up as the leader approached.

'He's not dead yet, sir.'

The leader leaned over and fired a single shot into the dying man's forehead.

'Zip it up,' he snapped.

Three Jeeps rounded the south corner of the pass and collected the ghost troopers. The leader was the last to jump into a Jeep. He checked his watch.

Four minutes. Perfect. He took a small radio transmitter from his pocket, pressed the Ready button, and then pressed Fire.

Behind him, high up on the cliffside, half a pound of C-4 ripped out the side of the cliff. The snow above it cascaded down, carrying trees and rocks. Rumbling in the darkness, the small avalanche swept down on the north side of the pass and engulfed the road.

The last Jeep wheeled through the south end of the pass. The leader set off a second charge. It was twice as loud as the first, starting landslides on both sides of the road.

The leader checked the luminous dial of his watch again.

Five minutes.

The hijacked semi vanished into the swirling snow.

Six

JANUARY 13, 4:35 A.M., EST

Marge Castaigne was wide-awake the minute the phone rang. Her night table was carefully arranged: night lamp with the press switch at the base, easy to reach and turn on; a digital clock so she could immediately tell the time; a safe, portable, hotline phone that connected with the White House. The first ring was not complete when she snatched it off the stand, looking at the green clock as she answered: 4:36 A.M. Not good.

'This is Castaigne.'

'General Castaigne, this is Claude Hooker. The President would like a meeting as soon as possible. How quickly can you be here?'

'Twenty minutes. What's up, Claude?'

'Don't know, but he's agitated. He had that look in his eye.'

'Uh-oh.'

'Your limo's on the way.'

'Thanks.'

Castaigne was passionately well-organized. Everything was prepared before she went to sleep, just in case the red phone rang, as it often did. Her clothes were laid out, briefcase repacked, coffeemaker ready to go. She threw on a robe, hurried to the kitchen, turned on the coffee-maker, then took a quick shower.

It could be anything. Somebody died. A cabinet member, maybe. Or a Supreme Court judge. No. That wouldn't agitate him. He was pissed, so it was some kind of crisis. The hell with it, she'd know soon enough.

She dressed quickly, sloshed a spoonful of sugar in a

109

plastic cup of coffee, took a sip, then went to the bedroom, took her 9mm Glock from the holster attached under the night-table top, and put it in her purse.

Showered, dressed, and out the door in nine minutes. The limo was waiting. Ten minutes to the White House.

Buffeted by the wind, the chopper roared down the Bitterroot Valley a hundred feet above the river, harsh beams of two searchlights leading the way. The chopper pilot leaned forward, squinting through the windscreen. He was a gruff man, husky, with rough hands and a heavy beard.

'You got big balls, Mr. Hardistan,' he said. 'Whatever happened down at Lost Trail ain't gonna go away, least until this weather shapes up.'

William Hardistan, Deputy Director of the FBI and the second most important man in the Bureau, huddled in an arctic jacket loaned to him by one of the agents in Butte and didn't say anything. His eyes were focused straight ahead, watching the river race by below them.

The pilot suddenly pulled the chopper up, rising a couple of hundred feet. They lost sight of the river in the swirling snow, and the searchlights were swallowed up in the darkness. Hardistan stiffened and shifted uneasily in his seat.

'Don't get nervous, we're passing over Sula. It's just a crossroads, but they got a church. Hate for you to end up hanging on the steeple.'

'I appreciate that,' Hardistan said in a low gravelly voice without a hint of nerves.

'You do this kinda thing often?'

'Not if I can help it. How about you?'

The pilot laughed. 'Only when there's nothin' better t'do.'

Hardistan watched the little village slide below them. There were a few lights on in houses, otherwise the town was dark.

'Another ten minutes we'll be there.'

'That's good news, not that I fault your flying, Sid.' Hardistan didn't know the pilot's last name. He was introduced as Sid and that ended the introduction. The pilot was unaware that his passenger was the number two man in the FBI, a veteran who had kept out of the limelight and managed to weather the Hoover regime, Waco, Ruby Ridge, Oklahoma City, and the FBI lab scandals, and had risen continuously through it all.

Ahead of them, Hardistan thought he saw lights reflecting off the snow. 'What's that?' he asked.

'Your people got some searchlights down there?'

'Probably. They brought a service van down from Missoula. Has everything in it but a sauna.'

'Ah, a sauna, now there's a happy thought.' A moment later the pilot said, 'Yeah, looks like they got a coupla ten-thousand-watters set up. This'll be easy.'

He guided the helicopter over the lights and checked for wires, then lowered the chopper down between the light poles. It settled gently on the frozen ground. Fifty feet away in the hazy, snow-speckled light, rocks, trees, dirt, and debris clogged the entrance to Lost Trail Pass.

'What happened, they have a landslide?' Sid asked as Hardistan unbuckled.

'Looks like it.'

'FBI investigatin' avalanches now?' the pilot asked with a grin.

Hardistan smiled wanly. 'Looks like it. Thanks, Sid. If I ever need a good chopper pilot again, I'll call you.'

'Praise from Caesar,' the pilot said, and shook Hardistan's hand. The FBI Deputy Director jumped out of the chopper and ran, stooped over, out of the windy circle whipped up by the rotors.

Geoff Isaac met Hardistan as he left the chopper. Isaac was agent in charge of the Missoula office, and at twenty-nine was the youngest agent in charge in the Bureau.

'Mr. Hardistan,' he said, shaking the older man's gloved hand.

'Hey, Geoff. I can't believe you drove the van down here in this weather.'

'I can't believe you flew down here in a chopper,' Isaac yelled over the clatter of the chopper as it lifted off. 'Let's get in the RV, it's a little warmer than it is out here.'

The RV was a mobile laboratory, equipped with an array of electronic equipment, a satellite dish for visual reporting, two cots, and a kitchen. A heavy-duty generator roared outside. The wind buffeted the big land cruiser, sneaked in around windows and doors, and strained the heater.

Isaac had spread two maps out on a table. He quickly explained to Hardistan where they were and the hazards posed by the weather. Then he gave Hardistan a quick report on the ambush itself, while the Deputy Director took copious notes in shorthand.

'Brilliantly planned, sir. Trapped the convoy here, in the pass, wasted the front and rear guard vehicles, killed all ten men in the convoy, set off explosions at both ends of the pass, and caused landslides that have us blocked on both ends. In the dark, in a blizzard, in and out in five minutes.'

'How do you know that?' Hardistan asked.

Isaac walked to a tape recorder. 'Listen to this. This guy's name is Norman Shields. He's a hunter, fisherman, and ham radio operator, lives somewhere up there . . .' He waved toward the mountains. '. . . and heard the attack. All the phones hereabouts are down, so he raised a radio buddy of his in – get this – Maine. His buddy puts him on the speaker phone, calls Missoula, and they patch through to us.'

'Miracle of modern communication.'

Isaac turned on the tape and Hardistan listened intently to the exchange.

'Mr. Shields, this is Geoff Isaac, agent in charge of the

Missoula bureau.'

'Yes sir, this is Norman Shields.'

'I understand you heard a disturbance tonight.'

'Disturbance is right. I hit the sack about ten, got no phone or electricity up here, they been out since about seven, and I wake up when I hear these explosions. First thing I do, I check the clock, and it's 10:27 on the button. First off, there's two explosions almost on top a each other, bam-bam, like that. Then what sounds like a lotta firecrackers, then boom! A big one, and about thirty seconds after that two more booms, even louder. That's it. It was all over at 10:32.'

'Did you hear any heavy vehicles after the second big explosion?'

'Didn't hear nothin' but what I just told ya. The wind was about to blow me off the mountain, I was lucky to hear anything. I judged it came from the northwest, probably two or three miles. I mean, it wasn't like it was in the backyard or anything. I got up and opened the window to get a better listen.'

'You're sure about the time?'

'I reset the clock every Sunday using the Greenwich signal on public radio.'

Isaac snapped off the recorder.

'We got an ear witness,' Hardistan said.

'Pinpoints the time. Five minutes, sir. We're talking real pros here.'

Hardistan nodded.

'I've got five men with me,' Isaac said. 'We've been out in the crime zone shooting video and Polaroids, but the equipment freezes up and you can't stay outside too long at a time. In another two hours the whole place will be under four or five inches of snow.'

'There goes whatever physical evidence there is.'

'I'm afraid so. We're trying to catalogue what there is. No tracks worth a damn. A lot of shell casings. What's left of the two Humvees.' Isaac went to the door. 'I want to show you something out there. You're not going to believe it.'

The Secret Service uniformed guard at the White House gate saluted when he looked into the rear seat of the limo.

'Morning, General,' he said, waving the limo through.

'Morning, Chet.'

The limo drove to the west wing entrance of the White House, and the FBI agent jumped out and opened the door. The Attorney General leaned out, poured the remaining coffee from the cup, snapped a Kleenex from a box in the back, stuffed it in the cup, and put the cup on the floor in the rear of the limousine. The guard watched her now-familiar ritual with the coffee and kept his eyes on her as she approached him. She was a handsome woman, five-five or so, with dark brown hair and hazel eyes, dressed smartly in a gray wool suit with a dark blue scarf around her neck. No coat. He snapped to attention as she neared his post.

'Good morning, ma'am,' he said.

'Morning, Ed,' she said, waving her ID holder at him. 'Who's here so far?'

'You're the first,' he answered, opening the door for her.

'Good,' she said, and winked as she entered the elevator to the first floor, where Hooker was waiting, unsmiling and stern-faced as always. The National Security Adviser never smiled. He was dressed in a dark blue suit, white shirt, and wine tie. As usual, he looked like he'd been up for hours.

'Coffee and pastries,' he said, ushering her into the Oval Office. 'He should be down in a minute.'

'Can't you tell me *any*thing?' she asked.

'Let's not spoil it for the President.'

'Who else is coming to the party?'

'The usual.'

Good old Claude, Mister Know-it-all-don't-say-

114

nothin'.

'You're just a fountain of information this morning.' She went to the silver service, poured a cup of coffee, opted for an apricot Danish, and sat down on the couch.

Lawrence Pennington burst through the door a minute later. He was a tall, deeply tanned, burly man with short-cropped graying hair over a hawk face and brown eyes. The slender seam of a scar from just above his right eyebrow to his jaw added a menacing touch to his rugged good looks. Every schoolkid and adult in the country knew he had earned the crease in a hand-to-hand fight with a Vietcong guerrilla in Vietnam, a fight that had earned him a Silver Star and a Purple Heart. They also knew that Pennington had graduated with honors from West Point, was a war hero in Korea and Vietnam, had been commanding general in Desert Storm, became the military's top gun, and retired his five stars to run for Chief Executive. The perfect President: a good-looking war hero. Now all they had to do was keep him in office. Pennington had been elected by an overpowering landslide, but a jealous Congress, dominated by his political enemies, had riddled his programs and made fun of his inexperience in dealing with the Hill. Now, two years into his tenure, he was more embattled than he had ever been on the battlefield.

He was dressed in a gray jogging outfit and white sneakers, his jaw set, his expression grim.

Uh-oh, this ain't a happy President, Castaigne thought as she stood to greet him. 'Morning, Mr. President,' she said.

'General.' He nodded. 'Sorry to get you up at this hour. And pardon my informality, I'm hoping to get a run in after our meeting.'

He took a can of Diet Coke from a large, sterling ice bucket, snapped off the tab, and took a swig. She knew better than to ask the big question. He'd tell her when he was ready.

'The house staff isn't up yet,' he said gruffly. 'I'm sure we can manage. Harry, Wayne, and Wendell will be here in a minute.'

Hooker, Simmons, Brodsky, and Harrison, she said to herself. *National Security, FBI, Department of Interior, the ATF, and the Attorney General. Now* there's *a mix.*

'How's Emilio doing?' the President asked, forcing a smile.

'Great, thank you. Finishes in June. Top ten percent. I can't complain.'

'Hell, I should think not,' he said, nodding sharply. 'Top ten at Harvard Law. You must be dancing in your shoes.'

'I am that,' she said.

There was a knock at the door, and Hooker ushered in Harry Simmons, Director of the FBI; Wayne Brodsky, Alcohol, Tobacco and Firearms; and Wendell Greer, Secretary of the Interior. Her mind played games. What could possibly have happened to get the Attorney General, these four men, and the President together at five in the morning? They said their good mornings and went to the coffee urn.

They all looked like they were supposed to look, Castaigne thought. Simmons was tall, had a health club physique, a pugnacious face, and a widow's peak of black hair that gave him a satanic look. He had served as police chief in Detroit and New York before taking over from Robert Lewis, whose administration had been riddled with scandal. Brodsky was bald and beefy and walked with a strut. He had worked his way up through the ranks to become top man at ATF, which was now fighting for its life to keep from being conscripted into the FBI. They had one appearance in common – intense, arrogant eyes – Simmons's deeply set, Brodsky's hooded by fleshy eyelids. Wen Greer had nothing in common with either of them. He was a slender stalk of a man, with a pleasant smile, passionate eyes, and blond hair. The hair gave him the

116

look of a surfer, which in fact he had been in his early years before joining the Forest Service and serving for twelve years in the Rocky Mountains. His maternal grandmother was a Cherokee Indian. Greer was the first person with Native American blood to serve as Secretary of the Interior, an ironic fact considering that Native Americans once owned *all* of the interior of the United States.

Hooker, tall, stoic, ex-Marine, ex-CIA, embraced paranoia as others would a lover, his eyes permanently narrowed into slits from years of suspicion about *everything*. An emotionless man whose lips hardly moved when he spoke, he was the perfect National Security Adviser. Hooker was an enigma. Rumors of dark deeds in 'Nam and Nicaragua swarmed about him like bees. He had the President's ear, a fact that he subtly lorded over the others. Hooker served the President well and discreetly, and Pennington had learned years ago as an Army officer that he didn't have to like someone to respect him and exploit his talent.

The President genuinely liked Margaret Castaigne, the first Puerto Rican Attorney General in history, a tough former federal prosecutor and later federal judge of the south Florida district. She was generally conceded by the media to be not only the most effective member of Pennington's formidable cabinet but, in terms of her position, its most powerful and feared member. She had been on the job only six months but quickly learned that her power rested in part on her alliances. Hooker played it safe and could not always be counted on for support. Simmons was not an ally. He was a political animal whose job was to protect the FBI and repair an image tarnished at Ruby Ridge, Waco, and in its own laboratories. The man who really ran the Bureau was in an RV in the middle of a blizzard in the mountains of Montana. Castaigne was also keenly aware that Simmons resented her as his boss and secretly lobbied friends on the Hill to have his position elevated to cabinet status.

They sat on twin sofas, facing each other across a coffee table. The President sat at one end of the table in a rocking chair, nursing his soda. Hooker sat apart from the rest in a chair near the door with a laptop computer on an end table beside him, drumming his fingers lightly on his knee.

'I have some disturbing news,' the President said gravely. 'There's been a terrorist attack on an Army convoy in Montana. Ten men are dead and an eighteen-wheeler crammed with weapons and ammunition has been hijacked.'

The reaction was shock and a sudden babble from everyone in the room. Questions started battering him. He held up his hand.

'The attack apparently occurred at about 2230 hours yesterday, Rocky Mountain Time.' He looked at his watch. 'Roughly five hours ago. That's pretty much all we know for now. We do have one break. Billy Hardistan was in Butte for a presentation. He took a chopper through extremely hazardous weather and is on the scene now. I expect to hear from him momentarily.'

There was a moment of silence as the cabinet members digested what they had just heard.

'Before anybody says anything,' Pennington said, 'I think we can assume this is not a foreign attack. I can't imagine foreign terrorists pulling off a trick like this.'

'All of the men were killed?' Marge said.

Pennington nodded.

'I find it hard to believe that Americans would perpetrate something like this.'

'Oh, come on, General,' Simmons said. 'How about the World Trade Center, Oklahoma City?'

'The Trade Center was foreigners. Oklahoma City was a couple of militia nuts. This was obviously carried out by a lot of people.'

'A handful. Ten or twelve,' Pennington said. 'They had the element of surprise, darkness, a storm. Ten men could easily have done the job. And very quickly. Bing, bang, boom, and out. Classic guerrilla assault.'

The red phone rang and Hooker snatched it up.

'Claude Hooker here . . . Hello, Mr. Hardistan, hold for the President, please.'

Pennington took the phone.

'Hello, Billy, sorry you're stuck out there, but I can't think of a better man to have on the scene. I'm putting you on the speaker.'

He pressed a button and hung up the phone. Hardistan's voice came in strong and clear.

'Thank you, sir. I'm afraid there's not much we can do right now. It's still snowing and probably will until mid-morning. It's colder than a witch's heart, and this is the darkest place I've ever seen in my life. Just setting the scene for you.'

'Perfectly,' Pennington said. He told Hardistan who was in the room with him. 'So what have you got for us?'

'Mr. President, this was a very carefully planned assault. They took out ten men and two vehicles, stole a semi rig, and sealed off both ends of the pass where the attack took place, all in about five minutes. The snow was a break for them. My assumption is they got inside information on what time the convoy was leaving, knew where it was going, and had rehearsed this operation to a fare-thee-well.

'The convoy left an arsenal near Spokane last night at five P.M. Its destination was the Air Force base at Mountain Home, Idaho. Normally about a five- to six-hour drive. There were three vehicles, two Humvees with four armed guards in each, and an eighteen-wheeler loaded with weapons and ammunition, a driver, and relief driver. The Humvees bracketed the semi.'

'What the hell were they doing out in that godforsaken place in a blizzard?' Pennington asked.

'It's SOP when moving this kind of cargo to drive at night when there's very little traffic, Mr. President. The blizzard was unexpected, a shift in the weather. I'm having a manifest of the cargo faxed to Colonel Hooker and the Director, but I think it's worth mentioning here that part of the cargo was a thousand pounds of C-4 explosives in half-pound packets.'

Pennington knew what a half pound of C-4 could do. That amount of the puttylike plastic explosive could take down a 747. Five pounds, placed strategically, could waste an entire shopping mall. It was also difficult to make and extremely expensive on the arms black market.

'My God,' Pennington said. 'What were they sending C-4 to an air base for?'

'The cargo was going to be air lifted to Fort Ord, sir. Anyway, one leg of the convoy's trip took them down U.S. 93, south from Missoula into Idaho. The road is bordered on the west by the Bitterroot Mountains. Very rugged. Peaks up to ten thousand feet. On the other side of the road is the Bitterroot River, and then the Anaconda Range, also very rugged terrain.

'At one point, 93 takes a jog eastward for a hundred yards or so, then turns back to the south. High cliffs on both sides of the road. It's called Lost Trail Pass. Aptly named.

'We have an ear witness who says the attack started at 10:27 and the noise ended at 10:32. Five minutes. Judging from the crime scene and the witness, when the convoy got into that straight stretch heading east, the front and back Humvees were hit with rocket fire. At the same time, a strike force jumped the cab of the semi and killed both men. Obviously they were careful to avoid any weapons fire on the trailer itself. All eight of the soldiers in the Humvees were also killed, several with an insurance shot behind the ear. Explosions were triggered at both ends of the pass, which created small avalanches and sealed off the pass. I'm surmising that the hijacked truck went south. Turning it around in that narrow space so they could head back north would have been difficult and time-consuming, and the description of the ear witness indicates the south end of the pass was sealed last. Two charges were set off there.'

'We have any leads at all, Billy?' Simmons asked.

'None. It was close to eleven before the explosions were reported, another hour by the time local police got there. The state troopers got there at twelve-thirty, and Geoff Isaac out of our Missoula office was on site by one-thirty with a fully equipped service van and five special agents. I got here at two-thirty in a chopper out of Butte. As of now, the ambushers have a window of almost five hours and we're hampered by a snow storm. The weather's estimated to clear by mid-morning, and by then we'll have up to a foot or more of snow over the entire area. Tracking will be impossible. If there are any hard tracks, they'll be covered and washed out when the snow melts. Hard evidence will also be severely compromised, if there is much hard evidence. These birds were very thorough.

'I have agents coming in from Butte, Boise, Missoula, and as far south as Salt Lake City. The Army is sending another fifty men down. I've ordered a massive chopper search of the entire area as soon as weather permits, but we're talking about mountain terrain, deep valleys, a lot of low-lying fog in some areas.

'Our men will coordinate the search for physical evidence and interview locals with the help of the sheriff's department. He knows everybody in the area.

'There's one other thing, Mr. President.'

'Yes, Billy.'

'They put all ten of the victims in body bags and laid them out military fashion beside the road.'

'My God!' The President's face flushed. He balled his fists and slammed them down on the arm of the rocking chair. *'God damn them!'*

'It gets worse, sir. We believe that one of the GIs was still alive. He was shot in the forehead while he was lying in the body bag. We recovered the bullet from the ground under his head. Probably a .50 cal Israeli Eagle pistol. So far it's the only piece of real evidence we've got.'

Pennington stood up and walked across the room to his desk. 'I want your candid opinion, Billy. You think this was a militia operation?'

'Well, it was certainly well-planned. A professional job from the front. And laying out the bodies could be some kind of warped military tribute.'

'Bunch of savages. An act of terrorism against the people of the United States, plain and simple. This smells like the Sanctuary to me. I think Engstrom has finally gone around the bend. He's declared open warfare on the U.S.'

'Yes sir.'

'You agree?'

'Sir, I've been on the site thirty minutes and I can't see across the road. I'd hate to make any guesses at this point.'

'That was an outstanding report under very difficult conditions, Billy. You are to be commended. Thank you. You'll keep us informed?'

'Absolutely, sir.'

'I want you to report directly to Claude Hooker.'

'Affirmative, sir.'

'Thank you.'

Hardistan hung up the phone and turned to Isaac.

'Top of the list, Mr. Isaac, find that goddamn truck.'

The President's face was red with anger after the call. He was grinding one fist into the palm of his hand.

'That bastard Engstrom,' he said.

'Excuse me, sir, but isn't that a bit of a stretch—' Simmons said.

'You heard what Hardistan said,' Pennington growled back, cutting him off. 'A well-planned military operation, and right in Engstrom's backyard. A cold-blooded ambush of American soldiers and equipment. A goddamn act of terrorism. Who else would be up to it?'

'The Posse, the Covenant, Aryans, some skinhead off-shoot. It could be any of them.'

'You think a bunch of pimply-faced kids with their heads shaved could pull off a stunt like this?'

'Some of the others could.'

Pennington walked back to the group.

'Think about that. The only militia group even close enough to pull it off is the Aryans in Utah. The others would have had to travel hundreds of miles into strange terrain. Not likely. And what would they do with the semi? Hell, what is *anyone* going to do with this eighteen-wheeler? It's hardly inconspicuous.'

'If they were smart enough to pull off this coup, you can bet they knew exactly what they were going to do with it,' Marge Castaigne said.

'And by sunup they'll have a six, seven hour jump on us. Let me tell you, Engstrom may be a religious nut, but he's a brilliant tactician. It smells like his work.'

'I'm just saying we have to be discreet. . . .'

'Oh, for God's sake, Harry, I'm not going to call a press conference and accuse the Sanctuary. But this goes on top of the agenda. We took forever to wake up to the fact that Engstrom and his outfit were serious threats. Now we have to make up for lost time.'

'Don't rub it in, Mr. President. We've got a file on the Sanctuary of the Lord that would fill the Smithsonian, and not one iota of evidence to prove they're guilty of anything.'

'Excuse me, Mr. President,' Marge Castaigne said, 'I'd like to make a suggestion.'

'By all means,' the President said.

'For over a year now we've been sniffing around General Engstrom and the Sanctuary, and so far we've got bupkus. If you're convinced that they are involved in serious crimes – murder, robbery, money laundering, crimes against the government – then I'd like to bring in a special prosecutor, set up a task force . . . and bring down a RICO case on them.'

'Oh my God,' Simmons said, shaking his head.

'What's that mean?' Pennington demanded of the Bureau director.

'I mean, what can a special prosecutor do that we aren't doing already?' Simmons complained.

'Focus on the problem,' Castaigne said flatly.

Simmons glared at her but said nothing.

'If there's a case there, we'll find it,' she added.

'Sounds like you have someone in mind for this job,' Hooker said.

She nodded. 'That's right, I do.'

'And who is this legal magician?' Simmons sneered.

'Martin Vail.'

'He the one that stole that Illinois case out from under Pete Riker?' Hooker asked.

'When it comes to RICO, nobody can touch him. Got the biggest RICO judgment in history. Ninety million.'

'That was the Atlas-Western case, right?' the President said. 'He put Tom Lacey and whatsisname from Atlas–'

'Grossman,' Simmons said.

'Right, Grossman. They both got some serious time, didn't they?' Pennington smiled. 'Never liked either one of them.'

'They never contributed a dime to your campaign,' Hooker said.

'Maybe that's the reason.'

They all laughed.

'Look, Mr. President, the Bureau is straining as it is,' Simmons implored. 'RICO requires a lot of FBI participation–'

'I'm aware of that, Harry. I also know if the Sanctuary – or any other paramilitary group – is getting this . . . dangerous, we need to give them A-priority attention.'

'We'll do that, sir. I've got the Deputy Director on the scene–'

'Luck, Harry, luck,' Pennington cut him off. 'Hardistan just happened to be a hundred miles away.'

Rebuffed, Simmons sat back on the sofa and stared at the floor.

Like all human beings, Pennington was a flawed man. His flaw was that he felt things too deeply, was too passionate in his friendships, in his work, in anger, love, war, and hate. His cabinet members recognized his seething rage, controlled but volcanic. He could end a discussion with a look, by the way he cleared his throat, or by stone silence. One moment he could handle a monumental calamity with inhuman calm, the next, a simple act of abuse or unkindness could set off an implosion.

At the moment, he was imploding just thinking about General Joshua Engstrom and the Sanctuary of the Lord and the Wrath of God. He did not feel compelled to explain to his assembled staff why he felt this rage or why he knew – *knew* – that Engstrom was behind the ambush in Lost Trail Pass.

The room fell quiet. Pennington walked to the window overlooking the rose garden and thought about his son and grandson practicing clever soccer moves on the lawn.

Supposing it was them, the President thought, *supposing they were stretched out in the cold in body bags. Innocent kids doing their job. Would I feel any more strongly than I do right now?* The answer was no. He had a quick flash back to Vietnam, sitting in his room in Saigon, writing letters of condolence to parents back in the World.

'This is a personal thing,' he said. He turned back to his staff. 'I understand what Marge is saying. You set up a task force and put the right person in charge, they'll make it happen. If it's there, they'll dig it out.'

'These things take years,' Simmons argued. 'It took, what, six years to get Gotti?'

'General, how long did it take your man to bring down Lacey and, uh . . .'

'Grossman,' the Attorney General said.

'Yes.'

'Less than two years,' Castaigne answered.

'And what will this entail?' the President asked. 'By that I mean, what's the scope of this project?'

'We'll have to gather evidence to prove criminal collusion between the entities comprising the Sanctuary.'

'They're churches,' Simmons said. 'That adds to the problem.'

'Not really,' the Attorney General disagreed. 'We make the case and we seek warrants against the principals and their underlings. Probably General Engstrom, the commanders of each of the four units, and a half dozen others, plus any citizens or institutions – banks, businesses, radio stations, anything used as a front for criminal activity connected to the defendants. If the institutions happen to be churches, so be it. Once we start, the gloves are off.'

'This is going to cost a bundle,' Brodsky remarked.

'A bundle,' Castaigne said with a nod. 'I couldn't even guess the cost. Once we get all this data together and have a case, we'll have to find a federal judge who'll grant us blanket warrants because the four churches are located in two different states. Once that's done, we can legally proceed against them, lien on property, including their weapons, vehicles, bank accounts, anything that was acquired with criminal funds.'

'And the fun begins,' Simmons said.

'What do you mean?' Pennington asked.

'Bringing them in. They won't go gently. And the trial could take two or three years.'

'I'll be out of office before that.'

'Mr. President,' Hooker said, 'you'll be here for at least six more years.'

There was general approval and agreement from the cabinet members.

Brodsky said, 'It could be a public relations coup for us

if we prove these people are hijacking trucks, killing people, robbing banks, money-laundering.'

'We're not going to have another Waco or Ruby Ridge,' Pennington said emphatically. He paced across the room and back and stopped in front of the sofas. 'I like it, General.'

'If we have the cases–' Simmons started.

'We'll have the cases,' Castaigne said sternly, cutting him off. 'We will take down the big shots, take all their toys away from them, put 'em out of business, drop the ringleaders for twenty years each, and fine them a couple of million dollars. That will make the biggest impression on the public . . . and the rest of these hate groups.'

'I don't want to give the impression we're against all militias,' the President said. 'Some of them are perfectly legitimate.'

Wen Greer stepped in. 'Sir, I spent twelve years in the Rockies, a lot of it in Montana. They're great people and I doubt that they're sympathetic to Engstrom and his movement, but they have an ardent sense of fair play and common decency.'

'I copy that, Wen.'

'If they're clean,' Castaigne said, 'they have nothing to worry about.'

'General Engstrom could be a problem,' Simmons said. 'He was a hero in three wars, battlefield commission in Korea when he was nineteen, held the line at Chosen Reservoir.'

'Who didn't?' the President snapped.

'Of course, sir. I'm just saying–'

'I know what you're saying, and I'm telling you he's a goddamn Bible-spouting glory boy. A sorehead. Made a fool of himself and retired in rank. Now he wants to get even by blowing up the whole country.'

'He's got people around him far more dangerous than he is.'

'He's the one in the kitchen,' the President said firmly.

'Of course, of course. I just mean, you know, he still has a following. We wouldn't want to create another John Brown.'

'We already have,' Brodsky offered. 'He's a raving lunatic.'

'If we do this,' Pennington said, 'I'd like them in court in eighteen months. It would be a great help in the next election.'

'What do we really know about this guy Vail?' Hooker said.

Castaigne opened her briefcase and took out a file folder. She handed it to the President. 'This is a top security check on Vail and his staff. Also a synopsis of the Illinois trial – I had the transcripts sent to me daily.'

The President was impressed. 'How long have you been thinking about this, A.G.?' he asked.

'Since we first started talking about Engstrom and the Sanctuary. About a year.'

He looked at Castaigne. 'Can he deliver a RICO case in a year and a half?'

'I really don't know. I'll have to ask him. I've never met him, by the way. He may turn us down. He's very independent.'

'What's he doing now?'

'Not a thing,' she answered.

'How soon can you talk to him?'

'I have to be in St. Louis tonight. I could fly up to Chicago on the way and have a talk with him.'

'Sooner the better. This is Monday. Can we have him here for a meeting at, say, nine Wednesday morning?'

Her expression did not change. 'Yes, sir, if he's interested in the job,' she replied.

Pennington smiled. 'If he proves difficult, tell him the President has a favor to ask.'

Seven

The cellular phone rang a second time before Vail turned over with a groan and felt for it in the dark, groping for the power button.

'Hello.' Sleepily.

'Mr. Vail?'

'Yeah?'

'Sorry to awaken you at this hour. This is Margaret Castaigne, the Attorney General.'

He did not answer for a few seconds. He raised up on one elbow and turned on the lamp. Jane made a noise and turned on her side, facing away from the light. The dog didn't move.

Margaret Castaigne?
Attorney General?
Of the United States?
Nah.

'Who is this, really?'

'I know this is rather unorthodox, Mr. Vail. This *is* Marge Castaigne. If you want to check it, you can get the number of the White House switchboard and call me back.'

'Uh . . . okay . . . I'll call you right back,' he said, and hung up. He sat up in the bed and rubbed the sleep out of his eyes. Jane turned back over and peered at him through sleep-swollen slits.

'Who was that?' she asked grumpily.

'Margaret Castaigne,' he said.

Her eyes popped open. '*The* Margaret Castaigne?'

'That's what she said.'

'The Attorney General?'

'Yeah,' he said. He got the number from information and, punching out the number on his cell phone, said, 'I've got to call her back at the White House.'

'The White House? Martin, are you dreaming? Why would the A.G. be calling you at this hour?'

'Tell you in a min– Yes, good morning, this is Martin Vail. I have instructions to call– Thank you ...' He cupped the mouthpiece with his hand. 'I think it's really her. The White House switchboard answered and they're– Hello, this is Martin Vail.'

'I like a man who's cautious, Mr. Vail,' Marge Castaigne said.

'Well, uh, one can never be too cautious, can one?'

Jane squinted at him, rolled her eyes, shook her head, and buried her face in a pillow.

'Mr. Vail, I'll be in Chicago in about ninety minutes. I was wondering if you can join me for breakfast?'

'Breakfast? In ninety minutes?'

'I know this is very short notice. I'm sorry about that.'

'I, uh, I can't get into town in ninety minutes, Ms. Castaigne.'

'Yes, I know. I understand you have a large open yard between your cabin and the lake. I can have a chopper set down there in, say, an hour?'

'Can you tell me what this is about?'

'Rather not on the phone. Do you have other plans?'

'Ms. Castaigne, I'm on vacation. The only thing I do before noon is take my dog for a walk.'

'One hour, then? You can still work in a short walk with Mister Magoo.'

'Right. Thank you, sir.'

'Thank *you*, sir. See you in about ninety.'

Vail turned off the phone and laid it on the night table.

'Well ... ?' Venable said.

Vail got out of bed and pulled on his bathrobe. 'It was her all right.'

'Martin, you called her sir.'

'Are you sure?'

'Yes I'm sure.' She waited for an explanation. 'Well?'

'We're having breakfast in town.' He headed toward the shower.

'When?'

'Hour and a half. She's sending a helicopter to pick me up. God, it's cold in here.'

'Is this a *joke*? It's always cold in here first thing. I always get up first and turn on the heat.'

'Oh. Thanks.'

'Marty? Are you serious?'

'Yes, it must be forty in here.'

'I mean about the A.G.?'

'Yup.' He got up, stepped over the dog, who was sound asleep on the floor beside him, and went into the bathroom. A moment later he stuck his head back out and pointed to the dog. 'That's a pedigreed, pure-bred white German shepherd, distant relative of the wolf, which is the smartest animal on four legs. You'd think the phone would wake him up, maybe get a bark or two out of him, wouldn't you?'

'Why? He doesn't have to answer it.'

'I didn't think of that.'

He went back in the bathroom and then stuck his head around the corner again.

'She knew his name.'

'Who?'

'The Attorney General. She knew Magoo's name.'

'She's the Attorney General, for God's sake. The FBI works for her.'

'Oh. That explains it. On the other hand, maybe it's a joke. Maybe I'm going to get up and dressed and whoever called is going to call back at six and say something like, "Happy January Fool's Day."'

'Go take a shower.'

'Right.'

She stood by the kitchen window, nursing a cup of coffee, watching Vail and Magoo playing down by the lake. He had never owned a dog in his life and was obviously skeptical when she gave him Magoo for his birthday, a twenty-pound bundle of white fur with gold eyes and enormous pointed ears. Now the two were inseparable and Vail was suggesting they get a mate for him. He was nine months old, ninety pounds and still growing. He looked like a ghost, trotting through the trees, his pointed ears moving to the side and back at every sound, his nose raised and sniffing the cold morning air for the scent of a rabbit or a stoat. She heard Vail whistle, saw Magoo turn sharply and gallop back to his side, and they headed across the snow-encrusted yard toward the house.

Vail admired the house, as he always did when he walked up from the lake. It was a two-story converted barn that Jane and an architect had fashioned into a perfect getaway house. On the first floor there was a guest bedroom, which no one had ever used, and an enormous living room, which towered to the peaked roof of the old barn. There were two fireplaces, one in the living room and one in the corner of the sprawling kitchen. On the second floor, their bedroom and Jane's bath were on one side of the house, and their office on the other side. The rooms were connected by a bridge across the back side of the living room. Vail had his own bath adjacent to the office.

'Know how lucky you are?' he said to Magoo, who was trotting beside him, his nose to the ground. 'Think about it, what a deal you've got. A nice cabin by the lake, great apartment in town with a view of the lake. A rich, beautiful mistress. Me.'

Magoo stopped and checked out a hole in the snow, then trotted on.

'Until Janie and I decided to live together, I never gave a second thought to owning a dog or a country place.

Never gave it a first thought. You could've ended up in some dinky house with a little fenced-in backyard, you know. Think about it.'

Magoo looked up at him and yawned.

'Know what I think, buddy?' Vail said, his breath condensing into swirls of steam. 'I think you need a girlfriend. Every man needs a little love in his life.'

He stamped snow off his boots before he entered the kitchen. Magoo scooted ahead of him and went straight to his food dish. Jane handed Vail a cup of coffee.

'You two make a beautiful pair.'

'He keeps getting smarter and smarter.'

'Are you going like that?' she asked casually.

'Why not?'

'You're having breakfast with the Attorney General of the United States. Don't you think a jacket and tie might be more appropriate than corduroys, a flannel shirt, and a bomber jacket?'

'She probably wants to raise hell with me about stealing the Grand County case from her department,' he said, sipping his coffee. 'Why should I dress up for that?'

'I'm sure she has better things on her agenda.'

'I really don't know that much about her. Wasn't she a judge down in the second circuit?'

'Yes, darling. And a former fed prosecutor, and before that a demon in the defense community – like someone else I know. You two have a lot in common.'

'The only time I ever worked for the government was in the Army, not a pleasant experience.'

'She's tough, Marty. I hear she kicks ass all over the Hill. When she first took the job, a bunch of decrepit congressmen decided to whip her into shape, walk all over her, teach her the Washington way, whatever the hell that is. She did the whipping and still does. You know about her husband, don't you?'

'Died, didn't he?'

'He was defending a lawyer friend in a money laundering case two doors down from where she was holding court, dropped dead cross-examining a witness.'

'Not a bad way to go.'

'I wouldn't tell her that.'

'I'm sure her husband's nose dive in court won't come up.'

'They were quite an item. The tough federal judge married to the hard-boiled lawyer.'

'How come you know so much about her?'

'She's the top lawyer in the country. I like to know about my competition.'

'You planning to enter government service?'

'I mean, I like to see a woman rise to the surface in D.C. Some of those old bastards in Congress can't stand it when one of their cronies gets passed over, particularly by a . . . *woman*.' She made quotation marks with fingers when she said 'woman.'

'I'll give you an in-depth appraisal when I get back,' Vail said. 'By the way, the guy her husband was defending got a mistrial when Castaigne died. Made a deal and never served a day. Some people think Castaigne dropped dead just to win the case. I always did appreciate a man who'll do anything to win. Of course, dying was a bit extreme.'

He stepped over and kissed her. 'Let's have corned beef hash and eggs for lunch. I'll cook.'

'You won't be back for lunch.'

'How do you know?'

'Woman's intuition.'

'Well, I'll tell Ms. Castaigne you're a fan.'

'And don't call her Ms. Castaigne.'

'What do I call her?'

'General, of course. How quickly you forget.'

'It always made me uncomfortable when people called me "General." I think of a general as, you know, standing in the back of a jeep waving at all the people he just liberated. Patton, Eisenhower, Stormin' Norman, now those were generals.'

'Martin?'

'Yeah?'

'Call her General.'

'Right.'

'Gonna change clothes?'

'Nope.'

Magoo heard the chopper first, its blades beating the air. He walked to the picture window in the living room, stared across the lake for a moment, and then growled.

'The phone rings in his ear and he sleeps right through it. But he hears a helicopter ten miles away.'

'I told you why. He doesn't have to talk on the phone.'

'What's he going to do, fly the chopper into town?'

'Wouldn't surprise me at all.'

He put his arm around her and they stared at the sky.

'What the hell do you think this is about?' he said, half to himself.

Jane did not answer him. But she knew in her heart that their life was about to change.

Radically.

Lawrence Pennington stood at his desk, running his finger down the appointments list for the day. His secretary, Mildred Ewing, waited patiently.

'What's this Missouri delegation coffee at seven-thirty?'

'It's the entire congressional delegation. The veteran's thing?'

'Oh, right. What time is it?'

'Seven twenty-three, Mr. President.'

'They here?'

She nodded.

'Give me five minutes.'

'Yes sir.' She turned and left the Oval Office, and Hooker came in the room.

'Got a minute, Mr. President?'

135

'What is it, Claude?'

The security adviser walked around the desk and stood behind him. He leaned over and whispered in the President's ear. He always whispered when they were alone, fearing tape recorders might pick up his words.

'This is a risky trick, General. This RICO thing.'

'How so, Claude?' the President said without turning around.

'If this man doesn't deliver . . .'

'Everything's a risk in politics, Colonel.'

'But if he doesn't bring this case in . . .'

'Don't worry about it, Claude, that's Marge Castaigne's problem.'

'If this doesn't work, it could backfire in the next campaign.'

He turned and faced Hooker. 'I know the risks,' he said flatly.

'He's not a player, Mr. President. This Vail's a real wild pony.'

'Oh?' the President said curtly. 'I'll tell you what, Claude. Stay out of his way, but keep an eye on him. Since you're so concerned, Mr. Vail will be your responsibility. If he *is* a wild pony, he's *your* wild pony.'

BOOK TWO
WILD PONY

For one who has been honored,
Dishonor is worse than death.
– Bhagavad Gita

Eight

The helicopter settled gently in a remote corner of O'Hare. A tall black man who appeared to be in his early thirties was standing nearby, his hand stuffed in a fur-lined jacket. There was a badge on the collar of the jacket. Vail jumped out and, as he ran in a crouch under the blades, the man came up to him and offered his hand.

'Mr. Vail?'

'Yes.'

'Roger Nielson, FBI,' he said. 'Follow me, please.'

Above them in the flight tower a man scanned the skies with binoculars. He swung them toward the chopper that had just landed and followed Nielson and Vail as they walked across the hard stand to a white 737 parked in a hangar. The jet had a U.S. flag painted on the tail and UNITED STATES JUSTICE DEPARTMENT on the side.

'Afraid I'll have to pat you down, sir,' Nielson said apologetically. Vail held his arms out to his sides, and Nielson's hands expertly checked him for weapons.

'Thank you, sir.' He motioned Vail up the stairs, where a younger man, short and dark-haired, in a dark blue suit, was waiting at the top of the staircase.

'Mr. Vail, I'm Paul Silverman,' he said. 'I'm the steward. Please come in. The A.G. will be out in a second, she had to take a phone call.'

Vail stepped aboard the plane. To the left of the door was what appeared to be a small combination dining and conference room that stretched the entire width of the plane. Ten easy chairs bolted to the floor surrounded an ebony table. A thirty-five-inch TV set was built into the wall of the room, and a door led to the front of the plane. To the right was what Vail assumed to be a sitting room.

A large sofa hugged the hull of the plane, with a coffee table separating it from three easy chairs. The twenty-seven-inch TV built into the interior of that wall was tuned to WWN, but the sound was off. A fresh copy of *USA Today* lay on the coffee table. The plane's interior color scheme – tan carpeting and royal-blue furniture throughout – was pleasant and unobtrusive.

'Coffee, sir?' the steward asked.

'That would hit the spot,' Vail said.

'Three sugars and one cream, right?'

Vail looked at the steward with surprise and nodded.

'The A.G. took the liberty of ordering breakfast. Cantaloupe, eggs Benedict with hash browns, and rye toast. Will that be satisfactory, sir?'

Vail kept nodding. They knew his dog's name, how he liked his coffee, and his favorite breakfast. What the hell else did they know? he wondered.

'Make yourself comfortable, sir.'

'Thank you, Mr. Silverman.'

'Please call me Paul, sir.'

Vail sat in one of the easy chairs, and the steward brought his coffee in a Spode china cup. Vail glanced at the TV and recognized Valerie Azimour, the reporter who had attempted to interview him during the Atlas-Western trial. She was bundled up in a fleece-lined parka, its fur-lined hood framing her face, her breath steamy from the cold. She was standing in the dark, looking serious as she spoke into the mike. Since the sound was off he couldn't tell where she was or what calamity she was covering now, so he turned his attention to the newspaper and scanned the headlines. A moment later the Attorney General entered the room.

Margaret Castaigne was a little shorter than Vail had imagined, a trim, dark-complected woman with jet-black hair turning gray and dark brown eyes. She was handsome, not beautiful, a well-groomed lady in her mid-fifties. She smiled with her lips, but he could see eyes

140

coolly appraising him.

'Good morning, Mr. Vail,' she said.

'Good morning, General,' he answered.

She had a handshake like a stevedore.

'Welcome to the AMOC,' she said.

'AMOC?'

'Air Mobile Operations Center. Don't ask me where these acronyms come from, probably some Phi Beta Kappa who does nothing all day long but dream them up. Thanks for getting up at the crack of dawn to join me. I hope it's worth the trip.'

'We'll see how the eggs Benedict go before I make a commitment.'

She laughed and nodded. 'Fair enough. Like to see how the Department of Justice lives?'

'That depends,' he said with a smile. 'What's the tour cost?'

'Not a thing.' She smiled and pointed toward the front of the plane. 'Up front is the flight deck, the galley, and the conference room, which doubles as a dining room. This is the sitting room, usually reserved for polite conversation. And this . . .' She led him into the next compartment. '. . . is my office.'

It was a simple compartment: a desk with a stuffed chair behind it and two chairs facing the desk. The desk was empty except for a single picture of two young men, its frame anchored to the desktop, and two phones, one black, the other red. There was a thirty-five-inch TV monitor mounted in the wall.

'Your sons?' Vail asked, nodding toward the photograph.

'Yes. The younger one on the left is Emilio. He's about to graduate from Harvard Law with honors. Arnie, on the right, is the family maverick. He's an archeologist. Right now he's in Egypt, hot on the trail of Alexander the Great's tomb or something.'

Vail smiled and looked around the small office.

'You people watch a lot of television?'

'They're all interconnected, Mr. Vail. We can have a visual conference with just about anyone in the world or watch closed-circuit feeds of live events. The TVs are also tied into the computers in the ComOp. All coded and secure except for the normal cable and network channels.' She opened the door to the next compartment. 'This is the ComOp, the heart and soul of AMOC.'

The long, cell-like, dark compartment was a maze of electronic equipment: a computer-video system with six monitors, a satellite scan, secure phone and fax, a red alert phone direct to the White House, a live surveillance monitor, digital video cameras, DSS tape recorders, direct video to AWACS, and a cable/network satellite TV with still another thirty-five-inch monitor. Castaigne described the equipment, although she seemed a bit bemused by it all.

'My electronics genius went into the terminal to get a local pa-per,' she said. 'Actually, I think he likes to check out the girls in the airport.'

'Are there girls in the airport at this hour?' Vail said sardonically.

'Well, if there are, Jimmy will find them,' she answered. 'Back there is another small conference room, with a computer and TV, and the commander's private bedroom. Commander is a highfalutin title for whoever's in charge of the aircraft. We have a crew of eight plus a flight crew of four, and space for twenty others.'

'And my tax dollars pay for this?'

'You'd be surprised how many hours I spend in this jet,' she said, a bit defensively. 'In fact we have four AMOCS. They're operational most of the time.'

'I wasn't complaining,' Vail said.

'Why, I didn't think you were, Mr. Vail,' she murmured as they walked back toward the front of the jet.

Silverman appeared and announced that breakfast was ready. They went into the dining room, which was set out with sterling silverware and linen napkins. All the comforts of home.

'So, any questions?' Castaigne asked when they had settled down to eat.

'Yeah,' Vail said. 'How come you know my dog's name?'

She laughed. 'I confess I did my own private security check on you – read all Jack Connerman's articles,' she answered. 'Connerman seems to know more about you than anyone alive. Are you two friends?'

'We occasionally have a drink together.'

'I also have a transcript of the Grand County trial. I consider it the textbook on RICO. Brilliant job.'

'Thanks. I figured you dragged me out of bed to lean on me about that.'

'Why? Because you snatched the case out from under Pete Riker?'

'I didn't snatch it away from him, he lost his grip on it.'

'It was a federal case, Mr. Vail.'

'And I made it a state case, General.'

'Why don't you call me Marge? Everybody else does.'

'All right, you can call me Martin or Marty or . . .' Vail paused and smiled. '. . . whatever Riker calls me.'

She smiled back. 'Not in polite conversation.'

'Ahhh, that's what this is then, polite conversation?'

'I would hope so.'

'Good. Then I can politely tell you that I didn't snatch anything out from under Pete Riker. He waited too long. He didn't have the link.'

'The link?'

'You know how complicated RICO is. Ultimately you have to find a link, something or someone that can tie all those cases together. I got lucky, I had the link, he never did. That's why he was sitting on the case.'

'You lucked out?'

'I said I got lucky, General, I don't luck out. Luck doesn't win cases, but a little luck always helps.' He paused a moment and said, 'Did you get the breakfast menu from Connerman, too?'

'He put me on to your favorite diner. He also says you're an edge runner, that you like taking chances.'

'Well, Connerman doesn't know everything. Right now I know three things I'm sure he doesn't know.'

'Oh? What are they?'

'He doesn't know you're such a big fan of his, he doesn't know I'm here, and he doesn't know why.'

She laughed. 'Point for you.'

'Are we ever going to get around to why?'

'Maybe I just wanted to break bread with the guy who took down Tom Lacey and Harold Grossman.'

Vail chuckled. 'Sure. And I came to check out Paul's world-famous hollandaise sauce.'

She tapped her lips with her napkin and said, almost casually, 'The President has a favor to ask.'

Vail's back stiffened. He sat up in his chair and put down his fork. He stared across the table at her for several seconds.

'You play your trump card early in the game, don't you?' he said finally.

'Sometimes.'

'That's a pretty good one.'

'I know.'

'Is this going to be twenty questions?'

'No,' she said with a laugh. 'I thought we'd finish breakfast before we got serious.'

'We're going to get serious, then?' He put down his fork. 'The breakfast was delicious and the hollandaise was unimpeachable. Now what's on your mind?'

She liked Vail. The arrogance and irreverence she had heard about were there, but he also was relaxed and had a playfully skewed sense of humor, and, as Connerman had told her, he was disarmingly blunt.

'What do you know about the militia movement in this country?' she asked.

He thought for a moment, then shrugged. 'What I read in the papers, which isn't much. I followed Waco and Oklahoma City. Bunch of neo-Nazi skinheads and religious fanatics. We always have that kind of nut fringe in our society.'

'Do you consider them dangerous?'

'I don't consider them at all.'

'I want to show you something,' she said. She got up, and Vail followed her back to the ComOp. A moment later her electronics whiz came in.

'Martin, this is Jim Hines. Mr. Vail, Jimmy.'

'Hi, Mr. Vail,' he said, and took his seat in front of the sprawling console. Hines was husky, his body obviously molded in the gym. He had flaming red hair, the pale skin and freckles that go with it, and a mischievous smile. He might have passed for a teenager. Vail estimated his age in the mid-to-late twenties.

'We may be getting a live feed from Hardistan,' Hines said. 'The reception is still bad but they're working on it.'

'Good. Bring up the H-file while we wait,' Castaigne said.

'Right.'

He closed out the file he was working on and switched back to the main screen of the computer.

'What level?' he asked.

'Alpha,' she said. 'Let's show Mr. Vail how it works.'

Hines popped the cursor over an icon and a blank screen appeared, followed almost instantly by the words:

'Security check: Voice. Prints. Visual.'

Castaigne placed her hand on a small pad with her fingers splayed out, looked straight ahead and said, 'Margaret Castaigne, Attorney General.'

All three of the boxes turned green almost instantly.

'ACCESS APPROVED. ID NAME?'

Hines typed in Castaigne's code name, which appeared as six asterisks on the screen. The screen cleared briefly and the words, 'PRIORX ALPHA. FILE?' He typed in 'HATE

145

GROUPS\INDEX,' and another menu appeared.

'We have a lot of security checks on the network system,' the electronics whiz said. He pointed to the bank of monitors and recorders in front of him. 'There's a palm-size digital video camera right there. It sends the visual signal to the security force at the same time as the voice and hand prints go over the line. If they don't cross-check electronically, access to the computer is denied.'

'Grab a seat, Martin,' Castaigne said. 'I'm going to give you a fast briefing on hate groups in the United States.' The screen filled with an impossibly complex chart that traced the emergence of hate groups from England and Tennessee through a labyrinth of interconnected lines up to the present day. Proper names were in circles, organizations in rectangles. It looked like a molecular chart with each name exploding into other names and groups. As Castaigne spoke, Hines moved the cursor around the chart, tracing the evolution of hate groups in the U.S.

As she described the start of the Klan in Pulaski, Tennessee, in 1866, which had burgeoned to half a million members within four years, photographs and movie clips appeared on the screen. They were dark and disturbing images from the past: hooded figures saluting a blazing cross; a man hanging from a tree limb while a crowd of men, some of them mere teenagers, gathered beneath it, smiling at the camera; a burned corpse, its arms death-frozen in a pleading posture; a church engulfed in fire while its black parishioners stared mutely and fearfully at the camera.

'Then in the 1920s, a more ominous threat came from England,' Castaigne went on. 'The Christian Unity Church, a white supremacy bunch that claimed that white Anglo-Saxons were the true Israelites and God's chosen people, while Jews, blacks, and other nonwhites were 'on a spiritual level with animals and have no soul.' That's a direct quote. They quickly found a soulmate in the Klan, and the 'Invisible Empire' awoke, more dan-

gerous than ever, and not just confined to the South. . . .'
Now the photographs and videos were even more chilling. These were not images from history, they were current events. There was a video of the death of Gordon Kahl, the maniacal member of the Posse Comitatus who wore a small silver hangman's noose pin on his collar. Kahl had killed two U.S. marshals and wounded two others, starting a manhunt that ended with Kahl, mortally wounded, screaming a mixture of biblical phrases and obscenities and firing his mini-14 from the burning farmhouse in the Ozarks that became his funeral pyre. 'The Klan grew to four million members, including forty *thousand* ministers. The Christian Unity spawned the Aryan Brotherhood, the American Patriots, the Liberty Lobby, the Birch Society, the Minutemen, the National Christian Democracy Union, and more recently, the Aryan Nations, the Covenant of the Sword and the Arm of the Lord, the Sword of Christ ministry, the Posse Comitatus, and the Order.'

Another photo flashed on the screen: two U.S. marshals lying dead on a Utah roadside. And then another of a black couple under sheets on a North Carolina street, gunned down by an Army skinhead as part of an 'initiation.'

'Kahl was martyred by the entire movement, the same as David Koresh and Randy Weaver would later be martyred,' Castaigne said. 'The most violent of all the hate groups was the Order, a spin-off of the Aryans. I'll get back to them in a minute. The point is, they were cloaking race hatred in Christianity, and then they added independence from the government. The Klan has a pamphlet called "The Bible Answers Racial Questions," which begins by quoting the First Amendment . . .'

'*Congress shall make no law respecting an establishment of religion, or prohibiting the free exercise thereof,*' Vail said.

'You know your Constitution,' Castaigne said, impressed.

147

'A lot better than I know the Bible,' Vail answered.

'They hide behind churches and the Constitution and condemn the government as the enemy of the people. They want government returned to the local level. Posse Comitatus, for instance, is Latin for "power of the county." The Minutemen's *Principles of Guerrilla Warfare* preaches all-out revolution. Their answer is "raid, snipe, ambush, and sabotage. . . ." Another direct quote.

'The primer for all these groups is a book called *The Turner Diaries*, which predicts a guerrilla war against the U.S. government and all minorities. It's a textbook on guerrilla tactics, how to modify weapons, how to make bombs. The book describes how to make a high potential bomb with fuel oil and ammonium nitrate fertilizer, and uses it in the story to blow up a federal building. *The Turner Diaries* was Timothy McVeigh's favorite book.'

A shot of the gutted Murrah Building in Oklahoma City flashed on the monitor, wires and conduits dangling from its gaping holes like entrails.

'Point is, Martin, violence has been the trademark of the militia movement since long before Oklahoma City. In the early eighties the Order went on a felony spree. They didn't miss a trick: counterfeiting, bank robberies, kidnapping, armored car heists, murder. They bombed synagogues, killed members they suspected had turned, assassinated talk show host Alan Berg . . .'

Two more photographs flashed on the screen, a nightmare montage of violence: George Matthews, the founder of the brutal Order, dying in a barrage of FBI bullets on an island in the Puget Sound, and the bullet-torn corpse of talk show host Alan Berg, lying beside his car.

'So in 1984 the FBI organized a task force and went after them. The Order's response was to declare war on the United States. The Justice Department made a racketeering case against twenty-four members of the Order.

148

Sixty-some counts of racketeering for counterfeiting, murder, and robbery. George Matthews wasn't having any. He chose to die instead. Another martyr. The other twenty-three were convicted and the Order finally faded away. We suspect most of the members who weren't indicted migrated to other groups.'

'How big was the Order?' Vail asked.

'We're not sure, probably less than a hundred members.'

'You think the public takes these crazies seriously?' Vail said.

'Martin, the Anti-Defamation League estimates there may be as many as 75,000 active members of hate groups in this country. We say the figure could be as high as 750,000 if you include sympathizers who aren't actively involved in the militia government. The figures went up after Waco and the Randy Weaver affair. We expected that. What shocked us is that the figures also rose sharply after Oklahoma City.'

Where's she going with this? Vail wondered. *And what the hell am I doing here? When is she going to get to the point?*

'Jimmy, bring up the Sanctuary,' she said. And to Vail, 'Ever hear of a group called the Church of the Sanctuary of the Lord and the Wrath of God, Martin?'

He thought for a moment. 'Isn't some hotshot general from Desert Storm involved with them?'

'Joshua Engstrom. But he was a colonel in Desert Storm, not a general. He didn't make general until after he retired and became adjutant general of the Montana National Guard.'

A shot of Engstrom appeared on the screen, a bald, husky, tall figure, a bit thick around the middle, wearing khaki camouflage fatigues with a pistol at his waist, an automatic rifle cradled in one arm and a Bible in the other, standing beside a tank in the desert surrounded by a dozen soldiers. Most of the men were smiling, but

149

Engstrom's face was a cold, expressionless mask.

'That's Engstrom in Desert Storm, 1990.'

'I remember that picture,' Vail said, staring at Engstrom's eyes. 'He had a nickname. . . .'

'The Preacher.'

'Right.'

'Bring the other one up, Jimmy.'

A second photograph was in sharp contrast to the first, a snapshot, fuzzy, faded, water-stained.

'This is Vietnam, 1973,' Castaigne said.

Engstrom was standing with six soldiers in the jungle. They stared with disdain, almost angrily, at the camera. Engstrom stood in the middle, a hard-bodied man with a buzz cut and a beard streaked with gray. All the men were shirtless and had bandannas tied around their foreheads. They all wore camouflage pants and boots, some with knives protruding from them. They had bandoliers crisscrossed on their bare chests and sidearms holstered low on the hip, and were holding a variety of different weapons: Uzis, AR-14s, M-1As, all mounted with telescopic sights. It was a harrowing photograph.

Hines zoomed in on Engstrom's face. His gaze seemed fixed, his eyes fiery, almost maniacal, conjuring visions of other zealots: John Brown on the gallows; Jim Jones in Guyana; Vernon Howell, who would later change his name to David Koresh, outside Waco on the eve of his personal Armageddon.

'The guy to Engstrom's right is Robert Shrack,' Castaigne said. 'His nickname was Black Bobby. Next to him is Dave Metzinger. Shrack is Engstrom's deputy now, and Metzinger is the pastor of one of the four churches that make up the Sanctuary. The one on the right with the scar down the side of his face is Gary Jordan. The guy with the beard and sunglasses kneeling on the left is holding a 50-caliber with a Unertl sight. Sniper rifle, not government issued. He and the guy in the middle are either dead or we can't ID them.'

'Can't you pull up their Army records?'

'There aren't any. Engstrom led a group called the Phantom Project. Black ops. Their mission was so dark all records of it and its members have been destroyed. It isn't even mentioned in Engstrom's service record. All it says is that he served with Military Intelligence in 'Nam from 1967 to 1975.'

'That bad, huh?' Vail said.

'Depends on your point of view, I guess,' Castaigne said. 'Now look at the Desert Storm shot. The boys are smiling, all except Engstrom, whose expression hasn't changed in twenty years; Shrack, who is standing just behind him; and the two guys kneeling in front of him. The one in front of him is Gary Jordan and the one kneeling next to Jordan is Karl Rentz. Both of them are Engstrom's pastors, too.'

'Pastors?' Vail said.

'They are the pastors of the four churches under the Sanctuary umbrella.'

'Metzinger, who you mentioned before, is the third pastor. Who's the fourth?'

'James Joseph Rainey, late of the Texas Knights of the White Camelia.'

'The good general is playing the field.'

'Jimmy, pair those up with a Desert Storm shot of the President.'

'Sure,' the redhead said. A photograph appeared beside the other photos, this one of Lawrence Pennington standing in front of a map with a pointer in hand.

'It's ironic that Lawrence Pennington is the President of the United States and Engstrom is the leader of one of the most dangerous hate groups in the country,' Castaigne said.

'Why is it ironic?' Vail asked.

'Because Engstrom hated Pennington, and Pennington didn't even know Engstrom existed.'

And Castaigne told him the story.

Nine

On the first night of Tet, the Vietnamese lunar New Year holiday, the North Vietnamese celebrated by launching a massive attack on American and South Vietnamese troops. Eighty-five thousand Vietcong swarmed over the country, with another 85,000 in the backup force.

'Charlie Company, this is Fox, do you copy?'

'Copy that, Fox.'

'This is Colonel Walker, get me Colonel Pennington on the double.'

'He's right here, sir.'

The radioman handed the set to Pennington, who was crouched along the edge of a rice paddy. Occasionally a mortar round would erupt, showering his troops with mud and water. He was tired and his force was splintered. He had not changed his wet socks or clothes for two days. It was getting dark.

'Pennington here.'

'Larry, it's Lou Whitaker. What's your position?'

'We're about fifteen miles north of Khe Sanh. My troops are scattered all over hell and gone. What the hell's going on?'

'We got Cong up our ass and out our ears. We're under attack all over the damn country. A suicide squadron blew a hole in the embassy wall last night and invaded the inner perimeter. It took the MPs five hours to kill 'em all.'

'Christ, where are they all coming from?'

'Who the hell knows? The word is out they took Hue over on the coast, and we're under seige here in Saigon.

And buddy, you've got about ten thousand of 'em coming down the pike toward Khe Sanh.'

'What d'ya mean, *coming* down, they're all over the place.'

'Larry, you've got to set up a line and hit these bastards before they get to the city. We got five thousand Marines in there trying to hold the town, and they're already outnumbered five to one.'

'Who isn't! What the hell do you want us to do, Lou, go looking for them?'

'That would help.'

'Jesus, my people are dog tired. We're burned out.'

'Who isn't? Do your best, buddy.'

Pennington and his radioman ran back along the paddy wall, dodging sniper fire and mortars. He had lost his captain and two lieutenants the night before. For an hour he worked with Cobb, his first sergeant, to regroup his force.

'When we find the VC's reinforcement column, we're going to attack,' he told Cobb.

'What the fuck with, sir? We're running outta ammo, outta grenades. We already ran outta light.'

'I don't give a goddamn, Cobbie. Shoot 'em, stab 'em, kick 'em, bite 'em. Pass the word I want to hear rebel yells, I want to hear football cheers. If we can't do anything else, we'll scare the bastards to death.'

Two hours later Pennington and Cobb led the company into a wooded bay, and suddenly a face appeared through the darkness just a few feet from Pennington. They were nose-to-nose with the enemy. Pennington raised his pistol and shot his adversary in the eye. The woods erupted with gunfire. A chaotic hand-to-hand battle broke out. Pennington charged ahead, firing with his .45. He felt a bite at his shoulder, another in his side, and still kept going, slashing blindly with his knife, using the .45 as a club. Flashes of gunfire blinked in the darkness like fireflies. Men were screaming.

Behind him someone fired a flare, and the battlefield suddenly burst into garish red light. Pennington got a momentary glimpse of his surroundings. He and Cobb were twenty yards ahead of his main force, caught in a no-man's-land between the Americans and the Vietcong, his men pinned down.

'Get off your asses, goddamn it!' Pennington roared. 'Get out here. And let's hear some goddamn yelling!'

He and Cobb turned and charged toward the enemy. His men ran forward into the darkness. Beside him, Cobb grunted. 'Jesus,' he yelled, and fell to his knees. Pennington jumped to his side as several riflemen raced past them, firing blindly into the dark and yelling like banshees.

The sergeant's fist was jammed in a bloody hole in his side.

'Let's get you out of here,' Pennington yelled above the din.

'Where are we going?' Cobb moaned.

'How about Boston, Cobbie? Want to go to Boston?'

'Don't make me laugh, it hurts too bad.'

Pennington swung Cobb to a sitting position, swept him over his shoulder and started back to the edge of the forest. A bullet ripped into his thigh, and as he fell, a half-dozen men swarmed around them.

'You okay, Colonel?' a friendly voice said.

'Thank God it's you guys,' Pennington said. 'I didn't know where the hell I was. We got a medic handy? I think I'm bleeding to death.'

'Right here, sir. I'll just tie that right up for you.'

'How's Cobb?' Pennington asked.

'Touch and go, Colonel.'

'Take care of him, you hear? Don't worry about me, just take care of him.'

'Yes sir.'

Behind him he could hear the yelling and gunfire fading.

'Anybody know what the hell's going on?'

'I think the gooks split for Hanoi,' the medic said with a smile. 'We got 'em on the run.'

'Son of a bitch.'

'My feelings exactly, Colonel.'

At dawn the medevacs swept in and took the wounded back to Saigon. Cobb was on the first chopper out. Pennington left last. As the chopper lifted off, Pennington looked down at the battlefield. The land below was littered with dead. Vultures were already gathering.

A hundred miles away on the same night, Captain Joshua Engstrom and three men lurked on the edge of a river in the Delta. Their faces were painted white and they were stripped down to just their shorts. Engstrom tightened a belt around his waist and checked the waterproof pouch attached to it. The pouch contained a .45 caliber automatic with five clips and a map. He had a knife sheath taped to his right thigh and another hanging from his belt. His men were doing the same, checking their equipment, peering upriver.

On the opposite side of the river, Black Bobby Shrack was crouched in a blind with a sniper rifle. He saw Engstrom's shielded flashlight blink twice and returned the signal. They were ready. He turned his binoculars upriver, saw a speck of light, and fixed on it.

They had rehearsed the operation several times. Preacher was a stickler for rehearsing. Rehearsing and timing, rehearsing and timing. Nobody spoke. They moved quickly, almost like machines, using hand signals to converse. Hidden a dozen feet away, on Engstrom's side of the river, was a second sniper, a slender man with a black beard and long hair. He snapped his fingers and pointed upriver.

Faintly they heard laughter and the jabber of voices. The men spread out and waited. The boat appeared through the dark and headed toward them. It was a wide, flat-bottom skiff with twin engines on the back.

Engstrom drew his knife. Half aloud he said, '*And the Lord sayeth to Joshua, go thee and drive out the Semites and Canaanites and slay them and send them back whence they came. And Joshua went forth to do His bidding.*'

He put the knife between his teeth and slid quietly into the water.

There were five men on the wide skiff, two sitting on barrels near the bow smoking cigarettes, peering at two fingers of light from spotlights attached to the bow. The other three were bunched together near the center of the boat under a lantern, leafing through a dog-eared copy of *Playboy*. All five wore the uniforms of North Vietnamese soldiers. The deck was covered with oilskin packages, stacked three deep.

The crewmen did not hear Engstrom and his team catch the side of the boat as it muttered by or hear them crawl silently over the stern.

The team crept up to them like cats. Each of the team members positioned himself behind one of the three readers.

The two shots were barely audible. One of the men in the front of the boat flipped over backward, sending the barrel spinning against the rail. The other one stood up, turned slowly, and fell over the side.

The team attacked swiftly, each grabbing a target by the hair, snapping his head back, and slitting his throat. They were deep cuts, almost to the spine. Engstrom held tight to his victim as the man jerked violently in the throes of death. Air hissed from his windpipe and sprayed a fine mist of blood into the air. When the man stopped jerking, Engstrom let him fall to the deck.

'Clear,' he said. He cut the engines, and another member of the team tossed a bowline to the bearded sniper, who tied the skiff to a tree. Bloody knives flashed in the lantern light as the team slit open each package and dumped the contents over the side. Engstrom watched the brown crystals of heroin swirl and disappear. The bearded sniper hunched on the shore, watching the river. When the rest of the team had destroyed the entire load, he unlashed the boat. Then Engstrom cranked up the engines and turned it around and headed it back up river.

Metzinger tied down the wheel.

Engstrom leaned over his victim, who was lying face-down on the deck, and pulled back his head. His muscles bulged as he neatly sliced the heavy blade through the man's neck bone. He tied the bloody head by its hair to the radio antenna.

'Therefore David ran,' he bellowed, looking up the river, *'stood upon the Philistine, and took his sword, and drew it out of the sheath thereof and cut off his head therewith. And when the Philistines saw their champion was dead, they fled.* First Samuel, Chapter Seventeen.'

He turned, jumped overboard, and swam to shore. He stuck his knife in a tree stump and stood waist deep in the river, washing the blood from his arms and hands for a very long time.

The story of Pennington in Vietnam became legendary. It was the kind of story the Army loves and the media turns into legend; the kind of story that wins soldiers the Medal of Honor.

Engstrom was the army's secret weapon, commanding the Phantom Project with its Specter squads operating deep in Vietcong territory, all trained experts at guerrilla warfare, torture, assassination, explosives, their methods so excessive all records of the project were sealed after the war – or destroyed.

Pennington came home from Vietnam to parades, a general's star, and a Medal of Honor. Engstrom came back a major who couldn't even talk about his exploits in the war.

*

Lawrence Culver Pennington and Joshua Luke Engstrom were inducted into the Army on the same day, August 23, 1952. Seventeen years old and fired with patriotism, both had enlisted rather than waiting to be drafted, anxious to see action in Korea. Engstrom, the son of a Wyoming fundamentalist preacher, was an unsophisticated mountain boy who had barely slipped by in high school. Pennington was an Arlington, Virginia, high school ROTC honor graduate whose father was a career diplomat.

One night during basic training, Pennington noticed the lean young westerner sitting alone on the steps of the PX. He sat down next to him, shook a Chesterfield loose, and offered it to him.

'No thanks, I don't smoke,' Engstrom said.

'Homesick already?' Pennington asked as he lit the cigarette.

'Nope. Just never was anyplace this hot before.'

'Where you from?'

'Dexter, Wyoming.'

Pennington whistled. 'You are a long way from home. I'm Larry Pennington, Arlington, Virginia,' he said, sticking out his hand.

'Josh Engstrom.'

'You a cowboy?' Pennington asked cheerfully.

'Nah,' Engstrom said. 'Can't even ride a horse. But I delivered papers on a bicycle.'

'I sold *Saturday Evening Post* subscriptions door-to-door one summer trying to earn enough points to earn a bike. What a cheat that was. What do you want to get into?'

'Tank Corps,' Engstrom said.

'Tank jockey, huh. That's tough duty.'

'I used to dream about driving a tank,' Engstrom said, staring up at the stars. 'Like Patton. After this war's over I want to stay in the Army.'

'Career soldier, huh? Me, too.'

'I want to be an officer.' Engstrom looked at

Pennington and smiled shyly. 'I'd like to be a general someday.'

'Nothing wrong with dreaming,' Pennington said. 'I want to be Chief of Staff someday.'

They both laughed. They never saw each other again after that night.

Engstrom made it to the Tank Corps. Pennington went to Officer's Training School. After the Korean War, Engstrom was reassigned for retraining, and for the next few years he was just another shavetail lost in the reorganization of the postwar Army. Pennington was appointed to West Point, graduated with honors, and started up the military ladder. He was the kind of officer the Army dreams about: smart, charming, polished, diplomatic, a brilliant strategist, and socially acceptable.

Over the years, Engstrom languished in obscure Army bases, frozen in rank as a lieutenant, while Pennington rose steadily to the rank of lieutenant colonel. Sometime in the early sixties, just before they both went to Vietnam, Engstrom fixated on Pennington, remembering that night in southern Georgia. He grumbled constantly that he was a better field officer than Pennington but was passed over because he was a country boy whose outspoken religious beliefs made him socially unacceptable to the Army hierarchy. There was a modicum of truth to that. But records also show there were complaints that Engstrom was a bigot who purged his units of blacks, Jews, and Catholics, read the Bible aloud during training sessions, and objected to his troops drinking liquor and smoking. In Vietnam, the Army found the perfect place for both of them.

Years later on the eve of their respective retirements, both officers served in Saudi Arabia. Pennington was regaled by the media as one of the master strategists of Desert Storm. Engstrom earned a single photograph in the *New York Times* as the 'Preacher,' a tough colonel who led his men into battle with a gun in one hand and a

Bible in the other.

And a year later, when Pennington retired as Army Chief of Staff, an embittered Engstrom was retired in rank. He never earned his star.

Engstrom blamed Pennington for blocking his promotion to general when he retired. The irony was that Pennington had nothing to do with it. He didn't remember Engstrom.

He didn't even know who Engstrom was.

Ten

'So Pennington trades his war years for a ticket to the White House and Engstrom plans the second American Revolution,' Vail said.

'That's right,' Castaigne replied. 'Engstrom has built a private army in Montana. He got his star as adjutant general of the Montana National Guard, stayed just long enough to build a following and shanghai the best officers into his private army, resigned, and founded the Church of the Sanctuary of the Lord and the Wrath of God. Next he brought in old cronies from 'Nam and Desert Storm, enlisted members of the Klan, the Posse, and the Covenant of the Sword to become officers in the Army of the Sanctuary. When he resigned as adjutant general, the Sanctuary was already established as an umbrella for four churches. The preachers of the four churches are hardened veterans from Vietnam and Desert Storm.

'He envisioned an army disguised as a church that would eventually mobilize the other militias into a countrywide revolutionary force.'

'With himself as its Paul Revere,' Vail said.

'Yep. The architect of what Engstrom calls the New Revolution. He defined its mission, he directs its strategy, and he's its most effective recruiter.'

'And the FBI ignored him all that time?'

'They put a loose package on him, but they have budget problems just like everybody else, Martin. Hard surveillance costs money. And Engstrom wasn't considered a threat. He went on a speaking tour, and his message was against gun control and income taxes, spiced with evangelical fervor. No big deal. The Bureau didn't start worrying until he started weaving in government conspiracies, attacks on the Jews, and open rebellion against the government. By then he had proselytized fanatics into the four churches that were the nucleus of the Sanctuary. Each of the churches had become a unit in his private army. Klansmen from Georgia, South Carolina, Alabama, and Mississippi moved to Montana to become part of the army.

'Then last month Engstrom started a radio show called 'The Wrath of Abraham.' It started as an hour show once a week. Abraham was an extremist, and controversial from the git-go. His message is a mix of hate and border-line sedition, delivered with the kind of fervor that makes Engstrom sound like a Boy Scout. The show caught on overnight. It's now running five times a week, thirty minutes a night, and is syndicated in about thirty markets, mostly in the Far West and the South. The audience is estimated at four to five million.'

'And Abraham's rage is . . .'

'Taxes, gun control, gays, abortion, Jews, blacks, reds, yellows, Hispanics . . . everything but white Christian bigots. He openly preaches violence, advocates killing government employees like Forest Rangers and office workers. In just six months, he's become the national voice of the militia movement. The radio show is sponsored by the Sanctuary. Engstrom introduces it.'

'So now the Bureau and the DOJ are real serious, right?'

She nodded. 'But by the time the FBI started paying attention, Engstrom's army had grown to between five and six thousand active militiamen. They train every weekend in their hometowns and once a month at Fort Yahweh—'

'Fort what?'

Hines punched a few keys and a video popped on the screen, a helicopter shot of what appeared to be a military compound.

'Yahweh. It's a distortion of the Hebrew word for God

in the Bible. This is it, a ninety-thousand-acre compound in the Rockies north of Missoula. The homes and farms of hard-core members were deeded to the Sanctuary to beat taxes. Fort Yahweh is now the size of a small town. It's an armed military compound.'

She pointed out several buildings in the aerial shot. Two barracks, an armory, a communications center, houses for the officers, a farm with livestock, and a quadrangle in the center of it all on which there were a dozen squadrons in green camouflage, marching in perfect formation. Near the quad there was a gunnery range, every slot filled with men and women firing rifles and handguns.

'This was shot last August. For three months in the summer the Sanctuary sponsors maneuvers in survival, guerrilla tactics, weapons modification, hand-to-hand combat, martial arts, and marksmanship at the fort. It's a very tough course that attracts militiamen and -women from all over the country. Whole families spend their summer vacations training with the Preaching General. More and more members of the Sanctuary are deeding their homes and farms to the church. Of course, they can live there forever, and no taxes.'

'Which is perfectly legal.'

'Yes. The Sanctuary has become a major landowner in the state.'

'Offhand, I'd say the Preacher has done okay for himself. None of this is against the law, by the way. They're protected by the First, Fourth, and Sixth amendments.'

'The Bureau is pretty certain–'

'Pretty certain doesn't play, General. Can you prove they've done *anything* illegal?'

'Nope.'

'Anything wrong with training people in military tactics at that – what's it called – Fort Yahoo?'

'Yahweh.'

'Whatever. Is Fort Yahweh an illegal entity?'

She shook her head. 'Nonprofit church.'

'Marge, you ain't got squat on these bozos and you know it.'

'Let's go to my office. I need another cup of coffee.'

Castaigne ordered two coffees from Silverman. Vail sat across the desk from her.

'I don't know what you want to do about Engstrom and his army,' Vail said, 'but from where I'm sitting, the Sanctuary hasn't done anything illegal.'

'The FBI thinks they were involved in two bank robberies as well as the theft of military weapons and ammunition from the National Guard armory in Helena. The same M.O. was used in all three cases. Military planning, perfect timing–'

'Pretty certain ... thinks ... supposes ... you can't *prove* anything.'

'Not yet.'

'What do you want, Marge? What the hell am I doing here?'

She paused for a minute while she took a sip of coffee, then said: 'The President would like you to accept an appointment as an assistant attorney general.'

'To do what?'

'Special prosecutor. We want you to bring a RICO case against the Sanctuary and its four churches.'

Vail was stunned. The offer was totally unexpected, and for several moments he didn't react.

'You want to do a RICO on this bunch? Hell, the FBI can't even get them for illegal parking.'

'Bring the leaders into court for their crimes, convict them, fine them, put them away for a long time. The people will realize what this movement is all about if we take them before a judge and jury.'

'What crimes? They haven't broken any laws.'

'Martin, you're the best RICO prosecutor alive. We're offering to make you an assistant attorney general with the FBI, ATF, DEA, IRS, Justice Department, even the Army, if necessary, at your disposal. Full sanction of the President, working directly with the Attorney General.'

'What's the difference who's running the show?'

'It hasn't been a focused investigation. This will be a task force, Marty. A-one priority. William Hardistan, the number two man in the FBI, will be your point man. You'll have the power to part oceans.'

'It's politics, and I've had politics up to here.'

'You'll be in complete charge, Marty. Only answerable to the President and me. Billy Hardistan will take his orders from you.'

Vail stood up, walked to one of the windows, and stared out at Nielson, the FBI man.

'It could take years,' he said. 'Tracking down data, accessing the information, trying to make some kind of sense out of it all. I don't want to turn fifty and still be trying to make a RICO case because a nut case is running around preaching revolution and the President is taking it personally.'

Hines tapped on the door and stuck his head into her office. 'I think we have a visual report from Hardistan coming in,' he said.

'Thanks, Jimmy.' She turned to Vail. 'Maybe you'll find *this* interesting,' she said, leading Vail back to the ComOp. 'Last night an arms convoy was ambushed in the mountains between Idaho and Montana. Two Humvees were destroyed, an eighteen-wheel semi was hijacked, and ten soldiers were murdered.'

'What!'

'Hardistan is on the scene. Just listen.'

Hines said, 'The weather's so bad we haven't been able to make visual contact, but hopefully it's clearing up a bit.'

The picture on the monitor was distorted and they could hear Hardistan's voice crackling with static, and then suddenly the picture cleared. Hardistan was standing outdoors, bundled in his coat, clutch-ing a mike in his gloved hand. The sun had not yet peeked over the mountains.

'We copy you, Mr. Hardistan,' Hines said. 'I've got the A.G. right here.'

'Good morning, Marge.'

'Morning, Billy. You're coming in just fine.'

'We can't pick you up here so I'm going to give you a walk-through of the crime scene. I'm standing on the rubble on the north end of the pass. They touched off a small avalanche here and sealed off this end of the highway.'

Behind Hardistan several powerful spotlights had been set up on both sides of the road. The video panned away from the G-man and into Lost Trail canyon. Vail stared at the screen as the camera picked up both of the burned-out Humvees.

'What's that on the side of the road?' he asked.

'Body bags,' Castaigne answered. 'All ten soldiers in the convoy were either killed outright or executed after the attack and laid out in body bags there beside the road.'

'Jesus!' Vail said.

The cameraman walked toward the row of green bags and stopped at one. Hardistan entered the picture and zipped the bag open. A young face the color of marble stared out of the bag. There was a bullet hole in his forehead. Snowflakes drifted across the picture, twinkling in the beams of the spotlights.

'This is the man who was shot after he was bagged,' Hardistan said.

Castaigne turned her face away from the screen.

'We found something else interesting,' Hardistan said. He walked to the rear of one of the wrecked Humvees and knelt down. The camera moved in for a closeup. Burned into the rear bumper were the numbers 2-3-13.

'We have no idea what this means, but it was definitely

scorched into the bumper here at the scene. I've put our code specialists and cryptology people on it. Any ideas will be appreciated.'

Vail watched as the camera pulled back to encompass a broad shot of the scene.

'That's all we've got so far, A.G.,' Hardistan said. 'The snow and wind have either covered up or obliterated any tracks. The crime scene is severely compromised. All we have is some rounds and shell casings, the bullet that killed that young man over there, and these numbers.'

'Thanks, Billy. I'm glad you're there.'

'We'll be back in touch a little later.'

The screen went black.

Castaigne turned to Vail. 'They killed all those young boys. All of them have been shot once behind the ear after they were wounded or killed in the attack. All but the young man with the shot in his forehead. He was obviously still alive when they put him in the body bag.'

Vail said nothing. Hines had taped the satellite pickup. He rewound the tape to the close-up of the numbers and jotted them down on a slip of paper: 2-3-13.

'Could be somebody's birthday,' he said, half to himself.

'We don't know for sure that the Sanctuary is behind this,' Castaigne said. 'But the President considers this an act of war.'

They went back to Castaigne's office.

'There's still no connection to the Sanctuary,' Vail said.

'It's the only militia group within two hundred miles of the scene.'

'Doesn't mean a thing, Marge, and you know it. You're going to need access to bank and corporate records, wire taps, computer access, hard surveillance, if you want to even consider a RICO case. I couldn't get a federal judge to give me permission to scratch my head with what you've shown me so far.'

'If I can convince you there's more to this than paranoia, will you consider the President's request?'

Vail did not answer.

'Will you talk to two people?'

'What two people?'

'Gary Jordan is one of them.'

'Gary Jordan . . .'

'The man with the scar in the Vietnam photograph.'

'He'll talk?'

'He's somewhat of a braggart. He's in a federal pen. You can fly out there in this plane. He's been interviewed three times, twice by the Bureau, once by a member of my staff. I think you might turn up something we haven't. I hear you're very good at that sort of thing.'

Vail glared at her for a few moments. 'Who's the other one?' he asked.

'I can't tell you his name. But I can promise you this, you'll be home in time for a late supper tonight.' She pressed a button under her desk and a moment later there was a knock on her office door.

'Come,' she said. The man who entered was tall and husky. His leathery face was deeply tanned and topped by a shock of white hair. He was wearing a western-cut brown suede jacket with patches on the elbows, charcoal jeans, and cowboy boots.

'Marty, this is Sam Firestone. I stole him from the marshal service. He'll escort you for the day. I've got to fly down to St. Louis to give a luncheon speech. Take one day out of your life before you turn down the President of the United States.'

'You don't pull any punches,' Vail said.

'I don't have time to,' she replied with a smile. 'You have an appointment at nine A.M. Wednesday with President Pennington. He'd like your answer by then.'

As AMOC One took off, the man in the tower watched through his binoculars. He put them back in the case and stretched.

'I'm gonna take a break,' he said to his supervisor. 'Back in fifteen.'

'Okay,' the supervisor said. 'Bring me a hot dog with mustard and onions, and a lemonade, will you?' He handed the man a five-dollar bill.

'No problem.'

The man went to his locker and took out a small computer, a cell phone, and a modem, and went to the men's room. He sat in a stall, connected the modem to the computer and the cell phone to the modem, and punched out a number. It answered:

'HOREB CQ. U?'

'SIMON?'

'OF?'

'CYRENE. 2-3-13.'

'UR HOME.'

'FLT PLN AMOC & DEST MESA FLATS. ET 0930MT. NO FLT PLN BYND. AG NOTABD. SF, UNIDM, ONLY PASS.'

'CPY THAT.'

'CAN U GET FLT PLN FRM MF?'

'NO PRBLM.'

'SELAH.'

He clicked off the cell phone.

Eleven

'Now that we're safely in the air, can you tell me where we're going?' Vail asked.

'Coyote Flats, New Mexico,' Firestone answered in a deep, sharp voice that almost crackled.

'I don't think I ever heard of a federal prison in Coyote Flats, New Mexico.'

'Prob'ly not.'

'What can you tell me about Gary Jordan?'

'Not much. All I did was arrest him.'

'Where are we going from Coyote Flats?'

'Tell you when we get there.'

'You don't have much to say, do you, Mr. Firestone?'

'Mr. Vail, I worked the witness protection program for five years. I could get somebody killed just talkin' in my sleep.'

Firestone closed his eyes, folded his hands in his lap, slid down in his seat, and went to sleep.

'Paul?' Vail said.

The steward appeared at his side.

'I'll bet you don't have a six-ounce Coke in a bottle.'

'Of course, sir.'

He disappeared and was back in a minute or two with the soft drink wrapped in a linen napkin.

'Anything else, sir?'

'I'd be afraid to ask,' Vail replied, and went back to the ComOp.

Hines was scanning four different monitors.

'Got a minute?' Vail asked.

'You're the commander of this flight,' Hines said. 'Just ask.'

'How about pulling up the file on Gary Jordan for me?'

'Can do,' Hines answered. He flicked the keys and front and profile photographs of Jordan flashed on the monitor. His graying hair was clipped within an inch of his skull. Hard muscles stood out in his neck. His eyes looked almost sleepy as they stared at the camera. A thin scar stretched from his right eyebrow, through the corner of his eye, and almost to his jawline. Below the photographs the biographical data stripped rapidly across the screen. Hines read the data as it appeared.

'Gary NMI Jordan, white, male, age forty-nine. Born in Ada, Kansas. High school graduate. Entered the Army in 1965. Completed training as a paratrooper and applied for Special Services. In 1967 he transferred to Army Intelligence. Stationed in Vietnam, 1967 to 1975. Served in Desert Storm, 1990 to 1991. Honorable discharge 1992. Owned a small farm outside Butte, Montana. Married with two children. Joined the Sanctuary 1992.'

Hines turned from the monitor and looked at Vail. 'Jordan's a tax protestor. He beat up a tax collector who came to deliver a lien on the farm, then took a shot at an IRS agent when they seized the place for back taxes. Turned rabbit and was captured in Boise a month later by Sam Firestone. He's two years into a nickel for tax evasion, attempted murder, and battery. We also know that his tour in 'Nam was with the Phantoms, and we know he was the number three man under Engstrom in the Sanctuary. Black Bobby was number two.'

A series of surveillance photos appeared on one of the monitors: Jordan standing behind Engstrom at some kind of rally; another of Jordan, 'Black Bobby' Shrack, and Engstrom, their heads together, talking at a restaurant table; Jordan holding what appeared to be a press conference in his front yard; a shot of Jordan's farm with several official cars parked around it; another of him being led in handcuffs into a federal building by Sam Firestone.

'We have some newspaper clips that go with the photos. I'll bring them up.'

Vail scanned the clips but they added little to the bare biographical data.

'We also have the Q and A on three interviews with him, and synopses of the interviews, if you'd like to read them, but the A.G. would prefer that you didn't.'

'Why?'

'Maybe she wants to see what you can get out of him without any notes,' Hines said with a smile.

'Very funny.'

'She's tough, Mr. Vail. Usually gets what she wants.'

'Where'd she get you, Jimmy?'

'Secret Service. I was in line for presidential guard duty when she kidnapped me.'

Vail was mildly surprised to hear that Hines was Secret Service.

'Looks like pretty good duty to me.'

'Well, at first I was pissed, but then when she told me I could have any kind of equipment I wanted, I thought better of it. This is a hacker's delight.'

'You've done some hacking, have you?'

'I was a computer nerd in high school,' Hines said. 'It wasn't real serious, I hacked the school system's computers and changed the grades of a friend of mine. Got six months of community service. I figured I'd never get into the Secret Service with that on my record, but they liked my 'talent,' as they put it. The A.G. liked it better.'

He paused while he pulled up one of the Jordan interviews. 'By the way, sir, everybody on the plane including the pilot is either FBI or Department of Justice. We're very good bodyguards in addition to our native talents, and that includes Silverman. He can toss a mean salad, but he can also toss you through the side of this plane.'

'That's reassuring,' Vail said with a smile.

The highway was a two-lane macadam ribbon stretching

toward the horizon across the flat, yellow, arid desert. On both sides of it, stretching to the gray mountains on the horizon, flat-topped mesas rose from the tablelands like giant toadstools.

The prison appeared suddenly, off to their right, at first an indistinct wall wriggling in the heat monkeys that danced on the desert floor. As they drove closer, the walls grew taller and the place took on the appearance of a large gray square with gun turrets at its corners. Around its perimeter was a series of eight or ten jagged wire fences, perhaps ten yards apart and a dozen feet high, protecting the fortress from invasion and escape. Behind the fortress, a curtain of mountains draped from the hazy afternoon sun. This was the federal prison called Coyote Flats, the name of the nearest town, twelve miles to the east.

To the inmates the place was known as the Grave, a reference to the stone quarry ten miles away where the men toiled seven hours a day, six days a week, under scorching heat in summer and arctic cold in winter.

The outside fence, several hundred yards from the walls, was a fifteen-foot steel grid, trapping the prison and the wire fences within its perimeter. The inside and top surfaces of the triangular metal beams were honed to a razor's edge. An electrified steel mesh, three feet high, topped it.

Vail whistled softly. 'So this is what a maximum security prison looks like,' he said.

'This is what *the* maximum security in the country looks like.'

A guard house stood at the entrance to the compound, a ten-foot-square building with concrete walls six feet thick. Temperature controlled at seventy degrees, and furnished with cable television, comfortable chairs, a refrigerator and cupboard, and a microwave for the convenience of the guard who stood lonely vigil, it also had a bank of TV monitors scanning the inside of the prison and a video camera that taped everyone who entered the Grave. The windows were heavily tinted. Gatekeepers were only required to spend six-hour shifts in the desolate outpost.

A small drawer slid out of the wall, and the guard, a shadowy figure behind the dark glass, said in an abrupt voice amplified by a loudspeaker, 'IDs, gentlemen, please.' Firestone and Vail dropped their cards in the drawer.

'Mr. Vail, would you please step out of the car for a moment?' the loudspeaker ordered.

'Christ, now what?' Vail growled.

'Video identification,' Firestone said. 'Camera sends a signal to the main house, they run a comp scan against your photo.'

'And where the hell did they get my photo?' Vail asked as he got out .

'Driver's license from Illinois Motor Vehicles.'

'Christ, Big Brother's everywhere,' he snapped.

'Matter of public record, Mr. Vail.'

Vail saw the camera, mounted on a corner of the guard house. He stared up at it and smiled.

'Keep a straight face please, sir,' the loudspeaker told him.

The entranceway was a tunnel of iron and wire, with steel gates operated by electric eyes every fifty yards. As a car passed through one gate, it closed behind the vehicle and the next gate opened. Any vehicle entering the main prison had to pass three of these traps.

Nobody had ever escaped the prison confines, although two South American drug lords serving life without parole once tried to break out of the quarry. The guards casually watched them as they struggled across the desert floor. When they finally collapsed from heat and thirst, a helicopter swept down and hovered over them, blasting them from above for ten minutes. The sand, whipped to a fury, shredded their clothes from their bodies. They were returned naked and bleeding to the prison. Their sentence: no mail, no visitors, no contact with the outside world for six months, lights on in their cells for ninety days, twenty-four hours a day.

'Place is manned by Marines,' Firestone said. 'Duty's for one year. They get combat pay.'

'You're kidding.'

'No joke.'

'What in God's name are we doing out here?' Vail asked.

'You're gonna get the other side of the coin,' Firestone answered. 'Jordan's a card-carrying member of the Sanctuary, very close to Engstrom. He'll be Silent Sam for a bit, but you keep talking, if he thinks the General's on the griddle, that might loosen up his tongue. Anyway, he'll join the conversation just to stay out of the quarry for an hour or so. Won't give away anything. Whatever he tells you, we already know.'

'So why didn't *you* tell me and save us this god-awful trip?'

'Horse's mouth.' Firestone fell silent for a moment, and then, almost as an afterthought, added: 'For the purposes of this visit, you might say you are with the A.G.'s office. Just say it that way, 'I'm with the A.G.'s office.' No need to elaborate.'

'I think I can handle that,' Vail answered as they proceeded through the tunnel of barbed and electrified wire and steel-girded razor blades. He looked around and said, 'This place must've set the taxpayers back a pretty penny.'

'Actually, it's cost effective. Totally self-sufficient, holds twenty-five hundred hard-core felons – minimum sentence, five years. They grow their own vegetables, some fruit. No parole from here. Anybody gets the Grave is in for the duration.'

'What's the suicide rate?'

'Never asked.'

Once inside the main prison, Firestone and Vail were ushered to a small waiting room. The presence of the Marines was evident everywhere. The halls and rooms were spotlessly clean, metal surfaces glistened, desktops were polished to mirrors. Twenty-five hundred prisoners were hermetically sealed in the air-conditioned cell blocks of the Grave, one to a cell. On weekends they had two hours in the yard. No television, no radios, no pumping iron. Reading material could be ordered from a list each morning and was delivered to the individuals at night. They had two hours to read, write letters, or just stare at the ceiling.

A Marine was waiting when they entered the waiting room, a stern-faced youth in a starched uniform standing at parade rest. He snapped to attention when they entered and nodded curtly.

'Gentlemen,' he said. 'Welcome to the Coyote Flats Internment Center.' He stood in front of Vail, looked at his name tag.

'Mr. Vail, sir? Come with me please.'

Vail turned to Firestone. 'You coming?' he asked.

Firestone shook his head. 'I just deliver them, Mr. Vail, I don't talk to them.'

The Marine guard led Vail down a hallway, unlocked a steel door, and pushed it open.

'Do you smoke, sir?' he asked Vail.

'Yeah,' Vail said. 'I've been quitting for three years.'

The guard handed him a small metal ashtray. 'I'll bring the prisoner down,' he said. 'Don't let him get ahold of this ashtray – they can be shaped into a pretty effective shiv.'

'I'll remember that. What's your name?'

'Corporal Becker, sir.'

'Okay, Corporal Becker, thanks.'

The small room seemed familiar to him, interrogation rooms were all alike: a linoleum-covered table, two hard-backed chairs, a small, barred window near the ceiling, a garish light recessed in the ceiling and shielded by wire, the vague odor of Lysol. He sat down and lit a cigarette and waited for five minutes until the doorknob turned and the heavy door opened again.

The man stood in the doorway, his feet locked in irons separated by a six-inch chain that caused him to shuffle when he walked. He kept his shackled hands at his waist. He was an inch or two under six feet, his body as hard as the quarry in which he worked six days a week, his skin leathery and deeply tanned, his brown hair clipped an inch above the scalp. Two years in the Grave had hardened the lines in his face and around his mouth, but he had alert eyes which scanned every inch of Vail's face.

'Corporal Becker, you can remove the irons,' Vail said.

'Gotta stay on, sir. Prison rules.'

Vail stood and said, 'Well, I'm with the Attorney General's office and I say take them off.'

Becker stared at Vail for several seconds, then unlocked the cuffs and removed them from Jordan's wrists.

'We'll split the difference, sir. The leg irons stay.'

Vail thought for a moment and shrugged. 'Fair enough,' he said, and held out his hand to Jordan. 'I'm Martin Vail,' he said.

Jordan ignored Vail's hand. 'Gary Jordan,' he said in a voice as hard as a ball bearing.

Vail nodded toward the table and chairs. 'Grab a chair,' he said to Jordan, and to Becker, 'I'll knock when I'm through.'

'I'm supposed to–'

'I'll knock when I'm through, Corporal,' Vail repeated without looking at the guard, and sat down opposite Jordan.

'Yes sir . . .' Becker muttered, and left, locking the door behind him.

Jordan laughed. 'There's four remote-controlled steel doors between here and the yard. Then about fifty yards of wide open nothin', then a fifteen-foot wall with electric wire on top. And you saw what's outside the wall. But he keeps the leg chains on.'

Vail threw his cigarette pack on the table. 'Have a smoke,' he said.

Jordan ignored the offer. 'You come a long way for nothin'.' He had the gruff, drawling voice of a hard-dirt farmer.

'How do you know where I came from?'

'Hell, everyplace is a long way from here,' Jordan said. 'I thought I'd talked to everybody in the A.G.'s office by now.'

'I'm new.'

'Well, I hope the trip was pleasant, 'cause it was a waste of your time.'

'How do you know what I want?'

'I been asked everything there is to ask. I can cover it all with one answer.' He leaned across the table toward Vail. 'I . . . don't . . . know.'

'You're a member of the Sanctuary of the Lord and the Wrath of God,' Vail said. It wasn't a question.

'Been so long I don't remember.'

Vail looked across the table at Jordan, felt a sense of sympathy and compassion for him. Still unsure why he was interviewing the tax dodger, he decided to play one of his old tricks from his Chicago D.A. days.

'What do you miss most?' he asked casually.

The question intrigued Jordan. He looked toward the window and seemed lost in thought. 'What do you want, poetry? The smell of rain when it first starts comin' down and the hay in the barn at the end of the season, hearin' my little girl laugh, the horses snortin' early on a winter's mornin'. . . .' He stopped and looked at Vail, and his voice turned to flint again. 'I don't miss nothin'. It'll all be there when I get out.'

'Gary . . . okay if I call you Gary? Good. I came here with an offer.'

'What're you gonna do, propose?'

Vail smiled. 'I suppose you heard about the arms heist.'

'Ya hear about robberies every day in here.'

'You know the one I mean.'

Jordan stared at Vail. 'When did it happen?'

'Last night.'

'Mr. Vail, we'll know about that when it's on the radio.'

'An arms convoy was heisted in Montana. Ten soldiers were killed. There's a move afoot to hang it on the General.'

'Engstrom?'

Vail nodded.

'*Shiiit.* No way.'

'How would you know? It happened last night, and you've been sealed up in here for two years.'

Jordan glared at the cigarette pack but did not take one. 'You *are* new at this.'

'I've been a prosecutor for twelve years. Nothing much is new to me. I might be able to get a couple of years knocked off your sentence. You could be out of here in six, seven months, if I get you moved to a country club like Panama City while you do the rest of your time.'

Jordan leaned across the table, and when Vail leaned toward him, whispered in his hoarse voice: 'I ain't got a thing to tell you.'

'You seem pretty sure Engstrom wasn't involved. Don't you give a shit about him?'

The question jarred Jordan. He leaned back in his chair and started to cross his legs, then remembered they were shackled. He thought for almost a minute, his eyes narrowing occasionally, as if he were having an argument with himself.

'Okay, pay attention,' Jordan finally said. 'I'll say this once. *One time.* I may or may not know some of those who took part in it. Wouldn't be no good to you anyways – be all hearsay and guesswork on my part. But I can tell

179

you this, General was in no ways involved in killing American soldiers. Unless . . .' He stopped for a minute, his eyes narrowing as if he was deep in thought.

'Unless what?'

'Unless they're casualties of war.'

'You think the Sanctuary declared war on the U.S. last night, like the Order did back in the eighties?'

'Now how the hell would I know that?'

'Maybe it was because three of the murdered soldiers were black.'

'I'll tell you something, mister, the General ain't no race hater. And he rides that Bible of his real hard.'

'Does he believe in the Bible in a literal sense? You know, word for word?'

'Pretty much so, although he does sometimes put his own spin on it.'

'How does he spin that garbage about the Canaanites and the Jews that the Klan preaches? They quote the Bible. Does he buy that?'

'The General's a logical man, Mr. Vail. He knows the difference between chickenshit and chicken salad.'

'You think that, Gary? That it's chickenshit?'

'I believe you can make of it what you want. That nut case, Abraham, shit, that son-bitch can make black outta white, turn night into day. He gets onto the radio and starts wilding, he's got his Bible thumpers buck-jumpin' and babblin' from the Ozarks to the Canadian border. Been rattler-bit so many times he's got a snake for a tongue and venom on the brain. I'll tell you what, if he's a preacher, I'm a Belgianfuckinwaffle.'

'Who is Abraham?'

Jordan shook his head. 'Man, you *are* a cherry. The voice of the Patriots, man. Blind as justice and crazier than a dancing bear. He raises Cain outta Hell six times a week on about fifty radio stations, preaching damnation to the government and all who don't ride on the back of his hay wagon.'

180

'I take it you're not a believer.'

'He gives me the crawlers.'

'The General supports the show.'

'The General does what he has to. When it serves his purpose. I told you, he's a logical man.'

'Uh-huh. So he has no problem lying down with dogs.'

'What's that supposed to mean?'

'You know, bank robbers, back-shooters, skinheads who go out on weekends and beat people to death because they're niggers or fags or kikes. That your idea of justice and democracy, Gary?'

'I told you, the General ain't no damn racist. He believes in freedom. Believes in justice. He just wants more of it – for all of us. And he can quote you that from the Good Book ten times over.'

'I can quote it back at him from the Constitution. Unfortunately for him, the Bible isn't the law.'

'It is out here.'

'Look, this situation could get fragile very quickly. Suppose they decide to charge Engstrom and arrest him?'

'Praise the Lord, there'll be hell to pay.'

'C'mon, that's a losing battle and you know it,' Vail said, shaking his head at the thought. 'Hell, nobody's crazy enough to take on the whole United States.'

'That ain't how we see it. We figure the military's gonna take *us* on.'

'There'll never be another Ruby Ridge. Or Waco. That won't happen again.'

Jordan laughed. 'Know what I think? I think maybe you're playing in a hornet's nest and you think all that buzzin' is houseflies.'

'That from the Bible?'

Jordan finally shook a cigarette from Vail's pack, held it up, and stared at it for a few moments. 'Brother Jordan's Words of Wisdom. Got a light?'

Vail lit the cigarette and Jordan dragged deeply on it, holding the smoke in his lungs for several seconds, then

181

blowing it out slowly, watching the thin stream of gray smoke as it danced through the harsh sun streaming through the window.

'Yeeahhh,' he sighed, closing his eyes. He sat with his legs stretched out, his head back, his eyes closed, and smoked awhile before he spoke again.

'Racism is for the Klan, the CSA, the Posse, the Aryans. That's their thing. The Sanctuary is mostly separatists. We want to get out from under the government. The General believes there's a Jewish conspiracy to take over the economy, but he don't hold that against all Jews. Me? I'd rather not have a Hebe with me on the line. Or a chocolate bar. But mostly it's the government we're scared of.'

'How many are in the Sanctuary?'

'Hell, I dunno. There's four separate armies, that ain't no secret. They operate pretty much on their own, except they train together and they look to the General as their spiritual leader. Maybe as many as a thousand or two in each unit plus another five hundred or so in the base unit.'

'Four, five thousand, more or less?'

He shrugged. 'And a lotta sympathizers.'

'And the General's outfit is called the Sanctuary?'

'The Sanctuary includes them all. The General calls his unit Fort Yahweh.'

'So, a couple of thousand men are going to take on the whole United States government?'

'They will defend themselves if necessary.'

'Against the United States?'

'These ain't weekend warrior types,' he said, and looked sideways at Vail. 'These are men and women who train constantly. Constantly. Focused, *real* focused. Zealots is what we are.' He took another drag, let it out slowly, and smiled. 'There's a word I like. Zealots. Survivalists, guerrilla-trained in every kind of weapon you can imagine. Some was in Desert Storm, some like

182

me even go back as far as Vietnam and Nicaragua. Hell, we – they – could disappear up in the Cabinets or over in the Bitterroot Range. Ten years from now you'd still be hunting us down. We'll be sniper-strikin', hittin' armories, robbin' banks, taking down buildings . . . no rules, Mr. Vail. Guerrilla warfare. The new revolution.'

'Terrorism.'

'Call it whatever you want. *I am Alpha and Omega, the beginning and the ending, saith the Lord, which is, and which was, and which is to come, the Almighty.* You're gonna have the Posse Comitatus, the Covenant of the Sword down in the Ozarks, the New Christian Crusade Church, the American Patriots, the Aryan Nations – all joining in once it starts. Does the IRA in Ireland ring any bells? It'll be kill and run. Buildings, bars, airliners, synogogues. *And snakes will fall from the skies and water shalt turn to fire and trees to rocks and the earth shall open up and turn to dust and vanish into the Heavens.* The American people can't handle that kind of shit.'

'You were in Desert Storm?'

'Oh yeah, picked me up a piece of Arab shrapnel. An inferior buncha whinin', goat-eatin' belly crawlers. Yeah, I done my share of bleeding so that pussy, Bush, could back off just when we had 'em by the gonies, bringing everybody home so he could have a parade and win the election. All's he did, shot himself in his own foot. Hell, we didn't win the war, we gave it afuckinway. Bastards'll be gassin' us all, next thing ya know.'

'You were an officer in the Sanctuary, weren't you?' Vail guessed.

'I was at Yahweh, aide to the General. But anybody who's done time in a federal lockup is gonna be treated with a certain amount of suspect back there when they get out.'

'They think you'll roll over on them?'

'Look around you. Everybody here's doin' the hardest

time there is. Anybody in the Movement, ends up in a federal joint, does hard time here.'

'You evaded your taxes for seven years and you assaulted a federal officer, Gary.'

'That's right. And I got five years. I owed 'em twelve thousand dollars and I got five years in here. And a ten-thousand-dollar fine I can't ever hope to pay. Lost m'farm, my stock, house. And I got this.' He wafted his arm around the room. 'A dozen men a year go stark raving crazy in this place. They got a whole wing where they hold the crazies, most of them in straitjackets. You come in here, they shave your head, take away all your personal belongings. You can't even have a picture of your family. Nobody to talk to. Alone all the time. Sometimes I'd give anything just to see a fuckin' cockroach walk across the floor. You do anything to piss them off, you get ten days. That's ten days with the lights on in your cell twenty-four hours a day. They degrade you, that's what it's about. Break your spirit, take away your identity. When you leave here, you're nobody, with a hate that's bigger than it ever was. That's if you ain't crazy.'

'So they spring you in three years and you're right back at it?'

'I've learned a few lessons. Let's just say if I ever get out of this shithole, I sure as hell ain't coming back.'

'No, you'll end up getting your brains blown out by some GI sniper. There's something to look forward to.'

'Nobody's looking forward to anything,' Jordan snapped, with bitterness in his tone. 'We're talking about survival. Don't matter whether there's fifteen hundred or fifteen thousand of us, it's the way it'll come down. Strike and vanish, like ghosts.'

'Or Phantoms?'

'Whatever you like.'

'You're talking about suicide.'

'Which is a helluva lot better than lettin' the government come, take away everything you got, and *then* kill you.'

'Tell me more about the General.'

'I'm sure you people have a file on him the size of a horse's dick.'

'I'd like your take on him.'

Jordan considered that for a minute or so.

'Best damn soldier who ever lived. That pussy, Pennington, is everybody's pretty boy. He don't know shit about makin' war. The General was the best. Nobody loved his men the way he did. We'd go out there in the fuckin' jungle, months at a time, he never passed a bitch. Tell you something else, when one of our boys got clipped, he was never left behind. We carried body bags with us to bring our guys back so they'd have a Christian burial. Six go out, six come back. Ten go out, ten come back.'

He got up and shuffled around the room as he continued.

'We done the dirtiest work there was over there. We did it with the General's prayers in our ears. *Vengeance is mine, sayeth the Lord.* And nobody done it better. Hell, Oz once took out a gook general from two thousand fuckin' yards out. You think about that. That's twenty football fields.'

'Who's Oz?'

'Don't matter, he's long dead. Thing is, we never was recognized for what we done. No medals, no citations. Not even a damn thank you from anybody. They took away our identity just like in here. But the General, he gave it back to us. His people love him.'

'And you're one of his people.'

'Fuckin-A.'

'He should know better than to pick a fight with the federal government.'

'People's rights are being taken away every day, man! Illegal searches and seizures. Breakin' in on people without a warrant. Keepin' track of our weapons. Dogs baring their teeth at you for no damn reason at all. The massacre at Marion. Waco. Ruby Ridge. Taxes. Fuckin' IRS comes in and takes everything away. House, furniture, everything, without even a trial.'

'So you start a fight you can't win.'

'Can't win? Victory is in the Bible, Mr. Vail. Some of the few verses I do know. I heard him speak them often enough.'

Jordan leaned his elbows on the table and stared straight at Vail. When he spoke, it was without emotion, as if he were describing a news event on WWN.

'*And the Philistines stood on a mountain on the one side, and Israel stood on a mountain on the other side: and there was a valley between them. And there went a champion out of the camp of the Philistines named Goliath of Gath whose height was six cubits and a span. And he had an helmet of brass upon his head, and he was armed with a coat of mail; and he had greaves of brass upon his legs, and a target of brass between his shoulders.*' He stood up and shuffled across the small room again, his voice rising slightly. '*And David hasted, and ran to meet the Philistine. And David put his hand in his bag, and took thence a stone, and slang it, and smote the Philistine . . .*' He stopped and smiled. '*. . . and the stone sunk into his forehead; and he fell upon his face to the earth.*' Jordan shuffled back, the chain clinking between his ankles, and stood next to Vail. He turned his head toward the ceiling and his voice became a preacher's voice. '*So David prevailed over the Philistine with a sling and with a stone, and smote the Philistine, and slew him; but there was no sword in the hand of David. Therefore David ran, and stood upon the Philistine, and took his sword, and drew it out of the sheath thereof . . .*' Jordan leaned forward, his face a few inches from Vail's. His voice became suddenly quiet, and he said, almost in a whisper, '*. . . and cut off his head therewith. And when the Philistines saw their cham-*

pion was dead, they fled.'

He wiped sweat from his forehead with the back of his hand.

'First Samuel, Chapter Seventeen.'

Vail thought for a moment and said with a sigh, 'You really think you can destroy the U.S. government with a slingshot and a stone, Gary?'

Jordan replied softly, 'It's what *God* meant, Mr. Vail. Nothin's impossible for the righteous.'

A chill suddenly coursed down Vail's spine, not because of the words, but at the quiet assurance with which they were spoken.

'I'm a God-fearin' man. I go to church, but I never been much for remembering the words. Except for a few verses of the Bible, I leave that up to the preacher.' He smiled faintly. 'Don't want to put him outta business, y'know.'

'Do you think General Engstrom will talk to me?'

'Why not? He ain't hidin' from anybody. Not yet anyway.'

'You say he's a logical man. Maybe he'll listen to logic.'

'Your logic?'

'Give and take. We'll listen to each other.'

'Yeah, we've heard that song before,' Jordan said bitterly. 'The government never keeps its promises. Broke every treaty they ever made goin' back to the Indians. Here it is 150 years later and they still ain't learned to keep their word.'

'What promise did they break to *you*, Gary?'

Jordan didn't answer.

'Look, if you don't pay your taxes like everybody else, you go down. Hell, if I try to screw the IRS on my taxes, they'll dump on me just as fast as anybody else. Trying to kill that agent didn't help.'

'What a joke. He was a hundred and fifty feet away. If I wanted to kill him, he'd be dead. I just scared the little bastard. Anyway, income tax is illegal. Nowhere in the

187

Constitution does it justify taxing people for doing a hard day's work.'

'Hell, if you told 'em you were sorry and it wouldn't happen again, you could have worked something out.'

It was the wrong thing to say. Jordan's eyes turned to fire, his back straightened an inch, his voice trembled with the fervor of an evangelist as he spat the words out.

'The strength of Israel will not lie nor repent: for he is not a man, that he should repent. First Samuel, Chapter Twenty-nine. Let me tell you something, when they come down on me, I had to listen to this little rabbit telling me I had to *suffer* for cheating Uncle Sam. Those were his words. *Suffer!* Who was that miserable little fag to be judging me! Some pencil-pushing prick couldn't get an honest job anyplace else, living off the taxpayers, giving me such shit as that. I fought a war for his scrawny ass. Repent? Tell such as him I'm sorry? I'll break rocks in this satan's brig for another *twenty* years before I'll break the word of God to a sorry little bastard like that.'

Vail leaned back in his chair and lit a cigarette. He had no desire to get into a discussion about taxes with Jordan or anyone else. He changed the subject.

'Is your family still out in Montana?'

'Stayin' with my wife's daddy. Least the IRS ain't robbed him yet.'

'Maybe you should move them out of there,' Vail said.

'Why? Something you heard? Is something going down?'

'Not that I know of.'

Jordan squirmed in his seat, then waved off whatever he was thinking. 'Where would they go to, huh? We worked hard all our lives for what we got, my father and grandfather and those before them. Go to New York or St. Looey or Chicago, live in a cardboardfuckinbox on a street corner? That's a damn go-to-hell suggestion if I ever heard one.'

'I'm not suggesting that. I'm saying get your family out

of harm's way–'

Jordan cut him off, his face deep red, his eyes darkened with anger.

'Fuck you. We got no fear of you and your heathen friends. First John, Chapter Three, Verse Eleven, says, *Love one another. Not as Cain, who slew his brother.* The feds are brother slayers and you're one of them.'

He shuffled to the door of the room and looked back at Vail, his eyes narrowed. The close-up of Engstrom's eyes on the computer monitor flashed in Vail's memory. Jordan's voice shook with wrath.

'*At the time of Parousia when there are great voices from the temple of Heaven and thunders, and lightnings, and there is such an earthquake as has not been seen since men were on the earth, and the cities of nations fall, and islands flee away, and the mountains will not be found . . .*

'. . . on that day when Armageddon comes, my family'll be the first to fly to Heaven. And you? God'll judge you and smite feds like you and send you all straight to Hell where you belong.'

Jordan rapped for the guard.

Later, when they were in the car, Firestone asked Vail what he and Jordan had talked about.

'Death and taxes,' Vail answered. 'Get me the hell away from here.'

Twelve

In the tower of the small airstrip outside the village of Coyote Flats, the pilot scanned the two-lane blacktop road through his binoculars. He checked his watch. It was 11:55 Mountain Time.

'They should be along soon,' he said to the air controller.

'Can't imagine them staying any longer than they have to.'

'Never been out there,' the pilot said. He sat on the corner of the large console and lit a cigar.

'I went out there once,' the controller said. 'Once was enough.'

'It looks grim enough from the air,' the pilot said. 'I don't need to see it close up.'

The terminal – if it could be called that – was just a one-room adobe shack with a fast-food machine, a coffeemaker, two long benches, and two rest rooms. The two-story tower was equipped with radar and a computer, and was manned by an air controller attached to the Bureau of Prisons.

Once a month an airline connector was permitted to land on the long concrete jet strip, bringing inmate visitors. Otherwise the field was closed to private air traffic. A bus took the visitors to the Grave. The field was surrounded by a twelve-foot electrified fence and guarded by Marines.

Neither the controller nor the pilot noticed the janitor standing outside the door to the tower. He stared into the room, watching the pilot walk to the sectional map of the U.S. The pilot held one end of the elastic measure over Coyote Flats with his thumb and stretched the string to the northeast.

'Twelve hundred miles,' he said to himself, then walked back to the controller's table and took a calculator out of his flight case.

The janitor tapped on the door and stuck his head inside. 'Okay if I clean up now?' he asked.

'Sure,' the controller said.

The janitor entered the room. The pilot and controller ignored him as he pulled his wheeled trash can into the tower room and emptied an ashtray into it.

'What kind of winds do I have to the northeast?' the pilot asked.

The controller checked the weather maps on his computer.

'Clear sailing all the way to Canada and east to the coast,' he said. 'Looks like about fifty at thirty thousand.'

The janitor quietly pushed his broom across the floor, an innocuous man moving silently around the room doing his chores.

'Looks like about two hours and fifteen minutes,' the pilot said. He took up his binoculars again and stared at the highway. Far off, a twister of dust rose from the road.

'Here they come now,' he said.

'See ya tomorra,' the janitor said, and left the tower.

After he left, the controller said, 'What's your destination?'

'Fort Wayne, Indiana.'

The janitor pulled his pickup truck into a deserted filling station on the outskirts of Coyote Flats and parked under the sagging roof beside two old, rotting pumps. He connected the minicomputer and modem to his cell phone and waited. At twelve-fifteen he saw the big jet soar off the desert floor and climb past him. He typed a number into the computer. It answered:

'HOREB CQ. U?'

'SIMON.'

'WHICH?'

'PHARISEES. CFLTS. 2-3-13.'

'UR HOME.'

'AML TO 12:15. DEST FTWAYNE, IND. ETA 2:30 CST.'

'UNID PASSENGER?'

'NO HIT.'

'SELAH.'

The man sat on a small folding chair meticulously grafting a twig from one rosebush into the stem of another. He had carefully prepared a bed for the new bush, measuring just the right amount of dirt and fertilizer in the trench before he replanted the mother bush. Then he made a thin slice in the bush, cut a branch from the donor bush, and trimmed the end into a point. He carefully inserted it into the sliver in the first bush and bound the graft tightly with string. When he was finished, he sprayed the graft with water and tied a tag to its base, one on which he had printed the date and words 'Elaine's Rose.'

The air inside the greenhouse was warm and moist, an ideal environment for his hobby. The cold air outside blowing across the warm glass created a thin mist inside, which settled on the blossoms and leaves of the rosebushes. The air was warm and humid, and the bushes were planted with exactly eighteen inches between each plant, assuring them ample room to grow. Waterproof loudspeakers murmured Mozart as he worked. Sweat dribbled down his face and off his chin. When he finished making the graft, he slowly folded the chair and leaned it against one of the two long boxes in which he raised his roses. The boxes were each eight feet long and six feet wide, and were lined to prevent rusting and wood rottage. There was a yard between the two tables and a yard between each table and the wall.

He had built the greenhouse himself, first drawing intricate plans for height and width, where water lines should go, and how big the glass panels would be. His wife of twenty years had taught him all about roses and assisted him in the planning and design of the greenhouse, but she had not lived to see him finish it. Cancer had taken her soon after he started construction, and he'd abandoned the project. Don and Elaine Woodbine had lived in the same house since they married. Childless, they were a devoted couple. When Warren Ferguson died, Woodbine had bought his hardware store and become one of Bad Rapids's most successful businessmen. The locals were particularly pleased that he chose not to change the name – it was still Ferguson's Hardware and Lumber Company. Elaine was vivacious and outgoing, a beautiful woman who was attracted to the shy, quiet, balding, plain man who was somewhat reclusive. Some of the town skeptics had predicted an early end to the marriage, but to their surprise, the Woodbines grew closer, stayed deeply in love. Woodbine also worked as a consultant for the government and frequently had to travel, flying his own plane, while Elaine managed the store during his absences. As time went on, he became more outgoing. The pair occasionally had cookouts for friends in the neighborhood, and for two seasons he coached the Presbyterian church Little League football team.

Almost to the very end, Woodbine had refused to accept the fact that his wife was dying, and that denial led to a deep depression when she passed on, two years ago. But after mourning for almost six months, Don Woodbine had suddenly gone back to work on their dream project, deciding to finish it as a tribute to her. And having finished it, he sought closure and solace in the hobby they had shared.

Now, Woodbine walked down the length of the shelter, carrying a small vase, stopping to check each blossom for aroma and color and size, occasionally cutting off a blossom and putting it in the vase. When he finished, he walked back to the house, his feet crunching on the frozen snow. He took off his shoes before entering the back door, and felt the familiar catch deep in his throat when he entered the simple three-room brick ranch house. He still expected to see Elaine standing there, smiling at him. Like the greenhouse, the place was fastidiously neat and clean. A cleaning service came twice a week, and between times he kept the place spotless. He occasionally fixed dinner for himself, but usually ate at Dressner's tiny café, where the food was as close to home cooking as one could find in the small central Michigan town.

Woodbine carried his muddy shoes into the garage, put them back on, and drove his Four Runner to the cemetery a few minutes away. He carefully placed the vase of roses in front of the headstone and stood for a minute or two talking in a whisper to his departed lover. 'I miss yoú, my dear,' he said.

He was headed into the village to grab a bite of lunch when the pager on his belt interrupted his sad reverie. He punched the button and read the number.

'Damn,' he said.

He turned around and drove back to the house. His study was in a corner of the place, and his computer, which was always on, was blinking. He checked the message, which said simply, 'Contact home.'

His fingers moved rapidly over the keyboard as he accessed the modem program and typed in a number. He sat listening to the phone buzzing, then the screech as it connected. Then the message appeared.

'HOREB.'

'SIMON.'

'WHICH?'

'SORCERER. 2-3-13.'

'UR HOME. SF ON THE MOVE. AMOC2 WITH UNID PASSENGER. U AVAIL?'

'WHERE?'

'AMOC ETA FTWAYNE, IND, 2:30 PM CST.'

Woodbine looked at his watch. It was 11:55. He sighed. He would have to hurry.

'CANDO,' he typed.

'GOOD LUCK.'

'SELAH.'

He brought up the weather on the computer screen while he dialed the hardware store.

'Ferguson's,' Charley Moore's cheerful voice answered.

'Charley, Don.'

'Hi, boss, what's up?'

'Gotta business thing. I'll be gone for a couple days. Any problem?'

'No, sir, Hazel and me can handle everything.'

'Good. When you gonna marry that girl?'

'Soon's you gimme a raise,' Charley said with a laugh.

'Poor child's destined to be an old maid.'

'I'll tell her you said that.'

'Give her a kiss on the cheek instead. I should be back before the weekend.'

'Safe trip.'

'Thanks.'

The weather was clear and cold from Michigan all the way south to the Ohio border. There was weather moving in from the west, but nothing bad enough to worry him. He walked briskly into the bedroom, took a quick shower, and changed into a plain gray business suit with a dark tie that he left knotted loosely around his neck. He went to the garage, swung a heavy worktable away from the rear wall. He reached inside his shirt and pulled out a silver chain with two keys hanging on it. They were the kind of keys used with safe deposit boxes; one had to activate the lock before the second key opened it. He used both to unlock a three-foot door and slid it sideways, revealing a carbon steel Malhauser safe. He twirled the dials and swung the heavy door open.

The safe contained two aluminum suitcases, a two-foot-high steel filing cabinet with two drawers, and two large strongboxes. He selected one of the aluminum cases, laid it on the floor, and snapped it open. Embedded in Styrofoam were the components of a .50 caliber fully automatic rifle, a telescopic sight, a twenty-shot clip, and a .50 caliber Eagle handgun with two sixteen-shot clips. There was one open slot in the Styrofoam tray. He unclipped the pocket in the lid of the case and lowered it. Secured in pockets in the lid were six boxes of steel jacket .50 caliber bullets. Three hundred rounds. He took each component from the case and studied it carefully: stock, barrel, silencer, scope, and telescoping aluminum tripod. Satisfied that they were clean and ready for action, he replaced them in their slots.

He opened one of the strongboxes. It was packed to the rim with neatly stacked ten-, twenty-, and fifty-dollar bills. He counted out a thousand dollars in various denominations, placed the packet of bills in the one open slot in the case, then snapped it shut. He reached up inside the safe above the door and pressed a button on a small black box. Then he closed the safe, twirled the dials on the lock, slid the door shut, and double-locked it. The house was wired with a pound of C-4 and several tubes of gasoline that he had built into the walls. The bomb could be deactivated only by using a remote controller that blocked the bomb switch attached to the lock of the safe door. If the safe was opened or blown, or the inside door to the carport was opened, the entire house would be instantly demolished and what was left would burn out of control. He swung the worktable back in place and carried the aluminum case into the house.

In his closet, he kept a small carry bag with a change of shirts, socks and underwear, and toilet articles, enough to last him five days. He quickly checked to make sure all windows and doors were locked, although there had not been a house robbery in Bad Rapids for years, and set the burglar alarm. He took the case, carry bag, and a briefcase, went back to the garage, and put them in the rear seat of his Four Runner. Then he drove the three miles to the landing strip on a ten-acre tract he owned.

The plane was a twin turbo prop Beechcraft Baron D-55 with 375-horsepower Lycoming turbo engines. It had a cruising speed of 300 miles per hour and a range of a thousand miles. The pressurized cabin provided a maximum altitude of 33,000 feet. It was hangared in a rebuilt barn at one corner of the lot. The landing strip stretched from the door of the barn, two thousand feet to the other end of the field, plenty of stretch for the plane. The Baron was fully fueled and always in flight-ready condition. He put the gun case and carry bag behind him on the floor of the plane, put the briefcase on the seat beside him, cranked up the ship, and pulled it out of the barn. He got out, put his car in the barn, closed and locked the doors. Five minutes later he was aloft.

He checked his watch. It was 12:27.

He brought up a United States atlas program on the built-in computer in the control panel and marked a course from Bad Rapids, Michigan, to Fort Wayne, Indiana; 206 miles. The weather was clear almost all the way there.

They had been tracking Sam Firestone for months, hoping he would lead them to Waller. So far, all dead ends. But as long as they continued to pay him ten thousand dollars to go on these wild goose chases, Woodbine was glad to oblige. And if he happened to get lucky and finish the job, the fee jumped to fifty thousand, which was fair enough.

He set his compass, leaned back, and turned on the CD player. Sarah Vaughn's 'My Ship' boomed from the stereo.

What a lovely day for a spin.

Thirteen

The big jet whined around the corner of the concourse and swung past Woodbine's small plane. He opened his briefcase, removed a palm-sized digital video camera, and stepping through the door, perched one foot on the wheel and braced the camera in the jamb of the door to keep it steady. He was casual about every move. No one noticed him seemingly resting in the doorway of the plane, a plain man in an off-the-rack gray suit. He watched the 737 as it followed the ground crew man to a designated spot on the tarmac and stopped. The ground crew rolled a portable staircase up to it and a moment later the door hissed open.

The video camera had a switch on the back that enabled Woodbine to shoot either video or still shots. He moved the switch to video and waited. A tall black man came out on the staircase platform and looked around. That would be Nielson. Behind him, the shorter guy in the blue jacket stepped out. Silverman. He had seen them before, always through the lens of a camera or through binoculars. A moment later Firestone came out with his passenger. He taped Firestone and Vail as they exited the AMOC and went down the stairs. The plane's captain followed them down. He stretched when he reached the tarmac and rubbed the back of his neck.

Vail and Firestone were chatting, Firestone occasionally pointing toward a small single-engine Cherokee.

Who is that guy? Woodbine wondered. *Doesn't look like a big shot, the way he's dressed.*

Woodbine switched the camera to still shot and snapped a half-dozen medium close-ups of the unidentified passenger. He slid back on the seat of the plane and put the video camera back in the briefcase.

They're heading for the Cherokee, he thought. *They're playing hard to get.* He nodded to himself. It made sense, all this security. *This is it. He's going to Waller.*

Firestone led Vail to the Cherokee. A man in a dark blue suit, wearing sunglasses, smiled and they shook hands.

'Al Ricardo, Martin Vail. Mr. Vail, Al is FBI.'

'The gang's all here,' Vail said, shaking Ricardo's hand.

'She's gassed and flight-checked,' Ricardo said. 'There's a two-door black Taurus waiting. Key's in the inside rim, right rear.'

'You're a good man, Al,' Firestone said, climbing into the plane.

'Be careful, huh,' Ricardo said. 'I had to sign for the car and Cherokee.'

'Trust me,' Firestone said.

'That's what you said the last time.' Ricardo smiled as Firestone pulled the door shut. Vail climbed in beside him.

'You flying this bird?' he asked Firestone.

'Yep. Been flying for thirty years.'

'What was that about the last time?'

'It's a long story.' Firestone laughed and, ignoring the question, said, 'You don't have a problem in small planes, do you?'

'I once flew seventy miles in a chopper in the middle of a blizzard at zero altitude,' Vail said.

'That when you were shagging Stampler down in Kentucky?'

'*You* know about that, too, huh.'

'The A.G. showed me your clips, Mr. Vail.'

'Do we have to be so damn formal? Why don't you call me Martin or Marty, whichever you prefer, and I'll call you Sam.'

'Fine.'

He tuned the radio to the tower frequency, advised the flight controller he was heading southeast to the Lima, Ohio, county airport, and asked for takeoff instructions.

'Roger, Cherokee N-32,' the tower responded. 'You'll take runway two. You have two aircraft in front of you. You got some weather moving in on Lima.'

'I read you, Tower. Maybe we'll beat it there.'

'Roger. Wait for your clearance.'

'Roger and out.'

Following close behind, Woodbine listened to the conversation on his scanner.

Lima, Ohio. So far, so good.

Above the Lima airport Woodbine held steady at a thousand feet, a half mile away, and watched through his binoculars. Vail and Firestone parked the Cherokee and drove off in the black sedan, heading northwest on the county road into Lima. A mile southeast of town the car turned onto Interstate 75 and headed south. The weather was working against Woodbine. Rocked by winds and turbulence, he flitted in and out of dark clouds and lost the car. He dropped down to five hundred feet to get below the storm. Cars whizzed north and south on the highway. He held at five hundred, scanning the road south of Lima, searching for his elusive prey. Finally, still battered by the turbulence and dodging in and out of black low-hanging clouds, he started a square search, checking the automap on his computer and sectioning off the area south of Lima. He flew a two-mile square east of the interstate, then did the same to the west, heading south in two-mile increments. Twice he thought he spotted the black car on narrow county roads, but checked them with his binoculars to no avail. He flew in the same two-mile squares until he was fifty miles south of Lima. Still buffeted by the bad weather, he finally turned and headed back north.

The interstate was almost empty.

He had lost the car.

Firestone had turned off the interstate onto a two-lane road. He drove for ten or fifteen minutes, then turned into a country filling station and parked under the roof over the pumps.

'Thirsty?' he asked Vail.

'Are you kidding?' Vail said with a pained expression. 'I've been eating and drinking ever since I got on the AMOC this morning.'

Firestone walked to an old-fashioned soft drink machine and fed quarters into the slot. He popped the tab on a can of ginger ale as he walked back to the car. He stood on Vail's side of the car, staring back at the road.

It was quiet except for a slight wind that rustled the frozen snow at the edge of the blacktop and the roar of a plane as it flew by half a mile to the north.

'Looking for a tail, aren't you?'

Firestone smiled down at him. 'Caution's my middle name.' He threw the can in a waste bucket and got back in the car. 'We're almost there.'

'Want to tell me who, what, or where 'there' is?'

'Ralph, Marty. That's what you'll call him, Ralph. He's going to tell you a story. Just listen, don't break his train of thought. You break his train of thought, he'll have to start over.'

'He's memorized this yarn, that it?'

'More or less. Once he's through, ask him anything you want.'

'WitSec, right?'

Firestone nodded.

'No wonder you're so cautious. Somebody must really want this Ralph bad.'

'Everybody in witness protection is on top of somebody's list.'

The farmhouse sat two hundred feet from the road, a

nicely kept two-story wood frame structure, white with gray trim. A dirt road led to a turnaround adjacent to a sagging barn, where a muddy, two-year-old Chevrolet was parked haphazardly near the door. As Firestone pulled up, white lace curtains parted in a front window and a young woman peered out with cautious eyes. Firestone got out of the car and she moved out of the window. A moment later the front door opened and she stepped out.

'Hello, Marie.'

'Hi, Mr. Firestone.'

'Where's Ralph?'

'Out in the field. The tractor's stuck in a hole.'

'Marie, this is Mr. Vail.'

'How do you do,' she said, and shook his hand. She nodded toward the door. 'Don't mind Noah. Come on in.'

She was a fragile young woman, with her waist-length ash-blond hair tied in a ponytail. Vail thought she had once been pretty, but her face was lined with the creases of harsh living, and the sparkle in her green eyes had long since faded. She was wearing jeans and a dark green flannel shirt, its sleeves rolled up to her elbows.

She led Vail and Firestone back toward the kitchen through the living room, which was cheaply but tastefully furnished. There was a large picture of Jesus on one wall, his hands out at his sides as if blessing the house, and a large leather-bound Bible on the coffee table. The kitchen was spotless. A large gas grill dominated the center of the room, and there was a breakfast nook in one corner with a painting of the Last Supper on the wall.

She opened the back door and yelled to her husband, who was twenty or so yards out on the snow-encrusted field, standing on the tractor, snapping the controls back and forth, trying to jog the John Deere out of a frozen mud hole.

'Ralphie. It's Mr. Firestone.'

He stopped what he was doing, turned the tractor off, jumped down, and trotted across the frozen earth to the house. He wiped his hands on his pants and shook hands with Firestone.

'This is Mr. Vail, Ralph. He's with the A.G., wants to hear your story. What say we just sit here at the kitchen table.'

'Sure. Marie, make up some fresh coffee, would you?'

He shook off his thick parka and threw it in a chair. He was wearing jeans and a plain white T-shirt, a good-looking young man, about twenty-five, short – five-six or – seven – and husky from working the farm. His black hair was trimmed short. A black beard covered the lower part of his face, and he had brown eyes that avoided direct eye contact. He looked at Vail's chin when he spoke. But what attracted Vail's attention was the tattoo on his right arm, an ominous black spiderweb that spread from the bicep through the inside of his elbow to his forearm. He remembered noticing a tattoo just like it in one of the dozens of photographs that had flashed across the monitor screen earlier in the day while the A.G. was briefing him on Christian hate groups.

Marie busied herself making a pot of coffee in an old-fashioned percolator.

'Where d'ya want me to start?' he asked in a flat western drawl.

'From the beginning,' Firestone answered.

I come from this little town called Wolf Point, near the Fort Peck Indian reservation along the Missouri Breaks in east Montana. We had us a little ranch ten miles or so out of town. Cattle and horses. I could break a jump-buckin' long-haired wild pony after they'd been running wild all winter by the time I was eleven years old. My ma was a nurse. Worked for Doc Zimmerman, who was a Jew, which was kinda rare around there, but he was the only one for a long ways around and liken it pissed off

203

my pa that she was workin' for the Jew but it was the best job she could get. M'pa was kinda short like me with big, callused hands, a God-fearin' Christian he was, read the Bible every night whilst m'ma played one of them old-timey pump organs. We'd sit around the fireplace and he'd read scripture and then he'd quiz us. My sister Lorraine and me had to learn a verse every night. Word-to-word, make a mistake and he'd glower down on us with them big black eyes a'his and shake his head and make us do it over. Everything we did, every decision he made, he took outta the Book. No dancin', smokin', drinkin'. No TV. We had us a radio which he used to listen to the patriot stations every night.

When I was twelve, Ma come down with pneumonia. We had a birthing shed where she had to stay four or five days a month when she was bleeding or when she had a baby, and she caught cold out there around Thanksgiving and just couldn't shake it. By Christmas she was havin' a real bad time breathin', and Lorraine took her place at the organ. I remember Pa and me goin' out and findin' a perfect Christmas tree, cuttin' it down, and bringin' it home. We all made ornaments for it and made Christmas as happy as we could. She made it through Christmas but she died on New Year's Eve. Shook Pa's faith up pretty good. He blamed Doc Zimmerman, said that was the problem with the country, that the Jewboys was takin' over and they was inferior in everything they did. He hated nigras, too, but I never seen one up close until I was almost growed. Pa was angry a lot after that, go out in the field and curse God, shake the Bible at the sky. But he still relied on the scriptures for how we lived day by day and the Bible readin' went on like always.

Long as I can remember, there'd be these men from down in Arkansas and over to Michigan who would come by once, twice a year. They'd sit down in the livin' room and talk about how the country was goin' to hell and what was wrong. When I was a little kid I couldn't sit with them but I'd lay at the top of the stairs listenin'. One such was Mr. Orin Plummer. He was fierce-lookin' 'cause he had lost his right hand makin' a hand grenade and he had bad scars all over his face and he always wore a pistol low at his hip. I heard later he was shot in the back by the ATFs. When he come to the house I'd run and hide in the stable and he'd stand in the door and laugh and yell at me to come on down there. And then Pa would order me down and Major Orin, which is what they called him, shook hands with this kinda plastic hand. It was always cold and kinda slick and it gave me the creeps.

When I was twelve, Pa let me come to the meetings. First time I ever saw a AK-47 was when Major Orin come to the house with a bunch of other fellas and he was carryin' one slung down from his shoulder under his arm. We drove out to the breaks and he let me shoot it. It was somethin' else, shootin' that piece. I got to tell you, I was almighty impressed. That Major made me feel like a man, like I was all growed and part of it even though I was just a kid.

The talk was always the same. We hated the government 'cause they wanted to take away our weapons. We hated the Jews 'cause they controlled the banks and the money. We hated the United Nations 'cause they was being readied to become the world police force and they were comin' into this country to take down anybody who didn't believe the way the government said to believe. We talked about robbin' banks and armories and stockpilin' weapons, and the Major talked about how the government made up the story about all the Jews Hitler killed and how the pictures of all them bodies stacked up was shot in Hollywood where the Jews owned all the movie studios, so that people'd feel sorry for them. We called the President and the Congress traitors and we called ourselves patriots and I was real impressed at bein' considered one of them. And we hated the tax man who could come and take away your house without so much as a howdy-dee-do. Major Orin called the IRSers a buncha low-bred kikes who couldn't get a job anywheres else and who lived off the public tit and treated everybody bad because they wasn't worth nothing themselves.

One such visitor we had was called Eddie Dukes and he was from down South somewheres and had a tattoo on his arm of a dagger with KKK on the handle. He spoke about the four B's, which was 'Bibles, bullets, beans, and bandages,' and I believed it all. Everything they said. They'd leave their little paper books for us to read and I had a whole shelf of them in my bedroom. They taught survival tactics and weaponry and there was one book called Satan's Kids which said how the Bible proves the Jews and nigras are God's fallen people and should be slaves. I remember it quotin' Revelations Two: I know the blasphemy of them which say they are Jews and are not, but are of the synagogue of Satan. Pa would quote from another book which was called The Bible Answers Racial Questions and his favorite was from Ezra Nine: Now therefore give not your daughters unto their sons, nor seek their peace or their wealth forever: that ye may be strong and eat the good of the land. My favorite of all the books was The Aryan Warrior, which was about survival and weapons and how to stance whilst shootin' and makin' foxholes and the like. One summer I went out to the breaks and dug myself a foxhole and I had my pack with some hardtack and my canteen and my thirty-ought-six and I stayed there for two days shootin' at Jews and nigras and government traitors – which was really rocks and the like.

My pa hated two things more than anything else and that was Jews and the tax man. When I was fourteen and Lorraine was nineteen she run off and married Ben Zimmerman 'cause she knew Pa would have no truck with her marryin' a Jew. They had been goin' together on the sly for a couple years while Ben was in college, and when he'd come home for the weekend they'd go off and shack up somewhere and Pa never knew anything about it nor did I. She tried to talk about it with him and he went into a rage. He was slammin' his fist on the dining room table and callin' her a whore and the like. The next day she was gone and she left a note but he never spoke to her or about her again. But one night soon after she was gone I woke up and heard all this racket downstairs and I went down and there was Pa, sitting in the living room with no lights on, just the fire in the fireplace with a bucket between his feet and he was smashin' all the framed pictures of her and lettin' the glass and frames drop in the bucket and he was burnin' her pictures in the fireplace. I never seen him look so ferocious. I don't know where she is neither, I ain't seen her since she left.

Pa refused to pay taxes because like he said it was just money goin' to the Jewboys who had the government by the throat. Finally they come after him. They was about ten, fifteen of them and they threw our things out front of the house, they took the ranch and sold it and sent my pa to the federal pen in Kansas. I was sixteen then and just afore he went away he sent me to Arkansas to live with the Posse at a compound they had in the Ozarks. I never saw my pa again for there was this riot at the prison which were the whites and the nigras havin' it out and they stabbed him to bits with a screwdriver. I hated them all. Hated the nigras and the kikes and the spics, I hated every last one of them for what they did to us and to my pa.

Reverend Zeke Longfellow, who was a leader of the Posse, adopted me, and from then on I was schooled in the Bible and the Constitution and history and the like for a couple of hours a day, then in the afternoons we would train in survival and guerrilla tactics. I learned how to make grenades and short-barrel a shotgun and where the kill points are on the human body and the making of bombs and incendiaries, and we was taught

207

how to take out bridges and telephone relay stations and radio station towers and airports and fuel storage tanks. Hit and run, hit and run, that was the big thing. In the summer we went off to camp in the north – Colorado, Montana, Idaho – and they would cut us loose in the mountains with nothin' but a knife and a canteen and we would have to find our way back and eat off the land whilst we was at it. I loved it all.

When I was eighteen, the Reverend sent me to the Army and I ended up in the 82nd Airborne and he give me the name of a man to contact when I got to Fort Bragg in North Carolina. He was a sergeant – name was Schmidt, Barry Schmidt – and he was a skinhead. They was about forty of us there and I fit right in. Had me a Nazi flag in my footlocker and I wore a Nazi Iron Cross on a chain around my neck. We wore our hair real short and we dressed alike when we was off the base. Jeans and bomber jackets, red suspenders, and black combat boots with red, white, or purple laces. We hung out in this bar called the Roving Eye and they had a back room which was like our private club. We'd get drunk, and the strippers would come back and perform for us and do other stuff.

Schmidt had this house off base and we'd go over there and read his Nazi literature and watch newsreels about Hitler on his video. He had a cold cellar and he had about five thousand rounds of small-caliber ammunition down there and more than a pound of explosives and blasting caps and smoke grenades. He'd give us orders for stuff and we'd steal it from the base and he'd pay us to do that.

And on Saturday night sometimes we'd go on huntin' trips. That's what we called it, huntin' trips. We'd scope us out a fag or a porch weasel, which is one of the ways he called niggers, or a Jesus killer, and we'd egg 'em on and pick a fight and beat 'em up good. Then this one night we was in this small town near the base, they was five of us and Schmidt, who had a souped-up Firebird, *and we see this nigger PFC and he's walkin' down the street with a white girl. Schmidt says, 'Lookit that ugly fuckin' jungle bunny with a blond girl.' He stops and we pile out and chase the girl off and the jig begins to get scared, he's sayin' to leave him alone and he wants to leave but we crowded around him. Then Barry gets a rope outta the car and he fashions himself a noose and we sling it around this nigra's head and he goes to screamin' and Barry pulls the knot tight and cuts off his voice. I never seen nobody as scared as that nigra soldier was. His eyes was big as a fry pan and he takes to cryin' and then Schmidt says, 'You lousy coward, die like a man' and he throws the other end of the rope over a tree limb and ties his hands behind his back. He says to me and one of the other boys to grab the rope with him and then we just, you know, just hauled him up off the ground and tied the rope to the tree and he was hangin' there, legs jumpin' and twirlin' around and he's gaggin' for breath. We stood there for the longest time while he hung there jerkin' on the end of that rope and finally he stopped and he fell real still and we piled back in the car and drove away. Next day it's all over the base that this nigger soldier was lynched and they're sayin' it was the Klan. Nobody said anything. None of us was scared or worried about it. Far as I know, they never did arrest anybody for that.*

When I got discharged, I went back to Arkansas. That's when I first heard about the Sanctuary. Reverend Zeke sent me up there. He said they was startin' an army and it was right down my alley. I was taken into the Church of Zorepath, which is one of the army brigades. There's four of them, each one a brigade in the Army of the Sanctuary. The preacher was Major Metzinger. I was made a lieutenant and I was feelin' big about that. They was organized, not like the Posse or the Nations, for the General had a vision. When I first met the General I thought, This is a real war hero. He stood there, straight as a phone pole with a voice like an avalanche and he says

209

to me, 'Son, the Lamb of God who died for our sins is returning to judge sin as the Lion of the Tribe of Judah. We are rising in power and anointing, which the gates of Hell shall not prevail against, which no man shall stand up to, which no enemy shall smother, which no kingdom can resist.' He was saying that directly to me and it brought to mind Revelations Ten: And I saw a mighty angel come down from Heaven, clothed with a cloud: And a rainbow was upon his head, and His face was as it were the sun, and His feet as pillars of fire: And He had in his hand a little book open: and He set his right foot upon the sea, and his left foot on the earth, and he cried out with a loud voice, as when the lion roareth: and when He cried, seven thunders uttered their voices. *It returned me to the Bible. It got me back to scripture. It got me back to the good life.*

We trained hard. For some of us it was a full-time job. Every weekend we trained in town and once a month we'd go up to Yahweh, spend a couple days in survival and layin' mines, stringin' razor wire, sniper-shootin', alterin' weapons, like that. It's a hell of an army. Even the women are tough and know what they're doin'. The instructors are ex-SEALs, ex-Berets. They're pros at stealth missions and tracking and guerrilla tactics. The General talks about Parousia and A-Day. They have mockups of banks and armored cars and armories and shopping centers and government buildings, everything. The control center has the best electronics equipment you can imagine. Computers, video cameras, satellite things, I don't even understand a lot of it. I heard they have a radio studio and a bunker full of weapons and ammunition. I never seen that, but I have seen AK-47s and Polish Skorpiens and other outlaw guns bein' used. There's a special group called the I.F., the Invasion Force, which is made up of the commanders of the brigades and hand-picked experts which plan what they call sorties, which can mean anything from a bank to an armory to a shopping mall or gun store. And they got Brother Abraham who is spreading the word.

They also got Colonel Shrack, who's the head of the I.F. and who is the best officer I ever met but he's cold-blooded as hell. About a year ago I was asked to join an I.F. force for a sortie. It was the National Guard armory in Helena. They had planned this job to a fare-thee-well. They knew exactly what they wanted and where it was located. They knew where the guards were, telephone lines, radio equipment, they knew everything. We had a mock-up of the building with toy autos and we ran through the operation over and over while Metzinger clocked us with a stop watch. We had mock-ups of the power box and phone network for the experts to practice on. Nothing was left to chance.

There was only three men on duty that night. Usually there was four, but one of them, which was really one of our boys, stayed home sick at the last minute. We set up a diversion. It was timed just perfect. There was two men on the phone and power lines, another one to go straight-aways in and make sure the radio and computers were down, two men who faked a fender bender in front of the main door, a driver and a shotgun in the van, four guys to get in, open the doors, and load up the stuff. Twelve in all, counting the man who stayed home and the commander of the operation, which was Metzinger, my preacher, and I guess that's how come I was asked in because he was my C.O. Metzinger was on the roof of a building about a block away with high-powered glasses, directing things because he had full view of the whole field of operation. I drove one of the fender benders and also jumped on the van and helped load. It went off like clockwork. Nobody got hurt, and we got what we went for, which was mainly C-4, grenade machine guns, steel jacket – that's bullets – a couple of grenade launchers, and a handheld missile launcher. The whole operation went down in six minutes. The guards was left duct-taped, hands, feet, and mouths. It was two hours before anybody even realized the lights and all was off. By that time we was long gone. The take was hidden in cars on an auto transport. Eight Toyotas. We . . . they own the transport and we . . . they got three car dealers in the army.

But after it was over some of the boys commenced to drinking and wanted to go to a whorehouse and it was like, they forgot all about what it was about, that it was a Christian war we was fightin' and we had to do it by the Book.

Then I got invited on another one, this time a bank job, and Metzinger told me they were checking me out to see if I was good enough for the I.F. because I done real good on the armory job. I was real thrilled about that. The bank job was a long way off. Denver. And from the start it gave me the worries. First off, it was a small operation – five men. A driver, which was me, three men in the bank, one outside with the radio, which was the commander of the job. He was a guy I didn't know. We went through the whole routine with the mock-up and everything just like the armory job and then we went into Denver to case the bank and make sure everything was cool.

It was two nights before the job. That night they all got roaring drunk and had women up to the rooms and they was up whoring and drinkin' all night long. It got me worried. I mean, to do a job like that everybody's gotta be in top form. Next day they went out to check out the escape routes and all and I stayed back at the hotel. We always kept one man in the hotel HQ when we did an overnight. I was sittin' there looking out the window and there was this movie playin' across the street that everybody said was a big lie. It was called Schindler's List and it was about the Jew murders during World War Two. I kept staring down at the theater and thinking about all the hell-raisin' they had been doin' so I sneaked across *the street and watched the movie. Most of it was in black and white and that was the part about the concentration camps and all and I thought, What a lotta bunk this is, but then at the end all these old people came up and gave witness. That part was in color. And I knew then that it was true. These people wasn't in any Hollywood studio, they was in Israel and they was outside. They gave witness and I started believing them and then I knew it was a big lie, all that stuff about the government and all. And I knew the bank job was gonna go sour, I knew that in my heart.*

So I walked out of the theater and I went to the government building and there was a marshal's office there, so I went in and there sat Mr. Firestone. I told him I'd give him the whole story but they would sure as hell kill me and I needed to go into the protection program. And I told him I wouldn't do no testifying once I was in because they're everywhere and you leave the nest they'll find you. And then like the cherry on a sundae, I give up the bank job. You probably remember about that. They was waiting when the I.F. got there and there was a big shootout, three of them went down and the other one was caught and got life but he never give up that they were an I.F. with the Sanctuary. And I come here. The government bought me this farm and gives me twenty-five thousand a year. I joined the church and that's where I met Marie and we was married six months ago. That's my story.

Vail was struck by the stoic monotone with which Ralph told his horror story. He showed no emotion or remorse in telling it. It was as if he were reciting the menu in a restaurant. Vail had taken no notes. He took a sip of coffee and stared at Ralph, who looked at Vail's chin.

'What does Engstrom mean when he talks about Parousia?' Vail asked.

'It's when Christ returns to earth. The second coming.'

'And what is A-Day?'

'Armageddon Day. The day of the last great battle between good and evil.'

'Is the Sanctuary planning a great battle on A-Day?'

'Yes sir, that's what I suppose.'

'And that's what he's preparing for? That's what the army is all about, stealing weapons, robbing banks, getting ready for the big day.'

'I'm just guessing that's what it means.'

'So the General is never explicit about that?'

'No sir, he has never said exactly when all this will take place.'

'Or where?'

'No sir. Don't you see? It's gonna be a holy war.'

'And A-Day is when it's going to start?'

'I guess that's it.'

'Like Hitler's war. The Third Reich was the Third Crusade in his mind. He exterminated millions of people in the name of Jesus Christ, Ralph, did you know that?'

'Well, yes sir, I'd heard some of that.'

'And if we bring the General into court, you refuse to give testimony?'

'I made that deal up front,' he answered nervously, and looked at Firestone for corroboration. The marshal didn't respond at first. After all, this was Vail's show. Finally Firestone said, 'We did have that understanding.'

'Well, *I* didn't,' Vail snapped. 'You've got a nice place here, Ralph. A lot of people live on less than the government sends you and Marie every month. You don't feel you owe something for that?'

'I give up a lot already,' he answered.

'What have you given up? A lot of talk? Life in the Sanctuary? You committed cold-blooded murder in North Carolina, Ralph, and armed robbery at the armory in Helena. The government has conveniently overlooked that. Now you're on top of Engstrom's hit list. They'll put a bullet in you and Marie in a flat second. They have no feeling for you anymore. You're dead meat in their

214

book. But you feel it's fair to live forever off the government and not help stop Engstrom's madness?'

'It ain't–' Ralph started, and then caught himself.

'It *ain't* what, madness?'

'They never killed anybody in these sorties and–'

'They killed ten United States GIs last night in the Bitterroot Mountains. That's the body count up there. Executed them, pal. You heard about that?'

'There was something on the TV but–'

'But nothing. They robbed the people of the United States and murdered ten soldiers in cold blood. There was nothing holy about it. What the hell is there to be proud of in that? You know something, Ralph, I make it a cowardly act of terrorism. Engstrom can wave his Bible around all he wants, I'll wave the United States Constitution right back in his face and we'll see which one the jury believes.'

Ralph did not answer. He looked at Firestone for support, but the marshal stared down at his coffee and said nothing. He turned to Marie, who stood by the stove, arms crossed at her chest, staring at the floor.

'Maybe it was–' Ralph started, and then stopped in mid-sentence.

'Maybe it was what?' Vail asked, and there was anger in his voice.

'Maybe it was an act of war,' he said in a whisper. 'Maybe it's A-Day.'

Fourteen

Vail sat quietly in the car as Firestone drove back toward the interstate. He knew why Castaigne had sent him to interview these two men. Jordan was the true zealot, a man who felt betrayed by his government, had given up on the legal process, and was devoted to the idea of revolution, like the hippies in the sixties. In many ways, his rant was more chilling than Ralph describing, without remorse, in a steady monotone, the lynching of an innocent black soldier. Jordan was a man of passion, far more dangerous than the young thug who had been trained almost from birth to be a psychopath, oblivious to the moral restraints imposed by his precious Bible. Ralph was a drone who did what he was bid regardless of the Ten Commandments. Jordan was a leader whose passion could instill civil disobedience and ultimately the violence that accompanies it.

Castaigne had made certain Vail heard both poles of the militia mindset.

The muscles in Vail's jaw twitched as he thought about Ralph . . . and he stared angrily through the windshield.

Finally Firestone said: 'Got to you, did he?'

'You could say that.'

'And Jordan didn't?'

'You know, I felt for Jordan's anger. I don't agree with any of it, but I can see how he got where he is. He's doing hard time, while this little scumbag is living off the taxpayers.'

'He gave us a lot of information, Martin.'

'Know what I think? I think the little bastard knew the bank robbery would go south and he didn't want any part of it. He knew they'd nail him or we would. One way he's dead, the other he has a murder rap and an armed robbery dangling over his head. So he played it smart. He gave up information and copped on testifying.'

'It's not that uncommon in witness protection deals.'

'Instead of ending up doing the full clock, no parole, he's got himself a farm and a pretty little wife who's probably just as fucked up as he is, and he's wiped murder and mayhem off his sheet.'

'You don't pull any punches, do you?'

'Look, I'm not knocking you for making the deal, I've put a few creeps in witness pro myself. I'm sure it sounded like a good move at the time.'

'It was the first break we got on the Sanctuary.'

'I'll tell you something else, I don't buy that rap about *Schindler's List* for a minute. This guy is as big a racist and hate monger as he ever was. He made himself a cool deal and the Bureau bought it.'

Firestone stared straight ahead at the ribbon of highway for several seconds before he nodded. 'I won't argue with that.'

'Like I said, I'm not knocking you, Sam. You want to know the truth, the only thing Ralph whatever-his-name-is is good for is corroboration.'

'His real name was George Waller,' Firestone said. 'You could figure that out with what you know about him. Hardistan and the A.G. are the only other people who know his real name and they have no idea what his alias is or where he is.'

'You're the only one who knows?'

'No, now there's two of us.'

Vail considered that for a minute and said, 'Helluva responsibility.'

'Yep. Don't have to tell you never to mention this guy to anyone.'

'I figured that out all by myself,' Vail said with a smile.

'The kid's right in one respect. If we blow his cover by taking him into court, they'll get him.'

'Sounds pessimistic to me.'

'Realistic.'

'Hell, it would be his word against theirs,' Vail said, 'and they'd gang up on him and make him the liar. I'll say one thing, he sounded dead serious when he called the ambush an act of war.'

'If we're to believe they have not hurt anyone thus far, then it certainly marks a serious change in their tactics.'

'Maybe they were desperate to get that arms truck and they wanted to avoid a firefight.'

'It changes the whole ball game,' Firestone said.

'That it does. I forgot to ask him who the surviving member of the Denver bank job is.'

'Name's Luke Sundergard. He's doing life without parole at Leavenworth.'

'What's he have to say?'

'Nothing. His lips are stuck together with Gorilla Glue.'

'Well, if I take this job and I need Ralphie-boy, he'll be in court and you can bet your paycheck on that, I don't give a damn what kind of a deal the government made with him.'

Firestone smiled. 'We heard you were tough,' he said.

'That's what you heard, huh?'

'Yep.'

'If he doesn't cooperate, you'll find out how tough I am. I'll tell him I'll drop a dime on him so fast he won't have time to pack his underwear before they come through the window after him.'

'I don't believe you'd do that, Marty.'

'No, but before I'm through with him, *he'll* sure as hell think I will.' Vail reached inside his jacket, took out a small tape recorder, and pressed the rewind button.

'You tape-recorded him?' Firestone said with surprise.

'I taped them both.'

Firestone didn't say anything.

'I know what you're thinking. You're thinking the

tapes won't be admissible in court since I didn't get their permission first.'

'It crossed my mind.'

'I would never put them into evidence.'

'Just research, huh?'

'I may just find a federal judge who'll listen to them and get nervous enough to give us some wiretaps, surveillance warrants, search and seizures, and maybe a computer hack or two. Without them we don't have dick.'

'You're gonna do the RICO case, then?'

'I didn't say that. That's *if* I decide to do this thing.'

'You'd blow off the President?'

'Sam, I've been playing political football for thirteen years, ten as a prosecutor, three as A.G. of the state. I'm sick of dodging political sharpshooters and PAC-whore congressmen and judges with too many friends in the wrong places.'

'Today didn't change your mind?'

'This is the first time in my life I've been free. There's a lot to be said for being rid of all constraints. I've been toying with a book. I've got an offer from Chicago U. Law School. I don't need the aggravation that would go with a case that'll be sitting on the President's desk every morning.'

'You gonna tell him that?'

'I don't know what I'm going to tell him.'

'For what it's worth, Marge Castaigne is as straight a shooter as you'll find in government. You tell her your ground rules, and if she agrees, so will Pennington.'

'And what happens if the IRS decides to snoop into our case looking for some easy-score tax money, or the FBI decides to go full-tilt on one of the supportive cases?'

'That's between you and the A.G. They all work for her.'

'It would be a tough call for her. Hardistan comes to her and says they got an open-and-shut on the arms job.

The FBI looks like a hero. The A.G. looks like a hero. And the RICO case goes down river.'

'She's the boss,' Firestone said. 'She's the one that decides when a case goes to court. The IRS or the FeeBees go to her and try to harpoon your RICO, she could put their cases on the bottom of the pile until the year three thousand, and they know it.'

'Politics,' Vail growled.

'Except this time you'll be two chairs from the top man, and if Marge wants to play by your rules, you haven't got a worry.'

'What's in this for you anyway?'

'I'd like to be the one who delivers the warrants. I'd like to put the cuffs on Engstrom and Shrack and the rest of these bozos and bring them in.' He looked over at Vail. 'By the way, I hate politics as much as you do.'

'How long you been a marshal?'

'Twenty-one years this June. Before that I was Montana State Patrol for six, and before that I was three years in the Marines, one in Vietnam.'

'That's an impressive résumé.'

'I'm like you,' he said, 'I like the action. Keeps you young.'

'Where you from?'

'Born in northeast Idaho. I'm half Nez Perce Indian.'

'No kidding? Then you know the mountains out there.'

'Grew up in them. For the first ten years of my life I lived on the Flathead Indian Reservation just north of Missoula in the valley between the Bitterroots and the Anaconda Range. Right in the middle of the northern Rockies. When I was ten, my mom sent me to live with my grandparents in Seattle. They were white, so I was brought up in both cultures.'

'Which do you prefer?'

Firestone did not answer for a long time, and then finally he said, 'I like the honesty of the Nez Perce. They have a way of cutting to the bone. And their religion is pure, not like all that Christian nonsense.'

'I think you and I are going to get along.'

'I'll take you to meet my father someday,' he said. 'He'll prop your eyes open.'

'I'll bet he will,' Vail said.

A few miles away Woodbine was flying lazy-eight patterns up and down the interstate, hoping he would spot the elusive black Taurus on its way back up I-75. Nothing. He gave up and flew back to the county airport. The twin-engine Beechcraft was still on the field. He decided to stay aloft, not wanting to take a chance of being seen if he landed at the field. The weather over the airport had cleared slightly. The bad weather was moving to the east, so he climbed to fifteen hundred feet and cruised up and down the county road that led to the interstate, waiting for the car to return. He laid to the north about half a mile so Firestone would not get curious if he saw the plane. With a thousand-mile range, he was not worried about fuel. Ten minutes later he saw the car turn off the interstate interchange, go down the county road, and turn into the airport.

He checked his watch. An hour and thirty-three minutes.

That narrowed the field.

Woodbine could not land at the Lima county airport. They would be checking everything in and out of all the small airports, and car rentals in the entire area. He checked his sectional, measuring distances to local county airports, then made a radical decision. He would land in a county strip northeast of Fort Wayne. From the airport it was a straight shot south on an interstate access eight miles to the suburb of New Haven and the intersection with Route 30, and another fifty miles into Lima. He checked it out on his AAA maps. They had a car rental office at the airport. He called and reserved a car, then checked New Haven for motels and found one at the intersection of the interstate spur and 30. An hour's drive from the motel to Lima. Ten minutes from the motel to the airport.

It was perfect.

He checked into the hotel an hour later, a nice corner room on the second floor. He called room service and ordered a sirloin strip, rare, mashed potatoes, a salad, and a bottle of French pinot noir, although he had to settle for Chianti. He got a map, a pair of dividers, and a compass out of his briefcase. He knew they were gone for ninety-three minutes. He knew they had gone south. He set out three options, each based on the length of time Firestone and his passenger might have talked to Waller, if indeed it was Waller they had gone to see. He estimated their car speed at seventy, which gave him some base figures. He took his calculator and figured how far the car would have driven in the event of thirty-, forty-five-, and sixty-minute interviews. If the interview had lasted thirty minutes, they could have driven seventy or eighty miles south on the interstate. He took his compass and drew an arc on the map on the outside and inside limits. Then he drew lines down both sides of the interstate based on his figures. When he was finished, he had a pie-shaped search area stretching south of Lima and intersected with three lines.

If they had gone to see Waller, he was somewhere inside that arc.

He would start at seven in the morning, first doing an air search, then scanning the area by car if necessary.

Five days max, he said to himself. *If I can't find Waller in five days, he isn't there.*

He took out the digital video recorder and checked the six single shot close-ups he had taken of the unidentified passenger. The photographs were excellent. He plugged the camera into his laptop computer and captured the best of the six shots in a file. Then he copied it into a fax file and hooked his cell phone to the computer. He dialed a number, and when it answered, he faxed the photo on.

Two thousand miles away at the communications center of Fort Yahweh in western Montana, the fax came over the machine. The sergeant on duty tacked the photo of Martin Vail on the bulletin board. Under the photo, Woodbine had written:

'Anybody know this man?'

Fifteen

Jane Venable stood at the big picture window of the cabin and watched Magoo, like a ghost in the twilight, darting through the woods near the lake, stopping occasionally to sniff at a rabbit hole or root around a fallen tree. Behind him, Martin dodged through the bushes, stopping to scale a Frisbee toward the white dog, who watched its arc and gauged it perfectly, leaping into the air and grabbing it. The dog dropped the platter at its feet and stood with his tail straight down, his head hunched down as he watched his master approach. The German shepherd waited until Vail was beside him, then turned and looked out at the lake, where two men had been fishing for most of the afternoon.

'I see them, pal,' Vail said.

Satisfied, Magoo turned and raced off again. Vail picked up the Frisbee and strolled closer to the shore. He watched the men for a few minutes. Occasionally one of them would pick up a pair of binoculars and scan the large lake, concentrating on the shoreline.

Fishermen my ass, Vail thought.

Magoo barked and Vail tossed the Frisbee underhand out into the large lawn between the house and the lake. The white dog ran like a racehorse but couldn't catch up with it. It hit the snow-frozen ground and bounced toward the house. The dog looked back at Vail with disgust, ignored the toy, and trotted toward the house.

Jane went to the back door and opened it as Magoo approached. He jogged past her and went straight to his food dish. Vail followed him in. He pulled off his gloves and rubbed his hands together.

'Damn, it's cold out there,' he said.

'Doesn't seem to bother your buddy,' she answered, nodding toward the dog.

'Hell, the colder it is, the better he likes it. I think he's got a strain of husky in him.'

She moved closer to Vail as he took off his parka and kissed him gently on the cheek. 'You were gone awhile.'

'Walked all the way down to the dam.'

'Notice the fishermen?'

'Yeah. Magoo is concerned.'

'Pretty lousy day for fishing.'

'If they're fishermen, I'm an opera tenor. The one in the back has been studying the lake through binoculars all day.'

'I noticed. Who do you think they are?'

'Nazi spies,' Vail joked. 'They're gonna blow the dam and flood the valley.'

'God, what an imagination. That trip has gone to your head.'

'I don't know what to do,' he said. 'I've been pro-ing and conning on our walk.'

'And . . . ?'

'Big decision, Janie. We've got a great thing going here.'

'I'm going to have to go back to work one of these days, darling.'

'Is that a vote in favor of my taking the job?'

'God no, I'm not going to get involved in that decision.'

'It'll affect us both. You have a right to cast a vote.'

'How about Magoo, does he get a vote, too?'

'Sure.'

The white dog came into the big room licking his chops, and Vail said, 'What do you think, Magoo? Take it or leave it?'

The dog snorted, plopped down in front of the window, and dozed off.

'What a life,' Vail said, and to Jane, 'Hungry?'

'Uh-huh.'

'I'll grill a couple of steaks.'

'I made some apple turnovers.'

'That's what smells so good. Ain't you the domestic one.'

'That's me. Martha Stewart.'

He went into the kitchen, turned on the electric grill, and set it on high. He took two T-bones, four frozen ears of corn, and the makings of a salad out and put them on the cutting board.

'I'll do the salad,' she said, and started breaking up the lettuce and washing it in a colander.

Vail melted butter and mixed it with garlic while he waited for the grill to heat up. The night before, when he returned from his trip, he had described the day, being careful not to give up too much of his interview with Waller. But he had played the tape of his talk with Jordan at Coyote Flats and told her about Waller and the lynching and arms robbery. She sat silently while he talked and saw his mood grow darker as he spoke. But she also heard something else in his voice: an excitement she had not seen or felt in him since the RICO case. She had worried about him, watching him halfheartedly pick away at his book or talk about teaching, and she knew he did not have the taste for either. In her heart she knew this was the perfect job for Vail. But she also had a sense of danger she'd never felt before. Like an omen. These were dangerous people, and if Vail took the job, she knew it would put him in harm's way.

So she made the salad while he marinated the steaks in his special sauce and boiled the water for the corn and finally put the steaks on the grill. A nice family scene, cooking together, with Magoo sitting by patiently waiting for the bones, while in Vail's head danced visions of cunning killers, death and destruction in the wilds of their own West. And for a moment she had her own vision, a vision of car bombs and assassinations and broken bodies in the Middle East, which suddenly seemed no farther away than Oklahoma City.

She cuddled closer to him under the goose-down comforter, seeking the spot on his shoulder that was her pillow. He hadn't discussed the offer since they had started making dinner. Before dawn the chopper would come and whisk him away for a meeting with the President of the United States. Between now and then he would make his decision, and she knew in her heart what that decision would be. Part of her wanted him to accept the position because he was right for it and he would do the job brilliantly. Part of her feared what the future held for them both.

She didn't ask. Perhaps he didn't know yet. No, he knew. Vail was not a man who postponed decisions. But she didn't ask.

Instead she asked, 'What time are they coming?'

'Five-thirty.'

'Jesus, that's terrible.'

'Yeah, I know. I guess the President starts early.'

'Well, he has a lot to do. Are you going to wear a suit this time?'

'The dark brown one.'

'What tie?'

'I have no idea.'

'I'll pick it out for you.'

'I was counting on that.'

'How long will you be gone?'

'Hell, I don't know. If I decide against the job, they'll probably send me back on the train.'

'Probably in a boxcar.'

'Yeah, I'll have to ride the rails like a hobo.'

'Just my luck you'll bump into some hobo-cutie.'

He slid his hand down her back and around to the inside of her thigh. 'There are no cuties in boxcars.' He scratched her lightly with his fingernails.

'Hah. Remember . . . uh . . . *Sullivan's Travels*?

227

Veronica Lake?'

He moved his hand up, felt her soft blanket, and laid the flat of his hand against her, curling his fingers against the soft muscles between her legs.

'That would only happen in the movies,' he said.

He turned to her, licked the forefinger of his other hand, and stroked her lower lip with it. She caught her breath and ran her hand down his belly until she felt him rising to meet her hand.

'You sure know how to shut a girl up,' she whispered.

Sixteen

Marge Castaigne was nervous. She had not heard from Vail since he returned from the trip the day before. She did not know how to interpret his silence. Was he going to turn down the President? Accept the job? Or was he going to wait and see how the meeting went before making up his mind?

Vail was an enigma to her. She'd read and reread Jack Connerman's articles, written through the years, charting Vail's career. As a young man, he was a cunning, dangerously clever and arrogant defense attorney who challenged the law at every turn. He snacked on prosecutors, including his lover, Jane Venable, sent more than one of them – including Venable – scurrying into the private sector, and was the bane of judges.

As a prosecutor he became a fearful opponent to his former colleagues, knew their every trick, most of which he himself had invented, could get inside a defense attorney's head, predict where the case was headed, and ambush his adversaries at every turn. He had put together a fearsome group of young lawyers which the press had dubbed the 'Wild Bunch.' Vail instilled in them a love of legal battle. Connerman had once written, 'Vail and his Wild Bunch see the courtroom as a Roman Colosseum; an arena where cunning and knowledge are adrenalized; where they are challenged to attack the law, its canons, traditions, statutes, and structure, in order to coax, maneuver, and seduce juries to accept their perception of the truth.' His brilliant opening remarks to juries were a forecast of doom for defendants; his summations were terminal. He was the bane of felons and their lawyers. And judges. He had once told Connerman, 'I love the law. My job is to kick it in the ass to keep it strong.' And challenge it he did, pushing every case to the edge and occasionally beyond. In the fifteen years Connerman had been following Vail's career, the lawyer had been cited for contempt no less than twenty times and paid $175,000 in fines, and had once served ten days in the county poke.

But if Connerman's facts showed Vail to be a daring, flamboyant, cynical, arrogant, legal magician, disdainful of authority and courtroom manners, his prose painted a somewhat different profile: a portrait of a sage and charming rogue who was unflappable, unbuyable, and unbeatable, and who, when Connerman once had quoted Disraeli's belief that 'Truth is justice,' had replied, 'Truth is perception, justice is an illusion.'

He owed allegiance to no one, a fact painfully apparent to Roy Shaughnessey, the state's most powerful political hooligan, who had appointed Vail Chicago's D.A. and, when Vail got too close to some of Shaughnessey's darker dealings, had him elevated to Attorney General, where he immediately set out to successfully take down Lacey and Grossman, Shaughnessey's two largest political supporters and contributors. Vail's unappreciative attitude had finally prompted Shaughnessey to proclaim, 'The trouble with Vail, he don't know who his friends are,' to which Vail had replied, 'I know who my friends are, I'm more interested in knowing my enemies.' On another occasion, when Shaughnessey had called Vail an 'ungrateful son of a bitch,' Vail had responded, 'Somebody ought to ask Roy what he means by gratitude.'

Marge Castaigne, whose career arc was not unlike Vail's, was canny herself. She had selected the two men Vail had interviewed the day before, hoping that the zeal and passion of one and the venality of the other would convince him that the President's fears of the Sanctuary were not without foundation. She also knew she was taking a political risk in recommending to the President a man who had disdain for protocol and titles, who got things done his own way, who was neither a team player nor a sycophant, and who was cynical enough to see past the facade of those who were.

All the things Washington political hacks hated.

But she also was certain that Vail was the only lawyer alive who could bring the Sanctuary to its knees. So she sat nervously in the dormer window, tapping her foot as she watched for the limousine that would bring Vail to her door and deliver both to the White House. When it arrived, she wasted no time in taking her seat beside him in the rear of the limo.

'Morning, A.G.,' Vail said. He was dressed in a dark brown double-breasted suit with a dark green tightly patterned tie.

'Good morning,' she said, appraising him. 'Beautiful suit.'

'I'll tell Jane you said so, she buys all my clothes.'

'Excellent taste.'

'I know.'

'How was the trip?'

'Interesting.'

Noncommittal. She should have expected as much. She decided to try another tack.

'The protocol for the meeting is relatively formal,' she said. ' "Mr. President" and "sir" will do for the man. The rest of us refer to each other as "Secretary," "Director," or "Mister" or "Ms." whoever . . . whatever's appropriate.'

'Okay.'

'I'll run down the players for you. Harry Simmons. He's the media head of the FBI, Billy Hardistan actually runs the works. Simmons was brought in to clean up the mess in the lab and the screw-ups in Oklahoma City. He'll be gone once the Bureau's image is restored. Wayne Brodsky is director of the ATF. He's fighting for his life. Simmons wants the ATF to become part of the Bureau. The ATF got

231

a bum rap at Waco and Ruby Ridge, it was the FBI that invaded the compound and ended Weaver's standoff, but the ATF got blamed for the screw-ups. Next is Ed Randolph, director of the IRS. He's been under the gun for a couple of years. The IRS is a mess internally, as everyone knows. The President is on record to clean it up. A few weeks ago Pennington caught Randolph lobbying some of his congressional pals to keep the status quo, and put him on notice. Shut up or get lost. Finally there's Claude Hooker, National Security Adviser. He's a nasty one. Claude and I are cordial, and that's about as far as it goes. He's ex-CIA, ex-Marine, ex, ex, ex, and he doesn't like women in high places. Thinks the cabinet should be a boy's club, that's how his mind works. But these guys are all pretty effective when they're not jockeying for position.'

'How do they feel about the RICO case?'

'Doesn't make any difference. The President wants to do it. End of discussion. You'll like Larry Pennington. He's direct, he's charming, he's tough, and he makes quick decisions. And he keeps his word. He likes straight talk and hates attitude. Stick to the point and don't get too passionate about anything. He doesn't trust ardor.'

'I'll remember that.'

He fell silent again. She waited a moment or two and then: 'You *are* going to do it, aren't you?'

'I'll tell you when we get inside.'

'Don't toy with me, Martin,' she snapped.

He looked at her and said with a smile, 'I wouldn't dare.'

'God, you're going to be a handful,' she said, looking out the window.

'I've got some terms,' he said.

'Oh? Okay, shoot.'

'I bring in my own top staff. I have the full-time use of an AMOC.'

'Done.'

'And I get Jimmy Hines and Sam Firestone for the run of the show.'

'You dog! They're part of my personal staff.'

'Jimmy's hip to the whole movement, Marge. And Sam Firestone grew up in the territory. I like them both. Jimmy thinks electronics were invented for his personal use, and Sam doesn't talk much but he says a lot. Hell, they all work for you, A.G. You want me to have the best, don't you?'

'What else?'

'I'm in full charge. I report only to you. Hardistan reports to me and works under my authority. Any problem there?'

'Absolutely none. I've already talked to Billy about it. He knows more about hate groups and the militia movement than anybody alive, with the possible exception of Jimmy.'

'I don't want any official announcement about this. I'd like to keep it out of the press until I have my team together and I have an idea what I'm doing. The longer we keep the Sanctuary in the dark about what we're doing, the better.'

'That could be a little tougher. This is Washington. Inside information is what makes it tick.'

'You mean gossip.'

'Uh-huh.'

'I'm sure you'll do your best.'

'I'll mention it to the President.'

'That ought to work.'

They drove past the White House and Vail's pulse quickened. Behind the pillared white walls lived the most powerful human being in the world. There was no denying it was a heady experience, meeting with the President. He was fascinated by the protocol entering the White House. It was cordial and efficient. But he felt a sense of awe when he followed Castaigne into the Oval Office. He looked around the room, noting little touches he had seen on the news and in photographs. Simmons, Brodsky, and Randolph were already there. Castaigne introduced Vail around and they got coffee. A moment later Hooker entered. He fixed his eyes on Vail as he came in.

'The President will be along in a minute,' Hooker said. 'He's stuck in a photo op with the president of Argentina. Mr. Vail? I'm Claude Hooker, NSA.' He offered his hand. Then he cleared his throat and looked at the other men in the room.

'While we're waiting,' he said, 'I'd like to discuss this RICO thing for a minute.'

Vail could see Castaigne bristle. 'There's nothing to discuss,' she said edgily.

'RICO cases can take years,' Hooker said. 'By the time we get them into court, the whole country could be a battleground.'

'What are you driving at, Claude?' Marge asked.

'Some of us feel a RICO case is a bit exorbitant, no offense to you, Mr. Vail. We think just as much can be accomplished by the FBI building individual cases, the A.G. taking them into court, the IRS burning them for tax evasion. Then we dangle the bastards in front of the press like the Nazis at Nuremberg.'

'Or end up with another Randy Weaver or Waco?' Castaigne said.

Brodsky, Simmons, and Randolph shifted nervously in their seats. Vail did not say anything. He sat relaxed in his chair and watched the power play. It became obvious to him that the National Security Adviser had discussed the 'problem' with the others in the room and had lined up some muscle in his corner. Everything was beginning to go political, as he had feared it would.

Hooker glared at her across the table. 'That wasn't necessary,' he said.

'Neither is this discussion,' Castaigne said. 'Mr. Vail has agreed to head up a task force and to actively pursue RICO, and the Department of Justice is behind that option. That was the President's decision. Period.'

Hooker's eyes turned to stone. He sat an inch taller in his chair. His lips curled in a sneer. 'Well, aren't we feeling feisty this morning,' he said.

The door opened at that moment and Lawrence Pennington entered the room, ending the confrontation. Vail was surprised. He seemed larger in real life than in his pictures. Or perhaps, he thought, the whole situation was larger than life. They all stood up. Pennington was wearing a dark blue single-breasted suit and a red tie. He stood in the doorway for a moment whispering to his secretary, then proceeded into the room.

'Good morning, Madame A.G., gentlemen.' He nodded and walked straight to Vail. 'You must be Martin Vail,' he said. 'What a pleasure to have you here.' He had a granite handshake.

'My pleasure,' Vail said, and was surprised at how small his own voice sounded.

'Sorry I'm late,' Pennington said. He sat down and immediately turned to Vail. 'Well, Mr. Vail, have you had time to consider my offer?'

'Uh, Mr. Presi–' Hooker started, and Pennington held up his hand and shut him up. Pennington leaned toward Vail. 'Shall I call you Martin?'

'That'll be fine, Mr. President.'

'Good. So, what do you think of the A.G.'s idea?'

Vail could feel all eyes on him, particularly Hooker, who stared straight at him. Vail looked directly at the President.

'I think it's an excellent solution to the problem,' he said. Peripherally he saw Hooker's jaws tighten and his eyes look down at his hands, which were folded in his lap. Then Vail added, 'If we can pull it off.'

'You have doubts?'

'I'm pretty much satisfied that the threat is real and dangerous, but it's going to take some doing, sir.'

'Can you do it?'

Vail did not want to seem evasive. This was a military man, not interested in excuses or apologies.

'Yes sir. If it's there, we can do it, and I believe that it's there. There will have to be some conditions.'

Castaigne looked over at him and for a moment he saw panic in her eyes. *Conditions? This is the President, Marty!*

'Let's hear them.'

'Mr. President, the objective of a RICO case is to lasso three or more racketeers or groups together and prove they are guilty of or have profited from serious felonies. My feeling is, charge them with crimes *nobody* can sympathize with. The slaughter of U.S. soldiers in the Bitterroots, theft of government property from the Helena armory, murder, armed robbery, and money laundering. As the case progresses we can probably add conspiracy and corruption of public officials to the mix. We do that, get them into court and prove our case, and the country will wake up to the threat. We have to set some guidelines up front, sir.'

'And what are they?'

'One man runs the show.'

'And that man is you, right?'

'Yes sir.'

'That's why you're here,' Pennington said.

'Good.'

'I notice you left out the tax angle,' Randolph interceded. 'That certainly needs to be part of the case.'

Here we go, Vail thought. He was prepared for his first battle.

'Mr. Randolph, I'd have to disagree with you on that,' he said bluntly.

Randolph looked shocked. Castaigne took a sip of coffee. Pennington looked a bit bemused.

'Why so, Martin?' the President asked.

'Tax avoidance is a major part of the militia's agenda,' Randolph said pompously.

'Let the man finish, Mr. Randolph,' Pennington said.

'The thing about taxes is, why risk it? We're talking about less than ten thousand dollars in most of these cases. Taking a man's farm because he owes fifteen hundred dollars in taxes and four thousand in penalties and interest is an onerous proposition with a jury. I don't want to have to fight that kind of case in a courtroom. A *dumb* lawyer would kill us. And if we lost just one of the cases we set out to prove, the whole RICO goes out the window.'

'Tax evasion is part of it, sir, and the easiest to prove,' Randolph said.

'I agree it's easy to prove, Director Randolph, but it's hell to sell to a jury, and in the end the jury's perception is all that counts.'

'You're saying you won't prosecute tax cases?' Hooker asked.

Vail ignored Hooker and continued to speak directly to the President. 'Mr. President, you invited me on this trip to make a RICO case against the Sanctuary. I'm saying if taxes is in the mix, the case will likely be compromised from the outset.'

'You'd quit over that issue?' Pennington asked.

'If I bring in this case, Mr. President, I don't want to lose it over taxes. There'll be plenty left over for the IRS when we're finished.'

'You think income tax evasion is that precipitous?'

'No question in my mind, sir. It's the one part of their agenda that could evoke sympathy with the jury. Remember, we're going after an army that's posing as a church. That's going to be touchy enough without tossing in income taxes. I know people who hate the militia but think they're absolutely right about their tax stand.'

Pennington leaned back in his chair and made a steeple with his fingers. 'Go on,' he said.

'The more complicated we make a case, the more it works for the defendant. We keep it simple, direct, and as uncomplicated as possible. If we bring taxes into the case, we could be introducing an element of doubt. People won't put up with murder, robbery, or money laundering . . . but you try to tie a tax case to it, it's apples and oranges. You're throwing an obstacle at the jury, and all it takes is one juror to sink a case.'

'Okay,' Pennington said. 'What else?'

'Full cooperation from the Bureau and the ATF. And the IRS.' He looked at Randolph. 'You people have access to records that we can't get to legally without a lot of hassle, Mr. Director,' he said.

'Our records are confidential, sir,' Randolph said.

The President had heard all he wanted to about the IRS involvement.

'Oh, I'm sure you can work around that,' he said, putting Randolph back in his box.

'I'd like to keep my appointment under wraps as long as possible, Mr. President,' Vail said. 'Let's not put the Sanctuary on notice any sooner than we have to.'

'Good idea,' Pennington agreed.

'There's one other thing: we need a sympathetic judge.'

'Sympathetic to what?'

'Wiretaps, hard surveillance, access to records, bank transactions, computer hacks.'

'Hmm,' the President said. He thought for several minutes and then turned to Hooker. 'How about Lucy McIntyre? She's in the Eighth Circuit. She's tough but she's fair, and my guess is, she'll look favorably on the request.'

Hooker nodded. 'Want me to talk to her?'

'Yes, but not directly to this point. Come up with another excuse to call her and mention it in passing. Don't give her the idea we're leaning on her. Then Martin can set up an appointment and make his pitch to her.'

'Yes sir,' Hooker said, and scribbled down notes on a legal pad.

The President turned to Vail. 'Anything else?'

'No sir.'

'We have a deal, then?'

'We have a deal, Mr. President.'

Castaigne muffled a sigh of relief. Pennington was delighted.

'Excellent,' he said. 'Welcome aboard. How soon can you start?'

'Tomorrow soon enough?'

Pennington looked at his watch. 'Still a lot of hours left today,' he said, and smiled. 'Marge, you can do the honors. Swear Martin in and let's get started.'

He stood up and shook hands with Vail. 'Congratulations, A.G.,' he said.

'Thank you, sir.'

'Gentlemen, I don't think Martin is asking for anything more than full cooperation from everyone, and I'm certain he will get it. This is A-priority, top of the list, clear? If there's a problem in that respect, I'm sure the A.G. can work it out. If she can't, I will.'

Pennington started to leave and then turned at the door.

'One other thing, Martin. I'd like this case in front of a jury within eighteen months. Thanks, A.G. Gentlemen.'

And he was gone.

Vail looked at Castaigne with shock. 'Eighteen months!'

'Didn't I tell you that?' she said as she was leaving the Oval Office. 'Must've slipped my mind.' There was a twinkle in her eye.

Vail followed her out.

'Think you can find us a Bible, Millie?' she asked Mildred Ewing, the President's secretary.

'Oh, I think we can handle that,' the secretary said. She left the office.

Vail whispered: 'Eighteen months? Are you crazy?'

'You just heard the man, you have the full force of the government behind you. Anything you need.' She winked at him as Mildred Ewing returned with a worn, leather-bound volume.

The secretary handed it to Castaigne. 'It's the President's family Bible,' she said softly. 'I'm sure he won't mind.'

'Thanks,' Castaigne said. She held the Bible out and Vail put his right hand on it, and there, in the doorway of the Oval Office, Martin Vail was sworn in as Assistant Attorney General of the United States.

Seventeen

That morning as Vail and Castaigne were en route from her house to the meeting with the President, Don Woodbine was having breakfast at a crowded diner. He had driven into Lima, leaving his motel at six-thirty. By seven-thirty he was ordering breakfast. He was dressed casually and wearing clear-glass wire rims, not a man anyone would notice.

The night before, he had changed his battle plan. Woodbine was not a heavy drinker, limiting himself to two glasses of wine with dinner and an occasional beer. But he was exhausted from two days of flying and trying to trace the journey Firestone and his mysterious passenger had taken. He had three glasses of the Chianti and it fired up his imagination. Lying in bed, he considered the facts.

Fact: Firestone didn't fly the AMOC jet into Fort Wayne, switch to a smaller plane, fly to Lima, then rent a car to meet just anybody. Assumption: The subject was in deep freeze.

Fact: The mysterious passenger with Firestone must be important. Firestone wouldn't risk taking even a family member to see someone in witness protection. Assumption: The stranger was involved in some way with the government.

Fact: He had lost the black Taurus in the clouds for perhaps fifteen minutes. He had flown fifty miles down the interstate and never seen the car again until it returned. Assumption: Firestone had turned off the interstate, either east or west, during the fifteen minutes he had lost sight of the highway.

Fact: Waller had grown up on a horse farm and

worked the farm when he lived with the Posse. Assumption: The government had bought him a farmhouse. Not big, it would draw attention. A small place somewhat remote from neighboring farms.

Conclusion: Firestone had come to see somebody in deep freeze, and the conversation had probably lasted an hour, at least. There was a good chance the subject was Waller. Assuming they had an hour-long conversation, that left thirty-three minutes for the trip to the meeting and back to the Lima airport.

He got up and consulted his map. Figuring the distances, he determined that Waller lived in an area ten miles to the east or west of the interstate and within ten miles south of Lima. The largest town in the area was Wapakoneta. There were half a dozen smaller villages within the search area.

He would search the arc closest to the airport first.

He had decided to check out the area by car, looking for small out-of-the-way farms, marking them on the map, and making occasional spot checks from his car on stores in Wapakoneta, stores Waller was most likely to visit – pharmacies, hardware stores, grocery stores – on the chance he might spot him. Woodbine had gone to bed with that plan in mind.

But this morning at breakfast he was reading the local paper and suddenly his eyes were drawn to the real estate page, in particular to two ads, both of which claimed they specialized in farm properties. He sipped his coffee, read each of the small block ads, and then quickly paid his check and sought out the nearest pay phone. He called the first realtor.

'Good morning, Buckeye Realty,' a woman answered, her voice irritatingly cheerful.

'Good morning. This is Walt Dempsey of the *Farm Journal*. Who is this?'

'I'm Marjorie Wilson, Mr. Dempsey. What can we at Buckeye do for you this morning?'

'Marjorie . . . is it all right if I call you Marjorie?'

'Everybody calls me Margie.'

'Margie, the magazine is considering a cover story on farm values in the Indiana-Ohio region. We've selected the area between Lima and Wapakoneta as one of several target areas. I was wondering if you could give me a little information?'

'My my, isn't that exciting! What's a cover story?'

'That means it will be featured on the cover, probably with a photograph.'

'My goodness, we'll be famous.'

'I certainly hope so,' Woodbine said in his most unctuous tone. 'What I'm trying to find out is how many farms have been sold in that area in the last nine months, how big they are, possibly get the names of the new owners and interview them. You know, what they like about the area, why they came here, that sort of thing.'

'Well, say now, Mr. Dempsey–'

'Walter.'

'Walter . . . that's easy enough. First off, farm properties usually sell in the spring and summer, not much turnover this time of year. We've sold eight farms since last spring. Wiggins Realty, which is our competitor, moved only two. Let me get the book. . . .' He could hear pages rustling. 'Let's see . . .'

She ran off the list, and Woodbine took notes on each of the six. When she finished, he scratched off five as being too large or because the ownership profiles ruled them out. He marked his map as she described the location of the three that might be his target.

'I'd be glad to show you around. Introduce you to folks. I'm sure they'd be delighted to talk to you.'

'That's really kind of you, Margie. I'll get back to you on that in a couple of days, if that's convenient.'

'Oh, well, that'll be just fine,' she said, sounding disappointed. 'The *Farm Journal*, you say. I don't know as I've ever seen the *Farm Journal*.'

243

'Well, you just give me your address and I'll put you on our mailing list. And I'll drop the current issue by later in the week.'

'Well, that's real kind of you, Walter.'

He had the same response when he called Buckeye's competitor using the same spiel. This time the secretary identified herself as Geri Bloom. The first farm was a thousand acres, too large and right on the state highway. The second one was a different story.

'There's the old Wainright place south of Uniopolis,' Bloom told him. 'Small place, about a hundred and twenty acres, kind of crowded in between two larger farms. We closed on May eighteenth.'

'Who owns it?'

'Ralph Anderson. Nice young man. Newlywed, you know. I don't have a phone listing for him.'

'Really. How do I find his place?'

'It isn't all that difficult. According to my sheet, it's 2.2 miles south of Uniopolis off Geyer Road 'bout half a mile. There'll be mailboxes along the highway.'

'Excellent,' Woodbine said, and put a star beside Anderson's name.

As Vail and Castaigne were exiting the elevator on the first floor of the west wing, Hardistan entered the White House.

'Ah, there's Billy. Time for you two to meet,' she said. 'By the way, among his many talents, Billy can chop through red tape faster than a boll weevil can chew up a cotton patch. In this town that's a very rare talent.'

'It's a rare talent anywhere.'

Hardistan was a husky man a little over six feet tall who looked more like a Texan than a Virginian. He had hard features, and brown eyes that seemed to be constantly on the move, checking out everything around him. There was also a resolute set to his jaw. He looked like a man who listened but rarely changed his mind.

Castaigne greeted him warmly and introduced him to Vail.

'We're in business,' she said. 'Meet your new boss.'

Hardistan nodded. 'We're gonna be busy,' he said in a quiet voice with just a trace of Virginia in it.

'Looks like,' Vail replied.

'How long you in town for?'

'I'm going back this afternoon. I need to see how my old crew feels about this job.'

'Have time for lunch?' Hardistan asked.

'Sure, my pleasure.'

'We have to go over to my office and fill out the usual forms to put Martin on the payroll,' Castaigne said. 'Why don't you pick him up when you're through here.'

'Fine. I have to fill in the man on Lost Trail.'

'Do we have anything?' Vail asked.

'Shell casings, rounds, an ear-ball witness, and some other people who think they heard something. Powder tracks from the C-4 they used to blow up both ends of the dogleg. And the numbers scratched on the back of the Humvee. They lucked out with the snow storm, but they were pros. It was clocked all the way. Six minutes and they were gone. We've got men crawling all over the mountains, but at this point I'm pessimistic about the outcome.'

'How about the semi?' Castaigne asked.

'Gone. And I don't think we'll ever see it again.'

Woodbine guided the plane south down Route 501. Ralph Anderson had real possibilities, he'd decided. The farmhouse had been purchased near the time that Waller had blown the whistle on the Denver bank robbery. It was small and isolated and Anderson did not have a telephone. He decided to scope the place out from the air.

Woodbine's heart was racing. This was the part he liked best. The hunt. Finding the perfect blind for the shot. Mapping the perfect exit.

The farmhouse was easy to spot. It sat alone a mile or so off the highway, an island in the middle of a sprawling farm. The house sat at one end of a small cultivated field. Three dirt roads crisscrossed the large farm, one of which obviously formed the northern perimeter of the Anderson farm. The house itself lay between two state roads that converged a mile or so north of Wapakoneta. He cut back on the throttle and banked down and around the small house, circling it at about seven hundred feet. He had the video camera out and zoomed to its maximum. As he leveled off he saw a man working on a tractor in the middle of a field. He started the video camera and flew past the house, swung around in a circle, and aimed the camera down at the man on the tractor. The man appeared to be stuck. Woodbine gunned the engine once and the man looked up, shielding his eyes against the sun. Woodbine wobbled his wings 'hello' and the man waved back. Woodbine pushed the throttle forward and climbed back up to fifteen hundred feet. He circled around once more, shooting the entire area before heading west.

An hour later he was relaxing in his motel room. It was four-thirty. It would be dark in another ninety minutes. He switched to a black fleece jogging outfit and hunting boots. Then he hooked his video camera up to the laptop and ran the footage. The house was situated about a mile from Route 198 to the west and 501 to the east. Two dirt roads crossed about a mile northeast of the house. He zoomed in on the intersection. Thirty or forty yards west of the crossroads there was a large oak tree sitting on a small bluff. He zoomed back and checked the sight line to the house. It looked clear. The closest house was about two miles away.

Next he traced his getaway route. He decided to drive due east on the dirt road to 501, north to 81, west to 116, south to 117, and then due west to U.S. 127, avoiding two small villages. He carefully measured the distance. If he held his speed to seventy, he could be on 127 in thirty to forty minutes. Another ten to Van Wert, and thirty miles back to the interstate access, then ten minutes to the airport. An hour and a half at the most and he would be airborne. He had made arrangements to leave the car keys in a night box at the county airport, and his motel room was paid through the next day.

Next he zoomed in on the target. He froze on the man on the tractor and zoomed down on him, digitalizing the shot for clarity as he did. The face became clearer as he zoomed in on it. Then he leaned back and smiled.

'Hello, Georgie.' He chuckled softly. 'Are you right with God?'

'Do you like Chinese?' Hardistan asked as Vail settled in the seat beside him.

'Sure.'

'I'll spring for lunch. I'm on the tab.'

'And I'm not?'

'Mr. Vail, right now you can have just about anything you want.'

'Good, start by calling me Martin or Marty.'

'Fine. I'm Billy. I told your driver he could go, I can run you out to the plane after lunch. You're about to have the best Chinese food you've ever eaten. The place isn't big on decor, but the food will stay in your memory for a long time.'

They drove out K Street to a section a few blocks from the White House. An ancient two-story, nondescript brick building was the lone holdout in the area. It occupied a square block dwarfed on all sides by towering, sterile glass towers. The street level of the small building boasted a Chinese grocery store, an antique shop, an herb market, a flower shop, and a pharmacy, but no restaurant.

'Is this block on the skids or going through rehab?' Vail asked.

'It's a holdout. There used to be a little pocket of Chinese culture hereabouts. The developers have gradually forced them out.'

Hardistan got his briefcase and led Vail through a narrow doorway and up a groaning staircase to a large room in a front corner of the building. Two dozen tables were arranged haphazardly in the main room and there were half a dozen booths lining the side of the dining room. The walls were painted a pastel blue. There were no paintings or tapestries, no dragons or fish tanks. Red tablecloths provided the only color to its otherwise stark interior. The odor was tart and strongly tinged with garlic. And most of the dozen or so customers were Oriental.

Near the head of the stairs was an ancient desk with only an abacus, a receipt tablet, and a pen on it. No phone. An elderly, white-haired Chinese gentleman in a dark blue suit and a red bow tie sat behind the desk reading a Chinese-language newspaper. He looked up and smiled.

'My friend Hardistan, how good to see you,' he said in elegant English as he led them through the room to a booth in a secluded corner of the room. 'I have missed you.'

'Missed you, too. Been busy, Mr. Keye.'

'I assumed. I read the newspapers.'

'This is Mr. Vail. After today, I'm sure he'll be a regular, too.'

'*Joy geen*. I would certainly hope so. Are the gentlemen drinking?'

'I'll have the usual.'

'Oolong for Mr. Hardistan. And Mr. Vail?'

'Beer, please.'

'May I suggest Yellow Dragon, Mr. Vail. It's Chinese beer. I highly recommend it.'

'Sounds delicious,' Vail said with a smile.

'I'll send the waiter over with some starters and menus. His name is Sam.'

'Thanks.'

The old gentleman walked away, his back as straight as a ramrod. Vail felt vaguely uncomfortable. Was the lunch to size him up, tell him the facts of life, pick his brains? Hardistan did not strike him as a get-acquainted kind of guy.

Vail looked around the place, marveling at its austerity.

'Don't worry, the booth isn't bugged,' Hardistan said.

'The thought never occurred to me. Should it have?'

'Not really, we're on the same side, remember? I thought we could enjoy lunch and a little privacy while I brief you. You won't find too many bureaucrats or politicians here.'

So that was it, he was to be 'briefed.'

The waiter brought a platter of fried shrimp and chicken with their drinks. The menu had a large variety of Cantonese dishes. Across the top was printed CHINESE RESTAURANT.

'That's the name?' Vail said. 'Chinese Restaurant?'

'I don't think Mr. Keye could think of anything appropriate so he opted for the obvious.'

They ordered lunch and noshed on the fried shrimp and chicken starters.

'How did you find this place?' Vail asked.

'When I was fairly new with the Bureau I was assigned to the Washington office. At the time this was a nice Chinese neighborhood, probably four or five blocks square. Little Chinatown. There was a homicide right down the street. A jeweler was killed, gunned down in his shop, but nothing was stolen. Most of the Orientals either couldn't or wouldn't speak English and the cops were getting stonewalled. We got called in because there was evidence that the killers may have come from San Francisco. Keye was an assistant chef at a restaurant called the Shanghai Gardens, just around the corner. He could barely speak English. He was also an illegal. No passport, no visa, nothing. But he came to us and told us the whole story. A tong on the West Coast had decided to move into this area. The murder was a warning. The locals were too scared to say anything. Keye realized the only way to put a stop to it was to tell us what he knew, even though it meant deportation to Taiwan. We cleaned up the West Coast gang and I prevailed on the Taiwan embassy and the Immigration Department and we got Keye a passport and a green card. He immediately learned English – superbly, as you can tell. When he became a citizen, I was his sponsor. And when he started the restaurant, I was his first investor. I own ten percent of the place. Not enough to retire on, but it pays for the groceries.'

'That's a nice story.'

'Well, we're not always bad guys,' he said. 'I eat here two or three times a week when I'm in town.'

'You're not married?'

'My wife died four years ago. I have a son thirty-one, a lovely daughter-in-law, and two granddaughters. Tony just got his seat on the New York Exchange. Thank God he didn't follow in my footsteps.'

'I don't suppose I have to tell you anything about my personal life.'

'Well, we never did establish whether you prefer baths or showers.'

'I'm a shower man.'

'I figured as much.'

'I could be a little paranoid, you know. The feds were really pissed off because I took that case away from Riker. How did you feel about that?'

'We spent a lot of time on that case.'

'So did we.'

Hardistan held up his hands. 'No argument. You did a helluva job. With a fairly limited staff, I might add.'

'Great lawyers,' Vail said, and after a moment added, 'I think they're all frustrated cops. Very intuitive.'

'Anyway, the Grand County RICO case is history. I'm glad you're on our side this time.'

'I may not fit into the bureaucratic mold.'

'I don't think it's quite sunk in yet, Martin. You are a special prosecutor and an attorney general of the United States. You've got awesome power. The power of the USA is at your disposal, compliments of the President. You're also my boss. My job is to back you up all the way on this, cut through the red tape, assist in gathering legal evidence, and make damn sure when you go into court there aren't any smoking guns to surprise you. It's your show. You need anything, you have the full force of the Bureau behind you. I'm here to make a nasty job as easy as possible.'

'How about the ATF and the IRS? I just smoked Randolph. I'm sure he doesn't like me.'

'It's immaterial whether he likes you or not. Unless you're interested in some kind of popularity contest.'

'Not hardly.'

'We need the ATF, we got 'em. We need the IRS, we got 'em. Randolph is a scared little loser. He was brought in to help Pennington develop a program to clean up the Service. It's rotten to the core, as everyone knows. Bunch of incompetent pencil-pushing sociopaths who get their jollies hassling innocent taxpayers. The man wants to abolish it, make the auditors tow the line. No more fishing expeditions in the guise of audits. They find something, they stipulate it, and that's all they can talk about in an audit. Any shenanigans will be turned over to the Department of Justice. The DOJ will have all the police powers. The IRS won't even have subpoena powers. Pennington made that clear when he appointed Randolph. So what does Randolph do? He runs to some of his pals on the Hill, promises them they'll never see an audit as long as they live if they'll scratch the President's plan. Pennington found out and keel-hauled him. He's through. Just a matter of time. So is the IRS.'

'I pissed Hooker off, too.'

'Well, Hooker fashions himself Iago to Pennington's Othello. The man knows it. He thinks for himself. He listens to Hooker and throws away about ninety percent of what he says. He's a high profile errand boy, that's all. As far as national security goes, he's very good. He's bloodless. Does that job. Write him off. There's nothing he can do for you that others can't do better.'

'You've been around a long time.'

'Twenty-five years.'

'How do you evade the bloodbaths when the guard changes?'

Hardistan smiled. 'I keep out of their way,' he said.

He gave Vail his official card. On the back he had written the private numbers of his home, his cellular phone, his beeper, and his car phone.

'Call me anytime,' he said. 'I'm a light sleeper.'

Nice speech, pal. If you want me to trust you, it's going to take more than talk.

'I've got a question,' Vail said. 'How come the Sanctuary got so important so quick without the FBI being on top of it?'

'Fair question. They're very slick. They learned from the mistakes the Klan and the Posse and the rest of the assholes made. They kept a low, low profile. Took their time. Moved very quietly. Their paramilitary units were and still are disguised as churches. They didn't cause any trouble, didn't go on the Internet with their message, didn't cavort with the other paramilitaries. They *just got good*. And they had themselves a genuine war hero to head up their outfit. Engstrom loves it. He's got his own private army.'

'So what makes you so sure they're involved in RICO?'

'You talked to two of them.'

'Nothing that will stand up in court.'

'You remember the shootout with Roy Marsden out in Oregon about two years ago?'

'He was the radical guy, robbed a couple of banks?'

'Right.'

'He and three or four of his people were killed, weren't they? Along with a couple of law officers.'

Hardistan nodded. 'Four. A sheriff, two state troopers, and one of my best agents. We recovered several weapons from the house. Marsden was using an M-16. The serial numbers had been removed with acid but our lab was able to reconstruct the number. The gun was traced to the manifest of weapons stolen from the Helena, Montana, National Guard armory two years ago. Then eight months ago George Waller turns himself in. He hasn't told us a lot, but during one of his debriefings he told us Marsden bought three M-16s from the Sanctuary. That's when they made our A list.'

'Maybe the Sanctuary bought them from the real thieves.'

'In that case they're brokering stolen weapons to other paramilitaries and they conspired in two murders.'

'So why didn't you take them down?'

'With what? Waller hears they sold the guns, blah blah blah. The same as the armory job in Helena. It's his word against everybody else in the heist. Would you proceed with that kind of evidence?'

'Nope.'

'There's your answer.'

'Have you been able to infiltrate this bunch?' Vail asked.

'We've tried. They're paranoid and very smart. Most have had military training of some kind, several in intelligence. Mainly we have people in the area working legitimate jobs and keeping their ears open. Except for Waller, we haven't been able to turn any of them. And we didn't turn him, he jumped in our lap.'

'I wasn't real impressed with little Ralphie. I think he got in trouble and found a home in the witness protection program. I don't think he's really changed. He's still a nasty little bigot and a thug at heart despite all that Bible thumping.'

'That's a keen analysis considering you only talked to him for an hour or so.'

'I've been at this game almost as long as you have, Billy. I don't have to hear nigger, kike, and spic more than once to peg a racist pig.'

'You got a man inside the club in Grand County, didn't you?'

'I have a young fellow who went into Grand County for six months before we started moving against them. He listened to the grumbling and the rumors. Instinctively he knew what was the McCoy and what was bullshit.'

'That would be Flaherty.'

'That would be Flaherty. Tough kid from Boston. Very streetwise, very instinctive.'

Hardistan nodded. 'One of the few prosecutors we ever permitted to go through the Academy. He was so good we tried to steal him from you.'

'I know, he told me.'

'I hope you don't hold that against me,' Hardistan said, trying a smile.

'On the contrary, shows you know your business.'

They both laughed.

'Anyway, Derm got a job in one of the mills, went to the commission meetings, read the newspapers, kept a log of all the lies they told, either outright or by omission. Made friends, kept his ears open. Pretty much put the case together. He had the whole link analysis in his head by the time we started building the case. He was the one who pegged Kramer as the weakest link in the chain. He was correct all the way across the board. And he loved every minute of it. The Serpico in him sneaked out.'

'How did Ms. Parver feel about his undercover work?'

'You subtly telling me how good your security people are?'

Hardistan said, 'It's something we're fairly effective at.'

'So I've heard. Parver and Flaherty have been living together for a year or so. Almost as long as Jane Venable and I've been together.'

'You considering sending Flaherty in on this job?'

'I can't. The Grand case was all over Court TV, World News, somebody would make him. In the Grand case, there was always the possibility someone might tumble to him and some trigger-happy local goon might put a bullet in his back, but out there . . .' Vail shook his head. 'We'd probably find him hanging from a tree somewhere with a note pinned to his chest.'

'They're more subtle than that. You wouldn't find him at all. But you're right, this is a deadly situation.'

'Uh-huh.'

'Grand County was about greed and power. A bunch of dirty old men who were really amateurs at the game. This is about fanaticism. The moral issues here are clear and concise. The hit on the arms convoy is a very clear statement. It changes the ball game. The body bag thing, that really got to the old man. He went totally ballistic over that.'

'Waller suggested it was an act of war. If that's what it is, moral issues become immaterial.'

'If they're at war, let them make the declaration.'

'I think they already have. In their heads, I mean. Making it formal is a tough call.'

'It just means they aren't ready yet,' Hardistan said.

'You've got all this figured out already, haven't you?'

'Some of it is logic. They have four units plus the headquarters command. That's roughly six thousand men and women ready to move out into the population and go undercover.'

'When I talked to Jordan at the Grave, he bragged about it.'

'Jordan likes to brag. We get more out of his bragging

255

than from Waller's confessions.'

'He says when it comes, it'll be guerrilla warfare. Hit and runs. Domestic terrorism.'

'Lost Trail Pass.'

'Uh-huh.'

'You think Lost Trail was a test run?'

'Hey, that's your call. I'm a neophyte, remember.'

'Not anymore. You got eighteen months to top your performance in Grand County.'

Vail was visibly shaken by the comment. 'News travels fast,' he said.

'I debriefed the President on the Lost Trail ambush. He told me you agreed to do the RICO and he also said the information stops with me. Hell, I'm working for you now,' he went on, 'weren't you going to tell me?'

'I just want a little lead time before the news gets out.'

'You've got that.'

'Getting back to the ambush, I think laying the bodies out was a military statement. They were honoring the men who were killed.'

'Well, it may have seemed like an honorable thing to them. Far as I'm concerned, it was barbaric. They've been reading too many comic books.'

'It shows a very dedicated mind-set.'

'I don't care what it shows, we're going to take them down.'

Vail smiled. 'Well, that's what I'm here for.'

Hardistan put his leather briefcase on the table and snapped it open. Inside were several videotapes, some booklets, and a small leather wallet about five inches square and a half-inch thick. He took it out and zipped it open. Inside were twenty plastic pockets. Each held a CD ROM.

'This is a lot of information. The CDs contain everything we know about this group, its ties to other paramilitary groups, some confidential reports, photographs and background on the key people, even some speculation. I had my staff put it together for you. The videos are mostly surveillance tapes. There are some government booklets, some hate literature we've gathered through the years from the Klan, the Posse Comitatus, so forth. Enough to give you an idea of what this movement is really all about.' He took out a small paperback book. 'This is a copy of *The Turner Diaries*. It's their textbook. The writing is terrible but the message is scary. An instruction book on urban guerrillas. The nice thing about the stuff on the CDs is it's indexed. The briefcase is yours. My treat.'

Vail moved things about in the case and studied the items, then picked up the leather wallet, turned it over, flipped through the sleeves.

'Lotta homework.'

'Look, you've got a year and a half to make a RICO case. That's impossible.' Hardistan pointed to the briefcase. 'But that's about two years' worth of hard work, so you're that far ahead of the game. It'll cut the odds a little.'

'Thanks,' Vail said, and laughed. 'I hope it doesn't take me that long to absorb it.'

'I don't want to sound presumptuous. I know one of your strong points is delegation, so this is probably unnecessary advice but I'll suggest it anyway. Divide up the material among your top people. Let each one become an expert in a phase of the investigation. And you've got me and Jim Hines for backup.'

'Of course. But the boss still has to know it all.' He put the wallet back in the case and started to close it.

'There's one more thing,' Hardistan said. He reached into one of the file pockets on the inside of the top of the case and took out a folder. 'This report is classified "Secret."'

'More surprises?'

'We jumped onto their computer for about three hours a while back.'

'You illegally hacked their computer network?'

Hardistan looked across the table at Vail for a moment. 'It was research. We just wanted to get a leg up on their operation. The only thing we got of interest was a reference to "Specter."'

'The Phantom Project?'

'Jimmy filled you in on that, huh?'

Vail nodded.

'Fully trained in every dirty trick known to man. Assassination, explosives, torture, the works. They were masters at the trade and extremely effective. There were a handful of them used in 'Nam and Nicaragua and later in the Mideast, all Engstrom's people. They were given assignments and cut loose. When they completed their mission, they'd come back in and get another folder. These guys were predatory in their efficiency. After Desert Storm they were considered too hot to handle and their mission was terminated. The military tried to rehabilitate them, but four of them left the program. One went to work for French intelligence and was killed in Algeria. Another one was an intelligence specialist in Desert Storm, also terminated. The other two are still out there somewhere, freelancing.'

'Hines says the file on them is sealed.'

'No, it's gone. No records whatsoever. Everything we know about them we got from interviewing people in military intelligence, ex-C.O.'s, and one or two guys who worked with them.'

'Any pictures?' Vail asked, leafing through the sheets.

'Just that one.'

'I've seen this. Hines showed it to me on the plane.'

'It's a Polaroid. A guy in one of the base camps snapped it.'

Vail pointed to the medium-size man with the hair and special rifle. 'I think this guy went by the name Oz.'

'Like in Wizard of?'

'That's what it sounded like. He was obviously a

specialist of some kind. Jordan says he once took out a Vietnamese general from two thousand yards, and I think that's the gun he used. But Jordan said he's dead. We know Jordan, Shrack, and Metzinger are Specters. I've got it on my tape.'

'You taped the interviews?' Hardistan said, his eyebrows arching.

After a moment Vail said, 'Only for reference.'

They both laughed.

'We think one of the other two who are still alive, maybe both, are working for the Sanctuary,' Hardistan said. 'That file contains all the information we have on them. Needless to say, it could be explosive in the wrong hands.'

'Like the media?'

'Or some members of Congress.'

'You know a judge named McIntyre?'

'Lucy McIntyre, Eighth Circuit. She's good people.'

'The President thinks we may be able to get the warrants and approvals for surveillance work from her. I was thinking of editing the tapes down, putting some salient points together to convince her. Maybe you'd like to come along.'

'You're the boss. I'll tell you up front, she's tough.'

'We need access to these guys, Billy. I'll throw the fear of God into Waller. Tell him I'll drop a dime on him if he doesn't testify for us. I'm sure he'll at least say he let me tape our conversation.'

'That might work,' Hardistan said. 'But I know the lady, she'll probably want to talk to Waller face-to-face.'

'How about a videotape? We could go down there and videotape him. Right now, he's the only card we can play.'

'It's certainly worth a shot,' Hardistan said. 'If she insists on a personal interview with him, we'll have to sneak him out for a meeting. That's risky business.'

'The whole thing's risky business,' Vail answered.

Hardistan slipped the file back in the pocket and closed the case. Vail ran the flat of his hand across the smooth leather top.

'You have good taste, Billy.'

'Thanks. Mind if I ask you a personal question?'

'Try me.'

'Why are you doing this? I mean, this is a shitty job. It's got failure written all over it.'

Vail thought for a minute and shrugged. 'I don't have anything better to do at the moment.'

Hardistan was jerked up by the remark. He looked at Vail, trying to decide whether the lawyer was joking or serious.

Vail took out his wallet and leafed through it, removed a worn business card, and slid it across the table. 'I used to pass these out when I was a defense advocate and later when I was D.A.'

His name was in the lower right-hand corner. In the center were his favorite two words.

NO COMMENT.

At dusk Woodbine left the airport outside Fort Wayne and drove the circuitous route to the dirt road north of Ralph Anderson's farmhouse, timing himself. It took forty-eight minutes. It was dark when he turned down the road, which was still caked with ice patches and rock hard. When he reached the intersection of the two dirt roads, he pulled off the road, turned around, and backed under some trees. He took the aluminum case from the trunk, assembled the .50 caliber rifle, then snapped the sight in place. He got out the pair of night binoculars and crept up the bluff to the tall oak tree and zeroed in on the farmhouse. He jockeyed his position a bit until he had a clear sight line to the farmhouse, then checked the area around the house: a small barn, a pickup truck parked beside it, what looked like a small shed of some kind. He moved the binoculars back to the kitchen.

A thousand yards. Piece of cake if he could get a clean shot.

He knelt down, augered a unipod into the hard earth, and set the rifle in its cradle. His heart was pumping hard but his hands were steady. He scanned the house through the scope, sweeping it slowly past the kitchen windows and back door, checking the small porch and the corner windows, where he picked up a television set. He assumed it was a recreation room of some kind. He moved the sight back to the kitchen and could make out the woman, obviously cleaning up after dinner.

But where was Waller/Anderson?

Woodbine wasn't in any hurry. He was dressed for the cold, and no matter how long he had to wait, he knew the escape route and how long it would take once the job was done. The time was relative.

He waited, sweeping the rifle back and forth between the windows of the house, waiting to catch a glimpse of his prey. He kept scanning the house, and then, as he was watching the window of the den, he saw the television station change.

Waller was in the room, watching television.

Woodbine had to lure him outside.

He turned to his binoculars, which gave him a broader view of the site. The tractor was still sitting in the field, its back wheels mired in a mud hole.

Woodbine sat back on his haunches and considered the problem.

The sequence was fixed in his mind. Take out Waller. Blow the tires on the pickup. This would leave his wife with no phone and no transportation. Unless someone happened to visit the Andersons, she would be trapped a mile from the state road. It could be an hour or two before she summoned help.

His other choice was to kill them both.

He waited, concentrating on the den window.

Inside the farmhouse, George Waller a.k.a. Ralph

Anderson walked into the kitchen.

'Want to take out the garbage?' Marie asked.

'Okay,' Ralph said. 'I'm gonna crank up the tractor for a few minutes and put a tarp over it. I'm worried it might freeze up on me.'

'Has plenty of antifreeze, doesn't it?'

'Yeah. Just makes me nervous. I got some wire fencing to put under the back wheels, get some traction. Maybe I'll give it another try. I'd feel a lot better if I could get it outta that damn hole and put it in the barn.'

'Watch your language, Mr. Anderson,' she admonished.

He put on his parka, took the garbage bag and a heavy canvas tarp, went outside, and dropped the bag in a large can. He picked up the roll of fencing, stuffed it under his arm, and trudged out to the tractor.

Over half a mile away Woodbine saw him leave the house and head out toward the tractor. Waller was walking straight toward him. He set the stock of the rifle firmly into his shoulder and laid his cheek against it. Waller was a silhouette, framed against the lights from inside the farmhouse. Woodbine followed him through the scope, watched as he leaned down and rolled out what looked like wire under the rear wheels of the tractor. Then Waller climbed up on the seat of the tractor and cranked it up. Woodbine saw a swirl of exhaust belch from the rear of the machine. Waller stood at the controls and, looking toward the back of the tractor, started working the controls.

Woodbine decided on a head shot. If he went for the body mass, even a dead-on shot could be iffy in the dark.

Then Waller turned on the lights of the tractor.

He was a clearly outlined target now.

Woodbine aimed at the center of his head, but the tractor suddenly jumped and wobbled out of the hole. He was about to become a moving target. As the tractor jumped onto firm ground, Waller stopped it for a moment and looked over the rear end.

Woodbine clenched his fist, felt the trigger tighten, heard the muffled report.

Pumph.

Felt the .50 caliber kick his shoulder.

Saw Waller's head snap back, watched as he fell against the control panel and then slid down, half in, half out of the rolling tractor. He charged another round into the chamber, leveled the rifle at Waller's body, and fired a second shot, saw it rip into the parka.

Inside the house, Marie heard the tractor start up and, looking through the kitchen window, saw it lurch out of the hole. Then suddenly Ralph's head seemed to jerk back and he fell over sideways. The tractor kept rolling toward the house.

She ran outside, saw Ralph hanging over the side of the tractor as it rumbled toward the house.

'No!' she screamed, and ran toward the tractor.

Behind her, she heard an explosion and turned to see the front tire of the pickup truck burst.

My God! Oh my God! What's happening?

She was frozen with fear, watching as the tractor rolled on with nothing to stop it. Then she turned and ran toward the farmhouse. It kept coming, struck the rear porch, ripped through it, and smashed into the kitchen wall. The wall crumbled and the tractor slammed into the kitchen sink. The water pipes burst as it ground to a stop. Water showered from the broken pipes.

Marie Anderson rushed to the doorway and stared inside, saw her husband lying over the side of the tractor, water pouring down over his body, cleansing the blood that rushed from the hole over his right eye.

She started screaming uncontrollably. But there was no one to hear her.

BOOK THREE
CHAOS

*Men never do evil so completely and cheerfully
as when they do it from religious conviction.*
— Pascal

Eighteen

At the penthouse apartment shared by Jane and Martin, the Wild Bunch was gathering for a staff meeting that Vail had requested earlier in the day. Jane had called their favorite restaurant, Avanti!, mastered by Guido Signatelli, who hosted the political kingmakers, lawyers, and media near the city hall in a bistro with the tackiest decor and the finest Italian food in the Midwest. Guido had acquitted himself with élan, heaping a feast upon the dining room table. The apartment had been Jane's before the two had decided to live together. It was spectacular, a two-story suite of rooms with a living room that soared to a spire on the top of one of the newest skyscrapers in the city. The living and dining rooms were faced with glass, affording both floors with a breathtaking panorama of the lake's waterfront.

One of the three bedrooms had been allotted to Vail for an office. It was a replica of previous Vail offices, dominated by a large, cluttered oak table that served as his desk. Built-in bookcases were jammed with volumes of every description from classics to law books, usually with dog-eared bits of paper stuck between the pages marking long forgotten passages. On a small table facing the window was Vail's old Smith-Corona electric typewriter. He eschewed computers, relying on his legendary secretary, Naomi Chance, to handle the electronics. Only Vail could find anything in the office, and he could put his hand immediately on even the most arcane notes, transcripts, and briefs from his twenty-some years of courtroom battles. Naomi had stayed with him after he stepped down as Attorney General of the state. The rest of his staff were still at loose ends, trying to decide what

267

to do without the adrenaline assignments Vail picked for them. Defending drug dealers, rapists, and armed robbers or working in staid law firms defending equally felonious big business clients was no longer their style. They responded eagerly when he called them.

Those who were there were what was left of the brilliant group Connerman had dubbed the Wild Bunch.

'Young, in their early to mid-thirties, they were aggressive, cunning, adroit, and resourceful, and although extremely competitive, they were bonded by mutual respect, talent, and a strong appreciation for teamwork,' he had written. 'Through the four or five years they had been together, each had become a specialist in certain areas and, like Vail, had become expert at walking the tightrope between statutory compliance and forbidden procedures, and they were not above taking risks if the payoff was high enough. They all loved the courtroom. As it was for Vail, for them the law was both a religion and a contest, and the courtroom was their Roman Colosseum, the arena where all their resourcefulness and cunning were adrenalized in the most intriguing of all blood sports.'

Naomi Chance was the den mother. She was a stunning, ramrod-straight black woman with high cheekbones and wide brown eyes, her black hair cut short and turning silver. She had earned her law degree at the age of forty-six, after working for Vail for twelve years, but chose to stay with him. She was indispensable. And she had recruited all of the Wild Bunch but one.

Shana Parver and Dermott Flaherty were a study in opposites who had changed their lives under similar circumstances. She had been brought up in a rich beachside community in Rhode Island; he was a product of Rochester back alleys, a tough, brawling street kid whose father had spent fifteen years on Death Row before dying of a heart attack, still appealing his death sentence.

She was not quite five-two, had a breathtaking figure,

jet-black hair that was clipped short, hooded brown eyes, skin the color of sand. Vail had expected anything but the beautiful, diminutive, and aggressive legal wunderkind.

'I want a lawyer, I don't want to give some old man on the jury a heart attack,' he said when he first saw her, to which Naomi had replied, 'What do you want her to do, Marty, get a face drop?'

A rebellious hell-raiser who made straight A's without cracking a book in high school, she had flunked out of an upscale New England prep school in her senior year. In the depths of depression she had decided to take her life in her own hands, became totally focused on school, and pursued her dream of becoming a lawyer. From that moment on she'd been an honor student, earning straight A's in college and law school, where her hero was Martin Vail. She also had pursued a place in the Wild Bunch.

Flaherty had been an angry kid, living on the streets, where he was constantly in trouble for fighting, shoplifting, and picking pockets, until one night, sitting in solitary at the juvenile lockup, he made the same decision, deciding to rely on his only asset – his brain. Back on the street, he had scrounged for a living, earned pocket money brawling in illegal backroom bare-knuckle fights, and focused his anger on books. Like Parver, he became a straight A student, went through college on a combination of scholarships and minimum-wage jobs, then hitchhiked west until he ran out of money in Illinois and won a scholarship to the University of Chicago. Inspired to become a lawyer to help his father, he walked off with honors, a sly, tough legal eagle who was as much cop as lawyer. Like Parver, he had idolized Vail before ever meeting him.

Vail's only personal choice was Ben Meyer, a specialist in fraud, embezzlement, computer crimes, and money laundering. A tall, lanky man with a long, intense face and a shock of black hair, he dressed impeccably and was a ferocious litigator. Meyer had been brought up in an

269

Hasidic family. The Hasids were the strictest of Jews, mystics who observed strict adherence to ritual law, opposed nationalism and ritual laxity, and turned their back on the fine arts and the pursuit of historic knowledge. They wore their hair in earlocks, dressed in black, and fervently studied the Old Testament and the Kaballah. Ben bore the brunt of his fellow students, who saw him as a physical freak who had no TV, did not read popular books or listen to their favorite bands, and did not go to movies or dances.

Meyer's father assumed he would become a rabbi. Until young Meyer was fourteen, he was a solemn, solitary boy who saw no alternative to his fate. One day he visited a friend after school. Left alone in the living room, he saw a book lying on the coffee table. It was a book of fiction, forbidden to his eyes. He circled it, staring over his shoulder as if he expected demons to attack him, and finally leaned over and fearfully opened the cover. He turned to the first page, and read:

In my younger and more vulnerable days my father gave me some advice that I've been turning over in my mind ever since.

'Whenever you feel like criticizing anyone,' he told me, 'just remember that all the people in this world haven't had the advantages that you've had.'

What advantages have I had? his inner voice screamed. Meyer could not put *The Great Gatsby* down. Suddenly the world opened before him, and he was intrigued, no *mesmerized*, by Fitzgerald's tapestry of the twenties as it wove gangsters, playboys, and bootleggers into its theme of bittersweet and unrequited love.

Meyer became a voracious reader, secretly poring over volumes of Hugo, Dickens, and Faulkner with themes he strongly related to: justice gone awry, bigotry, hatred, social malfeasance. When he finally informed his parents he was forsaking the ritual fervor of the Hasidic order to become a lawyer, he did so with panache, cutting off his earlocks, getting a haircut, and arriving at his father's home in jeans and a sweatshirt. He was promptly banished from the family by his father. Through the years that followed, his mother visited him often, bringing him homemade chicken soup and knishes, and secretly reveling in his success. His father never forgave him. He died three months before Meyer graduated from Yale at the head of his class.

His mother was proudest of him for the role he played in the Grand County case and its unraveling of political and environmental corruption in mid-America.

Harrison Latimore was the wild card of the Wild Bunch. He was its newest member and had acquitted himself well in Grand County as Flaherty's backup man. His father had lost both legs in Vietnam and died in a veterans' hospital. Latimore had become a lawyer to satisfy his father's dream for him, although he planned eventually to join the FBI. Naomi, who did most of the 'recruiting' for Vail, was attracted by his youthful good looks and casual air, which disarmed lawyers who faced him in court, and his skewed sense of humor, which concealed his voracious appetite for the jugular.

Another member of the Wild Bunch had been Harve St. Clair, a garrulous old-timer with the instincts of a wild predator and an encyclopedic memory. He had been killed two years ago in an automobile accident. A hunch player, St. Clair had a natural instinct for link analysis, putting together seemingly disparate facts and projecting them to a single conclusion. It was a trick Flaherty had learned from him and learned well.

But the man Vail would miss most was Abel Stenner, an ex-Chicago cop who had become Vail's closest friend as well as his bodyguard. Stenner had suffered a stroke in the weeks just after the Grand trial concluded and was living with his divorced daughter in Trenton, New Jersey.

Vail talked to him at least once a week, often seeking his wisdom and advice.

Vail's guests noshed nervously on scampi, salads, veal Avanti, meatballs, and pasta, and chatted with Jimmy Hines, whom Vail had introduced simply as a friend of the family. He was nervous about how the group would react to his news. Finally he tapped his knuckles on the table, and they all fell silent immediately.

'I've got a little entertainment for you,' he said. 'Let's go in the living room and get comfortable.' The Wild Bunch gathered there, sitting on the floor or lounging in easy chairs. Magoo strolled in, flopped down at Vail's feet, yawned, and went to sleep. No one said anything or interrupted while Vail played the two tapes he had recorded. When they were finished, Vail snapped the audio recorder off.

'The first tape was Gary Jordan. He's in the federal pen in New Mexico. The other one is in witness protection. Just call him W.P. The Sanctuary is the most well-organized, well-trained, and dedicated militia in the country. Four brigades posing as churches under the umbrella of Engstrom's Sanctuary. Six thousand soldiers expertly trained in guerrilla tactics and survival. They can justify anything, even murder, by quoting the Bible.

'So, at about nine-thirty this morning, I became a U.S. assistant attorney general. At the President's request, I've agreed to pursue a RICO case against the Sanctuary of the Lord and the Wrath of God.'

His announcement was greeted with stark amazement by everyone. Shana Parver finally broke the open-mouthed silence with a response that reflected everyone's reaction.

'*Huh!*'

Naomi was more specific: 'Uh-oh.'

Followed by a wave of nervous laughter.

'This is very sudden. I was offered the job by the Attorney General three days ago. I met with the

President, the A.G., and the man who runs the FBI, at the White House this morning and agreed to take on the job. I'll be in full charge, reporting only to the President and Attorney General Castaigne.'

'You met the President and the Attorney General?' Naomi asked incredulously.

'Yep.'

'And he *asked* you to do this?' Harrison said.

'Yep.'

'Holy shit,' Flaherty murmured.

'I need you all,' Vail said. 'This one's going to make Grand County look like a minor league warm-up. We'll use everything we've learned in previous RICO cases and still wish we knew more. We'll have three strong allies on our staff. Jimmy Hines here is one of them. He's more than a friend of the family, he's an electronics genius and can access any records we need and store all our data. Sam Firestone is a marshal who was brought up in the area. He's half Indian and knows the territory. He probably knows most of the answers we're looking for, but he doesn't say much.'

'Like Harve?' Flaherty said, and they all laughed.

'Yeah, like Harve,' Vail said, recalling the missing St. Clair. 'We also have Billy Hardistan working with us. Hardistan is the man who runs the FBI. He eats red tape for breakfast. Billy and I have a meeting tomorrow with a federal judge. We'll see how much room she's going to give us.'

'She?' Naomi said.

'Name's McIntyre. Originally from South Carolina. Ex-prosecutor, ex-superior court judge, and member of the Supreme Court there. I'm told she's tough but fair.'

'Judges,' Latimore growled. 'Good luck.'

Vail put the briefcase on the floor and opened it, taking out the case of CDs, the hate literature, and the Phantom Project file.

'These are CDs of the files on the Sanctuary and other

hate groups. I'll have copies made for everybody who joins up. Homework.'

Meyer groaned.

'Aw, you'll love it, Ben,' Vail said. 'It's like reading a thriller. Right now this is the background data the FBI has prepared. This is what we start with, this and one witness.'

'The W.P.,' Flaherty said.

'Right. I'm hoping that tape will convince the judge to give us all the necessary warrants and sanctions we need.'

'Will he hold up if we need him in court?' Flaherty asked.

'I don't know,' Vail answered.

'You don't see him as the link, then?' Meyer said.

Vail shook his head.

'What specifically is the case, Marty?' Parver asked.

'Murder, armed robbery, theft of government property, interstate transport of stolen vehicles, money laundering . . .'

'Yeah,' Meyer said softly.

'That's your job, Ben. The money. Naomi and Jim Hines can help you with that. Remember, a lot of this information may already be on record. The FBI and the ATF haven't been sleeping for the last two years. We want to know their banks, the directors and owners, the officers, how many branches they have, how much money they handle, what loans the four churches and the Sanctuary have. Also the specific real estate holdings of the Sanctuary.'

'That's going to be tough,' Hines said.

'We've done it before,' Meyer said, 'and legally.'

'It depends on how big a door the judge opens for us,' Vail said. 'Dermott, your job is hard felonies. We want to know every bank robbery, armored car heist, every armory that's been robbed, every hijacking, even gun store robberies, during the past two years.'

'What area?' Flaherty asked.

'Montana, Idaho, Colorado, and Wyoming.'

'We've probably got a lot of that information on file,' Hines said.

'Double-check everything. We don't want to miss a trick. We also want to know the M.O.'s on all these jobs. Jimmy, can you cross-reference this material?'

'No problem,' Hines answered. 'I wrote a program for the A.G. that will cross-reference by name, occupation, police record, real estate, driver's license, even similarity in appearance, or any other variable you want to throw in. Then it files alphabetically and by category.'

'Excellent. Naomi is an expert at RICO. She knows specifically what we're looking for and what matches are significant. Shana? The four churches. Who's in them, occupations, ages, what the chain of command is, where they're located. And eventually, you and I will do the interrogations of these people.'

'Great,' she said with a smile.

'Oh yeah, I want to know who the members of the I.F. are – that's their intelligence department. The W.P. mentioned it on the tape.'

She nodded.

'Harrison, I want you to concentrate on this radio nut, Abraham.'

'The FBI's been spot-taping his sermons, if that's what you want to call them – since he started,' Hines offered. 'Give you an idea of what he's all about.'

'Good,' Latimore said.

'I want chapter and verse on this guy. He preaches blowing up government buildings, looting courthouses and armories and banks, murdering judges and federal employees. I want to know who this guy is. Where did he spring from, where does he live, where does he record his shows, who's in business with him?'

'Gotcha,' Latimore said. 'You want the whole kahuna.'

'Whatever you want to call it. I've arranged a hard

surveillance of Fort Yahweh from ground and air. The FBI will handle that. Naomi, we need to advise all FBI, ATF, and marshal offices that we should be notified of any event – *any event* – involving the militia. That includes arrests. We'll screen them out. You're not gonna get much sleep on this trip, Naom.'

'So what's new?' she answered with a smile.

'That's about it,' Vail said, 'except for one other thing. We're opening a small office here in the city. But mainly we'll be operating out of an AMOC.'

'A what?' Latimore said.

'Air Mobile Operations Center – an AMOC. A 737 fully equipped with all the toys we'll need on this journey.'

'Our own jet!' Latimore said.

'Our own jet.'

'I hate to fly,' Naomi said.

'That's why you'll run the office here,' Vail said.

'Thank God,' she said. 'I have one question.'

'Shoot.'

'What's bugging you about this?'

'Nothing's bugging me.'

'Martin, I know when you're bugged, and you're bugged.'

He sighed and thought for a moment before answering.

'We have eighteen months to get this case on the docket,' he said finally. 'But I keep thinking about what the W.P. said. 'Maybe it's an act of war.' For all we know they may be planning to start Armageddon the day after tomorrow. Maybe next month is D-USA-Day. I want them before a jury before they go any further, and so does the President. I just want everybody to know from the front end, we're on the clock on this one. The President gave us eighteen months. I want us to pursue this case like eighteen months ends tomorrow.'

'Don't we always?'

'We had the time to develop the case on our own terms in Grand County. We don't have that luxury here. Dermott, I want you on top of everything. Put it in that matrix on the back of your eyeballs and come up with a link. Then we'll try to break him or her. I want the link. I want the one person who can tie these four churches to Engstrom. We get that, we can go for indictments, lean on them big-time, and build the case on the way to court.'

'That's risky,' Meyer said.

'Everything's risky, Ben. The difference is, the stakes are really high this time.'

'We need to follow the money,' Meyer said.

'What money?' Latimore asked.

'Hell, they're robbing banks, stealing weapons, and selling them,' Meyer answered. 'A lot of money is floating around. How are they washing it?'

'Work up options, Ben. Remember how we worked the banks in Grand County? Go straight for the jugular. Remember, you have the whole FBI working for you.'

Vail looked around the group. 'Are you all in?'

Their enthusiasm answered the question.

Then the phone rang.

Annoyed, Vail snatched it up. 'Vail,' he said sternly. The group watched him as his expression turned from annoyance to disbelief to anger.

'Martin, this is Billy. Our W.P. just got hit. He's dead.'

'My God!' Vail said.

'What is it?' Jane asked, but he held up his hand.

'Sam and I are taking a small jet to Fort Wayne. We'll go on to the scene in a car.'

'Where did it happen?'

'On the farm. Apparently, he was out in the field messing with that tractor of his. He was shot twice. Can you join us? We can drive in together.'

'Of course,' he said. 'I'll see you in Fort Wayne ASAP.' He cradled the phone and turned to his young colleagues.

'You all may want to change your minds,' he said.

'What happened?' Jane asked.

'We just lost our only witness,' he said. 'Somebody killed the W.P.'

Nineteen

Floyd McCurdy was the agent in charge of the FBI field office in Columbus, Ohio. The twenty-year FBI veteran was a soft-spoken man on the short side with a widow's peak of brown hair and brown eyes behind rimless glasses. He was wearing a dark blue FBI parka, old-fashioned galoshes over his shoes, and a dark blue ski cap pulled down over his ears. He had arrived at the scene of the Waller murder at three a.m. with twenty agents and John Nash, a forensics expert, and a field lab, which was parked near Waller's house. Twenty more agents were expected momentarily.

He stood in a bloodred early dawn, his gloved hands tucked under his arms and his shoulders hunched against the biting cold when Vail, Firestone, Meyer, Flaherty, and Hardistan arrived a little after six A.M.

'Good morning, sir,' he said as Hardistan got out of the car.

'Floyd.' Hardistan nodded and introduced the other four passengers.

'It's six below,' McCurdy said. 'We need more light before we start searching the area. Let's wait inside.'

The living room had been converted into a field head-quarters, with three bridge tables shoved together acting as a temporary desk. A map of the Waller site was spread out on the makeshift worktable. The agents were gathered in the den, drinking coffee and watching the early news on television. McCurdy led them to the kitchen doorway.

Vail looked into the wrecked kitchen. A small tractor was embedded in the kitchen wall, its engine buried under the rubble of wall, ceiling, and kitchen counter.

Stalks of water pipes, broken off and bent, protruded from the wreckage. The water had been turned off but the entire room was still sodden. A round battery-driven kitchen clock lay in the middle of the floor, the battery lying several feet away. Its hands were frozen at 6:23. Yellow crime ribbons were draped around the kitchen's perimeter. The only sound in the room was the solitary *plunk plunk* of dripping water.

'Here's what we know so far,' McCurdy began. 'At about six-fifteen last night, Waller took out the garbage, then went out to his tractor, which had been stuck in a mud hole for a couple of days. He had some wire fencing to use for traction to try and move it. He jogged the tractor loose. His wife was standing at the kitchen window over there and saw him stop the tractor for a minute and turn around, apparently to check the rear wheels to make sure they were clear of the wire. A second later his head snapped back and he fell sideways across the throttle. The tractor came straight across the field and rammed into the kitchen. He was shot twice, once over the right eye and once in the side. The bullet entered his side under his left arm and appears to have hit him in the heart.

'We found parts of his skull and some brain matter out near the hole, which is twenty, thirty yards out in the field, so we know that's where he took the kill shot. The insurance shot got him after he fell, somewhere between here and there. The body was at a local funeral home but our people moved it up to Lima to do the autopsy.'

'What kind of weapon was used?' Vail asked.

'Fifty caliber, probably a rifle.'

'He was using talons,' John Nash said.

'What's a talon?' Vail asked.

'It's a bullet that has small barbs in the nose,' Nash said. 'When the shot hits, the barbs splay out. It makes a nice neat hole going in and then spreads out the size of a pancake. We found this spent round near the head debris.'

He held up a Baggie. It contained a single round caked with blood and membrane. Small half-inch steel darts encircled the bullet.

'Jesus,' Meyer said.

'His wife went berserk, as you can imagine,' McCurdy went on. 'They don't have a phone, the nearest house is two miles away, and the road to town is a mile back down the dirt road you came in on. The shooter got off another hit on the front right tire of the pickup before the tractor got to the house. She never heard a shot. The loudest noise was the tire exploding. That bullet disintegrated when it hit the wheel rim.'

Nash, the forensics man, who was tall and wore an old-fashioned felt hat, picked up the story.

'We can triangulate the three shots. My guess is they cross about half a mile east of the house. There's a line of trees and shrubs out there. Beyond them he wouldn't have had a clear shot. He obviously used a silencer. I think we can safely assume for the moment that this is a professional hit.'

'The woman panicked,' McCurdy said. 'She pulled Waller's body out of the wreckage and realized he was dead. She finally got her wits together and drove the pickup, flat and all, down to the highway. About half an hour later a passerby picked her up and took her to the police station. That's when she called you, Billy. That was at 8:35, more than two hours after the killing.'

'He was halfway to China before anybody even knew what happened,' Hardistan said.

'The local and state police have been very cooperative,' Nash said. 'They set up a perimeter around the place to keep strangers out. We also have crime scene ribbons around the entire perimeter.'

'How about the press?'

'Nothing so far. We're pretty isolated out here. The nearest town of any consequence is Lima, about fifteen miles north of here.'

'Keep 'em out,' Hardistan said.

'Right.'

They all went outside, where the sun was beginning to spread long shadows across the field. They started walking across the hard earth toward the line of trees, still a dark shape a thousand yards ahead of them. Frozen snow crunched underfoot. Vail shuddered as the wind sheared through his jacket.

'I know how you must feel about this, Martin,' Firestone said to Vail. 'You shouldn't feel responsible.'

'I don't,' Vail answered calmly, his breath steaming in the frigid air. 'Waller wasn't my W.P.'

Firestone was shaken by Vail's blunt response. His jaw tightened and he straightened up and stared out across the field at the feds who were starting to scour the area on foot. Hardistan, too, was surprised at Vail's response.

'I didn't say it was your fault, Sam,' Vail went on. 'You took every possible precaution coming out here. Hell, for all we know we had a breach of security.'

'Not a chance,' Hardistan said defensively.

'I agree it's remote, but we have to consider every possibility. For all we know, the shooter was on to Waller and was already here when Sam and I arrived. I don't think that happened, I don't believe in coincidence. But I never rule it out, either.'

'It was dark,' Hardistan said. 'He could've walked across the field and plugged Waller at close range.'

'He wouldn't do that,' Firestone said. 'He'd take the long shot so he could get away fast. Wherever he was when he took that shot, we'll find a road nearby.'

'You're right,' McCurdy agreed. 'There's a dirt road behind the trees. Leads to State 501. From there he could have gone in any direction. He had two and a half hours before the police were even on the scene. He was 150 miles from here by then.'

'How the *hell* did he find Waller?' Hardistan said bitterly.

'I'm more interested in who the shooter is than where he was when he pulled the trigger,' Vail said.

'I'm more interested in how he found us,' Firestone said. 'We didn't file a flight plan to New Mexico until we were in the air. We didn't file a flight plan *out* of New Mexico until we were in the air, and we didn't file a flight plan from Fort Wayne until we were on the runway. We didn't even reserve a car, it was delivered by two marshals from Columbus.'

'Maybe he's telepathic,' Hardistan said sarcastically.

'Maybe he flies his own airplane,' said Flaherty, who had been quiet up to this point. Hardistan, Vail, and Firestone turned and looked at him.

'What are the options?' he said defensively, his hands held out at his sides. 'Either there was a breach of security, or you were followed. And if he followed you, he had to do it by plane.'

'He followed us to New Mexico in a private jet?' Vail said with a smile.

'Didn't have to. He's probably from somewhere within a two-hour flight from Fort Wayne.'

'How do you figure that?' Firestone asked.

'Someone picked up your flight plan on a scanner coming out of New Mexico,' Flaherty said. 'That person called someone who was close enough to get to Fort Wayne about the same time as you. That's two hours tops. He heard you file on the runway, followed you to the Lima airport, then followed the car by air, straight to Waller's door.'

'That's movie stuff,' Hardistan said.

'Then it had to be a security problem, which means there's a mole somewhere in the loop.'

'Nobody knew Waller's new name but Sam, the A.G., and me. Nobody,' Hardistan said. 'And Sam is the only one who knew he lived here, and he didn't put the data in the computer.'

'Then I agree with Derm,' Meyer said. 'We're looking

for an assassin who has his own plane, can fly it, is a dead shot, and lives within a two-hour radius of Fort Wayne.'

'Narrows it down to what? Fifteen, twenty million people, more or less?' Flaherty said.

'If that's true, he's a freelancer,' Firestone said. 'The Sanctuary hasn't got some hotshot shooter sitting out here in the middle of nowhere on the chance that somebody they want to terminate might drift through.'

'Maybe it's somebody they worked with in 'Nam,' Vail said.

'You mean somebody from Phantom?'

'Yeah.'

'They're all accounted for, Martin.'

'There are two unknowns in that photo. One of them is dead. Who said so? Gary Jordan. Nobody else so far. And there's no way of back-checking because there aren't any records.'

'They didn't have to phony anything,' Flaherty said. 'They just gave out the news that the guy is dead. Up until now, nobody gave a damn.'

'And it didn't have to be in 'Nam,' Hardistan said. 'The Phantom Project was in Nicaragua. And in Desert Storm. Somewhere along the line this guy quit and went into business for himself.'

Vail shrugged. 'It's a sidebar anyway. He's a pro. He planned his shot and his getaway perfectly. His first shot was a head shot at night. That's one very confident shooter. If we do find him, he'll never give anything up.'

'I want the guy who did him,' Firestone said.

'We all do. Let Billy worry about it. If this guy can be found, I'm sure the FBI will find him.'

Four agents were awaiting them when they got to the tree line, all wearing blue FBI parkas. The leader of the team was a tall black man, his hair trimmed close to the scalp.

'Billy, you know Dick Lincoln,' McCurdy said. 'This is Foster, Kravitz, and Sheridan. What've you got, Dick?'

'We've got tire tracks over there in the bushes. He left in that direction.' He made a chopping motion with his hand. 'We lose the tracks at 501. We got footprints in the mud leading from where the car was parked to that.'

He pointed to a large oak tree with the deep-set scar in its trunk. 'There's a small hole in the ground right here. My guess is he used a unipod, sat in that depression in the tree, and waited until he got a shot.'

'Casings?' Hardistan asked.

Lincoln shook his head. 'Probably took 'em with him.'

'You think a man can fit in there?' McCurdy asked, pointing to the split in the tree trunk.

Lincoln took out a flashlight and, straddling footprints leading to the tree, checked the depression in the tree.

'We got some fibers in here,' he said. 'Looks like fleece, dark, either blue or black–' He stopped and squinted as he looked at the inside of the tree trunk.

Nearby, John Nash had a steel tape measure and was checking the depth of a footprint. 'Adidas,' he said. 'Pretty well worn.' He walked around the tree and studied the tire tracks, measuring the depth of the depressions. 'Goodyears,' he said. 'New. Probably less than five thousand miles on 'em. Common as fleas.' He flicked a spot of dirt off one of the grids. 'Got a little scar on it. Looks like the tire ran over some glass.'

Sheridan, meanwhile, was squatted down in front of the tree with a pair of binoculars, studying the shot line.

'I make it twelve hundred yards and change,' he said. 'Almost three-quarters of a mile.'

'Somebody give me a Baggie,' Lincoln said. Kravitz handed him one and Lincoln reached into the scar for a moment, then handed out the Baggie with a five-by-seven photo and a pushpin in it. Hardistan took the Baggie and held it up to the light. It was a fuzzy photograph, obviously digitalized, of a man looking upward at the camera, shielding his eyes from the sun.

'It's Waller,' he said. 'The shooter must've used the

285

picture to make sure he had the right target.'

'Look at the back, sir,' Lincoln said.

Hardistan turned the bag around. They all stared at the printing on the back of the photo: 2–3–13.

'Son of a bitch! Son of a *bitch*! Every time we turn around these bastards are shooting us a bird,' Firestone said.

Flaherty studied the photograph. 'There aren't any trees by that tractor,' he said.

'So . . . ?' Vail said.

'So the picture was shot from above, pretty far above, judging from the quality. The shooter made Waller from the air.'

'Okay. Seal off this whole area, Floyd,' Hardistan said. 'I want molds of tire tracks, footprints, fibers that might be inside the depression in the tree, everything in this area. I want a hard target search of every landing strip within a hundred-mile radius of here. Check motels, rent-a-cars, filling stations, you name it. I want a door-to-door of all houses, barns, silos, stores, in the area. Somebody saw that plane.'

Firestone stepped away from the group and cocked his head to one side, then looked off to the north.

'Anybody hear anything?' he said. They all walked out into the clearing and followed his gaze. Then they heard it. *Chompchomp-chompchomp*.

'We got a chopper in the area, Floyd?' Hardistan asked.

'Not yet. Two on the way.'

'Then we got company.'

The chopper swung in over the trees and circled around them. In the open doorway, a cameraman supported by straps was shooting down at them. Behind him, leaning over his shoulder, Vail saw a face he recognized and quickly turned his back to the cameraman.

'That's Valerie Azimour from WWN,' he said.

'Too late,' Firestone said to Vail. 'You just got made.'

At five A.M. that day, as was his custom, Eddie Maxwell had arrived at the nerve center of World Wide News. Maxwell was a lean man, his rough and tumble life reflected in a worn and craggy face. He walked down the row of computers on what was known as the 'platform,' checking what the reporters were working on. Next, he checked the large Plexiglas atlas that covered one wall of the room and showed, in different colored lights, where reporters and camera crews were, where satellite vans were stationed, and, in red, where news stories were breaking. Then he went to his office, a glass bubble in the corner that gave him a panoramic view of the sprawling newsroom, which even at that hour was rumbling with activity. Directly across from him in the opposite corner was the major news studio, one of three on the floor.

This was the heart of the news department, where tips were received, reports phoned in, new agendas written, reporters assigned to write stories, and key news decisions were made.

Maxwell shook off his coat and sport jacket, threw them over a chair, poured himself a cup of coffee, doctored it with half a spoonful of sugar, got a can of grapefruit juice from a small refrigerator, popped the top, and sat down at a desk the size of a lake.

Behind him on the wall, plaques and awards traced a long and impressive career, from newspaper correspondent in Vietnam, to television in several B market stations, to the major markets, and finally news director of a major network. What was not on the wall were awards and memorabilia of the three years that Maxwell had been an unemployable drunk. But a successful rehab had drawn the attention of Ray Canton, executive VP of WWN, who brought him aboard as a reporter. Within a few months Maxwell had started moving up the ladder. There were Emmys three years in a row for producing, and finally a Peabody Award as executive producer and directing editor of the news division.

Maxwell got a sheet of paper from the wastebasket, folded it into a small square, and put the coffee cup on it. He took out a pack of Vantage Lights and lined ten cigarettes on the desk next to the writing blotter, one for each hour he would be working, unless the world came to an end, which was not uncommon. He drained the juice, threw the can in the basket, took a sip of coffee, and leaned back to check the morning line, to find out what was happening, about to happen, or no longer going to happen.

His secretary, Ann Wells, waited until he finished the routine before tapping on the door, which was always open except when he arrived in the morning or when something was breaking. He waved her in.

'Good morning, Mr. Maxwell,' she said, picking up the coat and sport jacket and throwing them over her arm. 'There's good news and there's bad news.'

'Arggh,' he growled. 'What's the good news?'

'Valerie Azimour is onto a breaking news story near Lima, Ohio.'

'Lima, Ohio? There's nothing in Lima, Ohio. I thought she was doing that thing in Akron?'

'She finished.'

'So what's the bad news?'

'She pulled one of the two video men who were with her out of the satellite van. And, uh ... she's rented a chopper.'

'Lima, Ohio? A chopper?'

'She's on the honker.'

He grabbed the red phone reserved for emergencies and roared, 'What the hell's going on?'

'I think I'm on top of a hot one, Eddie,' the reporter said.

'You *think*! You *better* be on top of the hottest one since the Lindbergh kidnaping. I repeat, what the hell's going on?'

'We finished up here about four this morning, and Sid wanted to drive back so we get in by noon. We're eating breakfast about five when my beeper goes off. An affiliate here in Akron says he was talking to a radio pal of his in Lima, Ohio, who says the FBI is all over a murder case ten miles south of there. I call the radio guy and here's what I know. A farmer named Anderson was apparently shot and killed about ten miles south of Lima early last night. The radio guy picked it up on a police scanner about nine o'clock last night, so he drove down to the funeral home, and the funeral director says Floyd McCurdy, FBI agent in charge of Columbus, called him and says nobody touches the body until the FBI gets there. So this kid gets curious and he hangs around and about three o'clock McCurdy shows up with an army. He says they have the place sewed up tighter than Scarlett O'Hara's corset.'

'Get to the point, Val.'

'I've got a chopper on standby. I've got Tommy Sewell with me, and the satellite truck's on its way down there. I should be there about seven—'

'What the hell's the story? Some farmer probably was running a hot car ring and got whacked in a shootout.'

'The G-boys didn't arrive until three A.M.'

'It's a waste of time.'

'Trust me on this one, Eddie. In two hours we'll know what's going on, and right now nobody else is on this story.'

'Nobody else wants it.'

'The whirlybird's warming up, Eddie. Gotta go. I'll call you back in an hour or so.'

'Listen . . . Val . . . Azimour! Goddamnit.' He slammed down the phone.

'Something wrong?' Wells asked from his doorway.

'Did I miss something? Has Azimour taken over my job?'

'Nooo.'

'She has a chopper, a satellite van, and a crew of five heading to some dipshit town in Ohio because a farmer got whacked last night.'

'You left out about the FBI.'

He glared at her. 'So . . .'

'So, if the FBI's involved, I'm interested in who this farmer is. And who whacked him.'

'Well, maybe you oughta be the directing editor.'

'Maybe . . .'

An hour and a half later Azimour was circling the crime scene, scanning it through binoculars. Blue FBI jackets were everywhere. There was a group huddled around a bay of trees, and the chopper circled it.

'Wait a minute!' she said, and refocused the binoculars. 'God damn, that's William Hardistan. What's he doing here?'

'Ya got me,' the video cameraman said, still shooting. 'Who's William Hardington?'

'He *runs* the FBI. How about the other guy with his back to the camera? I didn't get a look at him before he turned around.'

'Don't know. It'll be on the tape.'

'Jesus, look around here, Teddy. There must be thirty, forty FeeBees scouting that field.'

Teddy swung his camera around and shot back toward the house.

'Looks like somebody tried to park a tractor in the back of that farmhouse,' he said.

'Swing over there,' she ordered the pilot.

At seven-fifty Eddie Maxwell snatched up the red phone on his desk. 'Yeah,' he snapped.

'It's Valerie.' She was shouting above the noise of the chopper blades and the wind. 'We're freezing up here.'

'Too bad. This better be good, Azimour, or I'm taking the cost of the trip outta your next paycheck.'

In the chopper, she was staring at a freeze frame of the tape Teddy had shot twenty minutes earlier.

'Eddie, we've got a farmhouse sitting out in the middle of nowhere, two, three miles from the nearest building. We've got a tractor embedded in the back of the house. We've got a twenty-four-year-old farmer named Anderson who was shot twice, once in the head, once in the torso. We've got an FBI field lab here and FeeBees twenty deep crawling all over the place.'

'I'm not enthralled.'

'It gets better. Guess who showed up for breakfast?'

'Efrem Zimbalist, Junior.'

'William Hardistan.'

Suddenly Maxwell got interested. '*Hard*istan's there?'

'It gets even better, guess who's with him?'

'Oh for Chrissakes . . .'

'Martin Vail.'

'The lawyer?'

'How many Martin Vails do you know?'

Maxwell's mind started racing. 'Any competition there yet?'

'No, but it's just a matter of time. I just talked to the satellite truck. It'll be here in ten minutes. We'll set up for a live shot. We can use the flyover tape with my voice-over after my intro.'

'You need to get to Hardistan.'

'We're still in the air, Eddie.'

'You got Hardistan and Vail on tape?'

'You betcha.'

'All right, as soon as you can get the tape to the satellite truck, call me. I'll alert Julie Lane now, she's producing the news this morning. Think you can pin Hardistan down for an interview?'

'You know Hardistan, he never talks to anybody. And he's a chatterbox compared to Vail.'

'Okay, hold it to three minutes with a tease at the end.'

'Will do.' She looked down at the field behind

Anderson's house. 'Something big happened here last night, Eddie.'

'Damn good thing. Now find out what it was.' He hung up.

'Great,' Vail moaned as they trudged back toward the farmhouse. 'I'm on the job less than twenty-four hours, our only witness gets popped, and we're about to have our faces spread all over international television.'

'Welcome to the real world, Martin,' Hardistan said. 'Get used to it. She's gonna be dogging you from now on.'

They went back in the house, drew cups of coffee, and rubbed frozen hands over the hissing fireplace. Vail was quiet for several minutes, staring at the blazing logs.

'I tell you what we're going to do,' he said finally. 'We're going to leave for Fort Wayne. Billy and I have an appointment with a federal judge in less than four hours. Sam, Ben, and Dermott will go with us, that gets all of us out of here. Floyd, I'd like you to have a sit-down with Azimour, tell her we were on our way to Chicago and Hardistan stopped off here en route to another appointment to see what's going on. I'm with him on an unrelated matter.'

'An unrelated matter? I'll bet she buys that,' Flaherty said, and laughed.

'Floyd doesn't know what it is. Do you know why I'm here, Floyd?'

'Not yet.'

'Good, let's keep it that way for a while. That way he's telling the truth.'

'If she gets pushy,' said Hardistan, 'tell her we've got a lid on this investigation and she'll find out what's going on when everybody else does.'

'That'll put her on Jupiter,' Flaherty said.

'Screw her,' Vail said.

'She's got you on tape, Marty. If she doesn't get some

satisfaction, she'll be speculating about what you're doing here.'

'She will anyway.'

'Not if you give her a little sugar.'

'What the hell're you driving at?'

'Let Floyd give her a live minute. He can corroborate what she already knows and then put a cap on the investigation. She gets the first break – she ought to, she got here first – and maybe he can get her to lay off you.'

'How about Billy?'

'I don't think so,' McCurdy said. 'We'll have to give her more than that to keep Billy out of it.'

'Like what?' Hardistan snapped.

'Well, she already has an aerial of the tractor stuck in the house,' Flaherty said. 'Let her get an inside shot. She tracks through the kitchen window and gets a close-up of the actual shooting location. Explain that he was shot while he was on the tractor.'

'Worth a try,' McCurdy said.

'When did you start getting cozy with the press?' Vail said to Flaherty.

'She's the Dragon Lady, Marty. Why piss her off this soon in the game? You already blew her off once. Give her something to gnaw on.'

'Okay, let's do it that way,' Hardistan said. 'If she wants to play hardball, tell her I'll personally take her out of the press loop. She'll never get another word out of the Bureau, or an interview or a press release. She can see it on CBS.'

McCurdy raised an eyebrow. 'In just so many words?' he said.

'In just so many words.'

Twenty

The AMOC streaked off the runway and climbed to thirty thousand feet before banking toward the northwest. Vail sat quietly in the corner of the lounge compartment, mentally preparing himself for the meeting with the district judge in Lincoln, Nebraska.

He would be seeking a Title 3, federal approval for wiretaps of the Sanctuary's phones, cell phones, modems, and fax machines, as well as search and seizure warrants of the Sanctuary's headquarters, its bank accounts and financial records. To get the sanctions, he would need to convince her that the Sanctuary was involved in criminal activity.

He was also concerned about what was known as the rules of engagement, in the event there was armed resistance from Engstrom and his troops. Vail was determined to prevent a violent confrontation between the government and the Sanctuary. Rules of engagement were commonly established when there was a potential for armed conflict, and were intended to provide ground rules for such a confrontation. They were designed to limit the use of deadly force by government forces and also to make agents aware of the potential for violence. The rules were usually drawn up by the commander on the site, although in this case, Vail was certain Hardistan would be responsible for setting them up.

Vail was particularly concerned after reading the rules established during the Randy Weaver standoff at Ruby Ridge, Idaho, rules stipulating that 'any adult with a weapon observed in the vicinity of the Weaver cabin or in the firefight area could and would be the subject of deadly force.'

These rules would then be distributed to FBI personnel, federal marshals, and ATF agents. Vail was particularly interested in a clause that had advised agents that 'deadly force can and should be employed if the shot can be taken without endangering any children.' Weaver's fifteen-year-old son, Samuel, who weighed only eighty pounds, had been one of the first to die at Ruby Ridge. Not only was he shot in the back, his arm had virtually been shot off. Although there were conflicting stories on exactly what had happened that night, Vail was deeply disturbed by the report, as well as the fact that Weaver's wife had also been shot while holding her baby in her arms. That concern was compounded by the deaths of the seventy-two children at Waco several months later during Weaver's trial.

Vail was determined to avoid a violent confrontation with Engstrom's troops if he got the Title 3 sanctions. The question was how.

In the windowless communications center, Meyer sat beside Jimmy Hines, watching the electronics wizard scan the Justice Department network. To his left, a reel-to-reel was slowly and silently recording. Hines's nimble fingers clacked away at the keyboard of his master computer while on the monitor of another computer a live helicopter shot of Fort Yahweh swept across the screen.

'That's Yahweh, the General's army post,' Hines said. 'The FeeBees run a flyover two or three times a day to see if anything out of the ordinary is going on there. We can also pick up the place on the satellite scan.'

'He calls it Yahweh?' Meyer said. 'That's a tetragrammaton.'

'A tetra-what?'

'Tetragrammaton. In the original text of the Hebrew version of the Old Testament, the letters YHWH are used in place of the words *God* or *Lord* because God never identified Himself with the word God. It's in Exodus:

And Moses said unto God, Behold, when I come unto the children of Israel, and shall say unto them, The God of your fathers has sent me unto you; and they shall say to me, What is his name? What shall I say unto them?

'And God said to Moses, I AM THAT I AM: and he said, Thus shalt thou say unto the children of Israel, I AM has sent me unto you. It became Jewish tradition to use the tetragrammaton, YHWH. Christians bastardized it into Yahweh, so they can pronounce it.'

'So Fort Yahweh is really Fort God?'

'I suppose you could say that,' Meyer answered. 'It can also be translated, "I will become whosoever I please," or "I will be what I will be."'

Hines leaned forward and listened carefully as Meyer explained where the word *Yahweh* came from. 'You really know your Bible,' he said.

'Well, for the first fifteen years of my life all I read was the O.T. and the Kaballah.'

'That must've been rough.'

'Not until I discovered Fitzgerald and Dickens and realized what I'd been missing,' he said with a smile.

Hines laughed. 'I can remember pissing and moaning because I *had* to read Dickens and Fitzgerald.'

Meyer shrugged. 'You know what they say, one man's meat is another man's poison.'

'Is that from the Bible, too?'

'Not that I recall.'

'The Feebs have been spot-checking Crazy Abe pretty regularly,' Hines said. 'I thought I'd play his latest rant for the brass when I finish copying the tape.'

'Crazy Abe?'

'Calls himself Abraham. Has a radio show, "The Wrath of Abraham." Sonofabitch does go on. Thirty minutes every night.'

'What's he rant about?'

'Everything from gun control to the IRS to revolution. Pretty wild stuff.'

'I'm sure Marty'd like to hear a sample,' Meyer said.

'It's just about finished,' Hines said, holding one ear-piece of a set of earphones to his ear and checking the recording. 'I'll play it on the intercom.'

'Good. I'll tell them. I need some coffee anyway. You?'

'Thanks anyway. One more cup, I'll start talking like a tobacco auctioneer.'

'This was recorded last night at seven o'clock,' Hines said as Vail, Hardistan, Firestone, Flaherty, and Meyer settled back with coffee in the comfort of the lounge. 'I'll skip past the opening. It's usually some local preacher who introduces him, then there's the Heavenly Choir and a lot of crowd response.'

'Where does this Abraham preach?' Vail asked.

'He doesn't,' Hardistan said. 'He records his message and they dub in the bells and whistles later.'

The emotion-charged voice was deep and husky, almost a growl, except when he emphasized words, and then he bellowed, his voice shaking as though he were standing outside in the cold. He was interrupted at frequent intervals by voices from the crowd – voices that were dubbed in. The presentation was very professional.

'Blessed be Jesus!'

'Amen!'

'BLESSED be the CHRIST Jesus!'

'Amen!'

'Blessed be GOD!'

'Amen!'

'Blessed be YAHWEH and his ANGELS and his CHILDREN!'

'AMEN!'

'A-men . . . a-MEN sweet Jesus AMEN . . . He's here with us tonight, children . . . I feel his presence.'

'YES!'

'The Lamb of God is here . . .'

'YES . . .'

297

'. . . in our hearts and in our souls.'

'*YES!*'

'Tonight I take my words from Daniel, Chapter Two: *Ye have broken my laws and betrayeth my love, said God, and vengeance WILL BE MINE.*'

'*Amen!*'

'In a few weeks April nineteenth will be upon us. A holy day, children, for on that day in 1776 our forefathers fought for independence at Lexington. It is the day in 1992 that the DEMON HORDES from outta Washington descended on Waco, Texas, burned seventy-two sinless children to death, and killed Saint David Koresh and his disciples, and you know WHY?'

'*Tell us, brother!*'

'Because *they* fear ANY man who has a covenant with our sweet savior Jesus Christ.'

'*Amen.*'

'It *reminds* us of the day the government's assassins murdered Randy Weaver's wife with babe in arms . . . gunned down his teenage son . . . even killed his helpless little dog.

'Yahweh in his fury demanded VENGEANCE . . . he STRUCK DOWN the heathen Temple in Oklahoma City . . . he DESTROYED those who have turned their backs on Christ and who march with the Devil.'

'Damn him,' Hardistan snapped. 'Listen to that bastard talking about Oklahoma City. That shit . . .'

'First Amendment, Billy,' Vail said, staring at the loudspeaker as Abraham raved on.

'An army has risen . . .'

'*Yes, Lord . . .*'

'A holy army . . . prepared to emancipate the children of God at the Apocalypse when GOD in his glory will OPEN the gates of Heaven for all those who believe in His holy spirit and are ready to do war and purge the earth of the denizens of Hell. That day is upon us and I say AMEN.'

'*Amen to that, brother!*'

'It is foretold in Revelations Ten: *And I saw a mighty angel come down from Heaven, clothed with a cloud: And a rainbow was upon His head, and His face was as if it were the sun, and His feet were as pillars of fire: And He had in His hand a little book open: and He set His right foot upon the sea, and His left foot on the earth, And He cried with a loud voice, as when a LION roareth: and when He cried out, seven thunders uttered their voices.*

'God HIMSELF has trained us to be a CHRISTIAN army ready to fight with our Savior. As true Christians, we no longer have a choice but OBEDIENCE to the Lamb of God who died for our sins. When he returns he will return as the Lion of the Tribe of Judah and the armies of heaven will march behind him and will make war in the name of righteousness and the gates of Hell shall fall before this holy army and NO enemy nor ANY kingdom will resist its power and we WILL RULE THIS NATION with a cross of IRON.'

'*Yes . . . amen . . . amen . . .*'

'What has the ZOG government in Washington done for us? What has the Jew government in Sodom done for the children of God? NOTHING! They take away our arms so we are defenseless against them. We've given the country to the Hebe-Jeebies. The J-E-W-S who control every dollar that comes out of the mint. Remember what Daniel said: *Behold, I will make them of the synagogue of Satan, which say they are Jews.* And that damned IRS, seizing your homes, your cars, your bank accounts, humiliating and degrading you, a bunch of psychos in suits operating outside the Constitution so they can get themselves a little bonus. FIVE MILLION illegal seizures in one year alone. But if we marched a million strong to Washington, would anybody hear us?'

'*NO!*'

'That's right, children . . . because the Devil rules that

profane Hell on the Potomac. Our politicians are thieving, fornicating, liquor-sotted whores.'

'AMEN . . .'

'Tonight, I also speak of betrayal. Of traitors in our midst. As we march with CHRIST JESUS and come ever closer to the HOLIEST realm, we know many will LOSE faith, TURN BACK to sin, FALL to discouragement and fear, lose their VISION. Some have lost the faith and now march with the HEATHEN hordes. They have turned their backs on our Holy mission, just as Peter denied Christ in his final hour.

'In Turner's diary, those who often shouted, "You will never take my gun, unless you pry my cold, dead fingers off of it," were the first to surrender their weapons to gun control. They were victims of COLD FEAR, like the children of Israel who cried out in the wilderness, *Why have you brought us out here to die?*

'Our traitors have abandoned us and fled to the arms of our enemy, the ZOG government in Washington. They must die, must be led to slaughter, must be DESTROYED just as the denizens of Hell will be destroyed at Parousia. Their BLOOD will flow with the blood of all those who deny Christ.

'We of the Sanctuary of the Lord and the Wrath of God declare ourselves as a Nation within a Nation, whose citizenship is of the Kingdom of God and of our Savior Jesus Christ, and not that of this PERVERSE and CORRUPT government. As it is prophesied in Hebrews Twelve and Thirteen, we will sojourn in our faith to a land of promise, a new country. We have found that place and it has its foundations in God. We desire a better country, a heavenly place where God is not ashamed to be called God. God provided this city to us and it is called Yahweh, and Yahweh will wreak the Lord's vengeance upon this foul land and we shall RISE up from the great mountain, Horeb . . . on the day of Armageddon . . . on the plain of Parousia . . . as HE sayeth through the words of Daniel

300

... We will flood across the whole earth and our God of heaven shall set up a Kingdom which shall never be destroyed, but it will stand forever.

'I call on you to rise up with us against the heathen government. Shed the blood of tyrants. Kill the traitors. Create chaos in the gran-ite halls of the Satanists. Slay all who threaten us. Destroy their temples, bring down their leaders and their sycophants. Prepare for the Apocalypse. The hour of redemption and delivery is with us. Send the message that those who strike out against God shall PERISH and be damned to everlasting DARKNESS and MISERY in the furnace of Hell.

'We pray for this in God's name, in the name of YAHWEH and Jesus Christ, amen. Amen, a-MEN! Sweet Jesus.'

'*AMEN!*'

'Shut that damn thing off!' Hardistan said with disgust.

'A bit radical, wouldn't you say?' Flaherty said.

'A *bit* radical, hell. His fuse is lit,' Meyer said.

'Do you think sane people listen to that crap?' Flaherty asked.

'Them that do, do,' Hardistan said. 'He's been foaming at the mouth like that for months. I suppose even rational people can buy into it eventually.'

'The decent folks in Montana, which is most of the people out there, are scared to death of Engstrom,' Sam Firestone said. 'Six thousand crazies is a lot of crazies.'

'He's preaching sedition and anarchy,' Hardistan said.

'It's called freedom of speech, Mr. Hardistan,' Meyer said. 'Unless we can prove he's responsible for a specific act of violence, he can say anything he wants.'

'He's the mouthpiece for the movement,' Vail said. 'What time was he on the radio?'

'Seven, for half an hour,' Hines said.

'That whole diatribe about traitors was a reference to George Waller,' Hardistan said angrily. 'Abraham was on the radio preaching about Waller's murder thirty minutes after it happened, before anybody but Waller's wife and his assassin knew he was dead.'

'No,' Meyer said. 'There's an hour time difference.'

'That's right,' Vail said. 'He was preaching murder thirty minutes *before* Waller was hit.'

'He knew it was coming,' Hines said. 'That show was taped two or three *days* before the murder.'

'I think it's time we bring Abraham in for a little talk,' Vail said.

'We've been trying,' Hardistan said. 'We've been trying to track the son of a bitch down for months.'

'What's he look like?' Meyer asked.

'Who the hell knows?' Firestone said. 'He's the best-kept secret since the atom bomb.'

'The guy's on the air five nights a week and nobody's ever seen him?'

'We haven't been able to get a fix on him,' Hardistan said. 'He sends the tapes in to a radio station near Helena owned by a businessman named Lewis Granger. Granger's the syndicator but he claims he's never met Abraham, just talks to him on the phone occasionally, Abraham initiates the calls. Sometimes the tapes are post-marked St. Louis, next time it's Atlanta, all over the country. We've analyzed the originals, the packages they came in, tracked them back to the initiating post office. Zero-zero.'

'So why's he so shy?' Flaherty asked.

'Maybe he's hot. Maybe he's on the run.'

'Maybe he's got a side job. Traveling salesman.'

'Maybe, maybe, maybe. Let's put him on the A list and let's put this . . . what was the businessman's name?'

'Lewis Granger. Lives outside Helena on the lake.'

'What lake?'

'Canyon Ferry Lake. It's in the Black Belt Mountains. He has a million-dollar spread out there.'

'Is he connected?' Vail asked.

'To the Sanctuary? Not that we can determine,' Hardistan answered. 'He was very cooperative, let us review his telephone records, files on the show, air contracts, anything we wanted. Says he talks to Engstrom occasionally about the sponsorship but doesn't know him that well. Owns nine radio stations, most of them middle of the road. One station is definitely conservative. Carries Limbaugh, couple of other talk shows with a right-wing agenda, but the only radical program is the Abraham show. Our people have interviewed Granger several times, at his anchor station in Helena and at the lake house.'

'Put him under a microscope,' Vail said. 'And here's our new motto: Don't trust anybody.'

Twenty-one

Abraham sat in front of the TV with the sound beamed way up. He could hear Mordie and the girls in the kitchen putting together his breakfast. He pushed his white contact lens down under his lower lid and watched intently. He was interested in the WWN report of a murder in Ohio that had attracted the FBI. He knew the victim was George Waller. He knew the shooter but did not know his name. What he didn't know was why, for a brief moment, a face from his past was suddenly on the screen.

His nemesis, Martin Vail.

He was sure it was Vail, particularly after seeing the photo of him tacked to the communications center wall with the words 'Anybody know this man?' printed under it. Abraham knew him, all right, but he couldn't tell anybody. Even Mordie thought he was blind. Now there was Vail again, at the scene of Waller's execution.

What was he up to? Why was he interested in Waller? Hanging out with Hardistan?

For Abraham, tracking Vail's career was a psychotic obsession. During the Grand County RICO trial, he would sit alone in front of the TV set, send the girls and Mordie to town on some chore, push down his lenses, and daydream.

How many ways could he imagine? How many ways were there to kill Vail and make him suffer in the doing? His rage would build and then morph into a ravaging sexual hunger. When Mordie returned from his chores, Abraham would take the three young girls to his room and spend hours indulging in the most perverse sex acts. The young women, all in their early teens, were constantly in a 'state of grace,' as he called it.

Now Vail was back in Ohio. The first time could have been a coincidence. The second time could mean only one thing. Vail was either a consultant with the FBI or something related. The question was why? And what was he after?

As he watched Valerie Azimour, he knew how to find out.

At 11:05 A.M., Judy Shane, an operator on the WWN telephone switchboard, answered a call.

'World Wide News Network, can I help you?'

'Miss Azimour, please,' a harsh growl of a voice asked.

'I'm sorry, Ms. Azimour is out of town. I'll connect you with her editor.'

'I want to talk to Miss Azimour,' the voice snapped back. 'I know you can get her on her cell phone.'

'I think you need to talk to her assignment editor.'

'I said, I'm not interested in any damn editor. If she's interested in what really happened to Ralph Anderson out in Ohio, find her and have her on the phone. I will call back in three minutes.'

The line went dead.

The operator dialed Azimour's cell phone. It answered immediately.

'Ms. Azimour, this is Judy on the central switchboard. You just had a call. It could be a crank, but maybe not. I'll play back the tape for you.'

In the satellite van, Azimour listened to the message.

'Probably is a crank call,' Azimour said. 'But I'll hang on for a couple of minutes. Patch me in when he calls.'

'Will do.'

Azimour leaned back in her seat next to Sid, the sound man, who was driving the van, and held the phone to her ear.

'Some crank just called me,' she said to the driver. 'Claims he has the lowdown on the Anderson kill.'

'Probably the Psychic Hot Line,' he answered.

'Yeah,' said Teddy, the video man. 'Or maybe Nostradamus has risen from the grave to give you a scoop.'

They all got a laugh out of that.

On the outskirts of Missoula, Montana, Mordie and Abraham, formerly Brother Transgressor formerly Aaron Stampler, sat in Abraham's dark blue Four Runner. Abraham wore a dark beard that lined his jaw, like the beard of a Mormon elder. He was dressed in black, with a black pullover cap and a sheepskin coat. His hands were stuffed in his pockets. They were parked next to a free-standing phone booth just off the highway.

Mordie was watching his wristwatch.

'I don't understand,' Mordie said. 'Why are you tipping these people off? Shrack would kill you if he knew.'

'It's none of Shrack's business. That lawyer, Vail, wasn't at Waller's place by accident.'

'So what?'

'So, Mordie, I must conclude that Vail was there to make trouble for all of us. Why not let the world know? Whatever hand he's holding, it will be to our advantage to reveal it.'

'What you got against this Vail fella?'

'I had an experience with him once. In my previous life.'

'Previous or devious?' Mordie asked jokingly.

'Whichever you please,' Abraham answered.

'No offense, Brother,' Mordie said, embarrassed that he might have offended the preacher.

'You can't offend me, Mordie. How's the time?'

'About a minute to go,' Mordie answered, then added, 'These people make me nervous as all hell, T.'

'Have you ever had it so good? Nice house, TV, nice new auto, money in our pockets.'

'We always had money in our pockets, T.'

'He listens to me, Mordie. I'm Engstrom's prophet.'

'Prophet of doom, ya ask me.'

'Nobody asked you,' Abraham snapped.

'Sorry, sorry! Jeez, we're just talkin'.'

Abraham opened the car door and slipped out. He walked to the phone booth, using his cane although he could see through his milky lenses. He dialed the WWN number.

'World Wide News, may I help you?'

'Do you have Miss Azimour for me?' he asked.

'One moment, sir.'

He heard the click as she answered the call, and a moment later he heard her brisk answer.

'Valerie Azimour.'

'Hello, Miss Azimour?'

'Who is this?'

'Listen to me and do not interrupt. The reason the FBI is so interested in the man they call Ralph Anderson, who was executed last night in Ohio, is because his real name was George Waller. He was in the witness protection program. He was executed because he squealed on a bank robbery a few months ago in Denver. That's just the tip of the iceberg. If you're as good as I think you are, you'll get the whole story.'

'What do you mean *executed*? Can we meet? I need to–'

The phone went dead.

'Interesting,' Maxwell said. 'Any idea who this snitch is?'

'No, he spoke his piece and he was gone.'

'Okay, I'll get Research on the phone and see what we've got on bank robberies in Colorado in the last few months.'

'What do you want me to do?'

'Sit on it until I can get you some background.'

'Anybody try this on Harry Simmons?'

'Art Ferris is trying to get a comment now.'

'He won't say anything. He has a tape recorder that

keeps repeating "Ongoing investigation" over and over and over.'

'Well, that'll move the story a step or two farther. Where are you now?'

'We're going on up to Lima to see if we can get something on the autopsy.'

'Why don't you hang around there a little longer,' Maxwell said. 'If this tip turns out to be something, you can squeeze that FBI guy . . .'

'McCurdy.'

'Yeah. Maybe we can shake something more out of him.'

'He won't say anything else.'

'No, but he'll tell Hardistan and maybe you can squeeze a little more out of him.'

'That'll be the day, Eddie.'

'Hey, you already got enough to twist his arm. The thing about Vail, the witness protection stuff. The guy's name, what was it?'

'George Waller.'

'Yeah. See what else we can come up with, then you stick it to 'em, Val. That's your specialty.'

Twenty-two

Judge McIntyre's office was on the second floor of the federal building. Unlike most of the offices, which were cold and formal and furnished with dark wood paneling, her office was painted white, its windows bordered with flowered drapes. There were half a dozen photos of her son and his family on the bookshelf behind her desk. A vase of flowers held down one corner of the desk, and her high-backed chair was upholstered with a tan and green tweed material instead of wine-colored leather. Light tan carpeting completed the pleasing ambiance.

But, warned Hardistan, the cheery decor could be misleading.

'She's a tough lady,' he told the crew when they were ushered into the room by a secretary. 'She has an edgy sense of humor, and she runs that courtroom with a steel fist. Don't let appearances deceive you.'

'That's comforting,' Vail said.

'Just shoot straight up with her. She can spot a con in her sleep.'

'Fair enough,' Vail answered.

A moment later the judge entered the room, a pleasant but serious-looking auburn-haired woman, about five-five, in her mid-fifties, wearing a tweed pant suit.

Vail knew a little about her background, thanks to Naomi, who had supplied him with several articles about her. She had married while a senior in college, had graduated first in her law school class, and was president of the South Carolina bar while still in her thirties. At forty-five she was a member of the State Supreme Court. Her husband had started a small accounting firm a few years after graduation. By the time he was forty-five it had

309

become the most prestigious accounting firm in Columbia.

He was dead of a massive coronary before his forty-sixth birthday, leaving Lucy a pained and lonely widow.

A year later she had accepted an appointment as an Eighth Circuit judge and moved to Lincoln, where she served with distinction for eight years. It was rumored that she was high on Pennington's short list for appointment to the U.S. Supreme Court if Justice Lucas Frye did not survive a recent debilitating stroke.

It was a mark of her radical independence that she had chosen to move to a city she did not know, halfway across the country from her son, a research biologist with the Communicable Disease Center in Atlanta, her daughter-in-law, and two grandchildren, to accept the judicial post in the heartland of America and start her life anew.

Vail introduced himself, then introduced Hardistan, Firestone, Meyer, and Flaherty.

'Billy is a face from the past,' she said cordially. 'And your celebrity precedes you, Mr. Vail. I followed the RICO case in Illinois, although not as closely as I would have liked. There was a lot of talk among lawyers at the time, you know. You played some very interesting cards.'

Vail smiled. 'Shall I take that as a compliment?' he said.

'I like to watch good lawyers in action. You had very strong backup from those young people of yours. What is it they call them?'

'The Wild Bunch. A newspaperman invented that.'

'Very theatrical,' she said with a wisp of a smile. She looked at Flaherty and Meyer and said, 'And are you two members of the Wild Bunch?'

They both nodded. She turned to Sam Firestone. 'You look familiar, Mr. Firestone.'

'I delivered a defendant to your court once,' he said.

'Who was that?'

'Roger Buckhalter.'

'Ah, yes. Now I remember. He was a wild one, wasn't he?'

'Oh, we saddle-broke him okay.'

'Been a while since we last met, Billy,' she said to Hardistan.

'Nineteen ninety-five,' he said.

'As I recall, I had to slap your prosecutor's wrist a few times in that one.'

'He learned some lessons but he survived,' Hardistan said with a smile.

'I'm sure he did.'

'Judge, as you know, we're here to seek Title Three sanctions,' Vail said. 'We've prepared a brief to substantiate the request.'

Vail and Flaherty had prepared the brief on the plane with Hines's help, limiting it to five pages. It was an outline of what they knew about the Sanctuary, who the key people were, their stated objectives, and the relationship between the churches and the Sanctuary. It also included quotes from Jordan pertaining to guerrilla warfare and the coming revolution, but did not mention the taped interview with him. There were two photographs, an aerial shot of Fort Yahweh and the one of George Waller. Vail laid the file before her.

'You want me to read this now?' she said with surprise.

'We have the time if you do, Your Honor.'

'In a hurry, eh.' She leaned back in her chair, thought for a moment, then said, 'Well, I guess if it's important enough for you to fly halfway across the country to see me, it's the least I can do.' She opened the folder and read the treatise slowly, occasionally jotting down a note to herself. When she finished, she put it on her desk and looked at Vail.

'Anything else?'

He put his small tape recorder on the desk and pressed the play button. The judge sat quietly through the interview with the late George Waller. Toward the end she leaned her elbows on her desk, entwined her fingers into a triangle and leaned her chin on her fingertips. When the tape reached its conclusion, Vail snapped it off.

'You're going after a RICO case.' It was a statement, not a question.

'That we are.'

'Taking on the militia.' She sighed and shook her head. 'What's happening to our country?'

'The 1962 RICO act provides that racketeering activity is any act or *threat* involving murder, kidnapping, gambling, arson, bribery, extortion, or dealing in narcotics or illegal drugs. It also defines as racketeering any obstruction of justice, tampering with a witness, victim, or informant, retaliation of same, laundering of monetary instruments, murder-for-hire, and interstate transportation of stolen vehicles.'

'You left out obscene materials,' the judge said with a smile.

Vail smiled back. 'So I did, Judge. You know your RICO statutes.'

'Continue with your premise, counselor, you've got my attention.'

'A racketeering enterprise is defined as any individual, partnership, corporation, association, or other legal entity, or any union or group of individuals associated in fact, *although not a legal identity*.'

'Uh-huh.'

'The government's contention will be that the Sanctuary is an umbrella for four churches and they are involved in illegal racketeering under several of the 1962 statutes. It will also contend that the murder of George Waller was a case of retaliation, tampering with a witness, murder-for-hire, and obstruction of justice.'

'Just where are you taking this, Mr. Vail?'

'We intend to tie the four churches to the Sanctuary with charges of murder, witness retaliation and tampering, interstate transportation of stolen vehicles, murder, armed robbery, theft of government arms and ammunition, murder-for-hire, obstruction of justice, and money laundering.'

'That's quite a mouthful.'

'They're quite a handful.'

'You realize that churches are guaranteed certain immunities, particularly in regard to search and seizure. And to some degree, in deposition.'

'Yes, Your Honor. Unless, of course, we can prove they are involved in criminal activity. Then the rules change.'

'Yes they do. And you intend to prove all these allegations?'

Vail nodded. 'We may even toss in the radio clown Abraham.'

'Sedition is tough to prove.'

'Not for sedition. He's preaching murder and violent revolution almost every night. We may construe that as a threat under section 1A.'

'You're dealing with freedom of speech there.'

'We'll draw that line in the sand.'

She laughed and shook her head. 'Well, I'll say this, you've certainly filled your plate.'

'It's serious business, Your Honor.'

'You may run into trouble trying to sidestep the contention that these churches constitute an army and not religious organizations.'

Flaherty cleared his throat and raised his hand.

'Yes, Mr. Flaherty?'

'The religious angle could be moot,' he said.

Firestone, Vail, Hardistan, and Meyer looked with surprise at the young lawyer, wondering where he was going with his remark.

'How so?' the judge asked.

'Your Honor, we can contend that they are a group bonded together and associated in fact, as described in section 2C of the 1962 law. The question of legal identity or church affiliation then becomes immaterial.'

Flaherty looked at Vail, who turned back to the judge and nodded.

'Exactly,' Vail said.

She looked at him for a moment and nodded her head very slightly. 'Interesting,' she said. 'So you avoid the religious angle?'

'Not necessarily, Judge,' Meyer said.

'Care to pursue that?'

'Article One of the Bill of Rights states that "Congress shall pass no law respecting an establishment of religion, or prohibiting the free exercise thereof." I interpret that to mean that religious organizations should be treated without deference. They should get no special consideration, they are no different than a business or an individual. Unfortunately, there is a myth abroad that this is a Christian nation – at least the Christians think so. I don't think America belongs to religious fat cats who sell Christianity like snake oil on television or hide their political agenda behind Jesus Christ so they can cheat on their taxes. The Constitution takes umbrage with that notion.'

'I think you might have trouble convincing a jury of that.'

'I'll only use it if it's absolutely necessary,' Vail said. 'We're presenting it to you to justify the Title Three sanctions. The subpoenas and warrants we need.'

'Your legal arguments are very effective, Mr. Vail, but you're hurting for hard evidence.'

'Our hard evidence is dead, Your Honor. The man on the tape was in the witness protection program. He was murdered last night. The Sanctuary had him killed because he was both an informant and a potential witness. They used a professional hit man to do the job. That's murder-for-hire. Nobody else had a motive to commit this execution but the Sanctuary. If they feared him enough to kill him, they feared what he knew. They feared the truth.'

'Did you like this young man?'

'Not really.'

'Why?'

'I think his back was against the wall and he took his best shot, which was witness protection.'

'You disagree with that concept?'

'Not at all, Your Honor. I've used it myself. I'm not saying Waller shouldn't have been in the program, I just didn't trust his motives.'

She considered that for a few moments and turned to Hardistan. 'You haven't had much to say, Billy.'

'I'm just here for moral support,' he said, and grinned.

Meyer said, 'Excuse me, Your Honor, may I make a point?'

'Of course.'

'There was a code of sorts on one of the vehicles in the Lost Trail Pass ambush. It's a series of numbers: two-three-thirteen. These same numbers appeared on this.' He turned over the plastic Baggie that contained the photograph of Waller taken from the plane. 'If you'll look on the back of this picture, the same numbers have been written. This photo probably was used by the assassin to identify the victim. It ties both crimes together.'

She studied the picture and the back and laid it on her desk. 'Have any idea what these numbers mean?'

Meyer shook his head.

'Some kind of code,' Hardistan said. 'My people are working on it.'

'Looks like a date. Perhaps February third, 1913.'

'Or 1813 or 1713. Nothing significant happened on any of those dates,' Hardistan said.

She turned back to Vail. 'I like a man who comes into these things prepared, Mr. Vail,' she said. 'Most of the time they come in with a lot of vague accusations and they hem and haw their way through the meeting trying to keep their feet out of their mouths. Fishing expeditions. It's a pleasure to find someone who knows what he's talking about. Do they have representation yet?'

'Charlie Everhardt is their attorney, we assume he'll handle this.'

She rolled her eyes. 'Oh God, Charlie. He'll object to every warrant, every wiretap, every access sanction. . . .'

Vail nodded her through the list. 'That's why I wanted you, Judge.'

'How so?'

'They say you're tough but fair. I figure whatever windows you open for us will hold up in court.'

'Who suggested that you come to me?'

He thought for a moment and said, 'Somebody I met in Washington.'

Classy, she thought. *It was either the President or Marge Castaigne, and he's not going to play that card.*

'I've heard you have judges for lunch.'

'Only if they're digestible.'

Her response was a hearty laugh. 'And the rest of the time you just con them, is that it?'

Hardistan smothered a laugh. Meyer and Flaherty watched the interchange with fascination. Vail just looked at her with a cryptic little smile but did not answer her.

'Okay,' she said, 'what do you want?'

'Wiretaps, access to financial records, close surveillance including satellite observation inside houses, access to their computers.'

'That's a very big package.'

'They're a very big threat.'

Meyer sat and stared at the back of the photograph of Waller as they talked. Then suddenly he said, 'Of course.'

Everybody looked at him. Meyer explained the tetragrammaton 'Yahweh' to the group.

'It appears in Exodus, Chapter Three, verses thirteen and fourteen . . . two-three-thirteen. This is a code for the word Yahweh, which is the name of their commune and also the word for God. I think what they're saying is that

God committed these acts.'

Everyone in the room leaned across the desk and stared at the back of the picture.

'Nice hit, Ben,' Hardistan said.

'Or maybe Engstrom thinks of himself as God,' Vail said. 'He certainly has a messianic complex.'

Judge McIntyre stood up, walked to the window, and stood for a minute or two with one hand on her hip, staring outside. 'I am rather obsessive concerning the Constitution,' she said. 'I consider it the most important document ever written, and the most fragile. Easy to tear, almost impossible to repair. I am particularly concerned when individual freedoms are at risk . . . speech, religion, right to privacy, freedom from intrusion.'

'So am I, Your Honor. Remember, I was a defense advocate for ten years.'

'You're dancing close to the edge on this one.'

'Only way to win. It's their game, we're just trying to set the rules.'

The judge returned to her chair and fixed a deliberate stare on Vail for a long minute or two. Finally she leaned forward and lifted the phone.

'Mary? Come in, please, bring your pad.' She hung up. 'I'll give you your Title Three with reservations,' she said. 'You can have wiretaps on the headquarters and Engstrom and his leaders. You may have access to bank records of the Sanctuary and the churches, and I will give you search warrants for the fort and its surrounding buildings, but not private dwellings. I won't grant Title Three to their computers. In other words, no hacking, Mr. Vail. Understood?'

'Yes.'

'Also, I won't agree to wires planted in private homes. I consider that an invasion of privacy. But I will keep an open mind on these restrictions. If you can prove they are justified at some later date then I may revise my judgment.'

'Thank you, Your Honor.'

'Don't cross the line on this.'

'Understood.'

'By the way, I commend you on your choice of associates,' she said, nodding toward Meyer and Flaherty, who tried to look non-chalant but were obviously flattered by her remark. 'I have one other concern.'

'What's that?' Vail asked.

'If Engstrom is as dangerous as you say – and I'll reserve judgment about that – you may start a shooting war when you move on him.'

'It's a possibility.'

'How do you feel about that, Billy?'

'It's the chance we take when we step in with subpoenas.'

'We don't want another Waco, Your Honor,' Vail said. 'And we don't want a Mexican standoff. We'll be very careful in defining the rules of engagement. Or perhaps . . .' He paused.

'Perhaps . . . ?'

'Perhaps come up with a different strategy,' Vail finished.

'That should be interesting,' she said.

McIntyre turned to her secretary and started dictating the terms of the entitlement.

Twenty-three

The WWN news set was a simple glass-enclosed studio. The bustling newsroom, dominated by its enormous wall-sized map with flashing lights, sprawled out behind the anchor desk. The afternoon anchor was Sheila Boyle, a redhead – savvy, hard-eyed, all-business – who had been the top Washington correspondent for NBC when Maxwell stole her and offered her the afternoon news chair, his network's most coveted spot.

The TV in the lounge room of the AMOC was tuned to WWN but the sound was muted as Vail and his team settled down for the trip home. Vail was exhausted but his mind was still racing from the meeting with Judge McIntyre. He was staring at Sheila Boyle's silent image on the screen when the screen split and a map of the Lima, Ohio, area flashed on her left.

'Uh-oh,' he said, and unmuted the set. Boyle's no-nonsense delivery signaled trouble.

'In the small farming town of Wapakoneta, Ohio, a fast-breaking mystery story involves murder, the FBI, bank robbery, and possible connections to a right-wing extremist militia group . . .'

'Shit!' Hardistan snapped, sitting straight up in his chair.

'. . . Valerie Azimour is on the scene. Valerie, what's the latest?'

Azimour flashed on the screen with Waller's farmhouse a hundred yards behind her. As she spoke, a montage of scenes from the crime story flashed across the screen.

'Sheila, the death of a Wapakoneta, Ohio, farmer last night has taken a startling new turn since our exclusive

319

report this morning.

'The victim was originally identified by FBI agents as Ralph Anderson, whom they say was gunned down as he worked on a tractor in his backyard last night, a killing that has all the earmarks of a professional hit and is being investigated by at least thirty FBI agents here in this quiet farming community.

'Now WWN has learned that the victim allegedly was a twenty-five-year-old ex-soldier named George Waller. And we have information that Waller may have been in the federal witness protection program, although we have not been able to confirm this information . . .'

'Who the hell's she getting this shit from?' Hardistan said.

'. . . We also have information linking Waller to an abortive bank holdup in Denver five months ago. One of the bank robbers, Samuel Stevenson, was killed in that robbery, and a second man, Luke Sundergard, is serving twenty years to life in federal prison after plead-ing guilty to bank robbery and related charges growing out of that incident.

'WWN also has learned that both Sundergard and Stevenson were connected with the right-wing extremist group in Montana known as the Sanctuary. Waller's con-nection to the robbery and the Sanctuary is unclear at this time, as is the reason he was in the witness protection program.

'Floyd McCurdy, the agent in charge of the Waller murder investigation, talked to us in an earlier report today but now refuses any further comment on the case. In Washington, FBI director Harry Simmons stated that it is FBI policy to withhold comment in any continuing investigation. FBI Deputy Director William Hardistan was on the scene of the murder earlier today and can be seen in this videotape accompanied by noted attorney Martin Vail, shown on his left . . .'

The image of Hardistan and Vail froze on the TV

screen and held.

'. . . McCurdy earlier today stated that Hardistan and Vail stopped off while en route to Chicago on an unrelated matter. Neither Hardistan nor Vail was available for comment . . .'

The camera zoomed in on Vail's face. He stared grim-faced at the TV monitor.

'. . . Vail, you may recall, won a staggering multi-million-dollar verdict in an Illinois racketeering case last fall involving two of the nation's largest corporations. The CEOs of both corporations, Tom Lacey of Western Pulp and Paper, and Harry Grossman of the Atlas Chemical Company, were sentenced to prison terms, although their convictions are currently under appeal.'

The screen split again. Boyle was on the left.

'Valerie, does the FBI have any suspects in this murder case at this time?'

'We don't know. They're playing this one very close to the chest, Sheila. Except for the brief interview we obtained earlier today at the crime scene, they are refusing any comment at all.'

'Thanks. Valerie Azimour, live from America's heartland. In Phoenix, Arizona, today—'

Hardistan grabbed the remote and snapped off the television set. 'God damn her!' he roared. 'Doesn't she realize what she's doing?'

'She doesn't care, Billy,' Firestone answered. 'She's doing her job.'

'Job my ass. Where'd she get the information on Waller?'

'Who knows? A leak somewhere, obviously.'

'Maybe not,' Flaherty said.

'What do you mean?' Hardistan asked.

'Maybe it was a tip,' Flaherty said.

'From who? Who the hell would tip her?'

'One of them,' Flaherty ventured.

'Why?'

'Smoke us out. The more she finds out, the more they find out.'

'I'm sending a team in to find out where the hell she got her information,' Hardistan said.

Vail had remained silent during the discussion, but now he spoke up. 'Don't do that, Billy. She won't give up her source. And if you interrogate her, it'll confirm what she already knows.'

'You really pissed her off, didn't you?'

'This isn't about me. She's a pro and she smells a hot story.'

'So we let her get away with it?'

'Stonewall her. Everybody stonewall her. Then anything she gets has to come from the outside.'

'What good's that do us?' Firestone said.

Hardistan thought about what Vail said and finally nodded. 'You're right. We'll know what they want us to know, and maybe they'll slip up and give up too much.'

'Why not just put a wire on the WWN switchboard?'

'Whoever it is won't stay on the line long enough,' Hardistan said. 'Waste of time, and it brings Azimour back into the loop. We tried that in Ohio and she fucked us royally. Martin's right. We sit tight and say nothing.'

Later, Firestone was napping and Meyer and Flaherty were in the communications center running comparison tests on banks and robberies.

'How long will it take you to get the people together to enforce the warrants, Billy?' Vail asked.

'I'll need to know how many banks are involved. So far the warrants specify Fort Yahweh, the four churches, and the personal accounts of Engstrom, Metzinger, Shrack, Bollinger, Karl Rentz, and James Rainey, plus an unspecified number of bank accounts.'

'Pick a number. Ten banks. How long?'

'The way it works, I have the locations checked out, decide the size of the force at each location, order the necessary agents into the area with backup vehicles and proper weapons, write up the rules of engagement. You know we've got to be prepared for serious resistance, Martin. The rules of engagement will reflect that.'

Vail sighed and nodded. 'How long will all that take?'

'Busting ass . . . ten days.'

'How about a week?'

'We're talking about a lot of people, hardware . . .'

'The longer we wait, the more time they have to shred records, blow hard drives, hide weapons–'

'You letting this Azimour woman force our hand?'

'Hell, Billy, she could start speculating on our operation at any moment. She mentioned the Illinois RICO case already. I'll put my team on a twenty-four-hour clock, see if we can come up with the banks and any links they can turn up.'

Hardistan shrugged. 'Okay. A week.'

'Thanks.'

'I better get started then.'

Hardistan got up and walked to the rear office of the jet. Vail reached over and shook Sam Firestone. The big man opened one eye and stared at him.

'I hope this is important. I was enjoying the best sleep I've had since I met you.'

'Can you arrange a sit-down with Engstrom?'

'For you?'

Vail nodded. 'You know his people, don't you?'

'Some of them.'

'Can you get to him?'

'I can try.'

'Tell him he can pick the place.'

'Can I tell him why?'

'No.'

'Can you tell *me* why?'

'Later.'

'How many people are going to be at this summit?'

'Tell him he can bring his whole staff if he wants to.'

323

'How many people are you going to take with you?'
'One. You.'
'You're nuts, Martin.'
'So I've heard.'

Twenty-four

At six A.M., Henry Woo parked his car in the FBI lot and ran through a drizzling rain to the side entrance of the Hoover Building. It had been a good weekend for Woo. He had spent two whole days with his wife and ten-year-old son. The day before, the youngster had worn him down during their lengthy trek through the Smithsonian followed by dinner and a movie. It was the first time they had enjoyed the luxury of a weekend together in weeks.

But throughout the weekend the challenges of the coming week had lurked in the back of his mind. As Hardistan's logistics expert, he had to juggle investigative teams between Ohio and Montana, coordinate the FBI and ATF task forces and equipment for the service of warrants to the Sanctuary, and move men and equipment into the Fort Yahweh area without attracting too much attention. All this, and keep operational all the other cases with which the Bureau was involved.

Right down Woo's alley. He liked nothing better than a good challenge.

Hardistan was already in operations, a spacious room in the basement that was a mélange of electronic equipment, maps, and high-tech communications gear. Hardistan sat in the middle of the room staring dolefully at the large map on the wall. He sighed with relief when Woo entered.

Woo took one look at his unshaven, bleary-eyed boss and knew he had spent the weekend at the Bureau, grabbing forty winks when he could in a small, windowless room adjacent to his office, which contained a cot, a small refrigerator, a sink, and a shower. It was not uncommon. Since the death of Hardistan's wife, the

Deputy Director spent most of his waking hours on the job. He had not taken a vacation in four years, despite the urging of his staff and personal physician.

'We need to double our staff,' he growled when Woo came in.

'Maybe not,' Woo said cheerfully. 'I think we can move people around and cover all the bases.'

'Doesn't anything ever bother you?' Hardistan asked, reminding him of the overload on the Bureau's field staff.

'Love it, love it,' a smiling Woo said. Hardistan was continually astounded that the dull, boring job of keeping track of men, equipment, and operations obviously delighted the youthful Harvard graduate.

'We can bring two or three teams in from every district office and move them into say, Butte, Helena, Missoula, and Great Falls,' he said, pointing at the map. 'We'll bring in equipment at night. I've got Larry Olsen out there now, renting space for the Humvees and weapons. I figure we can move the force into the fort from all four towns in no more than two and a half to three hours. We can do that the night before we serve them. I won't need more than six to eight people to secure each of the banks and individuals. And we can move the teams from Ohio if McCurdy doesn't come up with something soon.'

As soon as Floyd McCurdy had taken over the investigation of George Waller's murder, he set up his plan of action. The initial assumption was that the killer had followed Firestone and Vail in his own plane, flown over Waller's residence, and taken Waller's photo from the air to assure a positive identification. He would have stayed in a motel or hotel and rented a car. His plane would have been parked at an airport during the two days he was in the Lima area. There was, of course, the chance that the killer lived in the area, but it was so coincidental that McCurdy ruled it out for the time being.

Hardistan sent in sixty-eight agents to scour the countryside. McCurdy used Wapakoneta as the headquarters for the search. The FBI rented a small storefront and immediately set it up as a search base. Phones and desks were brought in and a base team of ten was assigned to work the desks and also conduct phone interviews. They immediately set up interfaces with the AAA, the FAA, the state highway department, and the state licensing bureau. Experts laid out a huge map of the region, spotting airports, landing strips, motels, hotels, bed and breakfasts, rooming houses, and car rental agencies in the target area, a square divided into four segments, with Wapakoneta at the apex. Each segment was thirty miles square, with fifteen teams assigned to each segment.

Nine hundred square miles per team.

Four teams were also assigned to start a door-to-door canvass of the Wapakoneta area.

'You know the drill,' McCurdy told his search squad. '*Somebody* saw that plane, he didn't fly around here at treetop level and go completely unnoticed. I want to know the size, shape, color, number of engines, and anything else you can learn about it. The window is two days. We assume he followed Firestone into the target area from Fort Wayne on Tuesday morning and he made the kill Wednesday night about six-thirty. This guy's a pro, he planned this operation down to the minute. My guess is, he was back in his plane and on his way home one to two hours after the hit. Anything you get that looks promising comes into base. We'll coordinate all data.'

The activity served another purpose. In small communities like Lima and Wapakoneta, locals would gossip about the project, and anyone who did know something would either call or come by headquarters. McCurdy expected a lot of false alarms. Two were not.

The first hit came from a timid man named Kevin Young. He was husky, in his late thirties, wearing a plaid shirt and corduroy pants. He also wore a thick leather belt with tools holstered from it that clanked when he walked. McCurdy was hanging up the phone when Young walked in.

'Can I help you?' McCurdy asked the visitor.

'I think I may have seen something,' Young said tentatively.

'Seen something?' McCurdy asked.

'About that killing everybody's talking about. . . .'

'What's your name?'

'Young. Kevin Young. I work for the telephone company. Lineman.'

'And what's the information?' McCurdy asked the shy man as they shook hands.

'I was working on a pole about half a mile north of the Anderson place that Wednesday and I saw this plane from a distance. It was shining in the sun, that's why I looked over that way. It came flashin' up over the trees. Musta been flying almost on the ground because when he pulled up, it looked like maybe he just took off and I knew there wasn't any airfield around there, so I knew he was flyin' lower than the trees.'

'What color was it?'

'Well, it was either white or silver. I really couldn't tell from that distance.'

'One or two engines?'

'Engines? It was a twin-engine, I got a good look at the underside of the wings when she pulled up. But it circled around and was gone just like that.' He snapped his fingers.

'Do you remember anything else about it?'

'Sure was fast. Had a pointed nose. That's about it. Sorry I can't help more.'

'You did just fine, Mr. Young. If you should remember something else, give us a call.' He gave Young his card.

The second hit came from realtor Geri Bloom, who called in and spoke to an old-timer named Shuster.

'I'm a saleswoman over at Wiggins Realty in Lima?'

she started. She ended every statement as though it were a question.

'Yes, Ms. Bloom?'

'I don't know whether this is important or not, but I had a call on that Wednesday morning, the day poor Mr. Anderson was killed?'

'Yes, ma'am,' Shuster replied.

'The man said his name was Walter Dempsey from the *Farm Journal*. I never heard of the *Farm Journal*, but he said they were doing a story, actually he said it was the cover story, which means pictures and what have you?'

'Yes, ma'am, I know what a cover story is. What specifically did he want?'

'He wanted to know about farm properties that had been sold recently.'

'Did he say why?'

'Something about doing a story on farm values hereabouts.'

The FBI agent perked up. 'What did you tell him?'

'Well, there weren't that many, y'know. But one of the places I mentioned was the old Wainwright place.'

'Uh-huh.'

'That was the place the Anderson boy bought.'

Shuster paused for a moment. 'You told him where it was located?'

'Yes, sir. Did I do something wrong?'

'No, no, Ms. Bloom, not at all. When was this again?'

'That Wednesday just as I opened the office up. It was right at nine o'clock, A.M.'

'Do you remember anything about him?'

'I never met him. He told me he was going to put me on the mailing list. Quiet-spoken fellow, very personable. I think he was calling from a phone booth in Lima.'

'What makes you think that?'

'Well, I could hear traffic in the background. Cars stopping and starting and such as that, a couple of horns blowing? And then I heard the clock in front of the First

National strike the hour.'

'How do you know what clock it was?'

'Because they never turned it back at the end of the summer. It's still on daylight savings. Struck ten instead of nine. Kind of the town joke.'

A week after the murder, McCurdy reported to Hardistan.

'Billy, we got two breaks. We're sure now that the perp rented a car, unless he lives closer to Lima than we think. We're pretty sure he called a realty company from a phone booth on a street corner in Lima.' He recounted his conversation with the Bloom woman.

'She gave him Waller's location?'

'Yes.'

'Jesus.'

'Well, what'd she know? Also, this phone guy came in. He saw the plane, Billy. He was half a mile or so away but he ID'd it as light-colored and twin-engined. I'm narrowing my search down to airports and car rental offices.'

'You want to tighten it up that much?'

'We can always expand if we don't turn up anything. But this smells awfully good. We're only looking at maybe three dozen airports in the target area.'

'It's your call, Floyd.'

'I feel good about this.'

'How about the media?'

'Cooled off for the moment.'

'Let's hope it stays that way.'

'Amen to that.'

Geoff Isaac was handling the situation in Missoula. As Hardistan moved his teams into the area, Isaac kept them busy working the Lost Trail Pass case and interviewing people in neighboring towns. Others would be kept on alert in Butte and Helena. It was his job to keep the growing force of FBI and ATF agents spread throughout the area and less visible.

Nighthawks continued to fly over the mountains adjacent to the scene of the ambush, looking for any activity or sign of the missing semi. At night, AWACS made several swings over the area. The four-jet Airborne Warning and Control System E3s had a speed of 500 mph and a range of five thousand nautical miles. In addition to the flight crew of four, there were fourteen specialists aboard who were experts in its avionics, which included surveillance radar, navigation and communications data processing, display monitors, and 'look down' radar that could separate airborne targets from ground clutter. Its radar 'eye,' a six-foot-wide dish mounted near the tail, had a 360-degree view of the horizon. The trained observers could see ground objects more than two hundred miles away. Using body heat monitors, the technicians could detect personnel movement on the ground from 35,000 feet.

For days now they had been reporting frequent activity in the mountains next to Fort Yahweh. The AWACS located a dozen thermally heated survival tents capable of sleeping eight people, toe-to-head. One week after the Lost Trail ambush, during a sweep across the Yahweh area at three A.M., the crew reported seeing ninety-six people sleeping in the tents and another hundred scouting the mountains.

Stills and videos were shot and transmitted to Hines in the AMOC. Intelligence agents judged it to be the kind of survival training the Sanctuary normally conducted, but recommended increased surveillance sweeps.

By the end of the first week there was nothing new on the deadly ambush.

Vail decided to have a staff meeting of the Wild Bunch in the AMOC once a week. It was private. It was comfortable. And Paul Silverman, who was still chief steward on the plane, served a great breakfast.

Naomi recognized worry in Vail's face the minute she entered the dining room, but she decided not to mention it. The reports and updates were brief and inconclusive. Flaherty and Parver were gathering information on bank and armory robberies over an eighteen-month period prior to the ambush. They fed their info to Hines, who collated it and looked for matches or similarities in M.O. Meyer was building a database on all banks in the four-state area, looking for cross matches among the employees and officers.

The meeting was relaxed, yet there was an undercurrent of tension.

During a lull in the conversation, Shana Parver asked: 'Martin, what is Parousia?'

'Parousia?'

'Waller mentioned it in the interview you taped. In fact I listened to it twice and there's something on there that disturbs me. It's toward the end of the tape. I marked it. Listen.'

'. . . *the instructors are ex-SEALs, ex-Berets. They're pros at stealth missions and tracking and guerrilla tactics . . .*'

'Here it is,' she said.

'. . . *The General talks about Parousia and A-Day . . .*'

'I'm still not clear about Parousia and A-Day,' she said.

'Parousia's a Greek word,' Meyer said. 'It's a term for the second coming of Christ. The end of history as we know it. It's in Matthew. The disciples ask Jesus, *"When shall these things be? And what* shall be *the sign of thy coming and the end of the world?"* And Jesus answers, *"You shall hear of wars and rumors of wars . . . nation shall rise against nation, kingdom against kingdom. There shall be famines, and pestilence, and earthquakes . . . and no flesh shall be saved."* That's not exact, but close enough. I'm a little rusty on the New Testament.'

'Is he talking about Armageddon?' Shana asked.

'A-Day. Armageddon day,' Vail said.

'Jordan mentioned Armageddon during the prison interview. Waller mentioned it, too. And Abraham talked about it in the sermon I heard. The question is, what do they mean by Armageddon?'

'Maybe they've started it already,' Latimore said. 'Maybe they're taunting us. Could be the reason they flagged the convoy ambush and Waller's murder with the number code for Yahweh.'

'The last thing Waller said to me was, 'Maybe it was an act of war,' ' Vail said. ' 'Maybe it's A-Day.' '

'Maybe in Engstrom's mind, he's declared war,' Parver suggested.

'There's a landscape it would be interesting to explore,' Flaherty said. 'Engstrom's mind.'

Vail, who had seemed distracted throughout the meeting, now fell silent. He stared into his coffee cup for several seconds.

'Well,' he said finally, 'we'll never know whether Waller knew any more about it or not.'

'You're worried about something, Marty,' Naomi said. 'A little.'

'What is it?'

'I don't know for sure. I feel like we're on a truck going downhill without brakes. Everything seems to be escalating. The AWACS report there's increased activity at Yahweh. Waller talks about Parousia and A-Day. Abraham is openly preaching revolution on the radio. I'm not sure we have eighteen months to put together a RICO case. I'm beginning to think we'll be lucky if we have *six* months. Things are escalating too fast.'

'He's nuts, isn't he?' Flaherty said. 'Like Koresh and Jim Jones.'

'Far more dangerous. He's got several thousand people under his thumb.'

'Are you going to offer him a deal when you two meet?'

'We don't have any deal for him,' Vail said. 'I want to

see the enemy up close. I want to judge for myself what we're up against.'

Latimore listened but as usual was operating on his own wavelength. 'I've been thinking a lot about the shooter,' he said. 'I've got an idea I'd like to pursue.'

Vail shrugged. 'It's your job. Since when do you ask?'

Everybody chuckled.

'I mean right now.'

'Oh. Okay, why not?'

'Jimmy, who's the head of Army intelligence?'

Hines went to his machine, clattered the keys, and the information flashed on his monitor.

'Colonel Otis Maraganset. Age sixty-one. Had the job four years, looking to make general when he retires in two more.'

'How do I get in touch with him?'

'You mean one on one?'

Latimore nodded.

'I call him and tell him Assistant Attorney General Harrison Latimore needs to talk to him on a matter of importance.'

'Think he'll pick up?'

Hines laughed. 'Latimore, nobody ignores a call from the A.G.'s office.'

'Let's give it a shot. I'll go in the back office, Jimmy can patch the call into the speaker system so you guys can monitor the call.'

'That's not exactly legal,' Naomi reminded him.

Latimore smiled and winked. 'Just gonna be a friendly conversation. No big deal.'

'Colonel Maraganset, this is Harrison Latimore, I'm Assistant A.G. attached to Special Prosecutor Martin Vail's task force.'

'Yes, sir, Mr. Latimore, how can I help you?'

'The A.G., General Castaigne that is, and Mr. Vail need some information, Colonel. I was told you're the man to talk to.'

'At your disposal, sir. What kind of information?'

'It's a personnel matter going back to the late sixties, early seventies.'

'Vietnam?'

'Yes. Particularly related to intelligence units that were operating in the field.'

'I'm not sure I–'

'Let me be more specific. Black ops.'

'Black ops?'

'Yes sir. We're not interested in the men who served in those units, I know that's all hush-hush stuff. We'd like the names of the liaison officers who worked with the, uh . . . projects.'

'Mmmm, that's a bit sticky. Actually there were rumors about units working in the field, but–'

'Oh come on, Colonel, we know all about the Phantom Project and the others. No records kept, nonexistent, blah blah blah . . . that's not the information the A.G. wants. She simply wants the names of the liaison officers who worked with them. How many could there be?'

'It's classified information,' the colonel said abruptly.

'I see. Well, can I impose on you to give General Castaigne a call and explain that to her personally? I've got her number here and–'

'That won't be necessary,' Maraganset said hurriedly. 'It has been thirty years or more, Colonel.'

'Let me turn you over to my sergeant major, Steve Kosloski. I'm sure he can get the data a lot faster than I can. Is this a rush job?'

'You know the A.G., she even gets her junk mail overnight air.'

'Right. Hold on just a second, sir.'

'Thanks very much, Colonel. I'm sure General Castaigne will be most appreciative.'

He was put on hold for thirty seconds.

'Mr. Latimore, this is Sergeant Kosloski.'

'Good morning, Sergeant. Did the colonel tell you what we need?'

'Yes sir. I believe he pointed out that this is delicate informa–'

'I understand that,' Latimore cut him off. 'No one's going to know about this. It's purely for background, the data isn't going to get public exposure.'

'Right, sir. I'll need a little time. None of this stuff is in the computers.'

'How long would that be?'

'I'm sure I can have it by the end of the day.'

'Oookay . . .'

'Maybe sooner, sir. It's on first priority.'

'Fine, Sergeant. Let me give you my fax number.'

'I'd rather not put it on fax, sir. How about if I call you and give you the names over the phone?'

'That'll be fine, Sergeant.'

Twenty-five

It was a day Vail would never forget, not only because he would come face-to-face with his adversary, but because for the first time in a very long time, he would have a spiritual sense of the beauty of the country whose laws he had taken an oath to defend.

They had left Chicago before dawn, and the rising sun chased the jet across Wisconsin, the southern corner of Minnesota, and South Dakota. Now the big plane whistled over central Montana toward Missoula and the Rocky Mountains. It was following what is known as the Montana 'High Line,' which stretches from the plains of eastern Montana west to the fierce northern Rockies.

Firestone could have been a one-man Chamber of Commerce for the state. He entertained Vail as they ate breakfast. Between bites and sips of coffee, he described the land that slid below them and its history.

Long before Columbus discovered the Americas, the Blackfeet, the Assiniboine, the Cree, the northern Cheyenne, and the Nez Perce Indians roamed the great plains of Montana, hunting and fishing the Upper Missouri with free range over the 'High Line.'

The current inhabitants were descendants of the pioneers who first came to this land: immigrants, farmers, railroaders, gold miners, fur traders, mountain men, the plains Indians.

Vail was stunned by the rugged beauty of the Big Sky country, still abounding in wildlife, grain, horses, game fowl, and awesome open spaces. To the south of the plane was the winding Yellowstone River, and beyond it the gold-rich Black Hills where Custer met his fate at the Little Bighorn, creating a myth that still persisted.

Firestone knew his history, particularly when it concerned Native Americans. In the 1870s, to make room for white settlers, the United States government hunted down and defeated the Indian tribes of Montana one after another. The government lied, cheated, and broke its own treaties with the Indians, confining the great plains tribes to reservations on the poorest of lands.

The Nez Perce were the greatest horsemen, warriors, and hunters. In 1877, when the U.S. government tried to force them off their lands in the Wallowa Valley of Utah and isolate them on a barren, fallow reservation in Idaho, their leader, the eloquent Chief Joseph, challenged the United States:

'The earth was created by the assistance of the sun, and it should be left as it was. The earth and myself are of one mind. The measure of the land and the measure of our bodies are the same. Do not misunderstand me, but understand me fully with reference to my affection for the land. I never said the land was mine to do with as I chose. The one who has the right to dispose of it is the one who created it. I claim a right to live on my land, and accord you the same privilege to live on yours.'

When troops were sent to move the Nez Perce, Chief Joseph made a dash for the Canadian border and freedom. He led his tribe on an 1,800-mile running battle with the U.S. Army. For three months they used their knowledge of the mountains and survival skills to battle, outwit, and elude the U.S. Seventh Infantry. But at Bear's Paw, just forty miles from Canada, the Seventh caught up with the Nez Perce. After a bloody four-day battle, an exhausted and demoralized Chief Joseph called his beleaguered tribe together and said:

'Hear me, my chiefs, I am tired. My heart is sick and sad. From where the sun now stands, I will fight no more forever.'

The Army, as usual, broke its promise to the Nez Perce that they could return to their home. Instead, what was

338

left of the tribe was sent to a reservation in Oklahoma, where Chief Joseph died betrayed, his heart broken. But three hundred of the great plains tribe escaped Bear's Paw and made it to Canada.

Sam Firestone's great-great-grandfather was one of them.

'It was our holocaust,' Firestone said. 'The politicians practiced the worst kind of genocide. They destroyed our pride and our heritage. They outlawed our ceremonial dances and our tribal religions. They forbade us from speaking our own language. But the survivors, like my great-great-grandfather, kept the traditions alive and passed them down from one generation to the next, and finally some of us brought them back to the home country.'

'You practice that religion?' Vail asked.

'I think Native Americans have the right idea. They believe the spirits are in nature – the earth, sky, sun, the winds. Their faith is tied to the nature of things. God is an indescribable presence. Makes more sense to me than believing a spaceship's going to carry you off to heaven or praying to a human being whose mother was a virgin. But that's just my opinion.'

Vail did not answer. He looked back at the earth, then ahead toward the Bitterroot and Anaconda ranges of the Rockies. For a moment he sensed the great power of a religion that praised and honored the awesome beauty of nature. As the plane banked over the Missoula airport, he was wrenched back to the reality of his mission. He thought briefly about Jane and Magoo, waiting back in Chicago for him, then adrenaline fired his heart and he began mentally preparing for the confrontation ahead.

Firestone had made the arrangements. They were to meet Engstrom and his minions at a restaurant called the Retreat, which Sam described as an isolated cabin in a field near Fort Yahweh, about thirty miles southwest of Missoula, hard against the Idaho border.

As they headed down Route 93, Firestone pointed

straight ahead. 'Lost Trail Pass is down the road there about fifty miles,' he said. 'We can buzz it after the meeting if you'd like to take a look.'

A mile or so later he turned off the main road and took a narrow country road through the trees, toward mountains that rose sharply ahead of them.

'Pull over a minute,' Vail said. 'Gotta take a leak.'

Firestone stopped the car at the edge of the road. The forest was fifteen feet away, and Vail walked a few feet in front of the car to relieve himself. As he stood there, he suddenly felt he was being watched. It came to him like a chill across the back of his neck. He turned slightly and squinted into the dark shadows of the thick forest. The eyes were almond-shaped and gold-flecked and belonged to a white wolf. It stepped to the edge of the trees, its breath steaming from its open mouth, its eyes never off Vail's.

Vail was rooted in place. His mouth dried out. Then the wolf raised its head and a mournful howl echoed through the woods.

Should he stand still?

Run?

A moment later a second wolf stepped silently into the clearing, followed by two smaller animals, obviously their young. They stood behind the big white one and all stared at Vail. He started back toward the car, and as he did, the small wolf pack walked in the same direction, still hugging the edge of the forest. At the same time, Firestone eased the car forward and opened the door. As it pulled alongside him, Vail jumped in and pulled the door shut.

As Firestone pulled away, the white wolf stepped out of the protection of the trees and walked beside the car for a dozen feet before it stopped and turned back into the woods.

'What the hell was that all about?' Vail said breathlessly.

'Wolves are very curious fellows,' Firestone said.

'Curious? My heart's about to break a rib.'

'He wouldn't hurt you. Wolves don't attack human beings.'

'Easy for you to say, you weren't standing out there with your dick wagging in the wind. And how about that howling?'

'He brought his family out to meet you, Martin. I imagine he saw something special about you. Wolves are very mystic creatures.' He paused a moment and added, 'Maybe he smelled your urine. They can smell something three, four miles away and hear up to a mile.' He chuckled. 'Maybe he was attracted to you.'

'Lucky me.'

'Wolves have the most complex social order of any animal alive. They mate for life, they teach their young to play, they have a great sense of humor, and they're innately curious. I was in the high Rockies years ago stalking an elk. I was sitting under a tree catching my breath and this wolf saunters out. He was maybe fifty feet away. He knew I was there, he just didn't give a shit. He stopped in a clearing and then he did the damnedest thing. He watched a daisy open. He watched it, then brushed his nose across it, then lifted up his paw, and touched it. Then he went on his way. Beautiful thing to behold.'

'Great. Ferdinand the wolf.'

'The Nez Perce believe they're the most spiritual of all creatures. The Milky Way is called the Route of the Wolf. Leads the fallen horse soldiers to heaven. They can sense the purity of the human spirit. You got a pure heart, Martin?'

'I don't know how pure it is. Right now it's beating about eight to the bar.'

Firestone laughed. 'Whatever, Brother Wolf was certainly drawn to you. Brought out his whole family to meet you. Or . . . maybe he called his pack together to get a last look at you before you get your head blown off.'

'That's very calming, thanks!'

'Hey, if you go down, I'll go down right next to you.' He smiled over at Vail. 'Welcome to Montana.'

And a moment or two later they rounded a bay of tall pine trees and Vail saw their destination, a one-story building of stone and wood crouched alone in the open, with the mountains brooding a few miles behind it. Eight or ten cars were parked haphazardly around it and smoke rose lazily from the chimney. A rutted road, muddied in the snow, led back to it. There was a man in camouflage pants and a fur-lined parka standing by the highway with a .30-30 held across his chest, and two more with rifles by the front door of the restaurant. A small hand-painted sign over the door announced: THE RETREAT.

Firestone pulled to a stop as the armed guard held up his hand.

'Hell, he's just a kid,' Vail said.

'Yeah, they start 'em early.'

Firestone rolled down his window. The young man leaned over and studied them both. He couldn't have been more than fifteen or sixteen, the first sprouts of a beard checkering his chin and cheeks.

Firestone showed him his badge. 'Name's Sam Firestone, U.S. Marshal Service. This is Assistant Attorney General Martin Vail,' he said casually.

'You armed, sir?' the boy asked in a voice that wasn't as tough as he wanted it to be.

Firestone calmly reached over, unbuttoned his coat, and pulled it back. He was wearing a 9mm Glock under his right arm.

'You'll have to hand that over,' the boy said, dropping his voice half an octave.

'Sorry, son, I'm a United States marshal. I don't give my gun up to anybody.'

The boy was thrown off by the remark. He looked

342

toward the two guards at the restaurant, then decided to act grown-up and handle the situation himself.

'Then this is as far as you go,' he said.

Firestone nodded toward the vehicles parked around the restaurant. 'Judging from the vehicles, you have us way outnumbered. But . . .'

He reached under his arm with his left hand, took out the Glock, and dropped the clip into his other hand. He slipped it into his shirt pocket and ejected the round out of the chamber, caught it in midair, and dropped it in the pocket.

'That suit ya?'

The boy looked at him for several seconds, then took a cell phone out of his pocket and punched out a number. One of the men at the door of the restaurant answered it.

'This is Ricky. It's them,' the boy said. 'The marshal's still got his gun but it's dry.' He listened for a moment and nodded. One of the two guards at the restaurant door waved Firestone in.

'Thanks,' Firestone said, nodding to the young guard, and drove down the snow-encrusted roadway, swung around, and parked facing the highway.

'Just in case we have to leave in a hurry,' he said quietly.

Vail shifted uncomfortably in his seat. 'If we have to leave in a hurry, we won't get this far.'

'They ain't gonna start a war here,' Firestone said as they walked toward the eatery, their feet squeaking and crunching in the snow.

'That a guarantee?'

'Nothing in life's a guarantee.'

'You just keep reassuring me, don't you, Sam?'

The marshal smiled. 'Hell,' he said, 'you'll be able t'tell your grandchildren about this day.'

'That'll be a trick. I don't have any children, let alone grandchildren.'

'Never too late to start.'

'I'm a city boy, Sam. I wasn't cut out for this Wild West crap.'

'Never too late to start that, either. Besides, you're charmed, Martin. Brother Wolf said so.'

'Maybe you misunderstood him.'

'Not likely.'

The marshal took out a plug of tobacco, pinched off a piece, and stuck it under his lower lip.

'You're just transforming all over the place, Sam. Talking like Billy the Kid. Chewing tobacco.'

'Home country, I revert fast. Wanna chew?'

'Thanks anyway, I'm still trying to quit smoking. Wonder how many Engstrom brought with him?'

'Fifteen or twenty, judging from the vehicles.'

'Pretty shitty odds.'

'You dealt the hand. Let's play the sucker out.'

As they reached the door, the two guards stopped them. Before they could say anything, Firestone took out his pistol and pulled back the carriage. He held it up in front of them.

'Still have to pat you down, sir,' one of the guards said politely. He was a trim man in his thirties wearing camouflage pants and a heavy leather jacket with sergeant's stripes sewed on the sleeve.

'Is the General armed?' Vail asked before the man moved toward him. The remark caught Firestone off guard and surprised the sergeant.

'How's that?' the sergeant said, hesitating.

'If you don't trust the word of an attorney general, then we'll have to pat down the General.'

'I don't think so.'

'Then either open the door or we'll leave.'

The sergeant glared at Vail, tossing all the options around in his head.

'It's cold out here, Sergeant. Make up your mind.'

The sergeant shook his head but finally opened the door. Vail went in first and stood inside the door. It was a low-ceilinged room, L-shaped, with a counter and grill to the right and tables and booths in front of him, and it was dark, the only light coming from the windows. As his eyes became accustomed to the light level, Vail made out a moose head and a rainbow trout mounted on one wall. Beside the door were half a dozen pegs with old horseshoes hooked over them. The place smelled of coffee and freshly cooked bacon.

The tables in front of him were empty except for one in a dark corner occupied by two men. One man was as thin as a scarecrow, the other was beefy with a Mormon beard. He wore sunglasses in the dimly lit corner. The counter was crowded with men in camouflage, sitting at the counter or standing beside it. A stocky, ruddy, hard-looking man with colonel's eagles on the shoulder of his parka stood in front of them.

'Gentlemen, I'm Colonel Shrack,' he said in a brittle voice. He looked over Vail's shoulder and nodded to Firestone. 'The General wants to speak to Mr. Vail alone. Mr. Firestone, you can join me at this table here if that's acceptable.'

'Fine,' Vail said.

'I'll just tell him you're here.'

Shrack walked to a corner booth and leaned over, speaking to a bald, bullet-headed man who was sitting with his back to the front door. It was Engstrom. Firestone leaned close to Vail and whispered: 'I make it sixteen counting Shrack, Metzinger, Rentz, Bollinger, Rainey, and the General.'

'Gang's all here and in uniform.'

'You were right, he's showing off.'

Shrack walked back to them. 'Follow me, Mr. Vail.'

He led Vail to a corner booth where the General was seated. He was larger than Vail had imagined, and younger-looking. He was in trim condition, with broad shoulders and a bull neck, completely bald, with thick black eyebrows shading deep-set, fiery eyes that fixed on

345

Vail and stayed there.

He stood up, two or three inches taller than Vail, and his hand enveloped Vail's, closing on it like a snake squeezing a rabbit.

'My pleasure, Mr. Vail,' he said in a voice so harsh it sounded like he had a perpetually sore throat.

'Mine, too, General.'

'Have a seat. Want some breakfast? Coffee?'

'Coffee would be nice.'

Engstrom waved his hand but still did not take his eyes off Vail. 'I hear you're some kind of lawyer,' he said.

'Some kind,' Vail said, and smiled.

'And now you're with the A.G.'s office.'

'That's correct.'

'That Azimour woman really stuck a thorn in your paw, didn't she?' He said it without a trace of sarcasm or mirth.

'Well, you know how it is, the media's an occupational hazard.'

'Never said more than hello to a reporter.'

'I've tried not to say anything at all to them.'

One of Engstrom's men sat a mug of coffee and a pitcher of milk in front of Vail.

'You've come a long way, Mr. Vail. Must be important, what you've got to say.'

'I think so.'

'Well . . .' He raised his hands at his sides, palms up. '. . . here I am.'

'I'm going to put the whole deck on the table, General. Ten days ago an Army weapons convoy was knocked over in Lost Trail Pass. Ten American soldiers were murdered and left in body bags. A couple of days later George Waller, a.k.a. Ralph Anderson, was assassinated in Ohio by a professional hit man. He was in the witness protection program. There are some strings connecting these two crimes together. For one, Lost Trail Pass is in your territory. For another, Waller was a potential witness for the government against the Sanctuary. No other group or person we know of had a motive to kill Waller but your outfit.'

'It's a church, sir, not an outfit. A Christian church.'

'There was also a coded message left at the scene of both crimes. Numbers. Two-three-thirteen. It refers to the chapter and verse in the Old Testament that explains the use of the word "Yahweh" in place of God. As I'm sure you know, that's also the name of your compound.'

The restaurant was deathly silent except for the sizzle of bacon on the grill. Nobody moved. Sam Firestone suddenly wished his gun was loaded.

'And as far as this being our *territory*, we aren't some nigger street gang. We don't have a territory, this happens to be the parish of the Sanctuary.'

'According to your man Abraham, it's a Christian army.'

'He's not my man, Mr. Vail.'

'You sponsor his radio show.'

'Is that against the law now? Has the ZOG government finally outlawed the First Amendment?'

'His rants could be construed as a violation of certain federal statutes.'

'I don't think so.'

'I said construed, sir.'

'Is that what this is about? Brother Abraham speaks the truth and suddenly my church is under suspicion of . . . ?' He let the sentence die out.

'General, what we're talking about is a series of hard felonies. There's nothing in the Constitution guaranteeing the right to murder and steal.'

'Except in times of war. All bets are off in times of war, Mr. Vail.'

'Oh? Did I miss something? Are you at war with the United States?'

'Figure of speech.'

'Do you really want to lead your people against the

347

United States? You're a patriot, General, a war hero. Are you suggesting leading your people into a war with the country you served with honor?'

'Honor, eh,' he sneered. 'Do you know what I did in 'Nam? Do you know what I did in Desert Storm?'

'I know about the Phantoms. I also know the service lost track of these people after 'Nam. I know some of them became freelancers in the international intelligence community. Rogue agents, wet-boy assassins, dirty tricks operatives, you name it. They showed up in Nicaragua, Guatemala, wherever the job was dirty enough and the money was right.'

'If what you're saying is true, you also know that their biggest client was their own government, the government that trained them, robbed them of their youth and their souls, then cut them loose and used them for its own purposes. You know that, too?'

Vail didn't show his surprise. He stared at the General for several seconds, then nodded slowly. 'It would be a natural assumption.'

Engstrom leaned across the table and said in a rasp of a whisper, 'I saved their souls. I offered redemption, the forgiveness of Christ. I offered them the opportunity to march with Christ against the Devil.'

'And the Devil is the U.S. government?'

'Its minions and its servants. You know who you really work for, Mr. Vail? The Zionist government. The Jews. The niggers. The Irish sinners in Boston. Whoremongers and drunks. We are immaculately trained Christian soldiers, sir, the kind of men and women who would die the worst kind of death before uttering a word to the enemy or surrendering.'

'It's an exercise in futility, General.'

'Really? You read your Bible, Mr. Vail?'

'Not on any regular basis.'

'That's a shame. You ought to take a look occasionally. Are you familiar with the Philistines?'

Vail nodded. 'Jordan gave me that lecture. David and his slingshot against the nine-foot giant. Nothing is impossible for the righteous. Jordan laid it all out, General. I repeat, what can six thousand soldiers do except create a momentary crisis?'

'There are between fifty and a hundred thousand members of militia groups, Mr. Vail. With sympathizers, the numbers go as high as a million. Waiting for a sign. Waiting for the apocalypse to set them free. Waiting for the New American Revolution to kill political leaders, bomb buildings, carry out guerrilla warfare on the streets, refuse to pay taxes. This started long before I came on the scene, Mr. Vail.'

'But now you're the lightning rod?'

Engstrom's eyes blazed and his lips curled back. He stood up, raised his fist toward the ceiling, and glared down at Vail.

'I am the prophet of Yahweh!' he bellowed. 'The Lord speaks with my voice! *Give place unto wrath: for it is written, Vengeance is mine; I will repay, saith the Lord.* Romans, Chapter Twelve, Verse Nineteen.'

Across the room Firestone stole a glance at his watch. *Do it now,* he said to himself. *Do it, Martin.*

Vail reached into his inside pocket, took out a sheaf of folded documents, and splayed them out on the table like playing cards.

'General, these are Title Three search and seizure warrants against you, your key officers, and all your bank records. They were signed by a federal judge. They also permit a hard search of your facility known as Fort Yahweh.'

He took out his cell phone and punched out a number. Hardistan answered almost immediately. 'This is Billy. We're in place.'

'He's been served. Just a minute.' Vail looked at Engstrom. 'General, this is William Hardistan, Deputy Director of the FBI. He'd like a word with you.'

He held the phone toward Engstrom. The General stared at it as if it were a glowing coal. Finally he took it.

'General Engstrom,' he said slowly. Savagely.

At the front of Fort Yahweh, Hardistan faced the corporal at the gate. Behind him, Humvees and weapons carriers were lined up. ATF, FBI agents, and snipers in body armor and blue jackets were lined up like an army. Above them, Nighthawk choppers hovered like bats from hell.

'Sir, this is Billy Hardistan,' the Deputy Director said into his cell phone. 'You know who I am.'

'Of course.'

'The FBI and the ATF are in place and in force here and in seven other locations named in the search warrants Martin Vail just served on you. We don't want violence here, General. You've been served. These are legal search warrants. Please advise the young man at the gate – I believe his name is Starret – to step aside.'

Engstrom did not answer immediately. He had been tricked and he knew it. A confrontation at this point would be disastrous.

Finally: 'May I speak to Starret?'

'Of course.'

Hardistan handed the cell phone to the corporal. 'Your commanding officer wants a word with you,' he said.

The corporal, a hard-bitten veteran, glared at him, then took the phone.

'Corporal Starret, sir.'

'Starret, you recognize my voice?'

'Of course, sir.'

'Step aside, Corporal. Let them in.'

The corporal looked shocked, even though he knew there were only a handful of men on the base.

'Yes sir.'

Engstrom handed the phone back to Vail, who cut the connection.

In the darkened corner across the room, behind the sunglass lenses, Abraham's eyes glittered as he stared across the room at the man he hated more than he loved Satan. *He's fifty feet away,* he thought. *One bullet is all it would take.*

'We didn't want another Waco or Ruby Ridge, General,' Vail said.

'I could take you hostage right now.'

'You could, but it would be a dumb move and you know it. It would all end out here in the middle of nowhere. Your entire command staff is in this room.'

Vail punched out a number on the cellular phone and waited for an answer.

'Coming out,' he said. He clicked it off, slid the aerial back into the slot, and dropped the phone in his pocket.

'There are two Nighthawk choppers sitting about a quarter mile out there,' he said, waving vaguely toward the rear of the restaurant. 'They'll be real upset if we don't leave now.' He got up and slipped on his coat. 'Been a pleasure, General.'

'You're even more devious than I was led to believe,' Engstrom said, his eyes narrowed and cold.

'You had bad intelligence.'

Vail walked to the door and left, followed by Firestone.

Engstrom got up and stared out the window as the car drove down the road toward the highway. From out of the shadows, Abraham tapped his way across the restaurant. He stood behind the General and leaned close to his ear.

'He needs to be killed, General,' he whispered.

'That won't change anything.'

'It'll rattle them, slow them down. All we need's a little more time. *And I will set my face against you, and ye shall be slain before your enemies and they that hate you shall reign over you.* Leviticus, Chapter Twenty-six, Verse Seventeen.'

Engstrom watched the sedan turn onto the highway

and head back toward Missoula. A minute or two later one of the Nighthawks clattered across the treetops and swung in behind it. Engstrom's jaw tightened.

'Then let it come down,' he said.

Twenty-six

It was almost ten-thirty when Billy Hardistan showed his ID to the Secret Service agents and entered the service entrance of the Mayflower Hotel. He walked through the kitchen and ID'd himself again as he entered the stairwell. From the ballroom crowded with political contributors who had paid a thousand dollars to eat stringy chicken and asparagus and pay homage to the world's most powerful human being, he could hear the President wrapping up a rousing speech.

Hardistan took the stairs to the third floor. There were two Secret Service agents at the door to the corner suite that was Pennington's hideaway, a place where he could hold meetings not on the daily agenda. Hardistan nodded and showed his ID once again.

'Thank you, Mr. Hardistan,' one of the agents said.

'Anybody else here yet?'

'Yes, sir, the A.G. and Mr. Hooker.'

Hardistan nodded and entered the three-bedroom suite, which was tastefully furnished with American antiques. Both Hooker and Castaigne had poured themselves drinks and were seated facing each other on two sofas separated by a coffee table.

'Hi, Billy,' Castaigne said brightly when he entered.

'Marge, Claude,' the FBI man said, nodding at both of them.

Hooker smiled and raised his glass in greeting. 'How's he doing down there?' he asked.

'Sounds like he's wrapping it up now,' Hardistan answered. He put his briefcase on the table, took out a large manila envelope and his cell phone, attached a small audiotape recorder to it, and dialed a number.

'Echo, this is Coach. Have you got the run? Good, my audio is running, run tape please.' He listened for several minutes, then said, 'Excellent. Thank you, Echo.' He disconnected the phone and recorder.

'What?' Hooker said.

'More of the same.'

'Christ!'

Hardistan took out a videotape and several large photographs and spread them on the table. Both Hooker and Castaigne joined him and stared balefully at the display.

'My God,' Hooker said. 'What is the son of a bitch up to?'

'He's preparing to defend his mountain,' Hardistan said, almost casually.

'Since when did it become *his* mountain?' Hooker growled.

Before Hardistan could answer, the door opened and two Secret Service agents entered. They checked all the rooms, the baths, and the windows, then escorted President Pennington inside.

'Good evening, everybody,' the President said as he entered the room. He was obviously energized from his speech.

'How'd it go?' Hooker asked.

'Great. Full house. The National Committee ought to kiss my ass. So, Billy, where do we stand?'

'These photos were shot about 1600 Mountain Time. The AWACS just completed another run. I have a videotape of it, but these pictures should help orient you.'

There were eight photos in all. Four were taken from thirty thousand feet; the other four were digital blow-ups of the same area. Hardistan described the terrain as the others checked the overhead views of Engstrom's sprawling tract. They were looking straight down from thirty thousand feet. On the left side of the vertical photos, to the east, was Fort Yahweh, a cluster of buildings surrounded by a high fence. Rising sharply from the edge of the compound was a towering mountain capped by a nine-thousand-foot peak. The top half of the mountain was heavily forested in pines almost to its ragged, snowy crest. The bottom part of the mountain was precipitous, a series of sharp cliffs and waterfalls plunging straight down almost to the base. A narrow road wound up the side of the mountain to a small plateau about halfway to the top. A small bridge led across one of the gorges to a saddle at the edge of the cliffs.

The saddle marked the lower edge of the Sanctuary's training ground, a steep, harsh survival ground three miles wide and a mile high. Below the shelf were the deadly cliffs that loomed over Fort Yahweh.

The back side of the mountain, which marked the border of Idaho and Montana, was even more dangerous, a series of deep gullies and gorges stepped with shelves.

'Treacherous,' Castaigne breathed with awe.

'In more ways than one,' Hardistan answered. 'You can use these photos to orient yourselves while I play this tape. This was recorded thirty minutes ago.'

Hardistan put the video in a VCR and pressed the play button. The same view of the fort and its mountain sentry slid below the plane as an identification specialist described the scene in a monotonous but efficient tone.

'Sharpshooter, this is Echo One.'

'Copy that Echo One. Do you read our transmission?'

'Loud and clear, Sharpshooter. We are taping.'

'Copy that Echo. This is Sharpshooter on course due south from Canadian border over the Idaho-Montana border. Altitude 28,500, speed five hundred. Time: 1941 hours, Mountain Standard.'

'Copy that.'

'Approaching target. Do you read?'

'Roger. My God, they look like ants.'

Far below, heat sensors registered dots, like moving measles, all over the mountain.

'We'll run a grid on the video and get an accurate count. Looks like they've doubled since last night. Zooming in to ten-to-one.'

The camera zoomed down a hundred yards above the peak of Mount James. The ants now appeared as moving, white stick figures against the rubble of the forest.

'Those "ants" are Engstrom's soldiers, Echo One.'

'Copy that! What are those rectangles down by the entrance gate?'

'School buses. Thirty-eight passengers, up to fifty with standing room. Those three probably delivered 135 to 150 personnel.'

'They're moving out.'

'Going to pick up another load. And those barracks, the long buildings at the rear of the compound near the base of the mountain, hold ninety men each. That's another 270.'

'How about those thin lines all over the mountain?'

'That's wire. Look in the upper right quad of your screen.'

'Roger that.'

'That's a group of four or five men around a tree. They're stringing wire. Our profile indicates it's razor wire. Lower left quad, a single man appears to be burying an explosive device, probably a claymore mine or possibly a bouncing Betty.'

'Jesus!' Pennington said.

'They're on the back side of the mountain, too,' Echo One said.

'That's a roger. They're all over the terrain.'

'Turn that damn thing off,' Pennington snapped.

Hardistan turned off the recorder. 'It's more intense tonight. We don't have the grid count yet, but it will be in the six to seven hundred range. They're using eight-man survival tents in the target area, sleeping and working in shifts. And there's almost three hundred more quartered in the barracks.'

356

'What the hell are they doing?' Hooker asked.

'Digging in. They're bringing in their troops at night in school buses and vans. Been doing it since we searched the fort and served the entitlements.'

'What's he think he's going to do?'

'Defend his territory. This is their monthly training exercise. Usually only seventy-five or a hundred people.'

'Let 'em try,' Hooker snapped. 'Back in the early eighties, the Order sent a declaration of war to Congress. The Bureau took out Gordon Kahl, sent the leader, Wayne Snell, to the gallows, and put twenty-four of them away for life. And that was the end of the Order.'

'There were less than a hundred members in the Order, Claude,' Hardistan said. 'We're talking about several thousand trained troops, with almost a thousand in the area already, probably armed with automatic rifles, grenade launchers, antitank weapons, ground-to-ground and ground-to-air missiles, claymores, and three to four tons . . . *tons* . . . of C-4.'

'Jesus, that's enough to take out a city the size of Missoula,' Pennington said.

'That's right. They also have an enormous supply of AMFO – they've been stockpiling ammonium nitrate for two or three years. Every farmer in the Sanctuary has been buying it.'

'Which could be stashed all over the state,' Castaigne said.

'Exactly.'

'Can we provoke them?' Hooker asked.

'If Vail didn't provoke them when we delivered the warrants, I don't know what will.'

'What do you mean?' Castaigne asked.

'How about the attack on the convoy?' Hooker went on, ignoring her question. 'Killing U.S. soldiers in ambush. Can't that be considered an act of war?'

'We can't prove it was them. We're *sure* it was them, but we can't prove it,' Hardistan said.

'Any leads on the semi yet?' Castaigne asked.

'No. We've been all over those mountains with choppers, satellite scans, AWACS, and on foot. I think it's possible we'll never find it. But we know they've got AT-4 Vipers, 72-E5 66mm antitank guns, Dragon missiles, Stingers, M-16s, and enough ammo and rockets to start World War Three. And it's stashed in that mountain somewhere.'

'He's going to have to make the first move,' Hooker said.

'Christ, robbing banks, armories, killing people . . . if that's not the first move, what the hell is?' Pennington roared. They all walked to the sofa and sat down.

'Dave, draw me one, will you?' Pennington said to one of his Secret Service men as he took out a cigar. 'Sorry about smoking,' he said. 'I've been entertaining these money boys for four hours without a smoke.' As he lit the cigar, the agent poured him a stout glass of Jack Daniel's, dropped in two ice cubes, splashed water in the drink, and handed it to the President, who nodded his thanks.

'We need one hard case before we can mobilize a proper force, box him in, and order him to surrender his men and his weapons,' Castaigne said.

'Box him in?' Hardistan said. 'He's got those mountains mined, razor-wired, protected by well-trained guerrilla warriors. If I brought in every FBI and ATF agent I can find, I still wouldn't have enough manpower to box in a fortified mountain.'

'He'll never surrender. He's got to be taken out. And now's the time,' Hooker said.

Hardistan nodded. 'His entire staff and all his hand-picked personnel are either up there now or on their way.'

'We can't trust the National Guard,' Hooker said. 'Many of them have family who are members of the Sanctuary. What we need is highly trained specialists who can handle the terrain and get the job done.'

'Are you suggesting what I *think* you're suggesting?' Castaigne asked.

No answer. Then Marge Castaigne's eyes suddenly widened.

'Oh my God!' she muttered. They all looked at her. 'Do I have to remind you it's against federal law to use American troops against U.S. citizens?'

'Unless they declare war on us,' Hooker said.

'I don't think Engstrom will do that without aggressive provocation,' Hardistan said.

'Well,' Hooker said, 'one thing's for damn sure, the Boy Scouts can't handle this operation.'

The A.G. was becoming increasingly uncomfortable with the direction the conversation was taking.

'Marge,' the President said with a smile, 'why don't you go home. It's getting late.'

He stood up. She looked at him for a moment and got up and followed him to the door.

'I would never put you in a compromising position, Marge,' the President said softly. 'Just remember what Barry Goldwater said once, "Extremism in the defense of liberty is no vice. Moderation in the pursuit of justice is no virtue."'

'I was thinking of something else, Mr. President. Jonathan Swift said it: "It is a great disadvantage to fight with those who have nothing to lose." I think Martin Vail understands that. We made a promise to him. His people are working night and day on the RICO cases.'

He looked at her without expression. 'Good night, Marge,' he said. She looked at him for a moment more and left.

Pennington went back to the sofa and took a sip of his drink.

'Okay,' he said, 'where were we? How big a force are we talking about, Billy?'

'I would defer to the Army on that.'

'Then I think I should bring in Jesse James and get an'

expert opinion.'

Brandon 'Jesse' James was General of the Army and a former deputy to Pennington. He was a gung-ho commander who had been compared to Patton because of his garrulous and independent nature. He was also the best field officer Pennington had ever met.

'Will he do it?' Hardiston asked.

'I'll talk to him. Just the two of us, man-to-man.'

'Jesse has a mind of his own,' Hooker said.

'Well, the bottom line is, he'll do whatever the hell his commander in chief tells him to do.'

'Do you think there's a danger military action will provoke more terrorist attacks? Or will they back off?' Hooker asked.

There was a lull. Pennington looked at Hardistan, who raised an eyebrow for an answer.

'That depends on the body count,' the President replied.

Twenty-seven

The cab driver stared through the passenger window at the minister. He was dressed in a heavy black coat, a black felt hat, and a gray suit with a backward collar. He sat, leaning on his cane, on a bench overlooking the Oklahoma City park where the Alfred B. Murrah Building had once stood.

Aaron Stampler, now known as Abraham, had pushed his contacts down under his lower lids and was staring ahead through his sunglasses, past the wire fence draped with toys, flowers, and photographs of the victims. He felt his pulse quicken as he imagined the moment the truck had blown up. In his mind he saw half the building slide away, smelled the odor of fire and death, heard the clamor of destruction and the chaotic screams that followed it, saw the ruined building with wires dangling from it like entrails.

A masterpiece, he thought.

'Excuse me, Reverend.'

He turned slightly in the direction of the voice, saw the young woman standing beside him. She was holding a bunch of flowers and there was a gentle smile on her face.

'Yes?'

'I couldn't help noticing you. I thought perhaps I might describe the park for you.'

'What a nice thought,' he said. 'But I prefer to remember it as it was.'

'You've been here before?'

'No, but it's been described to me.'

'Did you lose someone in the explosion?'

He thought of the bomber. 'Yes,' he said.

'I'm sorry. I'll just go on, then,' she said.

'Thank you. You're very kind.'

'I lost my family here,' she said, and moved away.

Abraham sat for another two or three minutes and savored the moments, then went back to the cab.

'Airport,' he told the cabby.

He was surprised that the Sorcerer was familiar with the Oklahoma City jetport. Abraham's simple message had said: 'Sorcerer. Will be making a stop over at the Oklahoma City airport tomorrow, ten to noon. Hope to see you then. Fisherman.'

The answer was just as simple: 'Fisherman: Concourse Two. Brogen's. Ten A. Sorcerer.'

Brogen's was a restaurant with a bar facing the concourse walkway. Abraham sat down at the bar and ordered a diet Coke. The phone rang and the bartender snatched it up, listened a moment, then cupped the mouthpiece:

'Anybody at the bar who calls himself the "Fisherman"?' he asked.

Abraham waved his hand. 'That would be me,' he said. The bartender was surprised. He handed him the portable phone.

'Thank you,' Abraham said. 'This is Simon Peter,' he said into the phone.

'You didn't mention you were blind.'

'It didn't come up.'

'Go down the concourse to your left. Gate C is the second gate down on your right. There's nobody there right now, the gate doesn't get a flight for two hours. Go to the back of the waiting area. There's a row of chairs there. Count six seats over and sit down.' The line went dead.

Abraham laid two dollars on the bar, thanked the bartender, and left. He walked close to the wall on the right, pretending to feel his way along with the cane. When he reached Gate C, he followed Sorcerer's instructions.

Clever, he thought. Six seats over faced the wall. No window, no reflection. He sat down on the sixth chair and waited.

Across the concourse, Woodbine watched the blind man feeling his way down the walkway with his cane. He had chin whiskers and was dressed in black and gray. Woodbine turned into the gate area, found the seat and sat down, then waited for two or three minutes. Nobody was following Simon Peter. Woodbine who walked across to the gate and took a chair directly behind him, who opened a copy of *USA Today* and held it high enough to conceal his face but low enough to see over the top.

'I'm the Sorcerer,' Woodbine said in a low voice.

'Simon Peter,' Abraham answered, then added, 'the Fisherman, if you know your Bible.'

'You look like a Mormon preacher.'

'No, just a plain old Baptist Bible thumper.'

'No offense.'

'Of course not. Some of my best friends are Mormons.'

'How come you picked Oklahoma City?' Woodbine asked.

'I wanted to visit the Murrah site. I wanted to get a sense of that masterpiece of business.'

'Masterpiece my ass. He fucked the job up royally. That's what happens when you send an amateur to do a pro's work. Piss-poor planning and his getaway program was ridiculous.'

'Well, I got a certain amount of joy out of just being there, imagining what it was like. The whole side of the building collapsing. All the confusion. The sirens, people screaming, the smell of fertilizer and oil. I relived it in my imagination.'

'You're one sick puppy, Reverend.'

'And you're not?'

'I'm a businessman. If there wasn't a call for my services, I'd be selling hardware for a living.'

'Do you enjoy it?'

'What the hell kind of question is that?'

'Just curious. You're infinitely efficient. I figure a man that good has to enjoy his work.'

'I get a certain satisfaction out of it. The tougher the job, the better it tastes. I don't take just any job, you know. I like to think what I do contributes something to society.'

'I admire your rationale.'

'Let me tell you something, I don't share the General's viewpoint. The Army taught me a trade, made me very proficient at it. I've got nothing at all against the government. But if the General wants something done, it'll get done. I owe him that. I'll always owe him that.'

'Loyalty is an admirable trait.'

'You're not loyal to him?'

'I share his doctrine.'

'You want to get your ass handed to you on some mountainside in Mon-fucking-tana?'

'It may not happen that way.'

'Yeah, I know. You're all going to hide out in the hills and make guerrilla raids on shopping centers and filling stations and hang judges and shoot forest rangers.'

'It's a wake-up call. Things have to change in the country. We can't let the niggers and Jews keep running it into the ground.'

'I've got no complaints, Reverend. Things have gone very well for me. I may even retire.'

'Hopefully you have time for one more job.'

'Is it challenging?'

'Oh yes, I think it will easily meet your criteria.'

'Who's the mark?'

'You watch television.'

'A lot more than you do.'

They both laughed.

'A good one,' Abraham said. 'You recognize the name Martin Vail?'

'The lawyer who was with Hardistan in Ohio. He's with the Justice Department now, isn't he?'

'Assistant Attorney General, to be exact. A special prosecutor. He's aiming his big guns at the Sanctuary. Challenging enough for you?'

'It shows promise. You realize, of course, if you take him out, there will be more just like him.'

'No, he's unique, Sorcerer.'

'You know him.'

'Our paths have crossed.'

Abraham took a key from his pocket and laid it on the armrest of his chair.

'There's a locker key here. The locker's in the first bank after you leave the baggage pickup. There's a file on Vail in the locker. Clippings, articles, a videotape. He lives in a penthouse in downtown Chicago, but one of the articles mentions a secluded cabin where he likes to get away from things. Trouble is, nobody knows where it is.'

'I wouldn't call that a problem. I found whatsisname, didn't I?'

'Pure genius. That's why I'm here.'

'He's going to have a lot of weight around him.'

'Two or three FBIs all the time. That worry you?'

'Of course not, getting to him isn't going to be the problem. Getting out after it's done is the problem. Always is.'

'I'm sure you'll figure that out.'

'Oh yeah. How much will the freight bear?'

'A hundred. Usual arrangements. Half deposited in your bank before the end of the day, the other fifty when it's done. Sound fair?'

'If that's what the General can afford, then it's fair.'

'Out of curiosity, what would the fee on this job normally be?'

'Oh, I probably wouldn't touch it for less than a quarter mil.'

'Maybe you can write the other one-fifty off as a charitable contribution.'

'Very funny.'

'So I can tell the General it's done?'

'I'll need a couple of days.'

'I understand. This is a matter of some urgency. The weekend's coming up. He'll probably be at the cabin.'

'It will be done as fast as it can be done.'

'The General will be delighted.'

'Good. Now if you'll just stay the way you are for five minutes, I'll be on my way.'

Woodbine's hand reached between the seats and gathered up the locker key.

'Good luck with the Apocalypse.'

And he was gone.

Abraham waited for a few seconds and turned slightly, peering from the corner of his eye. All he saw was a stooped old man in a knee-length coat shuffling down the concourse toward the main terminal.

Twenty-Eight

The house, a two-story red brick structure with a wide front porch, was on a quiet street in a small village which boasted that its local hotel, the King's Inn, now a bed and breakfast, had been host to George Washington during the Revolutionary War. There was a tree house in the empty lot across the street and a two-wheeler lying on its side on the lawn next door. It was a house out of time and place, from an era when people never locked their doors and drive-by shootings were unheard of. The mailbox was neatly lettered:

Colonel Scott and Mrs. Barbara Grimes
424 Hawthorne Avenue

Latimore parked the car on the street and walked up a long slop-ing driveway to a brick path leading to the front door. The doorbell was answered by a pleasant woman in her early fifties wearing a plain housedress.

'Mrs. Grimes?' Latimore asked.

'Mrs. Grimes passed away two years ago,' she said. 'I'm Alice, the colonel's housekeeper.'

Latimore showed her his identification. 'My name's Harrison Latimore, U.S. Attorney General's office. I have an appointment with the colonel.'

'Yes, Mr. Latimore, he's expecting you. Come in, please.'

She led him through a small entrance hall to a bright sun room. A staircase led to the second floor, and there were French doors facing it, opening onto a terrace. The walls were covered with photographs of Grimes, a sturdy man with brown hair, in the company of soldiers, receiving a medal, standing with a group of officers in the jungle.

She walked around the room and pulled lace curtains across the windows, the rings zinging across the brass rods.

'The colonel has a problem with his eyes,' she said. 'Bright sunlight is painful for him, and he absolutely refuses to wear sunglasses indoors. Says he's not a movie star.'

Latimore chuckled along with her. She went to the foot of the stairs and rang a small dinner bell.

'Colonel,' she called up the stairs, 'you have a visitor.'

'Is it Gary?' a thin, reedy voice asked.

'No, Colonel, it's the stranger.'

'The stranger! Well. Right down.'

Latimore was shocked when he saw Grimes. He came down the stairs slowly, holding both railings and taking a step at a time. He was dressed in an old terry bathrobe and furry slippers, his face so ravaged by time and circumstance it was impossible to guess what he had looked like in his prime. His hair, haphazardly combed, was dirty gray, and there was a white stubble of beard on his cheeks, a day or two's growth. His eyes, once blue, were faded and lifeless. His arms were mere stalks, the skin white, the veins so close to the surface one could see his heart beating in his forearms. He was wearing only a yellowed upper plate and his lower lips sagged inward, and occasionally he tapped his mouth with a white handkerchief embroidered with his initials. His voice was a quivering memory and he gasped for breath between every sentence.

'You have a guest, Colonel Charlie,' the housekeeper said kindly. 'Mr. Latimore here came all the way from Washington to see you.'

'Oh,' he said in a faraway voice. 'Thank you. That's very nice. Don't get many visitors anymore, do we, Alice? Let me see, the last one was from an insurance company. Thought I'd passed.' He cackled at the thought. He offered a hand that was skeletal and tremoring with palsy. 'Washington, you say? Are you from the Army?'

'No sir,' Latimore said. 'Remember we talked? I'm from the Attorney General's office.'

'Ah, well. VIP, eh?'

'Not really, sir,' Latimore said with a smile.

'Have a seat over here by the window,' the old man said, motioning to a small table with two chairs near an alcoved window.

'Thank you, sir.'

'What time is it, please?'

'Three-fifteen.'

Grimes turned to Alice. 'May I have it now?' he asked.

'If you wish.'

'Perhaps Mister, uh . . .'

'Latimore. Just call me Harrison.'

'Mr. Latimore, would you like something to drink?' he asked.

'I'm fine, thanks.'

Alice whisked quietly out of the room. The old man squinted his eyes and stared through the thin curtains.

'Looks like a nice day,' he said.

'Yes it is, sir.'

'You have nice manners, young man.'

'Thank you. My mom would be glad to hear you say that.'

Alice returned with a bottle of Sappora beer and a single cigarette on a napkin. He took the bottle in both hands, stared at it almost reverently, licked his lips, brought it slowly to his mouth, and took a deep swallow. He closed his eyes and sighed.

'I saw a movie last night on the video,' he said. 'What was that movie, Alice?'

'Ace Ventura.'

'Silly, but it made me laugh,' he said, and took another

369

measured swallow of beer. 'Do you have a match?' he asked.

'Sorry,' Latimore said. 'I don't smoke.'

'Good for you. Alice?'

She lit the cigarette with a Zippo lighter. He very slowly inhaled, holding the smoke for a few moments, letting it out in a rush.

'Colonel Grimes, I'd like you to take a look at a photograph and tell me something about the men in it.'

Latimore slid the photograph of the Specter squad across the table. The old man took out a pair of rimless glasses and slowly and laboriously hooked them over his ears. When he focused on the picture, he looked shocked. His hand started to shake harder and he turned the photograph over and slid it back across the table to Latimore.

'I don't think so,' he said, and took another drag on his cigarette.

'Don't think what, sir?'

'Don't think I remember.'

'Take another look, Colonel. It's important.'

The old man smiled and shook his head. 'Nothing's important to me anymore, son. And most of what should be I'd rather forget.'

'Please take another look.'

Grimes looked at him through misty eyes. 'Why would you dig all this up now? Let 'em all rest in peace, if they ever could.'

'We need to know how many of the men in that photograph survived the war, sir.'

'If they did, I wouldn't call it survival.'

'Please try.'

'Son, I'm an alcoholic,' the old man said, stopping at every sentence to take a breath. 'One beer a day, every sip is ecstasy. I have emphysema. Four cigarettes a day, more if I can sneak 'em. I was an athlete once. Now I struggle to go up the stairs. I once wrote poetry, not very good poetry, but it gave me pleasure. Now my hands are so full of palsy I can barely hold a pencil. Every word is a struggle. I once loved a beautiful woman, now I'm impotent and she's dead. Why am I alive, young fellow? My body is rotten, my brain, my lungs, my balls, everything has given out, but here I am. And all those young men. All those young men, dead in swamps and filthy rivers or worse, corrupted by me and others like me. Did I know these men? I was a major in the headquarters company, of course I knew these men. They came to me, some of them just children, and I sent them off into the jungle and never saw them again. Oh, I heard stories, we all heard stories. Verbal nightmares. What they did. What was done to them. Engstrom always brought his dead back, you know. Why bother? We would send our young warriors to Engstrom and then their service records would be sent someplace, then someplace else, then someplace else, and eventually they would end up in a cardboard box and thrown in a fire. Young men fighting for their country and then betrayed. Erased. They said it was to protect them. What a joke. It was to protect the government. To protect the Army. To conceal what the Army asked of Engstrom and what he did to them in the name of patriotism and love of country. What he did to their souls. What we *all* did to their souls.'

He took another drag on his cigarette.

'You know, at first, every time I sent one of them out I would write a poem. I had in mind, when it was all over, it would be an epic poem about young men serving their country. Then I heard the stories. And I would write the poem and go out and drink a bottle of Scotch whiskey. And finally I stopped writing verses and just drank the bottle of Scotch. And one day when they came for the boxes with the service records, I threw the poems in the box. So here I am, young Harrison, without even the strength to put a bullet in my brain. All my memories are gone but the worst ones, and I sit with them, sleep with

371

them, spend my days with the ghosts of all those fine young men. Look at me, son, I don't have enough juice left in me to shed one lousy tear.'

Latimore, stunned by the old man's startling confession, stared at the pillaged face and then remembered why he was there. He turned the photograph over and slid it back across the table.

'Give it another try, sir.'

Grimes stared at him, took another puff on his cigarette. He had smoked about half of it and he carefully snubbed it out and touched the end to make sure it was out and put it in the bathrobe pocket. He leaned back over the photograph.

'Don't take no, do you?'

'The Attorney General doesn't take no, Colonel.'

'Hah, nothing changes.'

He tapped the faces with a forefinger.

'Shrack. Engstrom called him Black Bobby. This is Mez . . . Men . . .'

'Metzinger?'

'Metzinger, yes. Then there's Jordan. Engstrom here and Jennings. This one is . . . uh, Wayne . . . Wayne . . . Wayne something. Can't remember his last name.'

He stared at the photograph for a few more moments.

'One died,' Grimes said, still staring at the picture.

'You mean one of them was killed?'

'This was Engstrom's special squad. This is Specter One, nothing could kill them. Tunny, that's it, Wayne Tunny. Toughie from New York City.'

'Which one didn't survive?'

'I told you, no reports were filed, no official entries of any kind.'

'How about this one? You say his name is Jennings?' Harrison pointed to the man Jordan had called Oz.

The colonel leaned over closer and stared down at the picture for a minute or longer. 'Oscar Jennings.'

'Oscar. Os,' Latimore said.

'Os, yes. That's what they called him. From the Midwest somewhere, I think. Wisconsin?'

'And he wasn't killed?'

'I don't know anything for sure, but I do know Engstrom never put anybody from Specter One in a bag. He was very proud of that.'

'I thought all the squads were Specter squads.'

'They were numbered. Number One was Engstrom's personal squad, they were his boys. Engstrom lost a lot of men in those years. But not from One. That picture there probably was taken in the . . . late sixties, right in the middle of it.'

'So let me make sure I've got this straight. We've got Black Bobby Shrack, Dave Metzinger, Gary Jordan, Engstrom, Oscar Jennings, and Wayne Tunny.'

The old man nodded and slid the picture back to Latimore.

'What happened to Jennings and Tunny?' Latimore asked.

'God only knows.' He took a long sip of beer and tapped his mouth with the handkerchief. 'So, what does Harr . . . uh . . .'

'Harrison, sir.'

'What does Harrison Latimore do for the Attorney General of the United States?'

'Hopefully, the best I can, Colonel.'

Colonel Grimes threw back his head and laughed heartily. 'Oh yes. Didn't we all hope that, son. Didn't we all.'

'We suspect that one of these men, either Jennings or Tunny, has turned into a killer for hire, sir. A very dangerous man.'

'What's so surprising about that? They were all dangerous men.'

'But he kills for a living.'

Grimes stared at him, his eyes watery from the strain. He took out what was left of his cigarette and called to

Alice, who slipped quietly into the room and lit it for him. He drank his beer and smoked the cigarette.

'Most recently, we think one of them may have killed a man in the government witness protection program.'

'Ah,' Grimes said matter-of-factly.

'That doesn't surprise you?'

'Should it? If he kills for a living, who he kills is immaterial. I assume anybody might be fair game.'

Latimore put the photograph back in his pocket.

'Surprises you that I'm not shocked, doesn't it? Did it ever occur to you who hires these people? Ever occur to you that your own government might give them a ticket occasionally? A little job in South America. Kill a dictator in Africa. Somebody has to do it, son. And when they aren't busy doing for them, they hire out. Man has to make a living.'

'Who would know how to contact him?'

'I couldn't tell you that.'

'Who could?'

'Whoever hires him. Perhaps he was given a new name, new identification, a nice purse, and cut loose over there. Perhaps he did a few jobs, then came back to the U.S. Now, you want to contact him, you call a phone number. It's an answering machine in an office in some dump of a building somewhere. And he calls the machine from a pay phone and checks his messages, and takes the jobs he wants to do. No names, no addresses. The money is deposited in a numbered account offshore someplace. It's all very cut and dried.'

'That sounds like an extremely well-educated guess, Colonel. Are you sure you can't tell me anything else?'

'I can't tell what I don't know. And I can't know what never happened. The Phantom Project never *existed*. There never were Specter squads. And the Army buried them forever to make sure it was kept properly quiet.'

'So why are you talking to me?'

'It's over thirty years, son. Some probably died in far-

374

away lands, gunned down or tortured to death in stone dungeons in the Mideast someplace. Or maybe they just burned out and couldn't work anymore so they took out the old service .45 and ate it.'

'Somebody has to have the phone number of that answering machine.'

'Well, that was just a manner of speaking. There are probably much more sophisticated methods nowadays, with computers and whatnot.'

Latimore was trying to sort out what the colonel was saying. Only one man in Specter One had died, he said, but two of them were missing. Jennings and Tunny. But the one who died wasn't killed. Jesus. Grimes was like everybody else in the government, they never gave you a straight answer. Ask them if it's raining outside and they tell you the name of the weather girl on Channel 6.

'Well, I thank you,' he said. 'I guess I'll just check Graves' Registration in Washington.'

As Latimore got up to leave, the old man stared at him and smiled. The colonel's cigarette had burned down to the filter. He placed it gently in the ashtray and stared at it sadly, as if he were viewing the corpse of a friend in a funeral home.

As Latimore reached the door, the colonel looked over at him and said, 'Young Harrison?'

'Yes sir?'

'Just remember, what is, isn't. And what isn't, is.'

Twenty-nine

Ron Campbell's back hurt. They had been crisscrossing the area around Wapakoneta for two weeks and it was taking its toll. His partner, Ed Flores, was scrunched down in the passenger seat, sucking on a Tootsie Roll pop. That was good, it kept him from bellyaching. Flores had quit smoking four months before and was just becoming reasonable again after spending that time bitching and moaning about *everything*. Tootsie Roll pops, which he gnawed at constantly, had added ten pounds to his girth, but Flores blamed the added weight on his dry cleaner, complaining that they were using a new cleaning fluid that was shrinking his suits.

He took the lollipop out of his mouth long enough to say, 'What's the name of this one?' and popped it back in.

'Turkey Run.'

'God. We're really dragging the bottom.'

'We're down to landing strips and parking lots.'

'We're not gonna get a line on this guy, I can feel it.'

'That's what you always say, Ed. Don't you ever get tired of being wrong?'

'I can't quit now, the odds are with me,' Flores said. 'I'm bound to be right sooner or later.' He pointed off to the right. 'There it is. Hell, it's nothing but a shed and a couple of hangars.'

'Looks like it has landing lights.'

'Well glorioski.'

They turned down a narrow blacktop road and parked next to what passed for the terminal. There were three black automobiles parked near the door and, around the side of the building, two older cars. Nearby, a tall, lanky young man was tinkering with the engine of a single-engine plane. He wore coveralls and had an oil-streaked towel thrown over his shoulder.

'Hold it a minute,' Campbell said to Flores, who was headed for the terminal.

Campbell walked over to the mechanic, who looked over his shoulder and nodded.

'Hi there,' Campbell said. 'Got a minute?'

'What can I do you for?'

Campbell held out the wallet with his ID card. 'FBI. My name's Ron Campbell. This is my partner, Ed Flores.'

'Yes sir. Joey Bushkin.' He started to extend his hand and stopped. ' 'Fraid my hand's pretty greasy.'

'No problem, Mr. Bushkin. You work here?'

'Yes, sir. I pump gas, do mechanic work. Got a dozen or so regulars that base their planes here.'

'Get much overnight traffic, do you?'

'Nah. Don't have a terminal as such, just a coffee room, pay phone, a few sectionals, and a weather radio. Midwest Rentals has a cubbyhole inside, but Henry usually closes kinda early unless you call ahead. That's Henry Goshen.'

'Mr. Bushkin, we're trying to run down a plane that may have landed here on the sixteenth, two weeks ago yesterday. This would be a light-colored, twin-engine plane.'

Bushkin wiped his hands on the oily rag. 'That's an easy one,' he said. 'Don't see many like that anymore.'

'You remember the plane?'

'A 1983 Beechcraft Baron D-55 with twin 375 Lycomings. A rare jewel, and this baby was mint. I took a sneak peek inside. Built-in stereo, computer, the works.'

'How long was it here?'

'Let's see, he came in the afternoon that Tuesday and he was gone when I come in Thursday morning. Left sometime Wednesday night, early Thursday.'

'Happen to get a look at the pilot?'

'Nope. I was over at the hangar working on a Cherokee when he landed. Just kind of an average-looking fella from what I could see.'

'How was he dressed?'

'Well, lemme think. Tell you the truth, I remember airplanes a lot better than I do people. I think he was in a suit. Maybe a gray suit.'

'Did he refuel here?'

'No, sir. But the D-55 has a range of maybe twelve hundred miles. Could've come a far piece without gassin' up.'

'How about his call number?'

'Naw, don't remember that. Like I said, I can remember every airplane made, been my hobby since I was old enough to hold a book, but I don't pay much attention to people and numbers.'

'And the rental manager's name is Henry?'

'Henry Goshen.' He nodded and pointed to the terminal. 'He should be in there. He don't know much about planes, though.'

Goshen was in his late fifties. His shoulders were bowed and he was reading a newspaper from four inches away through glasses an inch thick. The room was painted pale blue. Goshen was behind a small counter on one side. Facing it was a worn sofa, a bottled-water machine, and a large map of the Fort Wayne area. The room was uncommonly warm, so Goshen had his jacket off. He was wearing a striped shirt, no tie, a belt and suspenders. He was chewing a toothpick. He looked up when Campbell and Flores entered the small office, slid his glasses down on his nose, and squinted over the rims.

'Help yuh?'

Campbell showed him his wallet. 'FBI, sir. I'm Agent Campbell, this is Agent Flores.'

'Well, well.'

378

'We think you may have had a rental on the sixteenth, late in the day. Do you remember that?'

'That's over two weeks ago.'

'Well, there doesn't seem to be a traffic jam around here, Mr. Goshen,' Flores said. 'Maybe you can remember back that far.'

Goshen was leafing through a box of index cards. He stopped and pulled one up. He looked on both sides of it, then pulled it out.

'Here it is,' he said. 'Remember him now. Didn't have a coat on.' He looked up. 'It was cold and rainy but he didn't have a coat on.'

'Remember what he looked like?'

Goshen looked at them for several seconds. 'Average-looking fella in a suit. No coat.'

'How about his hair?' Flores said. 'Long, short, black, brown?'

'Maybe he had a hat on.'

'Maybe?' Flores said.

'Would you recognize him if you saw him again?' Campbell asked.

'Look at my eyes, son,' Goshen said sardonically. 'These glasses is like reading through the bottom of a shot glass. He was clean-shaven and white. Anything else'd be guesswork.'

'Would you have a carbon of the rental slip?'

'Can bring it up on the computer.'

'Please,' Campbell said pleasantly.

Goshen tapped the keys, highlighted a date, and a copy of the rental agreement jumped on the screen.

'There it is,' he said.

'Can you print that out for us?' Flores asked.

'Nope. Outta paper.'

WASHINGTON, WEDNESDAY 12:42 P.M., EST

Hardistan and Firestone were en route to the airport when the FBI agent's cell phone rang. He answered before the second ring.

'Mr. Hardistan, this is Ron Campbell, I'm on the Ohio task force.'

'Sure, Ron, what is it?'

Campbell was sitting sideways in the passenger seat of the car with his legs barely touching the ground. They were in front of the Hoosier Chalet Motel on the outskirts of Fort Wayne.

'We got a break on the plane, sir. It's a white 1983 Beechcraft Baron D-55 with blue trim. Range about twelve hundred miles. The perp stayed in the Hoosier Chalet Motel on Route 30 about fifty miles from Waller's place. His rental car clocked 216 miles, which would be about right for two trips from Fort Wayne to Wapakoneta.'

'That's great, Ron. Have you reported this to Floyd?'

'Yes, sir, he told me to call you personally. That plane is kind of rare, Mr. Hardistan. I think if we notify the FAA and get their help, somebody might spot it.'

'Good idea. I'll call Jim Norcross at the FAA as soon as I hang up. Got the call letters on that plane?'

'No sir. It's probably a phony anyway. He checked into the motel at a drive-in window and paid cash for two nights. He also ordered up room service and paid cash for that, but he was in the bathroom when the bellhop brought it up, left the money on the dresser. The car rental guy was almost blind and doesn't remember what the perp looks like. Nobody remembers him. They all say the same thing, he's an average-looking white guy. He had a Florida driver's license registered to a Frank Pierce at 3224 Oceanview Boulevard, Fort Lauderdale. The license is a phony and there's no such address in Lauderdale.'

'Good work, Ron,' Hardistan said. 'We'll make a run on all licensed Beechcraft Baron D-55s and see if we get lucky. You and Flores did a good job. Tell him I said so.'

Hardistan turned off the phone.

'Chickens are starting to roost, Sam,' he said to Firestone. 'But we still don't know what the shooter looks like.'

International Security, Ltd., occupied two offices in an obscure office building a few blocks from the White House. The company kept a low profile. It avoided publicity, was not listed on any stock exchange, and never advertised. Its name never came up in congressional hearings or conversations. Most members of the two houses had never heard of it. The media was unaware of its existence. Yet the CIA and the National Security Agency had been using ISL as 'consultants' for thirty years.

Its president, David Worrell, was also unknown in political circles. Worrell never attended parties or official functions. He did not contribute to political parties or politicians. The phone number was unlisted, and the hard disk in his computer was removed every night and kept in a safe hidden in Worrell's office. He was a six-footer in excellent shape, with blond hair turning gray and a deep tan. He favored tweed jackets, gray Australian wool slacks, and dark-colored shirts open at the collar.

The other office was occupied by a paraplegic ex-soldier of fortune named Le Blanq who spoke five languages fluently. Forty years before, during the Algerian freedom fighters' rebellion against the French, he had lost the use of both legs when a bomb shattered his lower spine. Le Blanq was completely bald and had a barrel chest and massive arms offset by withered, useless legs. He looked awkwardly off balance in his state-of-the-art wheelchair.

Le Blanq and Worrell were talent agents. Their clients were the governments of Britain, the U.S., France, Germany, South Africa, and Israel. The talent was the cream of the freelance intelligence community: terrorists, soldiers of fortune, assassins, safecrackers, information gatherers. ISL referred to them as 'actors.'

Worrell was five minutes early arriving at the National Cathedral on Massachusetts Avenue. He entered casually, looked around the nearly empty shrine, and sat in a pew off to one side near the rear of the church. Two minutes later two Secret Service agents entered. They walked to the front of the cathedral, circled around the outside of the rows of pews, and came back past Worrell. They never looked directly at him. One of them stepped outside, and a moment later Claude Hooker entered. He sat behind Worrell.

'Good afternoon,' he said, his voice almost indiscernible.

'Hi, Claude. Got a problem?'

It was a natural question. Hooker and Worrell never met unless there was a problem.

'No,' Hooker said coldly, 'you do.'

Worrell turned sideways in the pew and leaned an elbow on its back. He looked straight at the ferret-faced National Security Adviser. 'With whom?' he asked.

'I'm not exactly sure. My information came from Maraganset's office.'

'Maraganset! Maraganset's an impotent pussy waiting to retire. I don't do business with Maraganset.'

'My informant is in his office.'

'What's this about?'

'I assume you're aware that this hotshot lawyer Vail has become Assistant A.G.'

'I've heard the talk.'

'It isn't talk anymore. That bitch Azimour told the whole world. Vail brought his own team with him, young hotshots, bunch of goddamn pit bulls.'

'Isn't that what they're supposed to be?'

'Not when you're on the end that gets bit.'

'What's the point here, Claude?'

'One of Vail's people made an inquiry about the projects.'

'The Vietnam projects?'

Hooker nodded.

'Christ, that was thirty years ago.'

'It might just as well have been yesterday. He got a list of all the liaison officers, and his big interest was Phantom. They gave him Grimes's name.'

Worrell resituated himself on the hard wooden pew. 'So? He's a dottering old fool. He's got a sieve for a brain.'

'David, Vail's after Engstrom. He's already got their bank records and searched that compound out in Montana.'

Worrell said nothing. He stared at Hooker and waited for him to go on.

'That government witness who was taken out a couple of weeks ago in Ohio? He was a former member of the Sanctuary.'

'ISL wasn't involved in that.'

'It could be.'

'What are you talking about?'

'It was a professional hit. Hardistan and Vail seem to think the shooter is one of Engstrom's old boys.'

'Now listen–'

'No, you listen. Let's just say he's right. Let's just say that you have somebody on your books who was with Engstrom over there. Let's just suppose Engstrom used this actor for the job in Ohio. And let's suppose the FBI nails him . . .'

'Impossible. There aren't any records and you know it.'

'I'm just saying–'

'There's no goddamn *way* to track back.'

Hooker folded his arms across his chest, stared at Worrell, and said nothing.

'Listen to me, Claude. Let's just say I do have this actor under contract. I wouldn't know how to find him. I don't know what he calls himself now, where he lives, what his cover is. I'd make contact through a series of shielded phone calls and computer mail. You really think a bunch of hotshot young lawyers can find him?'

'Hardistan might.'

'Then tell the son of a bitch *not* to.'

'Nobody but the Man tells Hardistan what to do, and I would prefer *not* to discuss this with the President. Don't you get it, David, the actor can be a threat to me, but he's a much bigger threat to you as long as he's on the loose.'

'What the hell are you suggesting, Claude?'

Hooker shrugged. 'Perhaps he's outlived his purpose.'

Worrell turned his back on Hooker. He stretched his arms out on the back of the pew and looked toward the altar.

'You know how long I'd stay in business if I took out one of my own people? All my actors would vanish overnight. I've lasted thirty-five years because they trust me and my clients trust me.'

'This has the potential to be a disaster for you. If this shooter happens to get caught and makes a deal–'

'You listen to me,' Worrell said, cutting him off, 'I had a man who died in Iraq with all his fingernails and toe-nails ripped out. He bit off his tongue and bled to death rather than give anything up. Get the point, Claude?'

'You need to get him off your books.'

'There aren't any fucking books.'

'Then you better get word to this actor of yours that he's hot. Tell him to go deep and stay deep.'

'I can try that.'

'Do better than try,' Hooker said nastily.

Worrell didn't answer. He hated to be strong-armed by government suits, and Hooker was one of the most oppressive. When they needed ISL, they were glad to put the national security in Worrell's hands. Now Hooker was concerned about his own skin. The existence of ISL and its mission would make Watergate look like a cheating scandal at a local kindergarten. But . . . if ISL went down, the NSA and the CIA would both go down with it. Possibly even the entire administration.

'Has this person ever been involved in any of our operations?'

'Shit, Claude, you know the goddamn rules. You put the money in the bank, I get the job done, no fucking questions asked.'

'Then I'll put it this way. I'll cover my end, you better damn well take care of yours.'

'Now what the hell's that supposed to mean?'

He waited for an answer. When it was not forthcoming, he turned in his seat. Hooker was walking out the door.

PEAKVIEW, MONTANA, WEDNESDAY 4:14 P.M., MST
The tellers in the bank eyed Flaherty curiously when he pulled a chair up to the front of the bank lobby, turned it around, and sat on it backward, his arms folded across the top. He stared at the interior of the room. To his left was a small entranceway and the reception desk, followed by a long counter with two tellers' windows. Next to the counter was a small conference room, then the safe deposit boxes and the shiny steel vault behind a metal gate. To his right was a small sitting alcove, the manager's office, a small loan office, and a teller's window that also served the drive-in window. A small entranceway served the rear door, which faced him in the far right corner of the large room. The combination storage room and employees' lounge occupied most of the rear wall of the bank and was adjacent to the vault. The room was spacious but compact, softly lit and user friendly, or at least it had been until three months before when it had been relieved of $229,000 by a swift and efficient crew of thieves.

What made the event unique was that at the same moment and with the same precision, anonymity, and

M.O., two other banks in the small statewide chain had also been robbed. They were all within seventy-five miles of each other in the western part of the state, and were all in an arc within a hundred miles of Missoula.

According to Geoff Isaac, the three robberies had been carried out with ingenious planning and military precision, not a difficult task since all three banks followed exactly the same procedures every day. At eight-thirty the manager arrived, entered through the rear door, and turned off the alarm. At eight-forty the vault lock popped. At 8:45 the six-person staff arrived at the rear door and were admitted by the manager. The three tellers signed off on their money trays and the banks opened at precisely nine A.M.

Isaac was particularly frustrated, since all three of the heists had occurred in his district. All were in small towns, the vaults in each bank were fat with payroll money, and the thieves had not uttered a single word while they pillaged the three institutions of almost a million dollars.

Adding to the unique quality of these three simultaneous events was the fact that the three banks were exactly alike. They had all been built from the same set of plans: free-standing, one-story structures, surrounded on three sides by small, landscaped parking lots, and on the fourth by the drive-in window. They were satellite branches of the chain's main bank in Helena, and the pride and joy of the Montana Trust and Security's board of directors, which not only had saved a lot of money by using the same plans, but felt it gave its customers a sense of 'family' no matter what branch they visited.

'Kind of like depositing your money at a Holiday Inn,' was the way Isaac sardonically put it when he described the thefts to Meyer and Flaherty.

Now, as Meyer was scrutinizing the deposit records on the bank' s computer, Flaherty eyeballed the interior and played back the robbery in his head as Isaac had described it.

'On a Friday morning in November, the manager of the bank in Peakview, population 5,600, arrives as usual. As he opens the door, he gets shoved inside the bank. He gets a brief glimpse of his attacker in a mirror. Black ski cap with holes cut for the eyes and dark coveralls, that's all he remembers. Duct tape is wrapped around his eyes and mouth. He hears what he thinks are two silenced shots and hears glass and metal hit the floor. His hands are taped behind him and he's led to a windowless storage room in the rear of the bank, shoved down on the floor and locked in. He hears no conversation, although he does hear the vault lock open. During the next ten minutes his other employees are also taped and locked in the room. Nobody can talk, nobody can see. Then they hear an explosion outside the bank. They're all terrified. Five minutes later there's a second explosion, this one closer. It's another fifteen minutes before anybody realizes the bank isn't open yet. The police ultimately break in and find the employees. None of them are hurt, none of them have any idea how many robbers there were. Both of the video surveillance cameras are shot out. The vault is empty. And nobody – *nobody* – sees the thieves leave the banks.'

'Nobody saw the perps vacate the banks?' Flaherty had asked Isaac with surprise.

'In Milltown we got a lady who says there were two guys in suits standing near the rear entrance to the bank about nine, and in Wild Bank a janitor says he saw a guy in work clothes walking across the parking lot about that time. But none of them were carrying anything and the descriptions of the three men were useless.

'This happened in Peakview, Wild Bank, and Milltown at the same time with the same results. All three had received large payrolls the night before. Three bank jobs

387

and nobody saw the perps. In all three towns, *nobody* saw them leave. Not one witness.'

'Why?' Meyer asked.

'Because at five to nine an empty storefront was blown up two blocks from each of the banks,' Isaac answered. 'Brilliant. Small towns, big explosions two blocks from the bank, who's looking at a bank that isn't open yet? Then at one minute to nine a stolen van blows up in each bank's parking lot. The police forces, such as they are, are busy dealing with two explosions. At Milltown, nobody even noticed the bank wasn't open until nine-twenty.'

'Like a magician using misdirection,' Meyer said. 'You look at his right hand while his left is doing the tricks.'

'Exactly,' Isaac said. 'By the time the police got their wits together, the perps had fifteen, twenty minutes' head start on them.'

'What was the take?' Flaherty asked.

'They took Peakview for $229,000, Wild Bank for $306,500, and Milltown was the biggest hit of the three – $383,500. Total take: $919,000.'

'Bet it killed them that they didn't break a million,' was Meyer's response.

Flaherty visualized the manager opening the door, turning off the alarm, and suddenly being shoved inside. His mouth, eyes, and hands are duct-taped while another member of the gang takes out both surveillance cameras with a silenced handgun. They relieve the manager of the keys to the vault room, put him in storage. They watch the second hand click around the face of the big old Seth Thomas clock above the vault. At eight-forty the buzzer sounds. The vault pops open and they go to work. They leave ones and fives on the floor of the vault. How many perpetrators? Three, four? Flaherty guessed four, two working the vault, two waiting at the door for the rest of the employees.

When they finish, one of them uses a remote to trigger

the bomb two blocks away. When it goes off, they step outside, pull the getaway car around past the drive-in window, throw the satchels in the trunk, and ease on out. While the town is going crazy, they cruise away, then blow the van they had stolen the night before the same way just to create more confusion.

Very cool.

How about the two guys in suits standing near the back door pointing in the direction of the explosion? How about the guy in work clothes in Milltown walking away from the bank? Were they involved? What did they carry the loot in, garbage bags? Too obvious. Satchels? How big a satchel would it take to haul off $380,000 and change?

Isaac was right, Flaherty decided. These guys were confident and professional.

Ben Meyer and Dermott Flaherty had been collating and cross-matching data on robberies and banks for two weeks, with the help of Hines and Naomi back in Chicago. The FBI files had been thorough and informative – two years of hard digging. But Meyer and Flaherty had decided the Bureau investigations had not been paranoid enough. So they had been playing devil's advocate. Relying on their experience in the Illinois RICO case, they took two years of FBI investigative work and tossed it like a salad.

In the previous eighteen months there had been seventeen bank robberies, nine solved, and three arrests with trials pending. That left eight unsolved. The three that had been committed the same day at the same time with the same M.O. seemed the most promising, since the banks were all members of the same small statewide chain. The two lawyers had decided to concentrate on them first.

'What we're looking for is laundering,' Meyer said early on.

'And we're looking at millions of dollars,' Flaherty said.

'Right. They may have hit some banks outside our zone, and if they're stealing weapons and selling them, the take could go a lot higher.'

'The biggest bank in this chain is the First Trust and Security in Helena,' Isaac had told them. 'It's the only one that hasn't been hit.'

'Too big?'

'Bad location. It's in a three-story building right in the middle of town. A very hard target.'

'You think these three hits were an inside job?' Flaherty asked Isaac.

'I would say so.'

'But they could've cased out everything but the information about the payrolls, and that was probably common knowledge in these small towns,' Flaherty said.

'True,' Meyer answered, then smiled. 'But let's assume there is somebody on the inside, just to be perverse.'

'I like that,' Flaherty said.

'Let's say this inside man planned the operations. The best time to do it, how to do it . . .'

'Okay.'

'This somebody also feeds them the information on payrolls, etcetera.'

'This somebody could also be laundering the loot through the banks,' Flaherty tossed in.

'That's good logic,' Meyer said.

'So how does he launder it?'

'If we can figure that out, that somebody could be the link Vail's looking for.'

Flaherty shrugged. 'Cooks the books?' he suggested.

'That's one possibility. So now we have the somebody plus a very slick accountant. Two moles in the front office.'

That had been two weeks ago.

*

Flaherty stood up, stretched, and put the chair back in the waiting area. He walked back through the bank and went out the back door. There was a seven- or eight-foot walkway beside the building with shrubs separating it from the drive-through. He went back inside as Meyer left the small conference room where he had been working. He pinched his eyes.

'I'm going blind, Derm,' he sighed.

'Let's get out of here,' Flaherty said. 'We've got a two-hour ride back to Missoula.'

'Can we stop for a decent cup of coffee along the way? Mr. Coffee doesn't crack it.'

They stopped at a roadside café at the edge of the small town. Meyer dumped sugar and cream into his coffee. He was quiet, staring into the cup as he stirred the mix.

'Something's bugging you,' Flaherty said. 'I can always tell when something's bugging you.'

'They got a nice edge. They got four banks they can work with. They don't have to move all that dirty money through one little bank.'

'They've also got bookkeepers, managers, tellers,' Flaherty said. 'I mean, you don't walk into some little bank in Montana and deposit three hundred grand without raising some eyebrows. Three crews took out a million bucks.'

'That's right.'

'So . . .'

'So maybe they pyramid the deposits.'

'What's that mean?'

'In the seventies and eighties, some banks in Miami needed to launder drug money. We're talking *big* money. Millions of dollars. The point is not to wave a flag at the IRS, which requires the bank to report any cash deposit of ten thousand dollars or more, so they came up with this pyramid scheme. The idea was to move these millions through their banks in increments of less than ten thou. They set up dozens and dozens of blind accounts. A computer program automatically sent deposits into these accounts when the big deposits were made.'

'I don't understand that,' Flaherty said.

'Okay, you have a company – the XYZ company, for the sake of argument. XYZ deposits a hundred thousand dollars cash into the XYZ account but the computer immediately redeposits that hundred thou into eleven other accounts, so instead of showing one account with the big deposit, they had eleven accounts with nine thousand and change in each one. The banks charged the depositors thirty to forty percent for making the deposits. That's the cost of washing the money. Then XYZ withdraws the small accounts and the money is clean.'

'So how does the Sanctuary work it? These yahoos walk into small banks with big bundles of cash to deposit?'

'Suppose the chief accountant for the main branch in Helena is the big man. Once a month he makes a swing around the branches and audits the banks. The thieves come in one at a time and bring in, say, a hundred thousand apiece. The accountant deposits all that money in one account, *but* the computer immediately spreads it over eleven accounts. So now you have the money spread over several accounts in all four banks. Nine thousand plus in each account. No reports to the IRS. And the program that deposits the money automatically is kept on a CD ROM, not in the computer, so the bank examiners never find it. And Mr. Accountant has four banks to work with.'

'How do we track it?'

'We can't, it would take a couple of dozen accountants months to track down all these accounts and try to figure which ones are the phonies, and we don't have that kind of time.'

'So what do we do?'

Meyer looked at him balefully. 'I haven't figured that out yet,' he said. 'We have to find out who the somebody is and who the accountant is.'

'And if we're wrong?'

'Then we're up shit creek.'

Two FBI agents sat in their car with the windows cracked and the heater on high. A state patrol car was slanted across the road, forming a road block. The ATF and FBI had set up blocks on all roads leading into Fort Yahweh, and with the help of the state patrol was running license and registration checks on every vehicle going in and out of the compound. Their objective was to harass Sanctuary members, check for illegal weapons, and hopefully discourage any further influx of troops into the mountain stronghold.

It was an effective ruse. There had been little traffic throughout the day. Harry Aiken, who had been called into the Montana task force from his home base in Georgia, had been bitching for three hours.

'It was seventy when I left home,' he said. 'What the hell am I doing out here freezing my ass off in the middle of the night?'

'It's seven o'clock, Harry, hardly the middle of the night,' his partner, Duke DeMay, who had been brought in from Virginia, answered.

'It's ten o'clock back home,' Aiken answered. 'I go to bed early.'

'Two more hours and we can go back to the hotel and grab dinner.'

'Midnight my time,' Aiken growled. 'A midnight snack. Fashionable if you're a member of the freakin' cotillion.'

DeMay cleared mist off the windshield and peered down the two-lane blacktop.

'What do you know,' he said. 'Company's coming.'

Aiken picked up his walkie-talkie and roused the patrol car.

'Turn on the carousel lights, boys, incoming from the compound.' He put on his thick gloves, turned up the collar of his blue FBI jacket, and eased the 9mm Glock from his hip holster. 'Hope this guy isn't a cowboy,' he mumbled.

The patrol car's red and blue lights flashed on and a blue Four Runner pulled onto the shoulder and stopped.

Aiken and DeMay got out of their car and fell in behind the two state troopers. The window of the Four Runner slid silently down.

'Keep your hands where we can see them, sir,' one of them told the driver. Aiken and DeMay walked around the back of the vehicle and checked the interior with flashlights. The driver was alone. They approached the passenger side of the car and stood ready.

'Sompin' wrong?' the driver said.

'May I please see your license and registration?' the trooper said.

'Yes, sir,' the driver, a tall, thin scarecrow of a man, said nervously. 'I weren't speedin'.' He handed the license and red slip to the trooper, who checked them with his flashlight.

'You Mr. Jessups?'

'Yes, sir.'

'This registration says your vehicle is owned by the Sanctuary.'

'Uh-huh.'

Aiken stepped beside the trooper and showed his credentials to Jessups.

'Sir, I'm Agent Aiken of the Federal Bureau of Investigation. Would you please step out of your vehicle.'

'What'd I do?'

'Nothing yet,' Aiken said in a flat, no-nonsense voice.

Jessups got out of the car, stuffed his hands in his jacket pockets, and stomped his feet on the road. He was obviously scared to death and close to hyperventilating. His breath curled from his mouth as he gasped for breath in the frigid night air.

'How come you rate a Four Runner, Mr. Jessups?' Aiken asked. 'What's your job at Yahweh?'

'I'm just kinda like a chauffeur,' the lean man said.

'A chauffeur, huh. Why don't we go over to my car for a minute and get out of the cold.'

He pulled one of the troopers over to the side. 'We may want to impound that vehicle,' he said.

'Want us to check it out for weapons?' the trooper asked.

'No. Just let it sit for now.' He took the license and registration and led Jessups to the FBI car after patting him down. They put him in the backseat and Aiken and DeMay got in the front.

'Let's see, you're Mordachai Jessups, that right?' Aiken said.

'Uh-huh.'

'So who do you chauffeur around in that Four Runner?' DeMay said.

Jessups didn't answer immediately.

'You Engstrom's driver?' Aiken asked.

'N-N-No, sir.'

'Then who?'

He hesitated before answering. 'Brother Abraham.'

Aiken and DeMay traded glances but tried to cover their surprise.

'You drive for Abraham?'

Mordachai nodded.

'Where is he now?'

Mordachai shifted uncomfortably in the backseat and wiped his mouth with his hand. 'Back there,' he said finally, nodding toward Yahweh.

'How come he didn't turn up when we searched the fort?'

'He . . . uh . . . he weren't there.'

'Where was he?' DeMay asked.

'Up on the hill.'

'You mean Mount James?'

'Yessir.'

'Where on the hill?' Aiken asked.

'L-L-Look, fellers, I can't talk about this. I could get me in a lotta trouble.'

'You're in a lotta trouble already,' Aiken said. 'Your boss could be staring treason in the eye.'

'Treason!'

'Every time he opens his mouth he speaks sedition,' DeMay said. 'He's preaching terrorism and murder.'

'He's most religious.'

'He's crazier than a one-eyed owl,' Aiken said. 'Where you from, you sound like a southerner, Mordachai – okay if we call you Mordachai?'

'Oh sure, yessir. I'm from Georgia.'

'No kidding? So am I. Where in Georgia?'

'Little town of Enigma just outside Tifton.'

'No kidding. I'm from St. Simons Island. Know where that is?'

'Oh sure. That's one beautiful place.'

'Well, it used to be before the vultures cut down all the trees and covered it with cement. I'm with the office in Savannah now.'

'So tell us about Brother Abraham, Mordachai,' DeMay said.

'You remember a spark-shootin' evangelist name a Brother Transgressor?'

'Can't say as I do,' Aiken said.

'Name rings a bell,' DeMay said. 'Snake handler, wasn't he? Blind man.'

Mordachai nodded. 'That's right. Abraham is Brother Transgressor.'

'He's blind?' Aiken said.

'Yessir. That's why I drive for him. We were partners. Was doin' real good, too. I mean, we was out in Nebraska, headed for Oklahoma, pullin' in a coupla hundred folks a night. In Omaha we had 'em fallin' outta the tent. Almost a thousand folk showed up that night. Took in a few thousand dollars. I drove and took care a business, he done the preachin'.'

'What happened?'

'Damn militia showed up one night and made him this offer. He was always kinda mystical about things. Like, he wouldn't let nobody take his picture. Hated the press. Why hell, if he'd a give out interviews we coulda riz up to be big as Falwell and Robertson and some of those fat boys. He wouldn't have no truck with TV though.'

'How come the Sanctuary was attracted to him?' Aiken asked.

'The night they come to see him he give one of the most rousing sermons I ever heard. Takin' down the government – no offense–'bout taxes and such.'

'Who came? Engstrom?'

'No sir, there was two of 'em plus a sergeant drivin' their car.'

'A real sergeant?'

'Militiaman.'

'Who were the two?'

'Colonel Shrack, call him Black Bobby. And some business fella who owned the radio station but I don't remember his name. Ain't seen him since. Made T an offer was too good t'turn away from.'

'What kind of offer?'

'Money. Nice place to live. Big audience. And they, uh . . .' Mordachai stopped and wiped his mouth again.

'And they what?'

'They, uh, kindly overlook his compulsion?'

'Compulsion?'

'He likes the ladies. Young ladies.'

'How young?'

'You know, fourteen, fifteen.'

'Jesus!' DeMay said.

'Runaways. He sanctifies 'em and they just follow him.'

'Sanctify them?' Aiken said. 'That's called rape where we come from, Mordachai. Rape and sedition. And you could be an accessory to all that.'

'I never done that. I didn't pimp for him. Tried to calm him down about that, but wouldn't do no good.'

'Why don't you tell us where on the hill he is, Mordachai,' DeMay said.

'Mister, they'll kill me. They'll probably kill me anyway for leavin', but tell you the truth, they're all crazier n' shit.'

'You're in our custody now, Mordachai. Nobody's going to kill you.'

'Has he got young women with him now? Up on the hill, I mean?' Aiken asked.

Mordachai nodded.

'Where?'

'They got a bunker up there, deep in the mountain. I never been up to it, only the I.F. gets to go up there.'

'What's the I.F.?'

'Intelligence Force. The planners. It's a regular command post from what I hear. Got a radio setup, too. That's where T makes his tapes.'

'What's his real name?'

'Ah, sweet Jesus . . .'

'You've gone this far, Mordachai. May as well give it all up.'

'I had to file taxes on him when he was on the road, get him social security.'

'His name,' Aiken said sternly.

'Elijah Wells.'

'Where's he from?'

'Albany, Georgia.'

Aiken turned to DeMay. 'I'll call Isaac. We'll impound the Four Runner and dust it for prints. You drive it back to town and Mordachai will come with me.'

Aiken dialed a number on his cell phone and asked for Geoff Isaac.

Thirty

Harrison Latimore got off the early flight from Washington and raced through the Chicago airport. He headed for a little-used gate at the far end of the concourse, where he flashed his credentials. He passed through the FBI guards and entered AMOC One. Vail, Hardistan, and Firestone were in the dining lounge eating breakfast.

'Welcome aboard,' Vail said. 'Grab a chair and have some breakfast.'

'Thanks,' the young A.G. said. He sat down next to Hardistan.

'Where have you been for the last two days?' Vail asked.

'New Jersey and Washington,' Latimore said.

Paul, the steward, put a cup of coffee in front of him. 'What can I get you?' he asked.

'Everything you've got back there,' Latimore answered, and laughed. 'I haven't had a decent meal for days.'

'How about a sirloin strip and eggs. Hash browns on the side. And some excellent cantaloupe to get you started.'

'Great!'

The steward left and Latimore wasted no time sharing his news. He took out the copy of the photograph of the Specter squad and slid it in front of Vail and Hardistan.

'I know who Os is,' he said.

'Os?' Firestone said.

'The guy who shot Waller,' Latimore said, and leaned

back with a self-satisfied grin on his face.

'Good,' Vail said, concentrating on his breakfast. 'Got his address and phone number?'

'No, but I think I know how we can get it.'

Everybody at the table looked at him. He pointed to Jennings and Tunny in the photograph.

'These two are the ones we never identified. The one on the left is Oscar Jennings. This one is Wayne Tunny.'

'So Oz is Oscar?' Hardistan said.

'Not necessarily. Hear me out a minute,' Latimore said. He recounted his conversation with Grimes. 'The last thing he said to me was, "What is, isn't, what isn't, is." My assumption was that our shooter was Oscar Jennings because Jordan mentioned him when Marty interviewed him at the Grave. So I went to Washington and checked Graves' Registration. Tunny is listed as KIA. Jennings isn't.'

'So Os *is* the shooter.'

'No. What is, isn't. Tunny isn't on the Vietnam wall. I went over and took a look. Guess who is?'

'Jennings,' Vail said.

'Right. I believe the *records* were dummied up a long time *after* the war. Look, Jennings is from Milwaukee. Brought up in a foster home, went into the Army when he was eighteen. Had no close friends or relatives. Tunny was from New York. Mother and father are dead now and he had no brothers or sisters. I think the CIA or some outfit enlisted Tunny before he shipped back. When Jennings was killed, he was sent back in Wayne Tunny's box. But when they collected the names for the memorial, Graves' Registration hadn't been altered yet. That's what Grimes meant by 'What is, isn't.' Jennings wasn't missed and Tunny was buried by his parents. The shooter is Wayne Tunny.' He pointed to the photo. 'That guy right there.'

'Sounds like the grassy knoll theory to me,' Hardistan said.

'I don't agree,' Firestone said. 'One of them is listed as dead in Graves' Registration, the other one is listed dead on the Vietnam wall. One of them has to be wrong.'

'What is, isn't . . .' Latimore said, and let the sentence trail off.

'That's great work,' Vail said. 'But it doesn't do us much good without some kind of identification.'

'It does if Mr. Hardistan takes this photograph and gets his artists to add twenty-five years to that face and run about six poses. With hair, bald, with a beard, without a beard, with sunglasses, and straight. Give it to WWN – they'll run it every hour on the hour. Then give it to the networks in time for the six o'clock news and follow up with newspapers the next day. Somebody will recognize him.'

'We'll have thousands of phone calls.'

'Not necessarily. When "America's Most Wanted" runs photos of at-large criminals they don't get that many phonies and they take down a lot of wanteds.'

'What do we tell the media – I mean, why are we looking for this guy?' Vail asked.

'Material witness in a continuing investigation,' Latimore suggested.

'You've given this a lot of thought,' Vail said.

'It's all I've been thinking about since I left here.'

'What if you're wrong, Latimore?' Hardistan said. 'What if it happened the way Graves' Registration says it did? We'll be looking for the wrong man and Jennings will go into deep cover. We'll never find him.'

'Then how did Jennings end up on the memorial?' Latimore asked.

'Why not do them both?' Vail said. 'Age up both pictures, release a story to the press, and say we're looking for both of them.'

'What if neither one of them died?'

'Then we'll get two for one,' Vail said. 'Give it to Azimour first. She'll have it on the air every hour on the hour. The nets will cover it a couple hours later and the press will have it the next day.'

Hardistan took a sip of coffee. He studied the photo for a few moments and nodded. 'It might work at that,' he said.

'I'm putting my money on Tunny,' Latimore said.

'Okay,' Hardistan said. 'I'll fax the picture to our best artist, Norm Friedkin. I won't even have to tell him what to do. He's been doing it for years.'

'I just have one request,' Latimore said. 'If we find him, I'd like to be there when you put the cuffs on him.'

WASHINGTON, THURSDAY 10:24 A.M., EST
President Lawrence Pennington sat behind his desk in the Oval Office. He had a few minutes to himself and he was pondering his situation. Engstrom had put him in an impossible position. WWN had carried photographs and some fuzzy video of the service of warrants at Fort Yahweh and rehashed the ambush at Lost Trail Pass and the murder of George Waller. The latest poll in the morning *New York Times* had him down three points. It was the first time his popularity had dipped in months.

There was a knock on the office door and his secretary looked in. 'General James is here, Mr. President.'

'Show him in, please, Mildred. And no interruptions.'

'Yes, sir.'

James entered the office. He was tall, a man in his late fifties, with white hair trimmed in a buzz cut. He was wearing his dress uniform and he entered the room briskly, like he owned it.

Pennington got up from his desk and moved around it to greet his visitor. 'Five minutes early, as usual, Jesse,' he said, and slapped James on the shoulder. 'You never change. You want coffee, a sweet roll?'

'No, thank you, Mr. President, I'm fine.'

'Don't be so damn formal,' Pennington said. 'It's just the two of us. For Chrissake, you and I have been running

402

together since 'Nam.'

The general smiled and relaxed. 'You were always a foot ahead of me, Larry. What's the problem?'

'I need some advice.'

'I'm going to give you advice? You were my boss. What do I know that you don't?'

'Let me show you something.'

He led James to his desk, opened a drawer, and took out a sheaf of the latest AWACS flyovers of Yahweh. He spread them out on the desk.

James leaned over them and studied each from a foot away. 'This that compound out in Montana?'

Pennington nodded.

'That lady on World News has sure been raising hell over that,' James said. 'Last night she was comparing it to Waco, only worse.' He looked up from the photographs. 'You looking at a siege here?'

'The Bureau and the ATF couldn't begin to contain this area. It would take most of their field agents, and that still wouldn't be enough manpower. And we can't trust the National Guard in that area. A lot of them also belong to the Sanctuary.'

'Looks like this mountain is crawling with people.'

'As of this morning the AWACS specialists are estimating seven to eight hundred.'

'Jesus Keerist!' James looked back at the photographs. 'That's about what? Three square miles? They must be bumping into each other up there.'

'Seven square miles counting the backside of the mountain.'

James picked up a magnifying glass and went over the pictures again. 'Are they *mining* this mountain?'

'And stringing razor wire. We assume they've got very sophisticated weapons. Stingers, Dragons, M-16s, probably AKs and .50 calibers. And a ton of C-4.'

'Been busy little bastards, haven't they?'

'They're on a monthly bivouac. Usually they meet on

Friday and wrap up on Sunday. They started gathering two days ago. If they don't come out and go back home on Monday, we have a situation on our hands.'

'And Engstrom knows it,' James said.

'Sure he does. And he's going to rub it in.'

Pennington opened a humidor on his desk and took out two Cuban cigars. He snipped the end off both of them, handed one to James, and lit them both with a specially made gold Zippo lighter. He went to the sofa, followed by James, and they sat down.

'If Engstrom's planning a standoff,' Pennington said, 'we have a major situation on our hands. They could send terrorist teams out of there at night, raise havoc, then bring them back a few nights later.'

'Have you got any legal recourse against them yet?'

'This man Vail is working on it. He's making a lot of headway already and he hasn't been on the job three weeks yet.'

'That's the RICO case?'

'Yes. But that could take months.'

James puffed on his cigar and stared into Pennington's eyes. Finally he said, 'What's on your mind, Larry?'

'What do you think it will take to dislodge them?'

'A lot of casualties on both sides, if they're as serious as you think they are.'

'How about a blockade?'

'Phew!' James said. 'A long, boring siege involving a lot of troops. It would cost a fortune.'

'It would be like a cancer, Jesse. A big tumor sitting out there festering while the taxpayers count the dollars.' He hesitated before he added, 'How about a preemptive strike?'

'You'd consider using the Army?'

Pennington didn't answer. He puffed on the cigar and blew smoke toward the ceiling.

'You can't do that, Larry.'

'We've been using the military on the southern border

for over a year.'

'Against wetbacks. These guys in Montana are American citizens.'

'Supposing they declared war against the United States?'

'I'm a military man, Larry. It's not my decision to make. What does the A.G. have to say?'

'I haven't discussed this with anyone but you. Supposing they attacked us first? We've got a couple of Nighthawks out there. Supposing they took one out?'

'I'd be very pissed. But I don't know whether that's provocation to launch an assault on several hundred American citizens. Have you thought about the public reaction?'

'Of course. I don't know how it would float if they started trouble.'

'Not my expertise, either. I think you need to talk to one of those hotshot P.R. firms in New York.'

'I'm talking to you, Jesse. I'd like you to do me a favor.'

'Of course.'

'Work up a plan of attack for me, estimate of body count, you know the drill. Just so I know what all my options are. Of course, this is just between you and me.'

'Between you and me.'

Pennington nodded.

'I'll have to consult with some of my people, Mr. President. Stryker, head of the Rangers, Joe Ringer with Special Forces. Norris with Logistics.'

'Tell them it's an exercise. Classify it top secret. They work for you, Jesse.'

'They work for you, Mr. President. You're their commander in chief. How soon do you want this proposal?'

'This is Thursday. How does Sunday sound?'

ALBANY, GEORGIA, THURSDAY 11:46 A.M., EST

'Just call me Laverne,' she said with a smile. She was a chubby, flirtatious woman in her mid-forties and not at all impressed by the credentials of an FBI agent named Buddy Harris, who had flown to Albany from Atlanta.

'Good, I'm Buddy, Laverne. Maybe you can help me.'

'I'd just love to,' she said, leaning on the counter in the Office of Vital Statistics. 'Are you spending the night? I can take you to the best barbecue shack in south Georgia.'

'Sorry, I'm out of here on the two o'clock plane.'

'Lunch?'

'Well, now, that's a possibility.'

'Okay, Agent Harris, what're you after?'

'A birth certificate for one Elijah Wells. Just want to take a look.'

She looked genuinely surprised, then shrugged, said, 'No problem,' and went away. She returned in a minute or two with a thick ledger book, leafed through it, found the entry she was seeking, and spun the book around to face the agent. She tapped the page.

There it was: Elijah John Wells, date of birth, March 12, 1962. Parents: Frank and Helen Wells. Born in the local hospital.

'You lived in Albany very long, Laverne?'

'All my life. Went to work for the county the day I graduated from high school. Done about every job they got. Worked in the sheriff's office for a while. Boooring. Transferred over here to Records about a year ago. Boooring.'

'You wouldn't happen to know Frank and Helen Wells, would you?'

'Sure would. Live right over on Oak Street.'

'Do you know their children?'

'Why, of course. I've known them since they were born.'

'Are they still around town?'

'Hazel went to Atlanta after she graduated from Georgia Southern. Frank Junior works with his father down at the lumber mill.'

406

'How about Elijah? Is he still around?'

She looked at him curiously. 'I can tell you exactly where he is at this very moment.'

'Really.'

'Uh-huh. Been there for over thirty years.'

'Here in town?'

She nodded. 'Tell you what, Mr. FBI man, I'll take you to see Elijah and then you can take me to lunch.'

'That sounds like a fair enough deal.'

They left the courthouse and she directed him across town.

'Turn left here,' she said, pointing to an arched drive.

'This is the cemetery,' Harris said.

'Uh-huh. Drive up there to the right.'

The road curved around through a blanket of green grass and old oak trees, past elegant tombstones surmounted by marble angels and crosses.

'Stop here,' she said finally. They got out of the car and she led him out across the expansive lawn to a large headstone. Across the top in fancy scrolled letters was the word *Wells*, and beneath it the names of Jeremiah and Edith, both of whom had died in the late seventies. There was a second smaller stone beside the larger monument.

Elijah Wells
Beloved son of Frank and Mary
Born March 12, 1962
Called home to God's bosom
March 14, 1962
Rest in peace our little angel

Elijah Wells had died two days after he was born.

Thirty-one

Vail liked to say that all it takes to win a RICO case is half a dozen good lawyers, hard work, no sleep, and a stroke of luck. In the Sanctuary case, that stroke came from out of nowhere. It started when Naomi took a phone call at the task force office.

'This is FBI Agent Alan Burger in the Bureau's Des Moines office,' a tough old-timer said. 'May I speak to Mr. Vail, please.'

'Sorry, Agent Burger, he's out of the office. This is Naomi Chance, I'm deputy director of the task force. Can I help you?'

'You tell me. I got one crazy galoot here who comes in off the street about half an hour ago and demands to see Martin Vail. He won't talk to me or anybody in this office but he says if Vail is looking for information on the Sanctuary, he's the boy.'

'Who is he?'

'Name's Ernest Gondorf. Kansas City address. This could be a lot of air, Miz Chance. The guy spent last night in the local drunk tank. Ran his car into a tree in the city park. He's driving a new Firebird with Montana plates, he's staying in an upscale motel here in town, and he had four thousand bucks in his wallet when he fell out of the car.'

'Interesting. Will he talk to one of us on the phone?'

'He says he wants to talk to Vail mano a mano. We invited him to leave but he won't budge. The guy appears to be scared, but he's putting up a tough front.'

'Scared?'

'Says he needs protection, that this guy Engstrom put out a hit on him.'

'Hold on just a minute, will you, Alan?' She put the agent on hold. Only Parver and Firestone were in the office. She explained the situation to them both.

'How about it, Sam, you want to play make-believe and see if this guy's for real?'

'Sure.'

Naomi got back to Burger. 'Is he nearby?' she asked.

'Right across the room.'

'Tell him you've got Vail.'

'He got back in a hurry.'

'Sure did.'

There was a muffled chuckle from Burger. She handed the phone to Firestone.

'Hello,' a voice on the other end said.

'This is Martin Vail. You wanted to talk to me?'

'Not on the phone. In person.'

'Mister . . . what was your name again, sir?'

'Gondorf. Ernie Gondorf. And I'm telling you I can put a dent in Engstrom and the Sanctuary, but I gotta have protection. You understand what I mean about that?'

'Des Moines is a long way from here, Mr. Gondorf. Could you give me an idea of what this is about?'

'Just come and get me, okay? You won't be wasting your time.'

A moment later Burger came on the line. 'He went back to his chair,' he said.

'And you don't have a hold on this guy?'

'Nope. Bailed himself out of the drunk charge, got his car out of impound, and came over here.'

'And he won't leave?'

'Nope. And he says if we make him leave, we'll be responsible for his death.'

Firestone cupped the mouthpiece of the phone. 'What do you think, Naomi? The guy won't leave the Bureau office over there, says they're going to kill him.'

'Phew.' She leaned back in her chair and made a face. 'Well, the plane isn't busy. What've we got to lose?'

'Mr. Burger, we'll come on over there. Two hours, probably. Think you can put up with him until then?'

'I don't have any choice. But hurry, will you?' Burger growled. 'He's sitting at my desk humming country songs and he's tone deaf.'

'On the way.'

Des Moines 5:13 p.m., CST

Ernie Gondorf was a wiry man in his late thirties, five-seven or so, with bad teeth behind a smirk of a smile, and hair trimmed in a crew cut. He was wearing a wool plaid shirt, dark green corduroy pants, and hiking boots. His narrow, paranoid eyes flicked around the small interrogation room when Burger led him in and left. Burger joined Parver and Firestone in the observation room.

Burger was a heavyset man with stringy, graying hair, cut short, and the beginning of a beer belly. He was dressed in a crisp white shirt, a green tie, and dark blue pants. His voice sounded like a gravel grinder. 'All yours,' he said.

Gondorf looked into the mirror, his face a few inches from Shana Parver's, separated only by the two-way glass. He straightened his hair and then, for some inexplicable reason, checked out his teeth.

'Sheesh,' Parver said. 'Hasn't this guy ever heard of a toothbrush?'

'Don't get too close,' Burger said. 'He's got the breath to go with it.'

Parver was dressed as conservatively as possible: a dark blue pant-suit and a wine blouse, her long, jet-black hair pulled back in a tight bun, and wearing glasses instead of her contacts. She was still beautiful. Firestone was dressed as usual, in a suede sport coat, Levi's, a dark green wool button-down shirt, and a pair of vintage black Tony Lama cowboy boots. He looked more like

John Wayne than Martin Vail.

Gondorf sat down behind a table scarred with cigarette burns, put his feet on the table, crossed them at the ankles, and crossed his arms.

'Beautiful,' she said. 'Looks like a real handful.'

'Slap his feet off the table when you go in,' Burger said. 'It works to establish chain of command.'

'I'll keep it in mind,' she said.

'Mind if I watch from here?' Burger asked. 'I got a kind of vested interest in this.'

'Sure,' Parver said. 'Is that video recorder loaded?'

He nodded. 'Always is.'

'Mind shooting the interview?'

'Don't you have to ask him first?'

'If he says no, turn it off.'

'Gotcha.'

She and Firestone entered the room, Firestone standing against the wall and leaving the field to Parver.

She said, 'Mr. Gondorf, I'm Shana Parver, Assistant U.S. Attorney General. This is U.S. Marshal Sam Firestone. Please take your feet off the table.'

'Where's Vail? I told him I'd only talk to him.'

'I'm authorized to speak in his behalf. Now put your feet down and we'll get started.'

'I wanna see Vail.'

She slapped his feet off the table. 'Listen, Mr. Gondorf, we just flew all the way over here at your invitation. You want some help from us? Stop acting like an asshole and start talking or we're out of here and you can go out and go get your head blown off for all we care.'

'Whoa,' he said, snapping to attention.

'We're videotaping this interview, I'm sure you don't mind.'

'Well I–'

'We'll start with your name, address, age, you know the drill, I'm sure.'

'I ain't ever been arrested, this is all new to me. I mean,

I ain't a criminal, y'know. I tied one on. Big deal.'

'Why are we here, Ernie? Okay if I call you Ernie?'

'Everybody does.'

'So, we're here. Give us a little bio on yourself and tell us your story.'

He hunched his shoulders and moved his head around. 'You the one interested in the militias, right?'

'Possibly,' she said. 'Let's hear what you have to say.'

'My name's Ernie Gondorf. I'm thirty-seven. Used to drive rods and then I had a ride for two years and did the whole southern circuit. Winston-Salem, Daytona, Atlanta. I looked good until I blew an engine and spun out at the Daytona 500. Gary Burrell was right behind me and he clipped my rear end, hit the wall and, you know, the car went all over the state and he ended up in the morgue. Everybody said I lost control, that it was my fault, yak yak. I lost my ride, lost the car, and it ain't been real cheery since.'

'When was that?'

'Two years ago.'

'You live here in the city, Ernie?'

'Uh-huh. I been moving around a lot.'

'What do you do now?'

Gondorf leaned across the table and said, very seriously, 'I never been arrested and I wasn't in the Army.'

'That's your career?'

'What I mean, my prints aren't anywhere, or weren't till last night.'

Parver stared at him but did not respond. She knew when to let them do it in their own way and in their own time.

'What I mean,' Gondorf said, 'until last night, nobody had my prints on record. Not by name, okay.'

'But the cops have your prints now, that it?'

'Yeah, they do now. They printed me when I got arrested last night.'

'That's the DUI?'

'The DUI.'

'So, what you're saying, correct me if I'm wrong, sometime back you left your prints where they shouldn't have been, that it?'

'Not here.'

'Well, where then?'

'Seattle.'

'Washington? That Seattle?'

'Only one I know of.'

'There's a Seattle in Maine.'

'Oh, I didn't know that.'

'So they have your prints in Seattle, Washington.'

'But not in my name. They just have, y'know, a set of prints, but no way to ID them.'

'And . . .'

'Last night I got nailed for this DUI, mugged, and printed. If they did another print run in Seattle now, they'd get a match-up, turn me for this other event.'

'What other event?'

'This thing in Seattle.'

'And what thing was that, Ernie?'

'Look, before we take this any further . . . I mean, if I tell you what I know, I want immunity.'

'Immunity from what?'

'From this event.'

'Now how can I do that, Ernie? I don't have any idea what we're talking about here.'

Gondorf leaned toward Parver and said quietly, 'If you're interested in the militia movement, I got what you want. Take my word for it.'

'Good. And if you have something we can use, we'll be glad to discuss some arrangements. And you can take my word for that. Sam Firestone is a U.S. Marshal. He'll cover you.'

Gondorf shrugged his shoulders, a nervous tic, and looked around. He wiped his mouth with his hand. 'Sure seems a little vague.'

'You're the one who's being a little vague, Ernie.'

'What I want is to get in the witness protection thing.'

'That's a tall order.'

'I got a tall story to tell.'

'Look at it this way, maybe I think you want me to think you've got something so you can get off the hook for the other thing, whatever that was.'

'Jeez, that's kinda inside out.'

'Like I said, it's the best I can do until I know more.'

'Well ... maybe that's, uh ... that's fair enough. Maybe.'

'It's give and take, Ernie. That's how it works.'

'I give and you take, huh? Heh heh.'

Parver didn't answer him. She just looked across the table and waited.

'What the hell.' Gondorf shrugged again. 'I just want you to understand this could get me killed.'

Parver waited silently.

'I mean, uh, there's no doubt about that, okay? Just sitting here talking to you could get it done.'

'I'm impressed with that fact. Can we talk about this event?'

'It was an armed robbery.'

'Armed robbery? What, you stick up a liquor store? All night jiffy? What?'

Gondorf looked around and lowered his voice again. 'Armored car. The take was almost four million.'

Parver was startled. 'Oh. Well ... that's armed robbery, all right.'

'It gets worse.'

'How much worse?'

'A guard got hit.'

'How bad?'

'Totallyfuckinbad.' Gondorf looked around the room. 'That makes me an accomplice or something, right?'

'Or something. I take it you didn't pull the trigger?'

Gondorf shook his head violently. 'I'm a thief, man. I

414

wouldn't kill anybody.'

'When was this?'

'Two months ago.'

'Now, let me make sure I understand this. Two months ago you were involved in a four-million-dollar armored car heist in Seattle, Washington, in which one of the other perpetrators killed a guard. And you left some prints around. That accurate?'

Gondorf nodded. 'We were all wearing those plastic-type gloves – like doctors wear – and I snagged mine. It just kinda peeled off and I didn't realize it at first and when I did, it was too late to go back and get rid of my prints. I, uh, I figured they aren't on file anywhere so I got nothin' to worry about.'

'And now you're on file and you do have something to worry about.'

'That's the news.'

'Why are you telling me all this, Ernie?'

Gondorf wiped his mouth again. Beads of sweat appeared on his forehead. 'I got snookered out of my end,' he said finally.

'How did that happen?'

'They conned me.'

'They being?'

'The guys I went into this with. I was in for ten percent. That's four hundred large any way you cut it. They gave me twenty-five grand and *invested* the rest of it for me. Twenty-five lousy G's for a four-million-dollar job.'

'How many others were involved?'

'Five. Five and the fixer. He wasn't along for the ride, he, uh . . . he set it all up.'

'You work with any of these people before?'

'One of them. He brought me into the job.'

'So you did two armored car robberies?'

Gondorf nodded. 'The first one was down in Modesto. That's in California.'

'I know where it is.'

'I thought maybe there was another Modesto someplace.'

'Not that I know of.'

'Anyway, it wasn't that big a deal. Two fifty, maybe. Hardly worth the trouble.'

'What did you do? What was your job?'

'I was the driver. I'm one helluva driver.'

'You weren't last night.'

Gondorf smiled sardonically. 'Pow, right in the kisser. One for you.'

'So, you want to give up these five guys in exchange for a deal?'

'There's a little more to it than that.'

'Oh . . . ?'

'I told you, I want into that witness protection program.'

Parver stared at him for a moment. 'That's a little more difficult than–'

Gondorf cut Parver off. There was genuine fear written in the lines on his face. 'You don't understand, Miss Parver. I'm a dead man already just talkin' to you. I gotta be buried somewhere. These people are everywhere. *Every . . . fuckin' . . . where.* One of them could be standin' outside that door right now.'

'Just who *are* these people, Ernie?'

'You're interested in the militias, aren't you?'

'You pulled an armored car robbery with members of the militia?'

'*Shhhh.* Hold it down.'

'Which one?'

'Ever hear of the Zaccariah Division? Call themselves the Sanctuary of the Lord? Huh? That's who you're interested in, ain't it. I saw it on WWN.'

'You've still got my attention.'

Gondorf nodded slowly. 'My deal was ten percent of the take. It was an inside job. I mean, we knew this was a multimillion-dollar job before we ever went into it. After it was over, we drove back to Montana with the loot. We were all spooky, that much money and all. Went in four different cars, we were carryin' about a mil apiece. We drove like little old ladies all the way back. When we hit Montana, the fixer hands me twenty-five grand and says they're investing the rest of it in the division. The fucking *division*. They expected me to go back, go into training with them. We were a great team, he tells me. We'll do other jobs. And in the meantime, I can be a patriot for freedom. Four hundred grand worth of patriotism? My ass. Like I wanted to join up with that bunch of Bible-beating Jesus freaks.'

'This fixer have a name?'

'We got a deal?'

'Maybe. Did the fixer say how they were going to invest this money for you?'

'He didn't have to. It's weapons. Ammo, explosives. Gear. Use it for training, summer bivouacs, shit like that.'

'You just said, go *back* into training. You trained for this robbery?'

'Are you kidding? It was like a military operation. It wasn't their first, either. They had a mock-up of the truck and everything. I spent two weeks in the Montana mountains. Survival training and learning the armored car trick by the numbers. The plan was to do four or five of these jobs. Only the take was so big everybody got a hard-on and wanted to get back to Montana, get rid of the money, and celebrate a little. Also, killing the people wasn't part of the plan.'

'People? What do you mean people? How many were killed?'

Gondorf shrugged again. 'It was, uh, it was four.'

Firestone had been chomping at the bit for the past five minutes. Finally he spoke up. 'You took down the Pacific Armored Transport.'

'You heard about it, then?'

'We're in law enforcement, Ernie. It's unlikely we would have missed a four-million-dollar armored car robbery that made all the front pages, particularly when four men were killed.'

'They ain't got a clue. We were outta the state before noon. Only thing is, if they happen to run another check on the prints, I'm road kill.'

'That's a fair assumption.'

'I been worrying about those prints ever since the heist. Then I go out, put a load on, end up against a tree in the city park. I don't remember nothin' until I woke up in the drunk tank. My fingertips were still black from the ink. Christ, my heart stopped.'

'That was this morning?'

Gondorf nodded.

'You didn't waste any time.'

'I figure I come to you, I'm a lot better off than if you come to me.'

'That's sound thinking.'

'I been seeing about this new guy who's looking toward the militia. Vail. On TV.'

'You know General Engstrom?'

'I met him. He talks a lot. Thinks he wrote the Bible, for Chris-sakes.'

'I've heard that.'

'So . . . Miss Parver, can you do something for me?'

'I'd say that depends on what you can do for me.'

'I can ID the whole bunch.'

'You'll have to testify, if we can make a case. Are you willing to stand up in court?'

'Hell, why not? I'm so deep in now I got nothin' to lose. The minute I split I was on their list because they know I was pissed that they screwed me outta my end.'

'What happened to the four million?'

Gondorf shrugged. 'I can't tell you that. I mean, I ain't got the first notion.'

'When you first got back to Montana, what happened

to it?'

'We went straight to the fort. We met up there, took the loot into one of the buildings, and then they took us over to the mess hall for something to eat. That's when they gave me the twenty-five.'

'And you never saw the money again?'

'Nope.'

'Who else was there when you delivered the package?'

'Three of us in the car, the fixer, couple of other guys.'

'You know these people? You can identify them?'

Gondorf nodded.

'Was the General there?'

'No.'

'Any big shots? You know, top guns in the division?'

'I'm deaf, dumb, and blind. I mean I got amnesia until we got a deal, Miss Parver.'

'What were you doing in Des Moines, Ernie? That must be seven hundred miles from where you were in Montana.'

'Makin' tracks. Drove for two days, grabbin' naps in rest stops. When I got to Des Moines, I figured I could relax. Checked into a motel, went out, had some drinks, lookin' to pick up a friend for the night. Guess I was a little drunker than I thought I was.'

'Why are you running?'

'They bought me a car. Actually, the bank financed it and then they just signed the sticker over to me. That was because I was bitchin' so much. They were gettin' the idea I wanted out. I didn't know it was in the game to kill those four guys. That never came up when we were rehearsing the job. Coming back, me and the guy I was driving are talking, he says they figured maybe I'd chicken out if I knew they were gonna waste them all. He says they planted some money in the driver's bank account to make it look like he was the inside man. Actually, it was the shotgun rider. I think his name was Baylor . . . they whacked him too 'cause they were afraid

419

he couldn't stand up to the heat. Then he says to me now you're in, you may as well stay in. I wanted out, but they owed me all that kale. So, we got a deal?'

'We'll take you back to Chicago with us,' Parver said. 'We'll keep you under wraps and you'll get to meet Mr. Vail. He'll make the final deal with you. Who was the fixer?'

'I swear to God I never got his name. Somebody said he runs some banks.'

'How about the show runner? Who was in charge of the heist, Ernie?'

He shifted in his chair a couple of times and wiped his mouth with the back of his hand.

'Colonel Shrack. They call him Black Bobby.'

Thirty-two

Billy Hardistan spread the doctored photographs of Tunny and Jennings on the coffee table in front of Vail and Jane Venable. The age transition of the two men in the Vietnam photograph was amazing. There were six views of each of the suspects.

'Floyd is distributing these to the media as we speak,' Hardistan said. 'WWN will have it on the air by noon. The nets have promised to feature them on the six and eleven o'clock news. And we'll get coverage in the print media by tomorrow morning.'

'Great,' Vail said. 'I just hope you aren't flooded with calls.'

'We will be,' Hardistan said. 'I have six people fielding calls. They know what they're doing. They can screen the nuts with a few well-chosen questions.'

'I want this guy alive if possible,' Vail said. 'So far we have a lot of strong circumstantial and corroborative evidence but very little hard stuff.'

'I think you've done an amazing job in three weeks,' Hardistan said.

'Thanks to the two years of data you provided,' Vail replied.

'It's your team that's making sense of it.'

Vail got up and paced in front of the picture window framing the sprawling lake and waterfront. He stopped and stared out the window. He quickly reviewed the case, such as it was, through his mind.

'We have the Waller tape, which spills all the beans, but even if we're lucky enough to get it in, it's corrobo-

421

rative evidence at best. We have the thief Shana and Sam brought back from Des Moines. That connects the armored car robbery to Shrack and the Sanctuary, but he's a turncoat witness and they'll blow him off on the witness stand. We've got the numbers on the semi and the photo of Waller, but we can't prove they were signatures left by the Sanctuary. What we don't have is the money or the weapons. We don't have a stick of hard evidence. We need a link, Billy. We need to tie all these crimes together. We find the link, we get the indictments.'

'Then Sam and his crew have to enforce them,' Hardistan said, his voice harsh and tentative.

'We have to lure the big guns off that hill somehow without starting a shooting war up there.'

'How about the banks? Have Flaherty and Meyer come up with anything?'

'Theories. It takes time, wading through miles of records looking for the paper trail. Flaherty's convinced the link that ties all this together is the banks. That's what cracked the RICO case downstate. But it could take six weeks or six months.'

'I don't know whether I can give you even six days,' Hardistan said. Vail had sensed an edginess in Hardistan since he arrived at the penthouse.

'What else is eating you?' he asked.

Hardistan looked at him through cold eyes and finally said, 'I've got some disturbing news.'

Vail smiled. 'That seems par for the course, Billy,' he said.

'This is personal, Martin.'

'It's all personal.'

'This is different. We know who Abraham is.'

Vail and Jane both looked at him intently, their eyes bright with curiosity. With everything else happening, Vail had almost forgotten about Abraham.

'Hell, that's good news,' Vail said.

'Yes and no,' Hardistan said. 'According to the IRS, his

name is Elijah Wells, born in Albany, Georgia. Thirty-six years old. Made a name for himself as Brother Transgressor, a snake-handling evangelist preacher, until last summer when he suddenly dropped out of sight. He was reborn as the Prophet Abraham.'

'What's so disturbing about that?' Vail said.

'According to the records in Albany, Elijah Wells died two days after he was born.'

Both Vail and Venable had been attorneys long enough to know what that meant.

'So who is he really?' Vail asked.

'We took several sets of prints from his van and ran them through the HITS network. And we scored. I hate to ruin your weekend, but it's a name from both your pasts. Abraham is Aaron Stampler.'

Vail and Jane were visibly shocked by the news.

'Aaron Stampler?' she said. 'How could that be?'

'No chance there's a mistake?' Vail said shakily.

'His prints were all over the vehicle, Marty.'

'Jesus! Stampler!' Vail walked to the window and stared out across the lake for a minute or two, then turned back and said, 'I don't know why I should be surprised. He's as close to the living Devil as anyone I've ever met.'

He looked over at the black eye patch on the woman he loved.

'Do we know where he is?' Vail asked. And now his voice was solid steel.

Hardistan nodded. 'He's up on that mountain in what his chauffeur calls the "bunker." The chauffeur's name is Jessups. He's never seen this bunker but he says it's a full-scale communications center. Also has a small radio studio, which is where Stampler taped his shows.'

'How the hell did he get out of that coal mine?' Venable asked.

'Maybe he rose from the dead,' Vail said. He stared at Hardistan and added, 'I want the son of a bitch alive. I want him to face a jury for the people he killed here.'

'You don't mind if we wait until Monday, do you?' Hardistan said. 'I'd rather not send somebody up there looking for him this weekend. We're looking at several square miles on Mount James with six or seven hundred armed men, mines, and razor wire. And God knows where the hell the bunker is.'

'Can the AWACS help locate it?' Venable asked.

Hardistan shook his head. 'They can't read through solid rock,' he explained. 'But we've got several surveillance aircraft up there shooting profiles of the mountain. We're getting as close as we can without provoking them. The Sanctuary has weekend maneuvers once a month. Hopefully, most of them'll go back to work Monday. Which will leave the command staff vulnerable, and they're the ones we want.'

'I hope we're that lucky,' Vail said.

'I hear that,' Hardistan said.

BAD RAPIDS, MICHIGAN, FRIDAY 1:19 P.M., CST
One hour after WWN ran the first photographs of Jennings and Tunny, the phones started lighting up in the special room set up in the Chicago FBI office. The first few calls were duds. But the release of the pictures paid off quickly.

Agent Lincoln caught the first significant call.

'Hi,' a woman said nervously. 'This is Mrs. Libby Dove. I'm from Bad Rapids, Michigan.'

'Yes, Mrs. Dove?'

'I saw the pictures of the man on the television news, the one you're looking for.'

'Which one of the pictures?'

'The one you call Wayne Tunny? I'm certain he's our next-door neighbor, Don Woodbine. Has he done something wrong?'

'We just need to contact him, Mrs. Dove. We have some questions to ask him. What does he do?'

424

'He owns the local hardware store.'

Lincoln rolled his eyes. 'How long have you known Mr. Woodbine?' he asked, tapping the eraser end of a pencil on the desk.

'Twenty years at least. His wife Elaine was one of my best friends. She died of cancer two years ago.'

'And how long has he owned the hardware store?'

'Since he came here twenty years ago.'

'Does he run the store himself?'

'Oh yes. Except when he travels.'

'Travels?' Lincoln said, beginning to show interest. 'Does he travel a lot?'

'He has some kind of consulting job with the government. That's why he has his own plane.'

Lincoln stopped tapping the pencil. Her revelation jump-started his heart. 'He owns a plane?'

'Oh yes. A beauty. Has his own hangar out on his farm a couple miles from town.'

'Can you describe the plane?'

'It's white with blue trim with, you know . . . the wing is on the bottom.'

'How many engines, Mrs. Dove?'

'Two.'

'Is he at home now – or at his store?'

'Golly, I don't know. He's somewhat reclusive and I'm not sure whether he's over there or not. You might call the hardware store and ask for Charley Moore. He works for Don. I have his phone number right here.'

'Now listen to me, I want you to do me a favor, Mrs. Dove. Do not call anybody. In fact, I want you to keep this information to yourself. And do not approach the Woodbine house.'

'Has he done something wrong?'

'We just need to talk to him.'

'All right, but I'm sure everybody in town's recognized him by now.'

She was right. The lights were blinking on several of

425

the phones. All the calls were from Bad Rapids. The agents answering the calls were all waving their hands, indicating that they might have a 'hit.'

'Tell me more about Mr. Woodbine, Mrs. Dove.'

'Well, he grows roses. He built a beautiful greenhouse in the backyard. He's been very reclusive since Elaine's death.'

'Any children?'

'No.'

'Lives alone, does he?'

'Uh-huh.'

'How long has he had the second job? The one requiring him to travel.'

'Since he came here. He must do well, he bought Ferguson's Hardware a couple of months after he arrived. I remember because poor Orville Ferguson died on my birthday, September twenty-third. And Don kept the Ferguson name on the store – it was kind of a tradition here. We always thought that was kind of him.'

'Were you friends?'

'Well, yes. Like I said, I was closer to Elaine. Don's a very quiet man. He coached Little League for two years. The Presbyterian team.'

'And he travels a lot?'

'Oh, not that much. Four or five times a year maybe.'

'Which of the photographs do you recognize, Mrs. Dove?'

'All of them. There's just no question. The man in those pictures is Don Woodbine.'

'Can you hold a minute?'

'Yes, sir.'

The agent cupped the mouthpiece.

'Anybody else talking to Bad Rapids, Michigan, about a Don Woodbine?'

Three other agents held up their hands and more lights were blinking on.

'May I have your number, Mrs. Dove?'

426

Hardistan had just returned to his hotel when the room phone rang. It was Floyd McCurdy, who had taken charge of the phone bank now that the investigation in Ohio was winding down.

'We got us a hit,' McCurdy said. 'Five calls and they're still coming in. The profile fits this guy like spandex underwear.'

'Who is he?'

'Name's Don Woodbine, Bad Rapids, Michigan. Estimated age is fifty. Owns a hardware store, but he also has a twin-engine plane and a consulting job with the government, which takes him on the road half a dozen times a year. Reclusive. Doesn't like to have his picture taken. I've got two men on the way up there. If it's him, I think we need a SWAT team in there.'

'No question. I don't want anybody approaching the house or the plane. Advise the local police what we're doing. I'll call Greg Fleming right now. He's one of the best and he's here in Chicago.'

'Are you coming up?'

'I'll hang fire until your man checks back in. Meanwhile I'll alert Greg.'

'Talk to you ASAP.'

Hardistan hung up, then punched out Vail's number on his secured cell phone. Vail answered immediately. He was en route to his cabin.

'Your man Latimore was right,' he told Vail. 'We may have a hit on our assassin.'

'Which one is he?'

'Tunny. He calls himself Don Woodbine. He's lived in Bad Rapids, Michigan, that's about 150 miles from here, for twenty years. It looks very promising. I'm going to alert my best SWAT team and get up there as soon as I have confirmation that he's our man.'

'Are you taking Latimore with you?'

'I wouldn't break a promise, Martin.'

427

'Good. Keep me informed.'

Hardistan's second call was to the SWAT squad of the regional FBI office.

'This is Billy Hardistan. Get me Greg Fleming, please . . . I don't care what he's doing, I want him and I want him now!'

Thirty-three

Don Woodbine's house was a modest one-story brick structure on a large corner lot. Two local police cars and an ambulance, their lights off, were parked a block away from the house. Several men and women and two children were huddled together on the sidewalk near four black FBI assault vans.

Dressed in body armor and a blue FBI jacket, Greg Fleming scurried up the darkened street and reported to Hardistan.

'We evacuated the families in the house across the street, the one next door to it, and the Dove house next door to Woodbine's place.'

'Good.'

Hardistan turned to the small group.

'Ladies and gentlemen, my name is Hardistan. I'm with the FBI. I'm sorry to inconvenience you, but this is a precaution we always take. You all know your neighbor, Mrs. Richards. She very kindly has invited you all to come into her house and get out of the cold. This shouldn't take too long.'

'What did Don do?' one of the men in the group asked.

'He's wanted for questioning in a felony,' Hardistan said simply.

'You need an army to ask questions?'

'We like to play it safe for everybody's sake,' Hardistan said softly. He entered one of the vans as Harrison Latimore walked through the crowd with Libby Dove, the woman who lived next door to Woodbine. She was a heavyset woman in her late forties, wearing a black, fur-lined parka. Mrs. Dove followed Latimore to the van Hardistan had just entered. He slid back the door and she went inside. It looked like a combination arsenal and TV station.

'Mrs. Dove,' Latimore said, 'this is William Hardistan, director of the FBI; Greg Fleming, director of the FBI SWAT division, and Roy Ware. Mr. Ware is a computer technician.' Ware was sitting at a table in front of two computer monitors, one of which was dedicated to the monitor of a heat scanner. Hardistan, Fleming, and Latimore watched while Libby Dove described Woodbine's house and carport to Ware, who roughed out a sketch.

'That's perfect,' she said finally.

Ware ran off ten sketches on a small copy machine.

'And there's no question in your mind that this is Don Woodbine,' Hardistan said, showing her blow-ups of the photos.

She tapped one of the pictures. 'It's him,' she said. 'That's Don Woodbine. Everybody says so.'

'Thank you,' Hardistan said. 'You've been a great help. Please join the others over there at Mrs. Richards's house. We don't want anyone on the street.'

The four black vans moved slowly in single file down the street, stopping when they reached the Dove house. The SWAT squad members emptied out of three of the vans and knelt in the darkness. Fleming was wearing a radio-controlled headset.

'Joker, this is Penguin. You copy?' Fleming whispered.

'Roger that, Penguin. Joker is in place.'

'Hold your positions.'

Fleming entered the lead van.

Ware was reading the heat scan of the house as the video camera slowly panned across it. He stopped it once, briefly, then moved on.

'There's a light on in the living room,' he said.

The camera completed its scan of the house.

'If he's in there, he's dead,' Ware said.

'You in place, Greg?' Hardistan asked.

'Ready to rock and roll. I've got fourteen men here, four in front, four in back, two snipers for backup in front and back. We've got ten at the hangar.'

'Excellent,' Hardistan replied.

'We'll hit them both at the same time.'

'Who's in charge there?'

'Oliver.'

'Okay, you know the drill. I don't care what the heat scan says, treat the place like he's there. Remember, this guy's a professional killer. A high-level professional shooter.'

'We know, Billy,' Fleming said with a smile. 'We go through this every time.'

'I just want to make sure, Greg. I want this man alive if possible, but this is an open range. Don't take any chances. I don't want any dead heroes here tonight. Go in fast and dust the place. If you get him, bring him outside, secure the premises, and the lab'll move in. And be careful.'

Greg Fleming shook his head and laughed. 'Got it all, Billy,' he said, and left the van.

'I'd like to go in with the team,' Latimore said.

'You stay here with me. These people are trained to do this kind of thing.'

'I qualified in SWAT training–'

'Latimore, this is not a Wild West show,' Hardistan interrupted. 'Put that vest on and be quiet. We go in when they clear the premises.'

'Yes, sir.'

'Joker, this is Penguin, move in,' Fleming said.

'Copy that.'

The team swiftly zigzagged across the lawn. One sniper stood behind a tree in Woodbine's front yard. The other was crouched behind the hood of a car parked across the street. They scanned the scene through night scopes. Blinds were pulled over the window. Through the slats they could make out a single light in the living room. The squad reached their positions and crouched against the house.

'Joker,' Fleming whispered, 'we're at the house.'

'In place here, Penguin. We can see through a crack in the door. There's a truck in there, no plane.'

'Count to ten and go in.'

'Copy that.'

Fleming counted to ten. 'Go!' he said.

Two men took down the front door with a battering ram. In the back, one of the agents smashed out a windowpane and unlocked the door. They rushed the interior of the house, gun lights fingering the darkness as they expertly cleared the rooms, closets, cabinets, any-place a human body could squeeze into. Nothing.

Fleming switched on some lights. The place was uncommonly neat and clean. It was also cold, the thermostat having been turned down to sixty.

In the rear of the house an agent tried the door to the carport. It was locked.

At the hangar, the heavy chain and lock were sheared with a pair of pneumatic cutters. Oliver shoved one of the doors open and his men dispersed, moving quickly through the large barnlike interior. The lights probed every corner of the enormous room.

Oliver checked the truck. The door was locked.

'Tony,' he said to one of his men, 'go get the jimmy. I got a locked vehicle here.'

'Right,' Tony answered, and left on the double.

'Penguin, this is Joker, do you copy?'

'Penguin copies.'

'The hangar's empty. We got a locked truck in here. Okay to jimmy the door?'

*

At the house, Fleming was walking back to the carport door. 'Do it,' he said.

'Roger that.'

Fleming walked past the agent and tried the doorknob. He looked around the doorjamb and checked in the kitchen for a key rack but found none.

'Kick it open,' he ordered.

The agent stepped back and slammed his foot into the door just under the knob. The lock shattered and the door swung open. The trip fuse to the plastic explosives set off the blast.

The house literally disintegrated, showering bricks, mortar, wood, and glass across the neighborhood. Car windows three blocks away shattered.

Inside the house Fleming and eight of his team saw only a blinding white flash before they were blown through the walls, into the ceiling, and out into the yard. They all died instantly, their bodies ripped apart by the force of the deadly plastic bomb, then scorched by the gasoline which sent a mushroom ball of fire swirling into the night sky. The explosion was heard ten miles away, and the fireball lit up three square blocks as it seemed to ignite its way upward.

Hardistan and Latimore were slammed back against one of the vans and battered with debris. They fell beside each other, stunned, bleeding from scratches and cuts, their bodies bruised from the force of the blast.

Hardistan raised himself on an elbow and stared at the fire with open-mouthed disbelief. He struggled to his feet and saw what was left of Fleming's smoking corpse lying in the front yard.

'Oh my God,' he muttered, and then repeated it, this time almost a shriek. Latimore got to his knees beside him.

'The hangar!' he cried out.

Too late. Another explosion rumbled through the night and the sky erupted in a second fireball.

Thirty-four

Hardiston trod past the wreckage of the Woodbine house like a man in a walking nightmare. The house and hangar barn had been leveled by explosion, ravaged by fire. Eleven of his men were dead; three more, including Latimore, had been flown in medevac choppers to a hospital in Chicago. FBI Director Harry Simmons had been given the task of informing the families of the victims and explaining the event to the press. Hardistan did not care what he told the media. Two investigating teams and a forensics team were on site. There was nothing further he could do in Bad Rapids.

He was heading in an FBI chopper to Vail's cabin to tell him in person about the tragedy when McCurdy called him.

'The plane's at O'Hare,' McCurdy said. 'A traffic controller going off duty spotted it.'

'You're sure it's his?'

'The registration's a phony. It's his plane all right.'

'What the hell would he go into Chicago for if . . . Jesus, Floyd, he's going after Vail!'

'Maybe he's—'

'Forget maybe, we can't take a chance. Treat this as an emergency rescue. I'll call the bodyguards and advise them to get Martin and Jane out of there. I want you to dispatch two choppers out to the cabin, just in case. You go with them, direct the operation there, and send two more teams by vehicle to the site. Stay airborne and check the woods. Contact the state patrol and the local police out there and tell them to get to the cabin. Are you still

434

with me?'

'Yes, sir.'

'I'm going to O'Hare. Get eight men and a sniper out there and set up tight surveillance on the plane. But don't move on him unless there's a danger of losing him. Get all the civilians off that tarmac and replace them with our people, but don't cause a big stir, make it look like a normal shift change. And for God's sake don't go near the plane, it could be booby-trapped. I should be there in twenty minutes.'

Hardistan hung up and called the secure line to Avery Baxter, the senior agent on Vail's bodyguard team.

There was no answer.

Earlier in the day, after the two FBI bodyguards had checked out the grounds and house, Vail and Jane had gone down to the lake and done some trap shooting. As usual, Jane had made him look like an amateur, while Magoo sat back near the cabin. The dog hated the sound of gunfire, and at one point howled soulfully because he was left alone.

'Thank God you're not a hunter,' Jane said as they walked back across the expanse of lawn, their shotguns unloaded while the dog trotted down to join them.

'I never even knew what a skeet was until I met you,' he said.

'You mean a clay pigeon?'

'Whatever,' he said with a laugh, and put his arm around her. Off in the woods he could see Avery Baxter, the senior agent, checking the grounds out. Cliff Mandel, the other seasoned agent, and Baxter had become their constant companions and protectors.

This was their first weekend away together since Martin had accepted the Sanctuary case, and it made Jane nervous seeing two armed men strolling the grounds. She also sensed a nervousness about Martin, which was uncommon. He had relaxed, as he always did the minute they arrived at their beloved getaway. Still, it was obvious to her that the case weighed heavily on his mind. A comforting fire hissed and crackled in the kitchen fireplace, and she made hot chocolate to take the chill off.

'Should we invite the boys in for dinner?' she asked.

'Not tonight,' he said. 'I thought we could have a nice candlelight supper. You know, just the two of us. Maybe you can fix plates for them before we eat.'

'Okay . . .'

They sat in front of the big picture window and watched the sun set on the other side of the lake. Then he took four T-bones out of the refrigerator and started the grill while she mixed up a salad and put potatoes in the oven.

Later, after Baxter and Mandel had eaten, Jane and Martin sat down together at the dining room table. Martin had lit a dozen candles, and the room had a soft, warm glow to it, made even cozier by the bottle of Taittinger's champagne he opened. And yet Vail still seemed distracted, at times jumpy.

'Are you scared about something, Marty?' she asked finally.

'Scared? No, why would I be scared?'

'You just seem . . . apprehensive.'

'Well . . . I, uh, I wanted to talk to you about, uh . . .'

He stopped in mid-sentence, as if he'd lost track of what he was saying.

'Yes . . .' she said, and smiled.

'Magoo really loves it here,' he said, looking over at the dog, who was sitting in front of the window.

'Uh-huh.'

'And, uh . . .'

'Marty, what's the matter?' she asked, touching his forearm. 'This case really has you on edge, doesn't it?'

'This has nothing to do with that.'

'What is it, then?'

He raised his champagne glass toward her and smiled.

'I love you very much,' he said.

'And I love you, darling,' she answered, tapping his glass with hers.

'Then . . . will you marry me, Janie?'

The question took her totally by surprise. They had been together for more than two years, and the word 'marriage' had never been mentioned by either of them.

'Is that what's been on your mind?'

'I just wasn't sure how to do it. I'll be glad to get down on one knee and ask you the old-fashioned way,' he said, almost stammering.

'Marty, you're blushing.'

'It's hot in here.'

'It is not hot in here, you're blushing. I think it's lovely. And of course I'll marry you. I didn't think you were the marrying kind or I would have asked first.'

'I'm the marrying kind now,' he said. 'I can't imagine spending the rest of my life without you.'

'We don't have to get married to spend our life together.'

'Oh . . . well, then, what'll I do with this?'

He took a black velvet box from his pocket, snapped it open, and held it out to her. The ring was a three-carat round diamond set in gold. Simple and elegant.

'This belonged to my grandmother,' he said.

Tears filled her eyes and she covered her mouth with the fingers of one hand.

'Oh, Marty,' she said. 'It's lovely. Was this Ma Cat's engagement ring?'

He nodded. 'I know she'd be overjoyed if she were here at this moment.'

Jane squeezed his hand. 'I'm sure she's close by.'

He slipped the ring on her finger and kissed her, a devouring kiss that lingered. Finally he leaned back in his chair.

'I wonder if the boys were watching,' she said, holding her hand up and studying the ring.

437

'Maybe we ought to invite them in to share a glass of champagne.'

'Are they supposed to do that? Drink on duty, I mean.'

'One glass of champagne?'

She laughed and said, 'I think it would be delightful to share the moment with our bodyguards.'

He picked up the walkie-talkie and buzzed Avery.

'Yes, sir?'

'Avery, will you and Cliff come here a minute?'

'Yes, sir. Is there a problem?'

'No problem.'

A moment later they appeared at the door to the kitchen, huddled in their blue FBI jackets. Avery was a tall man with silver hair and brown eyes. Cliff Mandel was shorter, his black hair trimmed neatly over his ears, his dark eyes always on the go, always checking things out.

'Come on in,' Vail said, and led them into the dining room. 'I know this is against regulations, but Jane and I would like you to share a toast with us. We're getting married.'

Both of the agents beamed at the news. Vail refilled their glasses and poured fresh ones for their two guests.

'Here's to both of you,' Baxter said. 'I hope you'll always be as happy as you are at this minute.'

She held out her hand and the diamond glittered in the candlelight.

'Beautiful,' Mandel said. 'I wish you both all the happiness in the world.'

Tears were trickling down Jane's cheeks and her damp eyes were glowing with joy.

'When's the big day?' Baxter asked.

Jane looked at Martin and raised her eyebrows.

'As soon as we wrap the RICO case,' he said. 'Suit you?'

'Do we have to wait that long?' she whispered.

The two agents finished their champagne.

'Gotta get back to work,' Baxter said. He checked his watch. It was nine-twenty. They went back outside.

Martin and Jane went into the living room, sat in front of the fire, and finished the last of the champagne while Magoo lay at their feet, lazily gnawing on a steak bone. Suddenly he stopped and looked up, his ears twisting and searching out a sound they could not hear.

'What is it?' Vail asked. 'Hear a rabbit out there?'

Outside, Mandel was walking along the six-foot-high wire fence Hardistan had insisted they put up around the forested ten-acre estate. His flashlight beam flicked along the ground and searched the area on the other side of the fence.

'Things are quiet out here, Avery,' he said into his headset.

'Here, too,' Baxter answered. 'Beautiful night if it wasn't so damned cold.'

'That champagne kinda took the chill off,' Mandel answered. He was thinking about Vail and the beautiful Jane Venable and how happy they seemed.

It was the last thought he ever had.

The figure seemed to grow out of the earth behind him, rising slowly from the leaves, eyes glowing in a blackened face, night goggles pushed up on his forehead, a jagged Marine knife glistening at his side.

Mandel did not hear him; he was talking to Baxter as Tunny emerged from the shallow pit he had dug in the ground. Tunny reached out swiftly, cupped his gloved hand under Mandel's chin, and snapped his head back. Before Mandel could cry out, the knife sliced through his throat, cutting jugular, esophagus, and air pipe. Breath whistled from his lungs. Mandel was dead when he dropped to the ground at his killer's feet.

The killer quickly stooped down, jabbed the bloody blade into the earth, cleaning off the blood, took the dead agent's headset, wiped off the blood with leaves, and put it on. He reached into the ditch and removed a plastic bag containing his rifle. He clicked off the flashlight, lowered the goggles over his eyes, and scanned the forest around him, being careful not to look at the lights in the house, which would have blinded him. He stalked through the forest looking for the man the dead agent had called Avery.

The day before booby traps had killed eleven agents, Tunny alias Woodbine had flown down from Michigan. He had read the newspaper and magazine articles Abraham had left in the locker at the Oklahoma City airport. One of the articles mentioned Vail's getaway cabin where he and Jane Venable spent weekends. The article said 'the cabin has a sweeping view of Lake Sloan.'

Tunny checked his sectionals and found the lake. Not that big. He set his course and flew to the lake. From the air he could see half a dozen shacks and small cabins on the lakeside.

But one was enormous, a barnlike structure. A link fence surrounded the large property. There was a locked gate and a long drive leading to the cabin, which could not be seen from the two-lane road that led past it. He circled the place. A large picture window in back of the house faced the lake. It was worth checking out. Then he crisscrossed the area across the road from the cabin. He finally found what he was looking for – an abandoned barn. It was a mile and a half from the Vail place. Perfect. A safe place to hide a car for the night.

Tunny had rented a car using a new credit card. He took his weapons case, his combat fatigues, and cap, and drove out to the lake late in the afternoon. Using a county map, he found the abandoned barn, changed into thermal long johns and his combat outfit, and waited until dark. Then he trotted to the county road with a sports gear bag over his shoulder. It was deserted. It took him twenty minutes to get to the fence surrounding the Vail property.

He slipped into the woods adjacent to the cabin, climbed the fence, and cautiously approached the house. He flashed his light in the window. It was the kitchen. On the floor near the sink was a large porcelain bowl with MAGOO painted on the side.

He circled the house. Glass everywhere. Excellent. Then he checked the woods. It was thick with pine trees and bushes. His first consideration was his getaway. He would have to take out the FBI bodyguards first, they were the big threat. Then it would be an easy shot through a window to drop Vail and Venable. She had to go, too, to prevent her from calling the police. He went back to the fence. If the guards patrolled the perimeter, they would pass by the fence. This was the place to be.

He opened the gear bag and took out a shovel and a tarp to wrap himself in. Then he started digging.

Inside the house, Magoo stood up, his ears twitching, his nose testing the air. He trotted swiftly to the front door of the cabin and growled low in his throat.

Vail followed Magoo to the door.

'What's the matter?' he said. 'You know Avery and Cliff.'

The dog scratched at the door, still growling. Vail opened the door and Magoo streaked out. Vail flipped a light switch, and a half-dozen floodlights mounted on the house and in the trees burst on.

Tunny shrieked with pain as the bright lights, amplified by the night goggles, seared his eyes.

Baxter rushed around the side of the house and yelled at Vail. 'Get back in the house and call the police! Turn off the inside lights.'

Magoo rushed through the woods, his nose and ears leading him toward Mandel's bloody corpse. Then he saw Tunny on his knees rubbing his eyes. He changed course and raced toward the assassin.

441

Through teared vision Tunny saw a white streak coming toward him, its teeth bared. He rolled to one side and fired a single shot from the hip. The bullet ripped into Magoo, knocked him into the air and sideways. The dog crashed to the ground and lay motionless.

Baxter zigzagged his way across the clearing in front of the house and dodged into the woods, dropped to his knees, and fell back against a tree.

'Cliff,' he whispered into his headset, 'you copy?'

A moment later a voice came back at him.

'Help me,' the voice whispered.

'God damn!' Baxter growled.

Tunny lay prone behind a tree stump and looked toward the house, searching the darkness for the surviving agent.

Vail raced through the house, turning off lights, while Venable ran into the dining room and blew out the candles.

'Jane, come here,' Vail whispered. She joined him in the living room and he pulled her into the doorway of the darkened guest room. He had retrieved both shotguns from the kitchen, where he had left them to be cleaned, but the gun cabinet with shotgun shells was across the room.

'What do you think's going on?' Venable asked. She seemed remarkably calm.

'My guess is it's Tunny, the killer who got Waller. I'm going over to the gun cabinet and get some more shells.'

'Stay here,' she pleaded. 'He'll see you in the light from the fireplace.'

'We've got to protect ourselves in case he gets past Baxter and Mandel.'

'Magoo's out there,' she said plaintively.

'I know it. Just stay here. Back into the room so he can't see you.'

'Where are Cliff and Avery?'

'I don't know, darling.'

He crawled away, slithering across the wide room to the gun cabinet. He opened the drawer, grabbed two boxes of shotgun shells, and crawled back. In the flickering light from the fireplace he shoved shells into the two .20 gauge shotguns.

Outside, Avery Baxter held his ground, listening for signs of movement. He decided the best place for him to be was in the house, where he could protect Vail and Venable. He got into a crouch, then ran toward the house, veering back and forth as he dashed for the door.

A hundred yards away Tunny watched him through his night scope. He waited until Baxter reached the back entrance and hesitated for a moment to open the door. Tunny got off one shot as Baxter leaped through the door. It hit Baxter in the back and spun him into the darkened house.

Baxter rolled over on his stomach and crawled through the entrance hall into the living room.

'It's me, Avery!' he cried out. 'Don't shoot.'

'Prove it,' came Vail's voice out of the darkness.

Baxter struggled to a sitting position against the wall and thought for a minute.

'Diamond ring,' he stammered. 'About three carats. Solitaire setting.'

Vail put his shotgun down and in a crouch ran to the entranceway. He could barely see Baxter in the failing light of the fireplace. He squatted beside the injured agent and checked his wound.

'Went right through your body armor. In the shoulder,' Vail said.

'Did you call the police?'

'Jane did.'

'Good,' Baxter said, pain wracking his voice. 'I dropped my weapon when I came in. It's by the door. An automatic. And turn on the lights. We got him at a disadvantage now.'

Vail crawled across the floor, feeling for the machine gun, felt its cool surface, and picked it up. Then he crawled to the door and flicked on the outside lights again.

Tunny was fifty yards from the house with a clear view through the windows of the kitchen and living room when the outside lights blazed on again. *Damn!* he said to himself. He removed the night scope, tossed it aside, eye-sighted the rear of the house, and fired a continuous burst from his .50 caliber across the back of the house.

Inside, the bullets stitched across the kitchen, sending splinters of wood and broken glass into the room. The steel jacket bullets ripped through the stove and microwave, shattered the blender and toaster, and tore into the free-standing gas grill in the middle of the room. One bullet ruptured the gas lines. Hot lead ignited the escaping gas and it exploded in a dull *whoosh*. Flames roared up from the ruined grill and set off the fire alarms and sprinklers. Flaming gas and cold water fused.

Another burst of gunfire ripped across the windows of the main room, shattering them and sending billows of cotton and cloth from ruptured sofas and chairs as the slugs tore into the furniture.

Tunny held his ground. He had heard the shotguns earlier in the day, so he knew Vail had shotguns in the house. He had caught a glimpse of Baxter's gun and guessed it was an Uzi. He moved quickly to the brush close to the house and checked it out.

Then he heard the sirens.

Tunny was too good a pro to continue what had suddenly become a losing battle. He turned immediately and ran back through the woods, past Mandel's body, leaped onto the galvanized wire fence, and, vaulting over it, ran toward the road. He dropped to the ground as a police car roared by and skidded into the drive leading to Vail's cabin. From the other direction another police car, an ambulance, and a fire truck entered the drive.

Cut and run, he thought. *Nothing's worth dying for.* Tunny dashed across the two-lane road and ran as fast as he could into the darkness.

O'HARE AIRPORT, FRIDAY 10:14 P.M., CST

When he arrived at the airport, Hardistan got the good and bad news from McCurdy, who was still circling the Vail cabin in the chopper.

'You were right, Billy,' he said. 'He took out Cliff Mandel.'

'Oh my God.' It was the worst kind of nightmare.

McCurdy went on. 'He clipped Baxter but he'll be okay. Vail and Venable are fine. The cabin's a mess.'

'Where are they now?'

'They went in the ambulance. Half the state patrol is escorting them. Apparently Tunny shot Vail's dog but it's still alive. They're taking it to the hospital with Baxter. A vet's going to meet them there.'

'And Tunny . . .'

'We're still looking.'

'Road blocks?'

'On all the main roads and the interstate. We're going to keep patrolling the area in the chopper. But Billy, there are dozens of little back roads up here.'

'If he gets through the road blocks, he only has one option left. He'll come to the plane.'

Hardistan sat down and his body sagged. He had lost twelve men to Tunny. He knew Vail wanted him alive, but he wasn't going to risk another man to take Tunny alive.

His cell phone rang and he answered it immediately.

'What the hell, who is this?' he said softly but sternly.

'It's Claude, Billy, we need to talk. . . .'

Hardistan stepped into an empty adjoining office and closed the door.

'God damn it,' he said, still whispering, 'I've got twelve dead agents and their families to deal with, and I'm in the middle of a stakeout. Not now.'

'Listen to me, Billy, this is to protect the Man, you understand what I'm saying?'

Hardistan was stumped for a moment. 'I understand that.'

'Don't bring him in.'

'What?'

'Don't bring him in.'

'You mean Tunny?'

'Take him out.'

'He could be an important witness for Vail–'

'Fuck Vail. If you do bring Tunny in and he agrees to testify, it could do us more harm than them. Understand what I'm saying, Hardistan. Put the son of a bitch down. Period. End of conversation.'

The phone went dead.

O'HARE AIRPORT, SATURDAY, MIDNIGHT CST

Hardistan and a young sniper were in a darkened office on the second floor of the concourse overlooking the parking bay. Eight agents dressed in utility clothes were busy doing inconsequential chores in the bay surrounding Woodbine's plane. Hardistan was wearing a headset and was scanning the tarmac below. He was sure Tunny would come back for the plane, it was his one way out. But Woodbine was an expert. He might have guessed they had a fix on the plane. Maybe he had an alternate route planned.

He continued scanning the tarmac, thinking about what Claude Hooker had just told him.

'What's your name, agent?' he said.

'Brandon, sir. Leo.'

'Leo, your mark is a professional assassin. He's responsible for the deaths of twelve of our agents earlier this evening, including your boss.'

'I know, sir. Mr. Fleming recruited me.'

'Keep that in mind.'

O'HARE AIRPORT, SATURDAY 1:32 A.M., CST

'We got a suit coming out on the tarmac,' one of the agents said into his lapel mike. 'He's carrying a sports bag.'

Hardistan quickly answered. 'Don't approach him, let's see what he does. Keep your eyes on that bag. It probably contains weapons.'

'How did he get weapons through the metal detectors?'

'I don't know and I don't care. Just watch the bag.'

The man walked casually into the bay and headed for twin-engine D-55.

Hardistan: 'Easy everybody.'

Tunny walked straight to the plane and stopped beside the wing. He looked around. What Tunny did not know was that he had been identified. He had been hidden at the Vail cabin since the news had been announced earlier that day and his house had blown up in the FBI raid. He felt assured and comfortable. He swung the bag onto the wing and climbed up after it. He checked inside the plane. The agents on the tarmac appeared to ignore him.

'Take him out when he reaches for the bag,' Hardistan said quietly to the sniper.

The sniper looked up at him for just a moment and then turned back to his rifle.

'All the way?' the sniper asked.

'Put the son of a bitch down,' Hardistan said.

Woodbine took out a key, unlocked the door, and opened it. He turned in a slow circle, casually scanning his surroundings, checking to see if anyone was watching him. As he reached for the bag he looked up toward the second floor of the concourse, his eyes moving past some darkened offices. Then he stopped. He squinted his eyes.

447

Was there something?

The flash in the dark window looked like a firefly. A moment later the armor-piercing bullet ripped through his chest. Woodbine was blown upward and back, landing on his back on the seat of the plane, his feet sprawled on the wing. He looked up at the ceiling of the cockpit, gasped once, and died.

Hardistan watched him through the binoculars.

'Take an insurance shot,' he said.

'He's dead, sir.' Brandon said. He stood up and cased his rifle.

'Well done, Brandon. I'll remember you,' Hardistan said. He took off the headset and walked away.

BOOK FOUR
ARMAGEDDON

*He that sets all the knaves at work must
finally pay them.*
– Anonymous

Thirty-five

Abel Stenner, the ex-Chicago cop who had become Martin Vail's confidant, friend, and partner in the years he was a prosecutor, had been one of the most intuitive detectives Vail had ever known. For ten years, while Vail was a defense attorney, he and Stenner had clashed many times in court. Each had a grudging respect for the talents of the other.

Their most notable confrontation was when Vail successfully defended Aaron Stampler for chopping up a Catholic archbishop with a carving knife. Vail had defended Stampler on the grounds of insanity, specifically that he suffered from multiple-personality disorder and was not responsible for his actions. During the trial, Vail had blistered the homicide detective on the witness stand, only to learn after the trial that the insidious Stampler had bluffed everyone, includ-ing Vail.

Disillusioned, Vail had become Chicago's chief prosecutor, and suddenly found Stenner a strong ally. When Vail had put together the 'Wild Bunch' of young, eager attorneys, Stenner became their mentor. His prize student was Dermott Flaherty, a tough street kid turned lawyer. Stenner had seen in Flaherty a hard-boiled young man who turned his education on the mean streets against the kind of criminals he himself might have become.

Flaherty had learned his lessons well. Stenner had approached every crime with cold calculation, often sitting for hours studying the scene of a crime, attempting to get inside the head of the perpetrator. It was that method that Flaherty used in studying the three simultaneous bank robberies in Montana. He had gone back to the scene of the Peakview heist twice, using it as a model for all three of the thefts. The bank employees observed him curiously, sitting quietly in a chair in the bank, at the front, watching every facet of its operation. He was cordial to them but asked no questions. He simply sat and stared.

While Ben Meyer pursued his theory that the small statewide bank chain was laundering the Sanctuary's IGG, FBI-speak for ill-gotten gains, Flaherty was more interested in the fact that nobody had seen the robbers leave the banks with the loot.

On the Saturday morning after the debacle at Bad Rapids and Tunny's attack on the Vail cabin, pressed by Vail's need to seek indictments against the rogue militia, Meyer and Flaherty were back in the Peakview bank, this time with Jim Hines. They were determined to find the 'someone' in the bank who was responsible for the money-washing scam. While Hines and Meyer were at work studying the bank's computer records, Flaherty took his usual position in the front of the closed bank and continued to study it. He was as thorough and as infinitely patient as his mentor had been.

Meyer, meanwhile, was convinced that the money gleaned from robberies and illegal arms transactions was indeed being pyramided, but he needed to study *all* of the banks' deposits, transfers, and payouts to find specifically how it was being done.

Hines, the hacker turned FBI computer expert, was there to help them. The search warrants Vail had secured permitted them to study the specific records of several of the Sanctuary's principals, but did not provide them access to every one of the bank's transactions. Without that access, Meyer was stymied. He particularly wanted to study similar deposits made on the same day, reasoning that a program had been written to distribute large cash deposits over several accounts to conceal them from the IRS.

And so, while Flaherty worked on the robbery aspect, Meyer had talked Hines into attempting to hack into the bank's most protected data. Since they were illegally gathering the data, it could not be used in court. But as Flaherty pointed out: 'If we shake whoever runs this scam out of the tree and turn him, he'll tell the whole story in court for us.'

Both Flaherty and Meyer were certain 'the link' that could tie all the aspects of the RICO case together was going to be found somewhere in the bank chain.

Two names continually popped up. One was Lewis Granger. The other was Dwight Wolf.

Hines had built up the data bank on both men. 'Granger looks good to me,' he said.

'Is he connected to the Sanctuary?' Meyer asked.

'No. He's a moderate Republican. Self-made man. Doesn't express any radical political ideas or belong to any radical groups. He's an elder in the Presbyterian church in Helena and a director in the National Radio Broadcasters' Association. Actually, Rocky Mountain Communications, Inc., is the main investor in the bank chain. Granger isn't listed on any of the boards and his title is General Manager of the key radio station in Helena, but . . . he's the largest stockholder in the company.'

'How much stock?'

'Fifty-one percent.'

'And what's the company's investment in the bank chain?'

'Forty-nine.'

'So all he needs is a shill with two points in the bank chain and he controls both companies,' Meyer said.

'Right. He also is the man who put Brother Abraham on the air and syndicated his hate show. And guess who his shill is? Guess who owns two percent of the bank's stock?'

Hines tapped the keys of his computer and another file opened.

'Dwight Wolf, chief accountant for chain, recommended for the job by Lewis Granger,' Hines said.

Meyer's interrogation of the staffs of the three branch banks had turned up the usual information – and one interesting item.

'Wolf makes a monthly visit to the all the branch banks,' Meyer said. 'It's not uncommon for an accountant to do that. But it is rare for the chief financial officer to audit the bank records personally every month.'

'Does he do it on the same day of the month?' Hines asked.

'No, but normally within the first three days, depending on where Sunday falls.'

'What's your theory?' Hines asked.

'My theory is that he personally makes the pyramid deposits.'

'So one of the thieves comes in, gives the loot in hundred-thousand-dollar chunks to Wolf, and he makes the deposit, which then automatically spreads across ten or eleven accounts?'

'Right,' Meyer said. 'And nobody in the bank ever sees the money. Wolf puts the cash in the vault, and the bank records justify it.'

'Can we find the program that does this?'

'It might be easier to scan their deposit and transfer records and see if your theory holds up.'

'So do it,' Meyer said.

'This is against the law, you know.'

'We're not changing anything, we're just taking a little peek.'

'That little peek could get us about ten years.'

'We're not even going to take notes,' Meyer said, and tapped his temple with a forefinger. 'I've got a ten-giga-byte brain.'

Hines rubbed his hands together and blew on his

fingertips, like a safecracker getting ready to feel out the combination on a lock. 'What the hell,' he said, and smiled. 'Reminds me of the old days.'

His fingers raced across the keys, attempting to access the bank files. The computer demanded a code name.

'Eight letters or numbers,' Hines said. He continually talked to himself as he ran the steps. He was using a combination of three or four hacking methods involving one program called Crackerjack, which scanned dictionaries at warp speed looking for letter matches, and another called SALT, which ran number combinations.

Hines leaned back and twirled a pencil in his fingers like a cheerleader's baton while watching line after line of numbers speed across the screen.

In the main room of the bank, Flaherty abruptly stood up and walked out the rear door. He strolled the length of the parking lot, crossed a street, and stared back at the free-standing building for several minutes.

'Yeah,' he said, and smiled to himself.

In the bank, the numbers and letters kept flashing across the monitor as the Crackerjack program decoded the bank's encrypted password. Suddenly the screen cleared and the codeword flashed on the screen:

'259HEWHAY176.'

And below it:

'ACCESS APPROVED.'

They were in.

'That was the easy part,' Hines said. 'Now we've got to start looking for patterns and deposits in transfers.'

'Let's start with November. That was the month they hit the armored car in Seattle. November nine to be exact. Run the data for one month starting on November nine.'

The monitor screen split into thirds. In one column was listed deposits, in the next, transfers, and finally a tally column. They were listed by individual branches. Hines entered '$8,000 to $9,999' in a search engine, and the cursor stopped on each deposit between the two numbers and moved it into the tally column. He ran the search engine on the three branches and main office.

Next, he collated them by date.

Meyer and Hines highlighted each entry and compared it to others.

'Here we go,' Meyer said.

November 23: three deposits of $8,750 in accounts in Peakview; four deposits of $9,860 in accounts in Wild Bank; three deposits of $9,910, Milltown. Total: $95,429.

All were escrow accounts.

'Beautiful,' Hines said. 'The money goes into escrow accounts for property, cars, whatever. The IRS doesn't check escrow accounts unless they're looking for something specific.'

'That's also how the Sanctuary became one of the biggest landowners in the state.'

'And the money was distributed to all four of the churches. There's your link, Ben,' Hines said. 'And look here. Here's a twenty-thousand deposit going to the Bank of Independence in the Virgin Islands.'

'Very cool,' Meyer said. 'The bank in the Virgin Islands then transfers that deposit to a corporation in Panama. And Panama by law will not divulge the names of officers or directors of its corporations.'

'So then they draw the money back here in legitimate bank transfers and it's completely laundered,' Hines said.

'Or,' said Flaherty, who was now standing quietly behind them, watching the records flash on the screen, 'they pay cash for arms they purchase from the international black market without a trace.'

'Yeah, no paper trails,' Meyer said. 'And most of it is legal. Even if we legally can get into the records, this information wouldn't be worth a damn in court.'

'I think I know what *is* illegal,' Flaherty said.

Hines and Meyer turned and looked up at him.

'I know why nobody saw the holdup men leave these

banks with the loot.'

'I give up, why?' Hines asked.

'Because the money never left the banks.'

'What!' Hines said.

'It never left the banks. Look, the thieves broke in, put everybody in the back room blindfolded. Emptied the vault, and put the money in safe deposit boxes in the bank. Then they took off their coveralls and put them and their weapons in a deposit box. When the explosion went off, they just stepped outside empty-handed in business suits and strolled on their merry way.'

'That's a good theory,' Meyer said.

'It's the only one that makes sense.'

Meyer considered the idea. 'And then they came back when Wolf made his monthly visit,' he said. 'Each of the three or four men in the crew had a safe deposit key, put shares of money in a briefcase, went into the private office, and Wolf made the deposits. Then he put the money back in the vault so the bottom line would even out.'

'Nice theory,' Hines said. 'The trouble is, we can't prove any of this.'

'So we need permission to get into those boxes,' Meyer said.

'Maybe we don't need to,' Flaherty said.

'We aren't breaking into the safe deposit boxes, Flaherty.'

'We won't have to, Ben. This is a game for the best bluffer alive. Martin will handle it,' he said.

WASHINGTON, D.C., SATURDAY 7:30 A.M., EST
In a room in the basement of the White House, President Pennington, General Jesse James, Colonel Stu Rembrandt, and Claude Hooker were studying huge blowups of the Mount James photographs.

'They've set up perimeters,' Rembrandt said. 'Zones of defense, starting down here at the saddle and going up to the snow line. Each zone is protected by razor wire and mines. Their troops basically are trapped in between the mine fields and wire.'

General James pointed to a ghostly image on one of the photographs. It appeared almost as a face hidden among the trees.

'We think this is where the bunker is located. The heaviest concentration of manpower is in this circle.' He drew an imaginary circle with his hand. 'That's where Engstrom is. That's where he'll be directing his force from.'

'I don't think Engstrom believes the FBI and the ATF will risk getting into a shooting war up there,' Pennington said.

'I don't, either,' James said. 'He thinks it will turn into a Mexican standoff. They can sit up there forever and send out their people on night forays.'

Pennington nodded. 'The provisional headquarters of the State of Sanctuary.'

'They'll tie up hundreds of Bureau and ATF agents and hardware in a blockade, Mr. President,' Colonel Rembrandt said. 'It will cost the taxpayers a fortune.'

'And become a P.R. nightmare,' Hooker said. 'We'd be on the six o'clock news every night. He'd harpoon you politically.'

'How close is Vail to securing indictments against these people?' Pennington asked.

'A week, a month, who knows?'

'Even if he gets them, who are you going to send in to arrest Engstrom and his key staff?' James asked. 'The marshal service isn't equipped to take them on. And the National Guard would get slaughtered up there.'

'Hell, the FBI and the ATF can't handle it, either,' Rembrandt barked. 'You want to break up this picnic, you'll need Rangers and Special Forces. They know how to deal with this kind of problem.'

'And that is . . . ?'

'Night drop. Fly in Hueys, drop the Rangers down on lines in specified areas . . .' He pointed to areas on the large map of the target zone. '. . . back up the drops with heavy air support. That way we control the situation. We can't use low drop paratroopers, the winds up there are brutal and unpredictable. The casualties could be disastrous.'

'Christ, this could make Waco look like a romp in the park,' Hooker said.

'What other course of action is there?' Pennington asked.

He paced the room for a long minute.

'Can I invoke the War Powers Act Johnson used to escalate the war in Vietnam? Or the antiterrorist acts?'

'Seems to me that's a question you should ask your A.G., Mr. President,' General James said.

Pennington sat down and stared at the wall full of photographs and maps. He rubbed his temples with two hands.

'What are we talking about in numbers?' he asked Rembrandt, who would command the force of specialists.

Rembrandt looked at the map. 'My recommendation is to drop five hundred men in the first wave. Lay 'em down at the edge of the snow line, which gives us the high ground. Back 'em up with another five hundred once we engage. Lower squads into trouble spots.'

'Body count?' the President asked.

'Once they realize what they're up against, they'll surrender in droves. Except for the diehards.'

'That's not what I asked.'

'Mr. President, if it goes smoothly, I'd say . . . we'd lose a hundred, max, against three hundred of the enemy.'

'And what if it doesn't go smoothly?' Hooker asked.

'Worst case scenario, we might lose as many as two hundred killed and wounded. I make the ratio three or four to one in our favor. Depends on how crazy they are.'

'They're crazy as hell,' Pennington said. 'Talking about Armageddon and the Apocalypse.'

'When it starts, they'll change religion real fast, sir,' James said.

'Damned if I do, damned if I don't,' Pennington mused, half aloud.

'It was Vail rushing in there with his damn search warrants,' Hooker said. 'He forced Engstrom's hand.'

'He was doing his job, Claude,' Pennington said. 'And I'm not interested in why. Why is yesterday. I have a decision to make and I'm out of time.'

He stood up, walked closer to the map, and studied the battle plan James and his commander, Rembrandt, proposed.

'How quickly can you move, Jesse?'

'We can have the necessary troops and equipment in a staging area at Travis like that.' He snapped his fingers. 'Stu has the units on base standby. We'll close the Missoula municipal airport, bring the troops in in C-140s, and load the Hueys there. It's fifteen minutes to the target.'

He looked at his watch. It was 7:51. 'It's 5:51 there. We can have our troops in Missoula by four P.M. Mountain Time. Start the incursion at first dark. The weather's good and there's no moon. We'll call it Operation Shining Armor.'

Pennington looked at James and Rembrandt.

'Put them on alert and get them to the staging area,' he said. 'Just in case.'

Thirty-six

The place was near the small town of Winston, twenty miles east of Helena. The two-story house sat on a knoll overlooking Canyon Ferry Lake, which meandered in an arc at the foot of the Big Belt Mountains. The brick wall surrounding the property vanished into trees on both sides. There was an iron gate at the entrance serviced by two video cameras.

'Guess he's not expecting us,' Shana Parver said.

'I hope not,' Vail said. 'I like surprises.'

'You mean when they get sweat under their nose and their Adam's apple starts bobbing up and down?'

'Exactly.'

'When they're not sure which of their crimes we're on to?'

'Yup.'

Vail stopped at the gate and a burly-looking roughneck in combat fatigues approached the car. Vail showed him his ID.

'My name's Vail, Assistant U.S. Attorney General, and this is Shana Parver, my associate. That's U.S. Marshal Sam Firestone in the back, and there are four FBI agents in the car behind me. Open the gate, please.'

The tough-looking man studied them both for a minute and said, 'I'll call the house.'

Vail handed him a search warrant that Meyer had obtained an hour before.

'That won't be necessary, just open the gate, pal. We don't want to have to shoot up the locks and all that Wild West stuff.'

461

The guard chewed on his lower lip for a moment and then activated the lock with a remote. The gates swung outward.

'Thank you,' Vail said. They drove through the gate and down a dirt road toward the house, followed by the FBI car. As they broke out of the trees, the house sprawled before them, a formal two-story faux southern antebellum mansion, a stunning and crass incongruity with the sparkling lake behind it. In back of the house a wooden stairway led down to a pier where a thirty-foot power boat and a single-engine pontoon plane rocked gently on the placid water. Two Mercedes sedans and a Rolls-Royce convertible were parked in a large turn-around in front of a free-standing garage.

Vail parked in front of the columned entrance and walked back to the FBI car. The agent in charge of the team, Harold Ellington, stared at the house.

'Well, you can take the boy out of the South but you can't take the South out of the boy,' he said. 'This joker should be arrested for bad taste.'

'We're going to drop him for a lot more than that,' Vail said. 'We'll go in and have a talk with Granger. Disperse your guys as you see fit.'

'Right. You going to arrest him right off?'

'Hopefully we're going to have a little chat first.'

Ellington reached around to the back of his belt and took out a pair of handcuffs. 'You'll need these,' he said. 'It's SOP.'

'Thanks, anyway,' Vail said. 'Sam'll do the honors.' He returned to the car, and Parver and Firestone followed him up to the door.

'Just follow my cue,' Vail said. 'I'll be making some of this up so don't be surprised.'

'We never are,' Parver said.

They rang the bell and another hard looker in camouflage opened the door.

'Mr. Granger, please?' Vail said.

'Who can I say's calling?'

Vail showed his identification. 'Martin Vail, Assistant United States Attorney General.'

'I'll see if he's in.'

'Just take us to him or we'll find him ourselves,' Firestone said. They entered the foyer, forcing the guard out of the way. Picture windows overlooked the lake and mountains. A marble swimming pool stretched the width of the room in front of the scenic view.

Granger was standing in the doorway to his office as they entered the living room. He was tall and florid-faced with thinning brown hair and a belly that was beginning to show the signs of the good life. In his younger days he would have been considered good-looking, but easy living had softened his features and dulled his eyes. He was wearing jeans, a plaid wool shirt, and cowboy boots.

'Mr. Granger?' Shana Parver said.

'That's right.'

'Lewis Granger, I'm Martin Vail, U.S. Attorney General's office,' Vail said, walking across the room. 'This is Shana Parver, a prosecutor for our office, and U.S. Marshal Firestone.'

Granger looked at his ID. 'So that's what one of those things looks like,' he said with a smile. 'Care for a drink?' Before Vail could respond, he went to the wet bar in a corner of the large room and poured two inches of Wild Turkey into a pebbled old-fashioned glass, dropped a single ice cube in it, and swirled it around with a finger, which he then licked off.

'No thanks,' Vail said.

'So, what is this about? Is the FCC annoyed with me about something?'

'That would be the FCC's business,' Vail said as Granger led them to his office adjacent to the pool. He sat behind a broad mahogany desk. Behind him, the lake and mountains were framed by sliding glass doors. He motioned them to chairs.

'Must be nice, traveling with a pretty young woman like Miss . . . was it Parlor?'

'Parver,' Shana said. 'Shana Parver.'

'What kind of name is that?' he asked, his smile bordering on a sneer.

'It's *my* name,' she answered coolly. 'And your name is Lewis Granger, is it not?'

'Oh, I think we've established that,' he said, and laughed.

'Good . . .' she answered, reaching into her shoulder bag and taking out a single-page document. 'This is for you.'

She handed him the warrant. He looked at it and the smirk evaporated, replaced for a moment by a cold, stolid stare. Then the bravado and the sneer returned.

'Murder, conspiracy, stealing government property, money laundering. My my, you left off speeding and illegal parking.' He wadded up the warrant and threw it in the wastebasket. 'I think we should invite my lawyer in on this little discussion,' he said, and reached for the phone.

Vail laid his hand over Granger's. 'First of all, we delivered the warrant,' he said. 'Second, we haven't read you your rights. Third, until you are Mirandized and formally arrested, you are uncharged. Would you like to talk about this before we go through that procedure, or call your lawyer from the federal building, where you will be treated like any other prisoner until you are arraigned?'

Shana Parver joined in. 'At that time you may be permitted bond, although I seriously doubt any federal judge would even set bail because of the charges. We would certainly fight any attempt to position bond. So, you'll sit in a cell until you are tried.'

'Which could be a year or longer, considering the case load on the court here,' Vail said.

Firestone retrieved the warrant from the wastebasket, shook it open, laid it on the desk, and smoothed it out with the flat of his hand. Then he took another warrant out of his pocket and placed it next to the first one.

'This is a search warrant for your home, office, bank accounts, cars, *everything*,' Parver said. 'Everything we haven't already legally checked – such as your phone records, computer data, etcetera. We will even search your son's school locker.'

Granger smiled. 'He'll be the hero of the school.'

'Okay, fine, act like a cocky asshole, but understand me,' Vail said. 'Right now, at this moment, you have the very last chance you will ever get to plea bargain. This is my case, Mr. Granger, and that's how I operate. You want to feel out a deal, get your hand off the phone. You want to play hardball ...' He took his hand off Granger's. '. . . Your decision.'

He leaned back in his chair and waited. Granger lifted the phone and stared at the dial. He looked at Vail, then Parver, then back at the dial. Sweat began to gather on his upper lip. He took a drink of whiskey, then finally reached out slowly and started to dial with his forefinger. Parver stood, reached over the desk, and pressed the disconnect.

'You weren't listening,' she said. 'The way it goes is this. We formally arrest you. We read you your rights. We handcuff you and take you downtown, where you will be fingerprinted and formally processed, *then* you get to make your call.' She gently took the phone from him and cradled it while Firestone took out a pair of handcuffs and placed them on the corner of the desk.

Granger nervously drummed his desk with his fingertips. 'What's there to talk about?' he said finally, staring at the cuffs. 'These charges are ridiculous.'

'You know Dwight Wolf?'

'The name sounds familiar . . .'

'It should, you talked to him about three hours ago. He called you from the federal building in Helena.'

'Wrong number.'

'Nope, you two had a five-minute chat. Now why would he call you instead of a lawyer?'

'I have no idea.'

'He works for you, Mr. Granger. He's the chief accountant in the bank you control. In fact, your office is in the same building.'

'I don't know everybody that works for me. . . .'

'Two of our associates had a very informative and revealing chat with him this afternoon.'

Granger stared at Vail for several seconds. He finished his drink, got up, and poured himself a second.

'Mr. Wolf is a bookkeeper, he doesn't know anything.'

'You're the bank, Mr. Granger. You're the bank, and the propaganda minister, and the money washer for the take from bank robberies, including the three-way job in Montana and an armored car robbery in Seattle in which four guards were murdered in cold blood. You also acted as the salesman for weapons and other government property stolen in the armory robberies around the state.'

Granger chuckled, but his bravado was unraveling. 'That's insane,' he said. 'You people are suffering a Rocky Mountain high.'

'We've got you cold, Granger,' Vail said. 'Conspiracy to commit, which carries the same sentence as actually doing the jobs. You're what we call the link. You tie the four church brigades to Fort Yahweh. They're separate entities under the Sanctuary umbrella, and that makes it a RICO case and that means we can take down everyone involved, everyone who knew these events were going to happen and profited by them in some way.'

'You know what a RICO is, don't you, Mr. Granger?' Parver said. 'That's when you lose all this,' she swept her hand around the room, 'and end up doing double digits in Coyote Flats.'

'Or?'

'Or you can corroborate what Mr. Wolf told us this afternoon. He says you came up with the pyramid scheme to launder money. He also says it was your idea to hide the loot from the three-way robbery in safe deposit boxes.'

'If you think that's true, what do you need me for?'

'Corroboration. You and Wolf can provide the testimony to make this RICO case stick. Without you, we'll rely on Wolf, and I assure you, you'll go to the Grave.'

'You think I'd live long enough to get to court?'

'We'll take care of that.'

'Like you took care of George Waller? Why should I put my life in jeopardy?'

'Because you won't go to the Grave, you'll go to a reasonable prison. You won't do life, no parole, you'll do five to ten, which means if you're a good boy, you should be out in three to four years. And then we'll put you in witness protection. Think about it. Which is it? The full boat? Or a chance to resume your life less than five years from now?'

'Why are you offering me this deal?'

'Because you'll just make it all that much easier. However, if you wish, I'll withdraw the offer. You washed several million dollars, and you personally made twenty percent off the top. You deuced your own people, and you made a fortune exploiting the message of your friends on your radio stations. In fact, you masterminded the whole scheme – sending squads to the West Coast to rob banks and armored cars, sending out wet boys to assassinate enemies. Those are facts we can prove.

'I can make a lot of hay out of you, Mr. Granger. Big businessman, banker, civic leader, guilty of conspiracy to commit murder, robbery, and so on. That'll put a big dent in the public perception of the Sanctuary and other groups like it.'

'Is that what this is about? Public relations?'

'Public information. You're not going to become folk heroes like Dillinger or Bonnie and Clyde – you're gangsters in camouflage suits. It's important for the people to

467

understand that.'

'And I'm the sacrificial lamb.'

'You just don't get it, do you?' Vail said. 'I'm offering you a way out. You want the deal or not? Take it or leave it. Now.'

'What happens next?'

'You take it, we arrest you, read you your rights, book you in Missoula, and then take your statement, including a declaration that you were not coerced, that you rejected the right to maintain silence and are making an honest and truthful statement of your own volition.'

'Then what?'

'We put you in protective custody and arraign you.'

'For what?'

'I haven't made up my mind on that yet. I'll probably stick to the finances – cleaning robbery money, marketing stolen weapons. It will be an all-inclusive indictment. That means whatever we charge you with will exonerate you from all other felonies to that date. We'll take everything you own in the deal, so the IRS'll lose interest. Nothing to get, won't be worth their while.'

Granger took out a cigar and rolled it between his thumbs and forefingers of his hands. He smelled it, closing his eyes almost in ecstasy at the odor. Then he carefully snipped off the end with a pair of small scissors and lit it. The ritual complete, he leaned back, took a deep drag, and blew the stream of smoke toward the ceiling.

'Cuban cigars,' he mused, almost to himself. 'Fifty bucks apiece. Never dreamed when I was growing up picking tobacco in South Carolina that someday I'd be smoking fifty-dollar cigars, living in a house like this, flying my own plane right out of my backyard. So here I am, not much of a future either way I jump.'

'Oh, I don't know,' Vail said. 'I think you might make three years in a minimum security lockup. You won't last a month in the Grave. I've been there.'

'Obviously you have a very low opinion of my ability

to survive.'

'Granger, you're a businessman, not a zealot. You're not even a good Christian. Fifteen years ago you came up here, saw a chance to get rich, and took it. Now it's pay-up time. Now . . . you looking for a bargain, or do you want to pay full price?'

'Hah. Excellent metaphor. Reduces it down to the simplest terms.'

'Yeah,' said Vail. 'Life or a living death in the Grave. They don't call it that to be funny.'

Thirty-seven

The Army had taken over a hangar at the airport and set up field headquarters. It was secured and heavily guarded. The airport had been evacuated, and Colonel Stu Rembrandt would direct the assault from the flight tower, which had been converted into a command post, taking his orders from Jesse James, who was in the war room at the White House with the President. Major Robert Barrier would set up a forward command post on the mountain, and Captain Larry Krantz would command the Ranger drop into the battle zone.

The hangar was filled with the most skilled Rangers in the Army, trained to fight effectively in any terrain and under the worst conditions. They were sitting on the concrete floor, leaning back against their packs, their faces already blackened.

Captain Krantz stood in front of an enormous map of the east face of Mount James and briefed the squads. The battle zone had been clearly defined. It appeared as a rectangle less than three miles wide at the bottom – a wide depression in the side of the mountain known as the saddle. Below the saddle, the mountain dropped straight down to its base. Above the saddle, the heavily forested area narrowed to a mile at the snow line a thousand feet from the peak. The north and south faces of Mount James were precipitous and barren, a no-man's-land impossible to inhabit or protect.

A roaring stream sliced through the mountain, forming a narrow forested corridor between the battle zone and the south face. An unpaved road led up the side of Mount

James to a small plateau perhaps the size of a football field. A wooden bridge spanned the narrow gorge formed by the swiftly running stream, connecting the plateau to the saddle. The plateau was bordered on the high side by heavy ridges that protected it from gunfire from the battle zone itself.

Major Barrier was to take several squads of Rangers in Humvees and trucks up the road to the plateau and establish a forward command post there. The plan was to rake the battle zone with machine gun and rocket fire from helicopters, then drop Krantz's Ranger force in a semicircle, along the snow line and down the north and south sides of the battle zone. Their mission was to drive down the mountain and in from either side, always directing their fire down the mountainside so they did not get in each other's line of fire. They would force Engstrom's troops into the saddle. The Ranger squads on the south side of the stream would command the bridge, and the militia force would be sitting ducks. Trapped in the saddle, they would be forced to surrender.

THE HILL, SATURDAY 4:33 P.M., MST

Twenty miles away, Engstrom gathered his officers and noncoms at the bunker for last-minute instructions. Beside him, as they had been in Vietnam and Kuwait, were Bobby Shrack, Dave Metzinger, Karl Rentz, and Ray Bollinger. The other commander was James Joseph Rainey, the ex-Ku Klux Klansman who had joined the Army of the Sanctuary early on. Two dozen men were crowded into the main room of the command post that had been carved into the face of the mountain.

The concrete bunker was located at the very center of the battle zone and was protected by a perimeter of razor wire and mines. It had concrete walls and contained a large room, which was the main communications center, sleeping quarters for the command officers, and a small radio studio with sleeping quarters adjoining it. Adjacent to the rather confined communications center, crates of ammunition, automatic rifles, rocket launchers, and rockets were hidden in a series of tunnels.

The most dangerous cache was nearly a ton of C-4 plastic explosives stored in one-pound demolition packs wired with fuses and blasting caps. This was Engstrom's 'secret weapon.'

Engstrom had his own battle plan if attacked – although he did not believe the Army would attack the mountain. It was his belief that the Army and the FBI would set up a blockade and eventually force him to surrender. But if they did attack, he was prepared to resist at all cost to protect what had become known as 'The Hill.'

The arrival of military forces changed all that. It now appeared that an attack on the stronghold was a possibility.

The previous night many of his troopers had deserted the mountain fortress. His diehard force was now depleted to about six hundred men, but they would all fight to the death.

Engstrom, a brilliant strategist if nothing else, had reasoned that an assault would be launched on three sides of the stronghold, driving down the mountain. His defense plan was to surround the bunker, his troops protected behind wire and mines. They would fire outward, away from the bunker and toward the invaders, thus preventing his men from shooting each other.

Engstrom knew he could not win such a battle. In his heart he knew the Apocalypse could be near at hand. Heaven was in the palm of his hand. He would die in the fields of Parousia.

At the back of the room, Abraham watched the General bolster his troops. In his private quarters, two teenage women had been 'entertaining' him for days. Abraham knew he could not leave the fortress. Down below, the FBI, the Army, the ATF, and Vail were waiting. Now would have been the perfect time to send the women out of the bunker. But he decided to keep them there. Why deprive himself? he thought.

'I'd like to offer up a prayer for all of us here gathered,' the General said.

'Amen to that,' one of the men said.

Several of the officers and noncoms got down on their knees. Shrack stood beside Engstrom, his hard features masking whatever he was feeling at the moment.

'I was thinking earlier today about Revelations,' Engstrom said. 'Chapter Fourteen seems appropriate. *And I saw another angel fly in the midst of heaven, having the everlasting gospel to preach unto them that dwell on the earth, and to every nation, and kindred, and tongue, and people. Saying with a loud voice, fear God, and give glory to Him; for the hour of His judgment is come: and worship Him that made heaven and earth, and the sea, and the fountains of water. Amen.*'

A chorus of 'amens' rose from the group.

'Well, I suggest you go out into this cold night and be with your men,' Engstrom said, and they began to filter out of the command center.

Shrack took out a cigar, bit the top off, and spit it in a waste can.

'Falling back on your old ways, Colonel?' Engstrom said.

'I prefer the taste of tobacco to the taste of ashes,' Shrack said.

'I never knew you to be doubtful of things, Bobby.'

'We've never been this far up the creek before, Joshua.'

'God's watching over us.'

'He sure as hell better be.'

WASHINGTON, SATURDAY 6:52 P.M., EST
In the war room at the White House, President Pennington paced back and forth before a large model of Mount James while battle maps were mounted on the walls. Several officers were in charge of keeping the map

up to date as the battle progressed.

Twenty minutes earlier, Abraham had gone on the radio live to preach about the coming Apocalypse, his fiery oratory filled with references to the rogue President who was moving troops into the Missoula area and the treachery of the government. General James listened intently, shaking his head as Abraham raved on for nearly thirty minutes. The preacher concluded with verses from Luke that sounded more like a warning than scripture.

'When ye shall hear of war and commotions be not terrified: for these things must first come to pass ... and great earthquakes shall be in diverse places, and famines and pestilences; and fearful sights and great signs shall there be from the heavens ... Then let them which are in Judea flee to the mountains ... for these be the days of vengeance, that all things which are written may be fulfilled ...'

'There he goes editing and paraphrasing again,' James said. 'He left out the part about leaving the mountains.'

'Turn that damn thing off,' Pennington said.

'Sorry, sir.'

Pennington looked at his watch. He had summoned Marge Castaigne, Jerome Brillstein, the Secretary of Defense, Claude Hooker, FBI Director Harry Simmons, and Wayne Brodsky of the ATF. He wanted them there if they did indeed launch an attack. Castaigne and Brillstein had disagreed with his decision to send troops into the area, and the legal aspects were murky, but Pennington had fallen back on the War Powers Act of the sixties and, more recently, the antiterrorist laws.

'I'll only order a strike if they provoke an attack,' Pennington had told them. But Brillstein remembered a previous discussion when Pennington had suddenly snapped at him. 'God damn it, Jerry, if we don't stop him now, the right-wing nuts in the country will think they can walk all over us.' Brillstein had decidedly mixed feelings about Pennington's motives.

Hooker and Simmons had agreed with him, likening the crisis on Mount James to a cell of terrorists plotting to overthrow the government.

Pennington had made his decision without fretting over it, especially after the fiery deaths of eleven FBI agents in Michigan and the attack on Vail that had left a twelfth dead. He was more convinced than ever that Engstrom had to be put down. In Pennington's mind it was a revolt.

Regardless of what his cabinet thought, Pennington felt his decision would be accepted by the voters, especially when he told them what a sustained blockade would cost in tax dollars. He was prepared to take full responsibility for the executive order that could send American troops against American citizens. His decision was firm. A single act of aggression by Engstrom's army would set off a civil war on the border between Montana and Idaho.

MOUNT JAMES, SATURDAY 5:56 P.M., MST
With darkness, a harsh wind moaned down through the trees from the peak of Mount James. Metzinger and his son were huddled around a small fire that flickered in the wind. It was raw cold but the youth did not complain.

'Chip, I think you should go back home,' Metzinger said. 'This is no place for a sixteen-year-old.'

'I been in the militia since I was fourteen, Pa,' the teenager answered. 'I'm not leavin' you.'

'Go down and be with your ma, she needs you now.'

'My place is with you.'

'Chip–'

'Forget it, Pa. I ain't leavin' without you. What would the General say, he heard you talkin' like this?' His father did not answer, and Chip asked, 'What do you think's gonna happen?'

'Aw, hell, at first light the General will sit down with

that Vail guy and get things straightened out.'

Chip shuddered and tried to shake off the cold. 'Wasn't like this in 'Nam, was it, Pa?'

'Not likely. Just the opposite. Hot, humid, buggy. You could grab a handful of sweat out of the air. In Kuwait it was hot and dry. Mouth'd be full of dust, you couldn't spit to save your life. But I tell you, it was better than this. I never did like the cold.'

Chip laughed. 'Then why'd you decide to live in Montana?'

'Because it's our home. It's God's country. I love it, just the nights that get me. Too cold.'

Behind them a voice said, 'You must be proud of your boy, David.'

They looked up, and Engstrom was towering over them, his eyes blazing from inside the hood of his parka.

Metzinger and Chip jumped to their feet and saluted. 'No need for that,' the General said. 'I just thought I'd have a prayer with the men. Sit down.'

Metzinger and his son sat and huddled near the fire.

'Any news?' Chip Metzinger asked.

'No. You scared, son?'

'Too cold to be scared,' the teenager answered.

'No matter what comes to pass,' Engstrom said, 'remember the words of Luke, Twenty-one to Twenty-eight. *And when these things begin to come to pass, then look up, and lift up your heads; for your redemption draweth nigh. Heaven and earth shall pass away: but my words will not pass away. Watch ye, therefore, and pray always, that ye may be accounted worthy to escape all these things that come to pass, and to stand before the Son of Man.*'

'Amen to that,' Metzinger said, but there was sadness in his voice.

'Amen,' Chip repeated.

The General moved on and they could hear him speaking to others in the darkness. '. . . *And in their mouth was found no guile: for they are without fault before the throne of God.'*

Metzinger put his arm around his son and pulled him close.

THE HANGAR, SATURDAY 6:05 P.M., MST

The sergeant walked through the crowded hangar, stopping occasionally to give the troops a pep talk. A young Ranger had moved away from the crowd. He knelt against a wall, sipping bottled water, and was obviously deep in thought. His blackened face was serious as he stared down at the concrete pavement.

'How ya doin', soldier?' the sergeant asked.

'Not sure, Sarge.'

'What do you mean, you're not sure?'

'I never thought we'd be killing Americans when I joined the Rangers.'

'What's your name, son?'

'Rizzo, sir.'

'Well, my name's Sergeant Williams. Jason Williams. I been in this man's Army twenty-eight years and I never thought so either. But our commander in chief says these men are traitors. They conspire against the government and rob and kill for their own glory.'

'I'm having a hard time thinking about killing a bunch of farmers from Montana,' the soldier, who was barely in his twenties, said.

'They're not farmers, they're highly trained guerrillas who mean to take down our government and disgrace the flag. Remember what happened in Oklahoma City, don't you? You think about that. Think about your mother and sister back home, what would happen to them if these renegades ever busted out of here.'

'Yes sir, I'll do that. I'll think about that.'

'Good. You'll do just fine. You'll do what you're ordered to do, Rizzo. I have no doubts about that.'

'Thank you, sir.'

When the sun dropped behind the western mountains, darkness quickly enveloped Mount James like a cloak. There was hardly a moment of dusk. As ordered, two Specter choppers eased around the south face of the mountain and flew to within a hundred yards of the battle zone. Night scanners searched the darkened face of the mountain, seeking the entrance to the bunker. The crew was looking for activity, and they found plenty. Figures scurried from the entrance carrying rocket and grenade launchers and M-16 automatic rifles, illegal weapons that had remained hidden until now. In the back of the chopper a specialist marked the locations of the surface-to-air rocket launchers on a grid of the battle zone and radioed the information back to the Missoula airport command center.

Colonel Rembrandt, an unlit cigar tucked in the corner of his mouth, turned to his adjutant.

'The rats are coming out to play,' he said, and transmitted the information back to the White House war room.

At the mountain a second government chopper swung in behind the first. Together they scanned the battle zone, studying the positions of the Stinger surface-to-air rockets.

In the bunker, Shrack, Engstrom, and Rainey, the Ku Klux Klanner rocket expert, watched, on night monitors, the two choppers move in closer.

'Seventy-five yards,' Rainey growled. 'They're spotting our positions, General.'

Engstrom pondered the situation. He did not want to fire the first shot, but he knew the assault on the Hill would have to come from a string drop. The heavy winds would prevent the use of paratroopers. The shoulder-mounted Stinger and 72-E5 rocket and missile launchers were their first line of defense. Their mission was to take down the personnel choppers.

Rainey, who had instructed the rocket squads, was cold and calm. He was a short block of a man with a handlebar mustache and a buzz cut. He watched the monitor with his hands on his hips, waiting for Engstrom to make a decision.

'General?'

Engstrom turned to Shrack. 'What do you think, Bobby?'

Shrack knew the consequences but he also understood the problem. 'Either we take them out and protect our missiles or we may as well give up,' he said. 'It's our first line.'

'We can fire a low shot and warn them off,' he said.

'Fuck that,' Rainey said. 'Either we take them out or roll over like a bunch of puppy dogs.'

Shrack hated Rainey but respected his opinions. 'If we can repel their first attack, it will shake up Pennington,' he said. 'He may not want to risk a heavy loss up here.'

'He wouldn't have moved his troops in here if he wasn't ready to go full barrel,' Engstrom said. He turned to Rainey. 'Fire a warning shot and see how they respond,' he said.

'Shit,' Rainey said disdainfully. He turned, walked down the long tunnel, and exited the bunker.

Two militiamen squatted near the entrance with shoulder-mounted Stingers. Rainey peered at the blacked-out Nighthawks through his night binoculars.

'Gimme that,' he said, and took the shoulder-mounted weapon. 'The General wants to play games with those birds.'

He aimed the Stinger low and fired a shot. The rocket whined out of the barrel and whooshed off into the night with its tail afire.

In the chopper, the pilot saw the flash, then saw the fiery tail of the rocket pass under his belly.

'We are under rocket attack!' he yelled into his mike.

Below him, near the saddle, a young militiaman saw

the rocket streak over and miss and thought the attack was under way. He fired several bursts from his M-16 up toward the sound of the chopper. Several rounds pinged against the underbelly of the Nighthawk.

'We are under rocket and ground fire, sir,' he said.

In the White House, James turned to the President. 'They're starting it,' he said.

Pennington looked at him and said, quite calmly, 'Tell them to return fire and move out,' knowing full well the consequences of his words.

Rembrandt heard his orders over his earphones. He relayed them to the chopper. The pilot lowered the nose of the craft and fired his machine guns toward the hill. The bullets stitched across the hard earth and ripped into the chest of one of the militiamen. He was slammed back into the side of the hill and was dead where he fell.

'Son of a bitch!' Rainey yelled. He grabbed another rocket. 'I'm gonna get me one of the fucking President's seventy-million-dollar play toys.'

He aimed the Stinger and fired. The rocket streaked through the night sky. As the Specter swerved to leave, the rocket ripped into its belly. The pilot felt the hit, felt his chopper spin on end and go out of control.

'Mayday, mayday!' he yelled, and a moment later the gas tanks exploded. The stricken chopper dipped over on its side, plunged into the side of Mount James, and erupted in flame.

In the bunker, Engstrom and Shrack watched as the chopper died.

Engstrom was as calm as the ice on a lake. He picked up a remote switch and pressed it. The bridge connecting the plateau to the battle zone was ripped to pieces by two C-4 charges. The debris collapsed into the roaring stream below it.

'General,' Shrack said, 'we just declared war.'

A hundred miles away, Martin Vail and Sam Firestone

were heading back to Missoula in Firestone's small plane. Vail had left Parver, Meyer, and Flaherty in Helena to continue interrogating Granger and Wolf. With their testimonies and Gondorf's he had enough to seek indictments against Engstrom and his staff. It would be the beginning of the end for the Sanctuary of the Lord. He was anxious to tell Hardistan in person and then call Marge Castaigne. Neither he nor Firestone were aware of what was happening in Missoula. They had not been listening to the radio and Pennington had not advised either of them about the alert. They had no idea what they were flying into.

Thirty-eight

The first drop was a disaster.

Led by assault choppers, two Specter gunships swept in over the south face of the mountain and hugged the snow line. Fighting the bruising winds that battered the peak of Mount James, they opened fire with 25mm Gatling guns and 40mm Bofors cannons, clearing a path for the big Pavelow choppers behind them. Below them, half a dozen militiamen with Stingers and 72-Es were waiting. The Specters raked the forest below the snow line with rocket and machine-gun fire. Behind them, hovering over the rim of the south face, Pavelow troop carriers waited to deliver the first Ranger contingent.

Rockets, 30mm antipersonnel shells, and machine-gun fire riddled the woods below. Rainey directed the rocket launchers, barking orders into the mike of his headset. Behind him, Metzinger's backup force was prepared to engage the Rangers when they were dropped on the mountain.

'Ignore the gunships!' Rainey yelled. 'Take out the big ones, get the personnel carriers.'

Rockets streaked through the night, some missing their mark, others clipping rotors, zapping into the fuselages, eventually finding the fuel tanks. The first two Pavelows went down in flames. Ninety Rangers and the crews of both choppers were killed instantly. But the Specters were taking a deadly toll on the ground. Rocket, cannon, and machine-gun fire chopped up the forest below the snow line. Trees were snipped off, the ground erupting with deadly missiles. Men screamed as mortar fire ripped into them.

Rainey watched as the rocket snipers around him were taken down one after another. He grabbed a Stinger, jammed a rocket into it as the ground exploded, and sent a rocket into one of the Specter gunships. The chopper keeled over and ploughed into the hard earth. Its rotors shattered and caterwauled down into the battle zone, chopping men down like cornstalks. Fire lit up the zone.

Rainey called up reserves from Metzinger's backup force. They rushed up, grabbing the missile launchers from fallen comrades, and desperately tried to fight back. The second Specter took a mortal hit. It plunged toward the battle line as its pilot tried vainly to get it under control.

Rainey was directly in front of it. He turned to run as it hit the ground, showering snow and dirt ahead of it. Like a burning, out-of-control bulldozer it followed him into the forest, a banshee of twisted metal and fire, and devoured Rainey before he could escape its path. Then it exploded, and the trees around it burst into flame.

In the eerie light of the fires, the big Pavelows rumbled over the side of the mountain and swept over the wreckage. Droplines were lowered and Rangers rappeled down, hit the ground, and sought cover in the tree line. Bullets peppered the ground around them.

'This is Metzinger,' the major said, his voice remarkably calm. 'We got Pavelows up here. They've made landfall and there are others coming in.'

'Tell Rainey to bring more rocket launchers up there,' Shrack ordered.

'Rainey's dead. I've got my people handling what we've got up here but I need reinforcements now!'

'We've got an intrusion along the north line and another on the south line. I can't spare anyone else.'

In the terrible first rush of battle, Chip Metzinger was separated from his father. He heard a rumble like thunder overhead and, looking up into the darkness, saw the grim shape of an enormous twin-engine Pavelow. It was directly overhead. Fear ripped through him like electricity. He raised his M-16 and fired at the shape, the gun kicking his shoulder as he emptied a clip into the black mastodon hovering above him. Wind from its big blades swirled around him, showering him with debris. Broken branches and dirty snow assaulted him, blinding him for a moment. When he opened his eyes, he saw half a dozen grim forms dropping down toward him. He was frozen with fear. His gun was hanging uselessly at his side as he stared up. He heard the deadly chatter of several assault weapons a moment before a dozen bullets tore into his body, knocking him six feet backward. He died staring terrified into the dark sky above him.

MISSOULA AIRPORT, SATURDAY 7:29 P.M., MST
The airport was a flurry of activity. Below them, Vail and Firestone saw two C-130s squatting on the tarmac while Specter and Penetrator gunships and enormous twin-engine Pavelow personnel choppers were taking off into the night.

'My God, they've got Specters and Penetrators down there!' Firestone said. 'And Pavelows.'

'I don't know what any of that stuff is,' Vail said.

'Gunships and troop carriers. The Specter is one of the deadliest aircraft made. The damn things cost seventy-two million bucks.'

Firestone radioed the tower for landing instructions.

'Sorry,' was the response, 'this field is closed to civilian traffic. I can reroute you to–'

Vail cut in. 'This is Assistant Attorney General Martin Vail with U.S. Marshal Sam Firestone,' he said sternly. 'I am supposed to be in charge of this operation.'

'Sir, General James is in charge. Colonel Rembrandt is the field commander but he's pretty busy right now.'

'I don't give a good goddamn,' Vail snapped back. 'I want some landing instructions.'

There was a moment of silence, and then: 'All right, sir,

if you will hold your altitude and circle southeast of the field we'll bring you in as soon as we have a clear runway.'

'Roger that,' Firestone replied. He banked and headed south of the field. 'They're in a full-scale attack,' he said.

'What the hell happened!' Vail said, not expecting an answer.

'I guess the Man got pissed off,' Firestone said laconically.

'Pissed off? Pissed off! He's the President, for Chrissake, he's not supposed to get pissed off.'

'*You* can tell him that if you want to,' Firestone said. 'Far as I'm concerned, he's the Man. He can do anything he wants to.'

'We've got a *war* going on over there, Sam!'

To the southwest the sky was lighting up like the Fourth of July.

'Judging from what I can see down below, I don't think it's going to last long.'

THE AIRPORT, SATURDAY 8:44 P.M., MST
'Colonel, what the hell is going on? What is the military doing here?' Vail demanded.

'Executive Order of the President,' Colonel Rembrandt said. 'They shot down one of our choppers. We have engaged the enemy.'

'Where's Hardistan?'

The colonel pointed to the plateau opposite the saddle on Mount James. 'He's there with the field commander, Major Barrier.'

Vail understood immediately that the command post was no place for him to be. His first thought was to get to Hardistan on the plateau.

'I need to be up there with him,' Vail said.

'I'm sorry, sir, I can't authorize–'

Vail ignored him. He took out his secured cell phone. 'I'll see what Attorney General Castaigne says about

485

that,' he said.

'Sir, I wouldn't bother those people right now. The cabinet is with the President at the White House.'

'Then I'll call every damn one of them.'

Firestone laid his hand on Vail's arm. 'I wouldn't,' he said. 'We were cut out of the loop.'

Vail's shoulders sagged. Betrayed, he didn't know what to do next.

'Colonel,' Firestone said, 'I'm a qualified pilot and have a lot of hours in choppers. Suppose I fly Mr. Vail up there in the FBI helicopter that's sitting down on the flight line.'

Rembrandt's earphones were squawking with the sounds of battle. He waved his hand in frustration.

'Check with the dispatcher and make sure you have a clear flight path. We got Specter, Penetrator, and Pavelow choppers all over the place up there. I don't want you people getting eaten up by one of them.' He turned back to the battle.

Mount James, Saturday 9:54 p.m., MST
The big Pavelow helicopters proved the most effective weapons against the militia. Backed by the deadly Specter choppers, they were big enough to resist the heavy winds on the mountain, and with their seats removed, could transport forty-five men into the battle zone.

Wave after wave of the big choppers swept over the mountain, then hunkered down and dispelled their cargo. But the plan to form an arc of troops and force the Sanctuary down the mountain had to be abandoned. Men scrambled over the mountain, trying to avoid mines and wire. The militia held stubbornly, refusing to give up their ground. At the top of the mountain, on the snow line, Metzinger had taken down another Pavelow. He had fallen back only when overwhelmed by numbers. In the insanity of the battle he had lost track of Chip and prayed that his son was farther downhill, away from the brutal close-quarters fight to hold the snow line.

Now Metzinger was forced to retreat. He and what was left of his four squads backed down the mountain, firing their M-16s and AK-47s into the dark woods. Around him was the constant din of gunfire, bombs exploding, and the worst sound of all, men screaming for help in the dark.

In the bunker, Engstrom tried to follow the war going on outside on large plastic boards but it had become futile. The Rangers were closing in on three sides. Rentz was holding the line on the north side of the battle zone, but the south side was in total chaos and he had no idea what was happening.

And still the Pavelows came in, bringing more Rangers and more firepower, their crews spraying the ground from the windows with Gatling guns, the barrels spinning in giant cylinders.

Rentz and his people were dug in a hundred yards from the rim of the north face, but the withering fire from the Specter and Penetrator helicopters was ripping his force to shreds. In the darkness, the bizarre whine of the Gatlings was terrifying as it sprayed thirteen hundred 25mm rounds a minute at the militiamen. Cannon shells ripped into Rentz's troops, dismembering and maiming them. They inched back on their bellies just ahead of the withering firepower of the Specters.

Then Rentz heard the rumble of a Pavelow. It rose over the side of the north cliff and headed in to drop its payload. Inside, Captain Krantz directed four more airborne troop carriers as they invaded the zone from the north face.

Rentz slammed a rocket into a Stinger and aimed it straight at the cockpit. Chopper and man were almost eye-to-eye, separated only by scorched earth and the stumps of pine trees. He fired the rocket and watched it squirrel through air. It was a direct hit. The cockpit disintegrated. The stricken troop ship dipped and crashed into the north face. Inside, Captain Krantz and forty-five of his men were thrown around the interior of the big ship like Ping-Pong balls as it scraped down the side of the mountain and smashed into the bottom of a thousand-foot cliff.

A moment later a second Pavelow dropped safely on the ground and its cargo leaped out. Sergeant Williams led the charge, a 30mm Gatling gun whining and spitting in his enormous arms. He laid down a barrage and his men followed him as they charged Rentz's tattered line. Williams saw the major stand, his teeth bared, an M-16 pointed to fire. He swung the Gatling gun around and sent a dozen 30mm slugs ripping into Rentz. They stitched up his body, ripping him to pieces, and blew off his head. His headset soared through the air and fell on the ground.

Williams kept going, the Gatling spraying death in the path before him.

THE PLATEAU, SATURDAY 11:18 P.M., MST

It had taken two and a half hours for Firestone to get clearance to take off. He guided the little chopper in from the south, skirted the cliff side, and slipped under the high ridge that protected the plateau, setting down near one of the three Humvees comprising the small command post. At the back of the plateau and hard against the side of the ridge, Hardistan, Major Barrier, and four Rangers were huddled over a map spread on the hood of the Humvee.

Vail was stunned. He was not prepared for the enormity of the battle being played out before him. The entire hill was ripped with grenade and rocket fire. The wreckage of burning choppers lit the night sky. Vail had expected a skirmish. He had flown into a war.

Barrier ignored Firestone and Vail as they jumped out of the chopper. Hardistan was genuinely shocked to see them.

'Are you two nuts! What are you doing up here?'

Vail glared at him, jerking with every explosion.

'This started out as my operation,' he said. 'Are you forgetting you work for me.'

'Go back to the base,' Hardistan said without rancor. 'This is far too dangerous and you can't do anything more.'

'I thought you'd like to hear firsthand. We got the link. I could have gotten the indictments.'

'Congratulations,' Hardistan said.

Vail looked across the gorge at the battle zone. He picked up a set of earphones and held one side to his ear, listening to the sounds of battle. Men were yelling for support where there was none; dying men were crying out for their wives and mothers; some damned God, others were praying.

'Waste of time,' Vail said bitterly. 'All a big fucking waste.'

'Marty, there'll be plenty to do when this is over. There are five or six hundred men over there in the zone. There are another four or five thousand out there somewhere.' He waved his hand toward the valley.

'I can't tell shit,' Barrier barked into his headset. 'We got a half dozen Pavies down and four or five Specters. Cap'n Krantz is dead. Our people are all over the hill. It's madness over there.'

Vail stared hard at Hardistan. He was remembering photos in the vast data files he had studied. Photographs from Murrel Bay when the FBI took down Matthews. Arkansas when Gordon Kahl got it. Waco. Ruby Ridge. Even the other night at Bad Rapids.

'You're always there, aren't you, Billy? Sitting in the background in a Jeep or standing in the crowd, always ready to give the big nod. That's it, isn't it, Billy? You're the one that always pushed the button. You're the fucking Angel of Death.'

Hardistan was unfazed by the remark. 'I didn't give

the nod on this one, Martin. This one went right to the top.'

'Am I just paranoid? Was I brought in just to give Pennington the ammunition he needed to take down Engstrom?'

A mortar shell sighed overhead and exploded twenty feet away and Hardistan never answered the question.

MOUNT JAMES, SUNDAY 2:21 A.M., MST

The battle was continuing insanely. In the eerie light of burning helicopters and trees, the two forces were locked in deadly hand-to-hand combat, fighting with knives, pistols, bayonets, even fists. The militiamen ran over their own mines and were engulfed in their own razor wire. In close-range firefights, Rangers and militia both were shot down by their own friendly fire. The militia was overwhelmed by numbers and technology.

And there was no letup. The battle blazed on relentlessly. Some of the troops were deaf from the constant sound of gunfire. Others wanted to surrender but died before they could, as Army troops charged over their decimated positions.

Metzinger shot at targets of opportunity, making out the dark Army combat uniforms in the light of fires that speckled the entire zone.

He heard the now familiar *chunchunchun* overhead and looked up to see a squad of Rangers rappeling down their lines. He opened fire, which was immediately returned. He felt the vicious kick of a .30 caliber bullet tear into his thigh and another nick his shoulder.

He dragged himself away from the descending marauders and ran into a bank of razor wire. It sliced through his clothes and flesh as he rolled and kicked his way over the fence. He got to his knees and crawled forward. His hand felt the mine in the soft earth a moment before it exploded in his face.

Sergeant Williams had been carrying Rentz's headset in his pocket since he had killed the militia officer. He took it out of his pocket and spoke into the mike.

'This is Sergeant Williams, U.S. Army Rangers,' he said. 'Anybody there?'

In the bunker, Engstrom heard the soft voice. He hesitated and then pressed the button on his mike.

'This is General Engstrom, Sergeant,' he said.

'Sir, I feel compelled to inform you that you are defeated. Why not give it up and save what few men you have left.'

'I appreciate your concern, Sergeant, but we are committed to a course of action. I'm afraid there is no turning back.'

Behind him, Stampler, alias Abraham, said, 'There are two women back here, General.'

Engstrom turned and looked at him with mild surprise. He had forgotten Abraham's concubines.

'You and your goddamn whores!' Shrack snarled.

'I didn't know it would come to this.'

'You're the great Prophet Abraham, I thought you knew everything.'

Stampler merely smiled at him. 'How about it, General? Can I bundle up these young ladies and get them out?'

'You should have done that hours ago.'

'I was busy informing the world what's going on up here,' he said.

'Like they won't find out,' Shrack said with disgust.

'Not from our point of view. They know now.'

'That's enough,' Engstrom said. 'Do they have warm clothes?'

'Yes.'

'Well, hurry it up, then.'

Stampler went back to his quarters.

The two teenage girls cowered in his small bedroom.

491

The bed was a snarl of bedclothes. Pillows were half out of their cases.

He handed them both heavy jackets and dark woolen caps.

'They're going to let you go back down the Hill,' he said.

'Are you coming with us?' one of the girls asked.

'Afraid not tonight. I'll join you later down below.'

One of the girls stood up and put on the jacket. Her woolen skirt hugged her ankles. She pulled the cap down over her ears. 'I'm leaving,' she said. 'You can do what you want, Reba.' She left the room.

In the command room, Engstrom spoke to Sergeant Williams. 'Sergeant, there are two young ladies in the bunker. They are not combatants. May we release them?'

Williams was surprised at the news. Women? In the bunker? The old general was randier than he thought.

'Yes, sir, I'll have a man standing by on the right side of the door.'

'You're very kind, Sergeant.'

'I got two daughters of my own,' Williams replied.

In his quarters, Stampler held out his hand toward the other girl.

'Come say good night, Reba darling,' Stampler said. She came to him and he put his arms around her. 'You were always my favorite,' he said. He kissed her throat, stepped around behind her, and, putting his arm under her chin, snapped her neck with his other hand. She fell without a sound. He threw her across the bed and quickly stripped off her dress. He put the dress on, then the jacket, and pulled the woolen cap down over his forehead and ears. He left the room, closed the door, and, slumping down, walked through the combat headquarters to join the other girl.

Engstrom and Shrack were staring at the maps. They paid no attention as Stampler and the young girl walked down the long tunnel and unlocked the double steel

492

doors. Behind him, Stampler could hear Shrack's heavy boots coming toward them. He took the girl by the arm and hurriedly left the bunker.

A Ranger was waiting for them. He escorted them away from the bunker and into the trees. Here and there in the darkness there was the *pop pop* of intermittent gunfire.

'I'll lead you up the south side,' the Ranger said. 'We can take you out in the next chopper.'

Stampler fell in beside him. As they walked through a dark patch of trees, he pulled a knife and stepped up so close the Ranger felt his hot breath on the back of his neck. Stampler snapped his head back and deftly cut the soldier's throat. The man gasped once and fell dead at Stampler's feet. The girl turned wide-eyed and looked at him. He slashed her viciously from the front, killing her instantly. He threw off his jacket and pulled the dress quickly over his head. He took the Ranger's body armor and field jacket and put them on. Then he blackened his face with dirt, put on the soldier's cap, took his gun, and headed up the hill as fast he could.

Sergeant Williams stood on a patch of unscorched earth and spoke into Rentz's microphone. 'General, I admire your guts, but this cause is lost. Give it up now before anybody else dies. Let's you and me see the sun rise together.'

'Those are kind words, Sergeant. Where are you from?'

'Charleston, South Carolina, sir. My daddy fought in World War Two. He was the first black man to run for Congress in South Carolina. Got beat, but at least he had the privilege of running.'

Shrack chuckled and shook his head. 'Wouldn't you know,' he said.

'You want to surrender, Bobby?'

'What the hell for? To do life in the Grave or end up strapped to a table with a needle in my arm?'

The General flicked up the black metal cover that protected the red button. It was connected to detonation cords that fused the C-4 cache nearby.

'We did pretty good, Bobby, considering they sent the whole U.S. Army against us,' Engstrom said. He smiled at Shrack and they shook hands.

High above, Stampler reached the snow line and dashed south, toward the narrow corridor of land that led down the hill to the plateau. With luck he could make it there, maybe even find Mordie and get the hell out.

'Sergeant Williams?' Engstrom said.

'Yes, sir?'

'Do you know your Bible?'

'I read a verse every night, sir.'

'This is from Revelations. *And the seventh angel poured out his vial into the air; and there came a great voice out of the temple of heaven, from the throne, saying it is done. And there were voices, and thunders, and lightnings; and there was a great earthquake such as man has not seen since men were upon the earth. And every island fled away, and the mountains were not found.*'

He pressed the button.

A thousand pounds of C-4 exploded simultaneously, setting off rockets, missiles, mortar shells, ammo, fuel: all of the contraband the Sanctuary had stolen through the years and hidden in the mountain.

The side of the mountain erupted like a volcano. First, it burst with a great storm of concrete, dirt, and smoke.

The earth trembled like an earthquake for miles around.

Then followed the fireball. It was the size of two city blocks, boiled up from the furnace of death, swirling into the sky and lighting the night like a birthing sun. It thundered down the face of Mount James, creating a vacuum that sucked everything up into it. Pine trees were torn from the earth, sucked into the sky, and cremated. Men disappeared into the all-consuming orb. Snow turned to water, boiled, and turned to steam. The earth under the terrifying ball of fire was fried as the howling juggernaut of flame consumed everything in its path.

On the plateau, Firestone grabbed Vail and Hardistan and dragged them over the side of the embankment, but Major Barrier, knocked to his knees, stared dumbly as death engulfed him.

They tumbled down thirty feet and cowered under overhanging roots and earth as the great river of fire roared down toward them, was deflected by the high ridges around the plateau, and swirled off into the sky. Trees and debris went with it. The three men held onto each other and to the roots as the heat sucked at them, burst over them, and boomed into the sky. The command Humvee was lifted and thrown over the side of the steep cliff. It exploded as it fell down into the gorge and crashed a few yards from them. Major Barrier's body followed it. Scorched and burning, it dropped from the sky like a smoky scarecrow and thudded to earth nearby.

Vail gasped for air, felt its heat inside his chest, and gagged.

Then, just as suddenly, a rush of cool air followed the sphere of fire. Vail, Firestone, and Hardistan stared up at the great fireball, watching it rush away into the heavens. It was an awesome sight as it boiled into the sky. A few moments later ashes and burning refuse showered down on the destroyed mountain.

Stampler cowered in the wreckage of one of the Pavelows. The explosion was below him, but the force of it knocked him out of the wreckage, tumbling him down the side of the hill. He rolled in the snow to snuff out the flames that licked at his clothes and face. Then he raced into the trees on the high south side of the mountain and stood there as the bunker disgorged its cloud of death.

Twenty miles away the earth trembled and the windows in the airport control tower rattled in their frames.

Colonel Rembrandt stared in disbelief as the great fire-ball rose into the sky, turning night into day.

'Oh my God,' he gasped. He took off his headset and dropped it beside him on a table while General James demanded to know exactly what the hell was going on.

Thirty-nine

A bloodred sky greeted the morning, staining long fingers of thin cirrus clouds. Vail, Hardistan, and Firestone were huddled under the ridge that had saved their lives. Barrier and his men had not been as lucky. The major's body still lay at the bottom of the steep embankment where the devastating fireball had dropped it. One of the Humvees lay crumpled in the trees, where it had been tossed like a toy, several hundred feet away. The chopper and the third Humvee were still burning.

Barrier's three aides were nowhere to be found.

By dawn's light the road leading to the valley was a cluttered mess. Charred trees and debris had clogged it for several hundred feet. Across the gap, in what had once been Engstrom's sanctuary, only an enormous gaping hole remained. On the high side, wreckage of Pavelows and Specters were all that remained of the task force. The snow – from where the snow line had been halfway to the peak of Mount James – had melted. Miraculously, eight wounded Rangers who were awaiting evacuation had been spared.

A thin veil of ash covered everything.

The three survivors on the plateau were without communication, food, or water. In the darkness after the holocaust, they heard choppers and saw the thin fingers of searchlights perusing the ruins. With first light, they would be seen and rescued from their perch. So they waited.

The trauma of the explosion had left them shaking and in shock. They huddled together speechlessly. There was nothing to say.

*

Above them, Aaron Stampler – the Abraham of Engstrom's madness – staggered down the hillside, through shattered trees and ruptured earth, toward the ridge that protected Vail, Hardistan, and Firestone. He still wore the dead Ranger's clothes, and the side of his face was burned and his hair was singed to the scalp. Sweat from the terrible heat had erased most of the blackness from his face.

He, too, was traumatized, shaking so hard his teeth were chattering. He was carrying an Army .45 in one hand and a canteen in the other, having filled it with snow that had melted, providing him with water. There were three cartridges in the clip of the pistol and one in the chamber – in case he got into trouble. He had long since discarded his contact lenses.

Stampler stumbled down the hillside toward the ridge. The road was clogged with rubble but he knew he could get through the debris. Once in the valley, he felt he could escape the bedlam surrounding the battle on Mount James. He had found an ID card in the uniform he stole. As he approached the ridge he could see the burning chopper but was not aware that below him, under the ridge, was Martin Vail.

He struggled toward the plateau and as he neared the foot of the steep drop he stopped. Three men were huddled together in deep shadows. The sun was not high enough in the sky to shed light in the natural alcove and it was difficult to make them out. He backed up the ridge, out of their sight, and pondered what to do. Obviously, they were waiting to be rescued. Stampler decided his best option was to go back to the top of the ridge, play dead until they were gone, then continue his trek to the valley. But as he turned to go back a voice stopped him.

'Hey soldier!'

He turned. A tall man in an FBI jacket was standing below him.

'Come on down,' the FBI agent called to him in a

friendly voice. 'We'll be picked up shortly.'

Stampler sat down and skidded on his rump to the foot of the ridge. The agent stuck out his hand.

'I'm Billy Hardistan,' he said. As they shook hands, he added, 'Where the hell did you come from?'

'I was up on the snow line,' Stampler said. 'There's some wounded guys up there. I don't think anybody else made it.'

'You're one lucky soldier,' Hardistan said. 'That's an ugly burn, let me take a look.'

As Hardistan studied the raw flesh on the side of his face, Stampler could see the other two men emerge from the shadows.

'Got any water in the canteen?' Hardistan said. 'We need to clean that wound up a bit.'

'I'll be okay,' Stampler mumbled.

Then he looked over Hardistan's shoulder.

And stared straight into the eyes of Martin Vail.

Jesus!

His hand inched down and grasped the butt of the .45.

Vail looked at him and started to say something.

Then Vail's expression froze.

'My God!' he cried, his eyes widening with disbelief. 'That's Aaron Stampler!'

Stampler smashed his elbow into Hardistan's face and pulled the gun. Firestone's hand swept under his arm but he was a second too late. Stampler fired a single shot. A second later Firestone's Glock roared. The bullet tore through Stampler's neck. He reeled backward and fell into the burning chopper. His clothes burst into flame. He rolled frantically, trying to get out of the tangled mass of metal, but it only embroiled him deeper in the burning plane's wreckage.

As he shrieked in pain, Firestone turned to Vail.

The single bullet had ripped into Vail's chest. It felt like a baseball bat had hit him. He fell straight to his knees and leaned forward, supporting himself with one hand.

Firestone raced to his side.

But Vail did not see him. His mind tumbled madly back through time. He thought of Stampler, a trial many years ago and Stampler's blood spree when he was released from the mental institution. Then his fevered mind turned to Jane and Magoo.

Yes, he thought, *I can do that. . . .*

He looked up at Sam Firestone and the world faded to white.

He collapsed in Firestone's arms.

Across the plateau, Stampler had stopped screaming. His eyes bulged from the melting flesh of his face as the fire consumed him.

In a corner of the intensive care unit at the Missoula hospital a curtain had been pulled around Vail's bed. Jane Venable sat beside him, clutching his hand. An oxygen mask covered his nose and mouth, and behind him, past the lifelines and tubes that were sustaining him, the heart monitor beeped as the green lines of its graph charted his fight for life.

The doctor stepped into the cubicle every few minutes to check the instruments. His face revealed nothing.

The bullet had nicked Vail's heart and he had lost a great deal of blood before rescue teams reached him. Pints of blood had pulled him back from the rim of death but the prognosis was grim at best.

Outside in the hall, Vail's beloved Wild Bunch, Billy Hardistan, and Sam Firestone watched the clock. He had been in surgery for hours. Now there was the agony of waiting.

Venable spoke constantly to Vail, reavowing her love for him, talking about Magoo and how they would find him a proper mate, softly telling him of the plans to restore their cabin by the lake.

His hands were cold and his face was drawn.

Then she felt him squeeze her hand. His eyes fluttered

and opened and he smiled. Feebly, he moved his other hand to the mask and tried to pull it down.

Jane moved the mask down for just a moment and kissed him. Then he whispered something to her. She leaned over, her ear almost touching his lips, and listened. Tears flooded her eyes.

'Oh yes,' she said. 'Oh yes.'

She turned to the nurse.

'Is there a chaplain here?' she asked.

'Of course,' the nurse replied.

'Could you find him, please.'

Fifteen minutes later, while his heart struggled to keep the monitor beeping and his staff and new friends stood by, Martin Vail and Jane Venable were married.

Epilogue

For God's sake, let us sit upon the ground,
And tell sad stories of the death of kings.
– Richard II, Act III, Scene 2

It was a bright morning in April, unseasonably warm for Washington, when the limo pulled up to the main entrance of the White House. A young naval attaché was waiting. He opened the door and helped the pale visitor from the car.

'Good morning, sir,' the officer said. 'Welcome to the White House.'

The visitor leaned on his cane. 'Last time I came here,' he said with a wry smile, 'I came in the side door.'

The officer offered his arm and helped him up the steps.

In the Oval Office, Claude Hooker and President Pennington were in conference when Mildred Ewing, the President's assistant, tapped on the door and stuck her head in.

'He's here,' she announced.

Pennington nodded. 'Good. Good,' he said. 'Show him right in.'

A moment later Martin Vail entered the room. He seemed grayer than Pennington remembered from their first meeting and he had lost weight.

'Martin,' Pennington said, 'good to see you again. You remember Claude Hooker.'

They all shook hands and then Pennington said, 'Claude, will you excuse us, please?'

Hooker was obviously disgruntled at being asked to leave, but he nodded and exited the room.

'Well, Martin. You look just fine, just fine.'

'Thank you, Mr. President.'

'And how is Jane?'

'She's on extended leave,' Vail answered. 'Been playing Florence Nightingale to me and Magoo. He's our dog.'

'Yes, I remember. Quite the hero, as I recall.'

'He took a bullet that was meant for me.' Vail said.

'Let's sit over here.' Pennington led Vail to the two sofas and they sat opposite each other. Pennington was an arranger. He moved things around on the coffee table as they spoke, finally stopping when he had put everything in symmetrical order.

'I've been following your recuperation. The operations went well, I understand.' It sounded more like an apology than a statement of concern, as if Pennington were looking for an opening to get into the conversation.

'It took four operations to get my heart ticking properly but I feel fine,' Vail answered. 'Still haven't got my sea legs back.'

'I want to thank you for all you did,' Pennington said. 'You and your team did an admirable job putting the RICO case together. Unfortunately, Engstrom and his boys chose death before dishonor. But the dust has finally settled; things are shaking out nicely.'

Maybe for you, thought Vail, *but not for Marge Castaigne. Not for Jesse James and Harry Simmons.* All had 'officially' accepted responsibility for the holocaust on Mount James and taken the hemlock cocktail, retiring or resigning in the wake of the tragedy, thereby absolving Pennington of the decision to attack the Sanctuary with military force. In the three months since the attack, Pennington neatly had removed himself from the fiasco while publicly 'accepting responsibility' for it.

'So, what are you planning to do once you've fully recovered?'

'I haven't really thought much about it, Mr. President.'

'Your people have done well cleaning up the RICO

case. They certainly have proved our point.'

Vail did not answer. He just stared intently across the table at Pennington.

'I was thinking,' said Pennington. 'We expect to have an opening in the Fifth Circuit, probably before the end of summer. I think you would make an excellent judge.'

So – there it was. It had taken Pennington less than five minutes to cut to the chase. Vail had remained conspicuously silent during his lengthy recuperation, maintaining a 'no comment' posture for which he was well known. Now the President was offering up a respectable lifetime job as a payoff.

'I can think of a lot of judges who would turn positively apoplectic at the mere thought,' Vail said.

Pennington chuckled. 'Oh. I think not,' he said solicitously. 'You certainly have the experience and background. And your respect for the Constitution makes you an excellent candidate.'

'I appreciate the offer, sir,' Vail said. 'But no thanks.'

'I see,' Pennington said. 'Perhaps . . . you have something else in mind?'

'You don't owe me anything.'

'I think you misunderstand . . .' Pennington started, his tone turning more formal.

'I don't think so,' Vail said, cutting him off. 'When I took the job as Assistant A.G. it was with the understanding that politics would not enter into the assignment. I realize now how naive I was. I think your politics and my naivete are two of the main reasons I was chosen.'

Pennington's face clouded up. His jaws tightened.

'I invited you here today to thank you for a job well done,' he said.

'Oh, I'm sorry,' Vail said. 'I thought you invited me to thank me for keeping my mouth shut and offer me a nice, cushy job to *keep* it shut.'

The President glared across the table. 'That's an insolent remark, sir, and an arrogant assumption.'

'Probably. Tact and diplomacy have never been my strong suits and arrogance is one of my many shortcomings.'

'Let me tell you something, Martin. Life is politics. You play the game or you suck hind tit. It's just that simple. I think you can learn a valuable lesson from this experience.'

'You know what I think? I think I was brought into this game to give you an excuse to take Engstrom out. I think you counted on my political gullibility to build a case that would make Engstrom so repugnant in the eyes of the public that you could use all your powers to destroy him. You had a lot of reasons. Even if we made the case, you knew Engstrom would never submit to the indignity of the court trial. You were facing a long, costly blockade. You had a Bible-spouting maniac who was in serious danger of making a fool of you, who scoffed at the presidency, and who was building support out in the hinterlands. I think you needed to show the whole militia movement that challenging the government's power was a suicidal venture at the very least. And I think you knew that even if the whole thing went south, Marge Castaigne, James, and Simmons would take the gas pipe. Hell, if Stampler hadn't put a bullet in me I would have gone down the tubes with them.' Vail leaned on his cane and struggled to his feet. 'The irony of it all,' he said, before turning his back on the President of the United States, 'is that Engstrom was praying for Armageddon and you answered his prayers.'

Jane Venable watched as Jack Connerman walked across the big lawn toward her husband and Magoo, who were sitting down by the lake. Vail stood slowly and shook the hand of the reporter who had chronicled his career since the days when he was a young defense attorney turning the law inside out and having prosecutors for lunch. She had no idea why Martin had invited the writer to lunch.

'How you feeling, Marty?' Connerman asked.

'I'm doing fine,' Vail answered. They walked along the lake's edge.

'Looks like they're putting the cabin back together,' Connerman said. He indicated the workmen who were busy sawing and hammering.

'I'll be glad to have all those people out of our hair.' They walked a little farther, then Vail said, 'I was thinking about zealots the other day.'

'Zealots?'

'Yeah. When two zealots face off, nobody wins,' Vail said. 'One ends up a martyr and the other ends up riding off into the sunset. And all the people get out of it is the shitty end of the stick.'

'Interesting,' Connerman said.

'Well, I've had a lot of time to think about it. I want to tell you a little story,' Vail said.

'About zealots?'

'About zealots and a lot of other things, too.'

'Is this off the record?' Connerman asked.

'Not on your life,' Vail answered. He began to talk. And as he spoke, as Connerman wrote, Martin Vail began to feel that perhaps his wounds would one day heal after all.

Two days later, on April 19, a Transcontinental 747 flying from Denver to Washington, D.C., exploded a few minutes after takeoff. Two hundred and thirty men, women, and children died in the crash.

Etched into the side of the black box in the wreckage were four numbers:

2-3-13

Also by

William Diehl

PRIMAL FEAR

A nightmare of terror and psychopathology worthy of
The Silence of the Lambs.

Martin Vail is Chicago's most brilliant lawyer. So brilliant his
enemies have set him up to defend a case he cannot win.

Young Aaron Stampler was caught red-handed after a murder
that had the city reeling. He looks bound to fry, but he swears
he's innocent.

In a desperate gamble for justice, Vail must reach deep into the
recesses of a killer's mind to flush out a monster of infinite
cunning and evil.

Explosive, haunting and brilliantly suspenseful, *Primal Fear* is a
truly terrifying read.

William Diehl

SHOW OF EVIL

The chilling sequel to *Primal Fear*

Lawyer Martin Vail has never lost a case – now he must catch
a psychotic killer, or he'll lose his life.

When Linda Balfour, a young mother, is found butchered in
small-town southern Illinois, a coded inscription stamped in
blood on the back of her head brands her mutilated body.

For Chief Prosecutor Martin Vail, the bloody insignia drags up
memories he'd like to forget.

With his career – and even his life – on the line, Vail needs
some answers fast before the killer signs someone else's
life away.

MORE BESTSELLING TITLES FROM ARROW

❐	Primal Fear	William Diehl	£5.99
❐	Show of Evil	William Diehl	£5.99
❐	The Final Judgement	Richard North Patterson	£5.99
❐	Degree of Guilt	Richard North Patterson	£5.99
❐	Eyes of a Child	Richard North Patterson	£5.99
❐	Private Screening	Richard North Patterson	£4.99
❐	The Chamber	John Grisham	£5.99
❐	The Client	John Grisham	£5.99
❐	The Firm	John Grisham	£5.99
❐	The Pelican Brief	John Grisham	£5.99
❐	The Rainmaker	John Grisham	£5.99
❐	The Runaway Jury	John Grisham	£5.99
❐	A Time to Kill	John Grisham	£5.99

PRICES AND OTHER DETAILS ARE LIABLE TO CHANGE

ALL ARROW BOOKS ARE AVAILABLE THROUGH MAIL ORDER OR FROM YOUR LOCAL BOOKSHOP AND NEWSAGENT.

PLEASE SEND CHEQUE/EUROCHEQUE/POSTAL ORDER (STERLING ONLY) ACCESS, VISA, MASTERCARD, DINERS CARD, SWITCH OR AMEX.

EXPIRY DATE .... SIGNATURE ....

PLEASE ALLOW 75 PENCE PER BOOK FOR POST AND PACKING U.K.

OVERSEAS CUSTOMERS PLEASE ALLOW £1.00 PER COPY FOR POST AND PACKING.

ALL ORDERS TO:
ARROW BOOKS, BOOKS BY POST, TBS LIMITED, THE BOOK SERVICE, COLCHESTER ROAD, FRATING GREEN, COLCHESTER, ESSEX CO7 7DW.

NAME ....

ADDRESS ....

....

Please allow 28 days for delivery. Please tick box if you do not wish to receive any additional information ❐

Prices and availability subject to change without notice.